my (extra)
ordinary
life

Rebecca Ryan lives in Bradford with her husband and three young children. Although she always loved writing, it hadn't really occurred to her that she could do it professionally. She recently left her job as a teacher to pursue writing full-time. She enjoys walking in the countryside and takeaways (if that counts as a hobby).

my (extra)
ordinary
life

rebecca ryan

**SIMON &
SCHUSTER**

London · New York · Sydney · Toronto · New Delhi

First published in Great Britain by Simon & Schuster UK Ltd, 2023

1 3 5 7 9 10 8 6 4 2

Simon & Schuster UK Ltd
1st Floor
222 Gray's Inn Road
London WC1X 8HB

Simon & Schuster Australia, Sydney
Simon & Schuster India, New Delhi

www.simonandschuster.co.uk
www.simonandschuster.com.au
www.simonandschuster.co.in

A CIP catalogue record for this book
is available from the British Library

Paperback ISBN: 978-1-3985-0924-5
eBook ISBN: 978-1-3985-0923-8

Typeset in Bembo by M Rules

Printed and Bound in the UK using 100% Renewable
Electricity at CPI Group (UK) Ltd

MIX
Paper | Supporting
responsible forestry
FSC
www.fsc.org
FSC® C171272

For Elodie, Hugo and Kit. Always.

Chapter One

Apparently, wondering when and how you'll die is an integral part of the human condition. Unless you're me, that is. I already know I've got exactly fifty-four years left to live.

It'll most likely be heart disease that sees me off in the end. And if the sheer averageness of my existence is to be believed, I'll be kicking the bucket in a hospital. Seeing out my last mortal moments down some random corridor in Huddersfield General.

'And that's it. Death. The only certainty in this, The Human Life.'

The not-quite-David-Attenborough presenter delivers his final line as the credits roll on the BBC2 programme. I feel like I've been punched. Not that I've ever been punched, mind, I'm not that sort of a girl. (Woman. God, that makes me sound old.) So, I imagine that's what it would feel like. Being hit in the face. I'm wobbly. Disorientated. I clutch the edge of the couch for support, except it was so cheap it offers little resistance and I sink to the floor.

It was a documentary. One that made out that human habits are just as interesting as animals', when really no one knows or cares that the average human blinks 28,800 times a day. (Note to self, must blink less.)

All in all, the programme was pretty dull. What's left me stricken on the rug in the front room is the stuff Mr not-quite-David-Attenborough said. 'The average human this ...' and 'the average human that ...', and every single average life event he mentioned seemed to apply to my own mediocre existence. For goodness' sake, *both* my names were in the top five most common names. Emily Turner. Dull as dishwater.

I'm off the floor now, relieved Kaz isn't here to bear witness to my demented pacing.

Don't get me wrong. It's not like I've ever considered myself destined for greatness. I'm an ordinary person with ordinary thoughts living an ordinary life. I was never going to be the person to develop a cure for cancer or anything impressive like that. But no one wants their one meaningless life to be *entirely* average, do they?

It's Mum's fault that I even know so much about the ins and outs of my own existence. Surely people generally forget some of the stuff from the first ten or so years? No such luck for me. Mum's a compulsive recorder. Every moment of my life has been meticulously documented. I used to think it was weird. But now, you know, I'm thinking at least she's got a quirk. *I* don't have a quirk.

Anyway, there's a whole wall of photo albums in the dining room of Mum and Dad's semi, each one diligently labelled. If it weren't for that, then maybe I wouldn't have known how long it took for her and Dad to get pregnant (cringe), how long her labour was (newsflash, Mum, it wasn't my fault), when I got my first tooth, walked, talked. She even made me pose on the day of my first period.

Blaming Mum is something of a relief. It's her fault I'm the average height. Her fault I'm distinctly average to look at. On one of those completely sexist scales that men use to rate women based purely on their looks, I'd say I'm a solid six. A five on a bad day perhaps. I've got brown eyes and that hair that's halfway between curly and straight. A sort of less attractive, aging Emma Watson. I sometimes think I'd be a perfect person to get away with murder. I have so few distinguishing features that any eyewitnesses would be at a total loss recalling me. The only thing that sets me apart is a freckle on my right cheek. Even then you'd have to be looking pretty close to spot it.

It's not like I even do something exciting for a living. I'm a teacher. And I know some people see it as something of a vocation. A calling. I really admire those people. Those people deserve OBEs. Unfortunately, I'm not one of those people.

I have a stab of something that feels distinctly like guilt. Right under the ribs. Where guilt tends to get you. Except I've no time for guilt. Self-absorbed panic seems much less stabby.

Without ever planning for it, I've ended up as the most average person on the whole entire planet. And what's left? Marriage at thirty-one, three years away. Bloody brilliant. I'll probably meet my soulmate this year, then. Two kids. Then the inevitable trudge towards retirement. Teaching *Of Mice and Men* every day of my life until I retire at sixty-five, spend a few decades pottering in the garden, and then go hurtling into the deep abyss of nothingness, right on schedule.

This is bad. Really bad.

Kaz! She'll make me feel better.

> **Me:** Kaz, tell me something interesting about me.
> **Kaz:** This message is pretty weird.
> **Me:** Come on!
> **Kaz:** I've got lives to save.
> **Me:** Please.

Those little dots which show she's writing appear and disappear over and over. Kaz is my flatmate, best and only friend. And there's absolutely nothing ordinary about her. For one, she's an A&E nurse; she literally gets free stuff in Pret because her job is so impressive. And she has red hair and big green eyes. Like a sexy, modern *Little Mermaid*.

Finally, a reply.

> **Kaz:** You came runner-up in that poetry contest.

Kaz's observation falls down on many, many levels:

One: She's the person who knows me most in the world. It was Kaz I went to when Martin Stevens told everyone in Year 9 I was a bad kisser. It was Kaz I showed the *Zoo* magazines to, which Matt had hidden under his mattress. And it was Kaz who squeezed my hand so tight all the way through the funeral because Mum and Dad seemed to have forgotten I was there. And despite all of those timeless bonding encounters, this is the best she could come up with. I didn't even win, for goodness' sake. The devil's in the detail. *Runner-up.*

Two: That contest was in Year 10. Ergo, she suggests I've done nothing even remotely interesting for the past fifteen years.

I can't catch my breath. I feel like an elephant is sitting on my chest. What do they do on *Holby*? Tell them to breathe, in-out, in-out.

Well, that doesn't work.

Sure, it's just a programme. But no one, I repeat no one, should be forced to confront just how lacklustre their life is at ten o'clock on a Thursday night.

I bounce up the stairs clutching my chest in an overly dramatic fashion. Except there's no one here to see it.

I brush my teeth in the tiny bathroom, facing away from the mirror as usual. Obviously, I don't own my own home yet. According to the rule of averages which shape my existence, like one of the lesser-known laws of physics, I've another three years until I can look forward to ticking that one off on the old life list. I mean, it might be nice not to have quite so much mould growing in the bathroom. I don't care what Mr McGee, our landlord, says, it is not akin to abstract art. But maybe I'll stay anyway, for an extra year.

It's 10.15pm. I've been having my breakdown for fifteen whole minutes.

I message Kaz again.

> **Me:** That's not particularly interesting.

Those three little dots. I hate those little dots.

> **Kaz:** You're being extra weird today. It's like my Great Aunty Mary used to say. Some people in life are stilettos and others are slippers.
>
> **Me:** Did Mary really say that?
>
> **Kaz:** She used to wear those whopping great heels, remember? Even in the care home.
>
> **Me:** So, in this scenario I'm the slipper, right?
>
> **Kaz:** Yeah, but which one would you rather be long term?
>
> **Me:** Well, not a slipper, obviously!
>
> **Kaz:** You have 12 pairs of slippers and a single stiletto.
>
> **Me:** Only because the heel broke on the other one. So, you're basically saying that my life is as interesting as a pair of old lady slippers? What else, a onesie? A flannel? What other inanimate objects would you use to describe how dull I am?

I am incandescent with rage. Sort of. I'm pretty miffed at the very least.

Another three dots.

Kaz: Sorry, need to dash. Medical emergency.

Well, that's that. I flump onto the bed. It groans at the combined weight of me and my existential angst.

I've only one option left.

Mum answers on the third ring.

'Emily, love. Is everything all right?'

I flinch at the panic in her voice.

'Yeah, everything's totally fine. Maybe even better than fine. Fantastic, you could say.'

'Love?'

I do my best to rein in the hysteria. 'Sorry. It's just that, you know when I was younger?'

She does a big breath out.

'Mm-hmm.' She shuffles a little.

'Well, was there anything particularly unusual about me? Like, was I really early at doing stuff? Or even a bit slow? I didn't have an extra toe you decided to have lasered off?' I ask hopefully.

'Oh no, love. Nothing like that. I used to say to your dad that you and Claire must have read all the baby books before you came out. Did everything bang on schedule, the pair of you.'

I wince. Not just because Mum is confirming my fears.

'But did I have any unusual habits? Anything you and Dad secretly worried about?'

'Nothing at all,' Mum declares proudly, missing the salient point of the conversation entirely. 'You never gave us any cause to worry. Either of you. Well, not until, you know.'

Her voice goes quiet and I have the sudden urge to get off the phone as quickly as possible. It occurs to me that perhaps a parent isn't likely to admit that they'd spawned some weirdo.

'Right, that's great, Mum. Anyway, I've got to go, bye!'

'Hang on a sec. Love, now that I've got you, maybe we could talk about the memorial.'

I fake yawn. Because I'm a terrible human.

'Sorry, Mum, I'm really tired actually.'

I pause. I'm not so awful that disappointing Mum comes naturally. 'We can sort it soon though, don't worry.'

'Okay, love. Night.'

'Night, Mum.'

I ring off and let out the breath I've been holding.

It's official. There is absolutely nothing special about me whatsoever.

First-world guilt swells. It had to at some point. Quite frankly, twenty-five minutes is probably long enough to be wallowing like this. After all, there are people who would kill for a nice, ordinary – read *boring* – life. That woman who got famous after she tried to climb out of the window to retrieve a poo she couldn't flush in her boyfriend's loo and got stuck, for example. And people who live in war zones.

Annoyingly I might be ordinary but I'm clearly not selfless enough for perspective to be helping at all.

And I've exhausted everyone who could make me feel better.

My phone has gone black in my hand and I inadvertently catch myself looking into the screen. I hate it when that happens. When my reflection creeps up on me unawares. I slam the phone down on the bedside table harder than I should.

Claire.

The stabby feeling in my ribs gets sharper.

When was the last time I thought about her?

Too long. And though I've gotten incredibly good at not thinking about her, or talking about her, or doing anything that might remind me of her, *I* want to be the one deciding on the not thinking. Not my subconscious just blotting her out.

Urgh, this is awful. Mediocrity and guilt do not a happy marriage make.

Claire wouldn't be having this crisis.

There'd be no need. She wouldn't be average.

The tears come then.

Because it's all been a waste. Of two lives, not just one.

Chapter Two

When I wake up in the morning my pillow is wet. I wonder briefly why I've been sleep crying until I'm once again faced with the dawning realisation that I'm the dullest person alive. And while it might be nice to ration my soul-crushing realisations to just one a week, another realisation is there too. The one about Claire.

I blink back more tears into my already scratchy eyes and roll out of bed, pulling on my trusty work get-up: black trousers, white shirt, black shoes. No need to check the mirror, thank you very much.

I always wondered if I'd be one of those people who rocked up to work in a nice pencil skirt and heels, ready to take on the world. But it turns out that pencil skirts have zero give in them, and heels start to hurt about three minutes into your day. Quite frankly, I don't need the additional pain.

It's Friday. By far the best of the weekdays. And yet all I feel is mild dejection as I eat my Corn Flakes. I google them as I crunch, not in any way surprised to find that they're the UK's foremost breakfast cereal. I must endeavour to make less average food choices. I saw this thing once about grating courgette into porridge. Zoats or something I think they called it. At the time I thought it was probably an indication that the apocalypse was nigh. But now I'm not so sure. Maybe a change would be good.

I make it to work in time for staff briefing, though, at best, I'm ill-prepared for the day ahead. I'd had this vague notion that being an English teacher would involve helping kids to love books. Turns out I was wrong on many, many fronts. And five years in, I now find myself at a loss when it comes to mustering the requisite amount of enthusiasm for the latest pedagogical breakthrough. PLTS, Blooms, SMSC, objectives, effect sizes, personalisation. Who knew that teaching kids about books would be so bloody complicated?

On the way in I do another Google search. *Teaching is the most common job for women.* Fuck's sake.

I head into the staffroom. In the centre of the school, there is no natural light and a hodgepodge of mismatching chairs all in varying degrees of wear and tear. The blue carpet is so worn it's almost black and the walls are peeling. A staff wellbeing display includes faded leaflets on dealing with anxiety and stress. The whole place screams budget cuts.

I make a beeline to my pigeonhole, itself a veritable treasure trove of delights. Sixty Year 8 progress reports await my comments. There's a printout of my midpoint appraisal review, highlighting that I have yet to make a start on any of my three yearly targets. And finally, a poster for this year's school production of *Little Shop of Horrors*. There's a Post-it Note on the front, presumably from my boss, which says,

'Can you help with this?' Not bloody likely. Despite my lifelong dedication to musicals, I now refuse to entertain the prospect of spending any more time in this place than is absolutely necessary.

'Morning, folks,' Mr Hughes, the head, begins. I dive into the nearest seat and get a few shifty glances from the people nearby. Everyone has their own chair in the staffroom. Next to their best work friends. Except me, that is. I don't have a chair. I operate on the premise that being here at all is like finding yourself stranded behind enemy lines; you need to keep moving. When I dare risk it, I skip briefing altogether, having discovered a direct correlation between time spent in the presence of Mr Hughes and feelings of mild desolation.

'You'll all be disappointed to hear that we're skipping Focused Friday.' Some people make a noise to suggest that they might genuinely be disappointed by the lack of this Friday tradition in which we spotlight pupils who are making less than expected progress and discuss strategies to help them. And by help them, I mean consider ways to affect our whole school performance.

Mr Hughes carries on. 'However, as you may well know, following an illustrious career, Andrea Heartshill will be saying her goodbyes this morning. Come on up, Andrea.' Brilliant. A retirement speech. Nothing like an entire career commemorated in the three minutes before morning bell.

Andrea walks demurely to join Mr Hughes, turning slightly red in the process. I remember the time when she called him a 'bastard, wanker, tit' in the toilets following a particularly brutal lesson observation.

This morning, however, all thoughts of Mr Hughes being a bastard, wanker, tit are apparently now long forgotten. Andrea accepts her Co-op flowers and bottle of medium-priced wine with a flurry of 'you shouldn't haves' to polite applause.

'Thank you very much, Mr Hughes,' Andrea begins, unfolding a single sheet of A5 paper. There's a collective sigh of relief. No one appreciates long speeches. The less said about Mr Flerrin's song-based leaving extravaganza, the better.

'I'd just like to say I've really enjoyed working here.' Mr Hughes smiles as if she's paid him a personal compliment. No doubt, whatever pleasure Andrea has derived from her career will have been despite, not because, of his involvement in it.

'I'll really miss the maths department and of course, all of my ladies over in cake corner.' There's a whoop from some far-flung crevice of the staffroom. Five years I've worked here, and I didn't even know there was a cake clique. Normally cake and I always find each other.

'But it's time to hang up my whiteboard marker, or chalk as we called it in the olden days.' Gentle chortle. 'So, thank you everyone. I'll really miss you all. I might even pop in with some cake one day!' She raises her bunch of flowers in triumph.

There's another appreciative whoop from the loyal ladies of cake corner and that's it. A thirty-odd-year career reduced to a few platitudes and false promises. That's what I have to look forward to. And I don't even have any cake corner ladies who'd be willing to cheer me on through my leaving speech.

I sink further into my seat. I am Simba from *The Lion King,* that part where the stars realign to reveal his dad spouting off about his destiny. Except in my universe, all the signs are aligning to spell out, 'Your life is shit.'

For a Friday, the day takes an extraordinary amount of effort. At lunch, I eat alone in my classroom and spend the time scrolling through Google looking up random things to be average at. Height, five foot four and a bit. Check. Shoe size, five. Check. Skin type, combination. Check. Brown hair, blue eyes, check, check. I'm deep into an article about the most common blood group when I realise that I don't actually know my own.

I turn to Facebook. Admittedly this is an act which, when facing something of a personal crisis, is tantamount to the behaviour of those twelfth-century flagellants who wandered through the streets whipping themselves. But still, to Facebook I turn.

There are the usual inspirational quotes, mostly shared by Dad. And a smattering of political articles reflecting the left-of-centre political leanings of all good millennials.

I start randomly clicking on profiles.

Angela Senior: Feeling emotional. I said yes!!! Followed by a picture of her and her now-fiancé beaming on a beach somewhere.

Well, give it fifty years, Angela. Then you might not be quite so cock-a-hoop with your predictable life choices.

Katie Small: Feeling nervous. Wish me luck everyone #newadventures #movingtoCanada #promotion There's a picture of her passport in case any of her Facebook friends are particularly slow.

Steven Whitward: Feeling exhausted. His arms are raised in triumph as he crosses some Bupa-themed finishing line. Feeling smug, more like.

I'm just about to close the app when I spot a repost from my dad. And not his usual, 'live, laugh, love' drivel either. It's Matt, my brother. Matt's accepting an award at work. *Pete Turner: Feeling Proud: Proud dad! Congratulations* <u>Matthew Turner</u> *on being named accountant of the year.*

No. This cannot be. Matt's like me. Dull as sin. Except at least I'm boring and reasonably nice. Matt is boring and bad. Our relationship best described as 'strained'. And yet, here he is, winning awards left, right and centre. And okay, accountant of the year isn't exactly the Nobel Peace Prize. But he has a little plaque and everything. And here I am, decidedly plaque-less.

My palms grow sweaty as I consider Matt's betrayal. Goodness, I'm an awful person now. I can feel my heart beating hard. I genuinely wonder if it's about to give out. Like it's deliberating what the point in keeping me alive is. That other realisation, the one I'd been doing my best to avoid, is tunnelling with intent. Mining right into the centre of my brain.

Claire. Claire's life wouldn't have been like this.

Now that it's there, it's impossible to dislodge. My skin prickles as the bell to signal the end of lunch rings. I force myself to take some deep breaths, pulling air into my lungs. My Year 7s are at the door and I plaster on a forced smile as I wave them in.

A few of them give me nervous glances and I wonder if I might look a bit demented.

I manage only a distracted rendition of the adverb song I developed a couple of years ago. It's a very catchy tune if I do say so myself. But my performance is lacklustre, even for the last lesson of the day.

Normally on a Friday, I'd race home and be on the couch in my day pyjamas by four o'clock. Not that my weekends ever hold a particular amount of promise. But the prospect of not having to wear a bra for a couple of days, well, that appeals a great deal.

I scowl at the sight of my Ford Fiesta in the car park, my earlier internet trawl already revealing it to be the most popular car on the market. And it's silver. I've a mind to sue the salesperson. They'd described it as 'edgy'.

At the last moment I detour to Mum and Dad's. The three-bed semi that I grew up in comes into view. I'd had a moment of joy earlier, while googling house prices. Apparently, the average house sells for £251,000 these days. There's no way that Mum and Dad's house is worth that. Of course, it would mean we're poorer than average, which isn't exactly something to be celebrated, but at this stage I'll take whatever I can get. Obviously then I'd remember all those places in London that have a fridge in the bathroom that sell for a million quid. They were probably dragging the average up. So, I'd narrowed my search to just Yorkshire. I'd triangulated my findings with some Rightmove data to ascertain that I'd grown up somewhere average.

Pulling onto the drive, I wonder how I'll explain my impromptu visit. I never arrive unexpected. I never do *anything* unexpected. Mum will definitely anticipate the worst. She was rewired after Claire. She's at my window before I've even turned the engine off.

'Emily, love. What's the matter? Has something happened? You can tell me, I'm here for you,' she says all in one breath as I open the car door.

'No, don't panic. Nothing's happened. I just thought I'd call round for a cup of tea.'

'But why? It's Friday. We're expecting you on Sunday, aren't we? Usual time? I was going to do beef?'

We have a rota of beef, chicken, pork for Sunday lunch. Ten years ago, Gran declared lamb too fatty, and it got dumped. That I would suddenly turn against one prong of the meaty trinity seems ludicrous.

'Yes, I'll still be here on Sunday and beef sounds good. Honestly, there's nothing wrong. I just fancied a cup of tea. Dad still at work?'

I see her do one last sweep, no doubt for some grievous bodily harm that I've thus far kept hidden.

'Yep,' she relaxes. 'Well, it's a lovely surprise. Come in and I'll put the kettle on.'

I sit at the dining table picking at my fingers until Mum appears with tea and biscuits. Fearfully, not even the sight of custard creams is enough to rouse me from my melancholy.

'Are you okay, love?'

'Mm-hmm. It's just that . . . Do you ever think I'm a bit, well, dull?'

Instead of confirmation, I get on point maternal outrage. 'What!? Of course not. You're clever and funny and kind. You're lots of things.' She's lying. I'm only one of those things at best. And even then, I fear that *I* find me funnier than anyone else.

'But I don't *do* anything. I mean look at my life. It's completely average.'

She goes to interrupt, but I cut her off. 'I even counted how many times I weed today. Seven times. Bang average. What's my blood type?' I demand.

'Er, O positive I think.'

'Knew it, common as muck.'

'But that's, you know, biology, isn't it?'

'It's not just that. The rest is average too. Guess where the most common place to buy clothes is?'

She keeps quiet, sensing this is perhaps not a good point to interject.

'Next. Ninety per cent of my wardrobe comes from that shop. And the rest is from Primark, only the second-most common.'

I'm flushed. The abject misery of earlier is dissipating. Replaced instead by anger. At what or whom is anyone's guess.

'And don't even get me started on Colgate.'

'I ... uh ... well ...' Mum flounders. She can mount no defence because there is none. 'You *did* almost win that poetry contest, remember? Me and your dad both said you were robbed.'

For fuck's sake.

I slump my head on the table, making the tea tray rattle.

'What's brought all this on, Emily, love? Is it something to do with you calling last night? Only, I know you don't like to talk about her, but I don't think Claire would have seen it quite like—'

I leap up. I don't know why I came. Perhaps in the vain hope that Mum would know something I didn't. That it somehow wouldn't be the case that I'd completely failed Claire. That just maybe I'd been living a life she would have been proud of. Instead, I've probably just drawn attention to the fact that I haven't. I bet everyone already knows.

'So, it's been good to chat. I'll, um, see you Sunday.' I'm out of the door and halfway down the drive before Mum realises what's happening. She appears blinking at the window as I reverse away, my heart pounding hard again.

Chapter Three

The talent contest was the bit Claire liked best about Butlin's.
It was the bit I liked least of all.

'Right, and then you'll do a cartwheel that way, and I'll
do one this way. And then we'll skid down on our knees at
the front before the last bit of the song. Remember to keep
your arms straight, though. That's very important.'

'But I'm not very good at cartwheels. Not like you.'

I'm not very good at any of the things Claire is good
at. Like singing. Or dancing. Or cartwheels. I'd rather
not have lots of people watch me do the things I'm not
very good at.

'You're all right at them. You need to practise more, that's
all. I did twenty-seven already today. Even when I kept
falling over. Are you sure you can remember all the words?'

I nod.

We've watched the film over and over at home. And
Claire made us practise the song the whole drive here. By
the time we stopped halfway for a Happy Meal, Dad said

20

his ears were bleeding. I could see them, though, and there wasn't any blood.

A man and a giant bear in matching bright red coats come onto the stage.

The Skyline Pavilion smells of candyfloss and smoke, even though the smoking seats are a long way away.

'Right folks, we're just about getting ready,' the man in the red coat says. 'Filbert and I are so excited to see what you can all do.'

Filbert the bear gives a big thumbs up to show that he's excited, too. There's a big cheer. Claire joins in.

'So, anyone who wants to enter, come and put your name down and we'll call you onto the stage in order. Remember folks, you've got to be older than three and younger than thirteen! Have fun!'

He waves his hand to a little table next to the stage steps. A woman in a matching red coat with blonde hair smiles and waves.

I go to walk towards her.

'Wait.' Claire holds my arm. 'We want to be last so we can make a big impression. That's how you win.' She scrunches her face up and makes her eyes go small. Dad calls it her evil genius face.

Last year we didn't win. I forgot the words and then I stopped dancing. If we don't win this time, it'll be my fault. I know it.

When there's only one person left at the table, a bigger girl in a football kit, we go over.

'Claire and Emily Turner,' Claire tells the lady. 'We're going to sing "It's the Hard Knock Life" from *Annie*.' Claire hands over our cassette.

'Right you are, girls. And how old are you both?'

'Five.' Claire holds up five fingers in case the lady doesn't know her numbers.

The lady looks up and her eyes go all big. Mum tells us it's rude to stare, but me and Claire are used to it on account of the fact we're twins. Not just any type of twin, either. Mirror twins. I have a freckle on one side of my face, Claire's is on the other. Claire likes that we aren't just twins. We're extra-special twins. I like being a twin, too. You've already got a bestest friend when you're a twin. But I'm not bothered about the extra-special stuff.

Claire's the oldest twin. She's been alive seven minutes more than me. Claire says this makes her the wisest. I don't know about being wise but she's good at being in charge.

'Well, good luck,' the lady in the red coat says, after she's finished staring.

'Come on.' Claire tugs me back to the dance floor. 'Let's watch the competition.'

We wave at Mum, Dad and Matt, sitting at a table around the edge of the dance floor. Mum is drinking orange juice with a pink umbrella in it and Dad has some lager, like what he drinks at home, but it's in a glass this time.

The music gets really loud and the lights go down everywhere except the stage.

'ARE YOU READY FOR THE TALENT SHOW TO

BEGIN?' the man in the red coat shouts, even though he doesn't really need to because he has a microphone.

Everyone cheers. Everyone except me. My tummy feels like it does when I'm on the caterpillar rollercoaster, even though I'm sitting still.

'I SAID, ARE YOU READY?!'

Claire is bouncing up and down next to me.

The shouty man introduces the three judges. They're sitting facing the stage. They're all wearing nice red coats, too.

Everyone sits on the dance floor waiting for the first act. Me and Claire cross our legs like we do in story time. There's some twirly music on and a big girl twists and turns in a ballerina outfit. She's so beautiful, just like a princess. I'm jigging my leg like I do when we have to go to see the dentist. There's no way I can beat princess ballerina girl.

I think I'm going to wee my knickers.

'Claire, I need a wee.'

'But what if they call our name? You'll have to hold it in.' Princess ballerina girl is doing a curtsey.

Now a boy does magic tricks in a suit that's too big for him. Except one goes wrong and he drops the white rabbit teddy he's supposed to pull out of his hat. He goes off the stage after that.

They're going to call us soon. I can tell.

'Claire, I need to go for a wee. I'll be really quick.' And before she can tell me no, I stand up and run towards the toilets. Mum said we're not to go to the toilet by ourselves, but this is an emergency, so I think it'll be allowed.

The toilet seats are really high and it's hard to get my bum on. But I do my wee and then I stay there for a bit even though toilets are not a very nice place to sit.

There's a knock on the door.

'Are you in there, sweetheart?' It's Mum.

'Yes,' I say, and I wonder if I'm going to get into trouble for going to the toilet by myself.

'Are you coming out?'

'I suppose so.'

I open the door. Mum doesn't look mad.

'How about we stay in here together for a little while?' she asks.

'But won't Claire get mad?'

'You leave Claire to me—'

Except Mum doesn't get to finish what she's saying because Claire is at the toilet too now.

'EMILY! They're calling our names. Come on!'

'Claire love, Emily doesn't want to go on the stage,' Mum says.

Claire lifts up one of her eyebrows, like she always does when she wants me to do something. I never say no to Claire.

'No, Mum, it's fine. I do want to go on. I just changed my mind for half a minute.'

Claire is smiling now.

'Are you sure, love?'

I nod.

'Come on then slowcoach, they're waiting for us.'

Claire's talking really fast.

'There was a girl who did keepy uppys but she dropped the ball and went off crying, and those sisters from Splash World did The Spice Girls but they weren't very good.' We're at the bottom of the stage steps now. The carpet's a bit sticky and I think I'm stuck until Claire gives me a shove.

'Em, come on! Be brave!' Claire has a big smile on her face as she drags me into place in the middle of the stage. The lights are so bright I can't see Mum or Dad or Matt. I do some big blinks like you do when you want to go to sleep but you're pretending you don't.

Then the music plays, and my arms and legs start to move. I see Claire out of the corner of my eye and try to keep in time with her. Everything she does is bigger. Her singing voice is loud and clear.

I open and close my mouth, but I don't know if any noise comes out. I can't hear it. I move my arms side to side and do a couple of box steps. We skip around the stage and then hold hands in the middle and twirl under.

Then it's the bit where we need to do the cartwheel. I throw my arms up and the lights go upside down for a second. I land with a thud and skid along my knees for the end.

Claire falls to the side after her cartwheel and I panic that it's going to go wrong again, but then she's on her knees too and smiling her biggest smile.

My mouth hurts from trying to copy her.

We take a bow holding hands. As we walk down the steps,

she says that our clap was louder than anyone else's, and that hopefully no one noticed that she tripped up a little bit.

The disco starts up again as the judges huddle together to decide the winners.

'I hope Dad lets us have some chips.' I'm really hungry now that my tummy isn't feeling funny anymore.

''Course he will. Specially after the talent contest. I think the judges will pick us.'

We make our way to Mum and Dad's table. There's already a massive basket of chips.

'There's my little stars!' Mum smiles at us. 'You were great up there, girls.'

'Thanks. We'd better win. No one else was as good as us.'

'My teacher says it's the taking part that counts,' Matt says, looking up from his Sega. Matt is four years older than us. He likes to tell us things his teacher says. Claire says that Matt's a swot, but I don't mind if he is.

Claire scrunches up her eyes and rubs her head.

'Are you okay, sweetheart?' Mum asks her, trying to give her a hug.

'Mum!' She wriggles free. 'The judges are coming on stage – look!'

Mum keeps frowning. But she sees me watching and starts to smile again so I think everything is okay after that.

The judge reads out third place. The boy with the magic tricks.

Second place goes to the ballerina.

Claire has her eyes closed and her hands in fists at her side.

When they say our name for first place, she squeals and runs to the stage, dragging me behind her. I don't like being back on stage, but at least there's no singing this time.

Claire takes the mic and thanks everyone for voting for us. Except I don't think anyone has voted for us really. We get a real gold medal each, which is nice, and Claire looks so happy and I'm happy, too, because she's happy and the talent show is over and we're in Butlin's, which is our favourite place ever. Now we can relax for the rest of the holiday.

Chapter Four

'Rough night?' Kaz asks as I emerge on Saturday morning. She nods towards the pizza boxes piled by the sink. In the cold light of day, it *does* look an awful lot of food for one person.

I groan, clutching my stomach. 'I'm never eating pizza again.' This is a lie. One which I tell on a weekly basis.

'What's up?' Kaz is flushed, just back from parkrun. She's drinking a green-looking concoction – her New Year's resolution. I didn't bother, myself. Twenty days in and already this year promises the same disappointments as every other.

'Want some?' Kaz nods towards the toaster.

'Three slices please.' Overeating always makes me hungry.

Kaz is a flurry of activity. The toast is down, the kettle is on, she's unloading her washing, sorting through it on the breakfast bar I'm currently slumped at. If we were animals, she'd be one of those beautiful hummingbirds, flapping about like a maniac. Whereas I'm a slightly angry two-toed sloth.

'Do you have to do that there?'

'Do what?'

'Sort your knickers right in front of me? I'm feeling delicate.'

'They're knickers, they won't bite you.'

'Those ones might.' I point towards some red satin thing. 'At the very least they'll give you thrush.'

Kaz laughs as the toast pops and she sets to buttering. The offending knickers keep catching my eye. None of my knickers look like that. Instead, they all hover somewhere along the colour spectrum between grey and black. And I haven't worn a thong in at least a decade.

'Come on then, out with it.'

I realise that I'm staring at my toast.

Kaz is my best friend. I tell her almost everything. Partly because I've no one else to tell. But that's beside the point.

'Kaz, I think I'm boring.'

'No way. I'd never have a boring best friend.'

I carry on as if she hasn't spoken.

'I saw this programme the other night. All about the average human, right?'

She nods, waving her mug at me to hurry up. 'And I realised that that's it. I'm the average human. I'm exactly average.'

'Nope. Definitely not. What about your musical collection?'

Musicals? Please. Who in their right mind doesn't get a bit giddy when Sandy completely reinvents herself – even if it is just to please Danny, or when Maria von Trapp hauls herself across the Alps with seven kids in tow?

'Five of the top twenty films of all time are musicals. I'm in a majority here.'

My elbow is propped on the breakfast bar. My head feels ridiculously heavy in my hand. I wonder if I have a heavier than average head.

'What about Claire?'

'What about her?' My head snaps up.

'Not many people have a twin, surely.' I relax again a bit.

'No, you're right. Only 0.2 per cent of the population are identical twins.' I am a walking encyclopaedia of useless facts about humanity. 'But I'm not an identical twin.'

'Do you really believe that?'

Time stretches out as we stare at each other, Kaz peering down at me over her smoothie. I cave first. Because I'm a wuss who would never argue with Kaz. I need her way more than she needs me.

'Weekend plans?' I ask, employing my best evasive manoeuvres.

She holds my gaze for another second before letting it slide. 'Some of the other nurses are going to meet for a coffee in town later. If you're bored, you're welcome to join us?'

'No, thank you.'

'Why, because you can't squeeze us in?'

I give her a look. The magnitude of my crisis cannot be soothed with coffee in town.

'Might do you some good.'

'As would colonic irrigation.'

'How about the tip? I'm taking that dresser down there in a bit.'

Kaz's dresser met an unfortunate end some weeks ago,

the sexual prowess of Steve the lorry driver no match for the decade-old piece of furniture.

'Kaz, I might be a pathetic excuse for a human, but even I draw the line at weekend plans that revolve around a trip to Huddersfield tip.'

'Suit yourself. Just promise me you'll get dressed today?'

Kaz rinses her mug and leaves it by the sink.

'I can't promise anything.'

'You know, Em, I mean this in the nicest possible way, but if you really are unhappy, you could change some stuff.'

I pft, to demonstrate the fallacy of her sentiment. I wouldn't even know where to start. My head inches closer and closer to the faux marble countertop again. Mr Singh had arrived with a roll of stick-on paper one day and announced the kitchen was getting a 'makeover'. He'd upped our rent £50 a month to cover the costs.

Kaz heads for the stairs.

'Claire wouldn't have been unhappy. Just saying.' She holds her hands up like I'm about to shoot. I've whipped my head up so fast there's a good chance I've got whiplash. She darts up the stairs, banking on the fact that I won't have the energy to follow.

She's right.

Over time I've come to accept that my life holds little promise. And when you accept that, you're altogether more prepared for whatever it throws at you. As such, I take any day that contains only a modicum of disappointment as a win. It would never have been that way for Claire.

31

Kaz's words ring in my ears long after I've taken position on the couch.

I flick on *West Side Story,* only half-watching as the Jets and the Sharks wage a dance-based war against one another. Only half noticing as Kaz leaves for the tip.

The film ends and some Channel 4 programme about people moving to far-flung places around the globe comes on. I'm sure even the TV is mocking me. I've lived in Huddersfield all my life.

Lunchtime passes. In a life first, I don't move to get food.

Claire wouldn't have been unhappy. Not a chance. She'd have been some mega-successful actress. The sort who earn industry respect *and* hit it off with viewers. Like that guy from *Last of the Mohicans* who's won a ton of Oscars but also looks excellent shirtless. Or else she'd have lived off the land in some faraway country. Dedicating her life to a worthwhile cause. She wouldn't recognise *this* as a life at all.

'*You're a good sister, Emily . . .*'

Words from some almost forgotten memories float back to me.

I can't stop the guilt then. It doesn't confine itself to stabbing me in the ribs either. It smothers me, making it hard to breathe. All I had to do was live. Claire didn't even get to do that.

How do you fail at living when you're alive?

I drag myself upstairs in search of toilet roll. People like me don't have neat little boxes of tissues.

Wiping my eyes, I catch sight of myself in the mirror

and flinch. My cheeks are red, and my face is puffy. In my imaginings, adult Claire doesn't look like this. Her skin is less grey, her hair less dull and her eyes are more vivid than my own. As if through sheer zest for life, she managed to become more attractive.

I fight the urge to look away.

Well?

Mirror me is right. I can't carry on like this. Sleepwalking my way through the most average of existences.

Something has to change.

Chapter Five

Come Monday, I wake up bursting with determination. It's like a switch has flicked in my brain. I will make my life interesting. Even if it kills me. In fact, if it kills me, that's a bonus. At least it's a story.

It's quite unusual for me, waking up with a sense of purpose like this. With actual feelings. Even if those feelings do largely centre around the utter pointlessness of my existence paired with a healthy dose of guilt. Oh, and there's a sprinkling of hopelessness too. So that's nice.

It prickles the back of my neck, all this feeling. As if the cells in my limbic system are waking up after a year in hibernation. Shouting, *Ahoy lads, we're back in action* to each other while high-fiving.

I had hoped that I'd have had a sort of lightning bolt realisation as to the future of my life mere moments after I decided to make a change of some description. Instead, it's brought the loss of Claire to the very forefront of my brain, and I've been bashing my way through the emotional spectrum at warp speed. Despairing, excited, weepy, inspired, back to despair. It's not even 8am yet and I'm exhausted.

And yet, like an army in the final throes of battle, I must rally.

Getting dressed, I flout the school's all-staff-must-wear-a-suit Victorianesque uniform policy. A spotty cardigan – the beacon of my rebellion.

And I purposely stop brushing my teeth before the little buzzer goes off to tell me two minutes are up. Tooth decay. That'll show it.

I catch sight of myself in the mirror. There are big bags under my eyes. Two days into my quest and it's already breaking me.

By the time I grab my cheese sandwiches and jam rolls, I'm already running late. I silently vow that tomorrow my lunch will have more wow factor. Instagram tells me that kale is out. Avocado is in. I spend the drive to work considering all the ways I could mask the taste of avocado in order to eat it.

I park up, drumming my hands on the wheel to delay having to get out of the car.

The problem, as I see it, boils down to this. How can I possibly be trusted with making my life interesting when I've done such a poor job of it for the past twenty-eight years? God, I might have to hire one of those life coaches I've read about. I wonder how many there are knocking about in Huddersfield. I clearly cannot be responsible for my own fate.

The first bell goes, alerting me to the fact that I've missed staff briefing. Anyway, I think I have enough to contend with without having to sit through Motivational Monday. Ever since that time Mr Hughes treated us to a recording of Maggie Thatcher declaring, 'The lady's not for turning,' when word hit that Ofsted were in the area, I'd not found Motivational Mondays to be particularly motivating.

My mind has begun to wander when it hits me.

Teenagers.

There are teenagers everywhere. I'm surrounded, and quite literally. They flood past my car on their way into school. I ignore the odd bang on my bonnet as following it up would involve a lot of paperwork. Here I am, walled in by the most cutting edge of all the generations. They're a veritable hive of stupid, yet interesting, ideas.

I peg it to first period, hanging my coat as the second bell of the day rings. I quickly open the blinds and set my laptop on its ten-minute wake-up. Everything is as I left it on Friday, if a bit cleaner. The desks are worn. More than one penis is etched into their wooden tops. The displays are peeling. I remember when I'd got the job and I'd made a whole Pinterest board of classroom décor and felt an actual, genuine, kernel of excitement at the prospect of an *A Midsummer Night's Dream* theme. I'd even gone in in the summer to work on the display.

But then on the first day of September, I'd arrived to find that my Puck was in the bin, replaced instead by a massive, standardised poster outlining the many, many layers of the school's zero-tolerance behaviour policy. I'm of the opinion that having kids stare at a huge poster with EXPULSION at the bottom of an inverted pyramid isn't the thing to motivate them. But then I've long since stopped claiming to know what I'm on about.

It all seems so small now. Like the classroom is closing in on me, trapping me in this existence. Not anymore. I wave my fingers at the walls like a lunatic. I have a plan.

I swing open the door to find my form lined up along the wall with moderate to poor adherence to the rule that they must be in single file and silent before they enter.

'Morning, everyone! In you come.'

If they're perplexed by my unusually chipper greeting, they don't say so as they trudge past me.

First lesson on Mondays is spent with our form. Doing Life Lessons. On paper, a sort of citizenship, life skills mash-up-type lesson where we're meant to teach very important topics like money management and how to roll a condom onto a banana. That sort of thing. I'm not qualified to deliver at least ninety per cent of the content and so during our five years together, my form and I have found our own rhythm. We have a quick flick through the school-prescribed lesson and then they do a bit of revision while I crack on with some marking and we argue over which music to play through YouTube.

'Right, everyone, we're trying something a bit different today.' I clap my hands together and use my best teacher voice.

There's a hum of excitement. I have form when it comes to 'a bit different'. Like that time we covered alcoholism and I unearthed a YouTube clip of some guy doing shots of vodka through his eyeball.

However, they groan in unison as I hand out lined paper.

'But Miss Turner, we thought you were one of the cool teachers.'

Categorically not true.

'Yeah, you never tell us off when we forget our homework.'

Confrontation makes me sweat.

'You look tired, miss, don't worry about teaching us today.'

True, but I need to milk your brains. I'm extra glad the last sentence was in my head.

'Right.' I clap my hands together again, ignoring their protestations and plastering a fake smile on my face. 'Today we *should* be covering The Importance of Free Speech for a Democratic Nation.'

There is a particularly raucous groan as I read the official title of today's lesson.

'However, instead, what I'd like you to do is write the title, "What makes a life interesting?", and basically write me a list of things that you might expect to see in an interesting life.' It had sounded clearer in my head.

'What, like being a drug lord on the FBI's most wanted list?'

'No, not quite like that. "Good" interesting.'

'Can I put down Kim Kardashian?'

'If you want. Maybe you could draw on some literary characters we've studied over the years.'

Blank faces.

'What're we doing this for?' one asks, doubtful.

'It might help you, you know,' I wave my hands about in a vague fashion, 'later.'

They can smell blood. They know it isn't even close to a proper lesson now.

'Can we work in pairs?'

'If you like.' A wave of noise metaphorically flings me back against the whiteboard.

Amidst the current cacophony, I make the only sensible decision I can. I sit at my desk, close my eyes and begin to rub my temples. It does absolutely nothing for the headache now pulsing through my skull.

It takes me a moment to realise that someone other than a fifteen-year-old is shouting my name.

'MISS TURNER!'

I pinch the bridge of my nose in yet another futile hand-to-face action and then realise that it's actually the head, Mr Hughes, bellowing at me.

'Mr Hughes!' I half leap out of my chair. 'What a pleasant surprise.'

The class have gone silent. They know I'm in trouble. I don't even have the free speech lesson PowerPoint ready to go. My traitorous white board is still turned off.

Mr Hughes leans in to mutter to me, 'I noticed that you weren't in briefing this morning. We're starting the week with learning walks.' He gestures to Ms Higginbottom, the deputy head. Whereas Mr Hughes is an enormous hulk of a man, with a tight red face and short grey hair, Ms Higginbottom is like a twig. Tiny, with sharp edges. I'm sure they're banging. They spend hours every day locked in Mr Hughes' office. The official line is that they're preparing for the Ofsted inspection, a task which does, admittedly, lend itself to the same levels of preparedness as the D-Day landings. But still, that wouldn't account for all the grunt-ing that goes on in there. Ms Higginbottom gives me a tight smile.

'Miss Turner, would you be so kind as to explain to us the aims of your *own* lesson today?' she asks, in a sickly-sweet voice that fools no one.

Evan, one of the Year 11s right in front of me, raises his eyebrows. His meaning is clear. You're fucked.

A learning walk sounds like an innocuous sort of thing. Nice, even. Who wouldn't want to walk and learn at the same time? But really, it's the school equivalent of the stealth bomber. They're coming to destroy you. You just don't know when.

'The, *uh,* aims are for the pupils to work out what might make an, *um,* character interesting.'

If the class notice that I've changed the salient point of the lesson, and there's a very good chance that they simply have not noticed, they don't let on. If push comes to shove, I'd like to think they're on my side.

'Let's hear some of their suggestions, then.'

'Yes, excellent idea, Mr Hughes.' I throw the class a warning look that I hope screams *not one mention of a single Kardashian.*

Khloe puts her hand up.

'Yes, Khloe.'

'Well, miss, I think an interesting,' she pauses, *'character,* would be someone who doesn't have a regular life.' Khloe, a girl after my own heart. 'I mean, they might go somewhere really exotic. But mostly they wouldn't do what you're meant to. No one wants to read a story about someone who just gets married and knocks out a couple of kids.'

I've seen *One Born Every Minute,* and so dispute the ease with which 'knocking out' suggests that babies enter the world. However, now is not the time. Instead, I nod sagely and scribble her idea down on the whiteboard. It's a good start.

'Thank you, Khloe. Anyone else?'

Tim, whose tongue piercing I've been decidedly ignoring, puts his hand up. Asking him risks alerting Mr Hughes and his evil henchwoman to the silver bar through his tongue. To say they don't appreciate Tim's flair for originality is an understatement. Still, there's no one else.

'Yes, Tim.'

'What about an influencer or a computer gamer or some-thing. You know, like that kid who won millions playing Fortnite. Him, he's interesting.'

We're veering into dangerous Kardashian terri-tory, but I nod along. I note Tim's suggestions down. Influencer, Fortnite.

'And I have to say, miss, top-notch lesson as always. No one gets me to learn shit like you do.'

It's blatantly for the benefit of Hughes and Higginbottom. I resist the urge to bang my head off my desk.

'Thank you, Tim. Anyone else?'

They're growing in confidence now, assured that I'll let anything pass to get Mr Hughes out of here.

More hands.

'They might do a bungee jump.'

'Or something proper sporty.'

'What about Hitler?'

Why is it every lesson someone mentions Hitler? I scribble down 'fascist?', starting to sweat.

'Trump!'

'Zombies!'

'Thank you, everyone.' I manage to cut them off. I'm losing control. I take a moment to question the life choices that have led me here. Then I remember choice is perhaps too strong a word for my tumbleweed approach to life. Still, and I don't know what possesses me to do this, I add 'the undead' to my mind map.

'They could be vegan,' Casey with the dreadlocks shouts out.

Tim throws his balled-up worksheet at her. 'Everyone knows vegans are knobs.'

'Now, now, Tim.' I throw him a pleading look. Tim should be on my side. I bring him breakfast every day. Ever since I caught him trying to swallow a dry Weetabix in Year 8. 'I don't want to take your planner.'

Non-adherence to the school behaviour policy is one of the things that could make you fail a learning walk. I risk a glance at Mr Hughes, busy scribbling on his clipboard. Tim and I both know that I have an, at best, relaxed approach to the behaviour policy. I struggle to muster the requisite venom for a wrong shade of sock.

'Sorry, Casey, I was out of order,' he says sweetly.

Casey responds with a very rude hand gesture.

'Well, I think that's enough suggestions. Thank you, everyone.' I look at the sparse mind map on the board. There's some good stuff there, something to get me started at least. As long as I ignore their entreaties to turn to fascism.

There's another ten minutes of the lesson left. I'd hoped the learning walk would be over by now but Morticia and Lurch are both still waiting expectantly.

'So,' I begin, willing my brain to come up with something, anything, to save the job I'm not sure I like and am only moderately successful in.

'Next, what I'd like you to do is to complete a piece of creative writing. Create your own character and write the shortened version of their life story. The only condition is that you have to make them interesting.' This has nothing to do with Life Lessons in any way, shape or form. But still, thank you, brain. I promise the universe to shoehorn free speech into some future lesson.

Blank looks.

'So, you want us to write?'

'That's why we're here isn't it, Tim?' I say breezily. With my back to Mr Hughes, I mouth the words DVD and tilt my head to the side to indicate next week. Perhaps we'll watch some *West Wing*.

It seals the deal. Suddenly they're all nose to paper, scribbling away.

'Thank you, Miss Turner,' the head nods, as he backs out

of the door. 'I'll leave the feedback in your pigeonhole.' He waves his clipboard at me. 'See me if you'd like to discuss it.'

I'd rather gouge out my eyeballs with a rusty spoon.

The door swings shut.

'What a twat.'

'Tim!'

'Well, he is, miss.'

The door opens again.

'Tim, could you come to my office. Take out the tongue piercing on your way.'

Tim makes to leave, collecting his jam roll on the way out.

'Told you,' he says, as the door shuts again.

For once, and it is somewhat unnerving to admit this, I think Tim might be right.

Chapter Six

I retrieve my learning walk feedback at break. 'Requires improvement.' Which fits entirely with my sentiments about life. On the 'next steps' section there's the one word set to strike fear into the heart of any teacher. 'Competency.' It's only a threat at this stage but any more require improvements and I'm sure Hughes will have me on it.

Competency is the thing that headteachers do when they want to sack you but don't want to risk any sort of employment tribunal. It's to education what the rack was to Tudor torture chambers. On competency, you can be learning-walked at will. You have to set weekly targets. You have to produce evidence, beyond being in a classroom every day, that you've met all several thousand of the teaching standards. It's a means to make your life so miserable that they force you to leave of your own accord. Not that leaving would be completely terrible. If I knew what else I wanted to do, that is.

Stan, the English technician, sees me grimace at the feedback and gives me my photocopying for the rest of the week. He always does mine first. I once asked him why and he said it's because I have sexy ankles. I'm not sure if this is inuendo for something else and I don't care enough to find out. Low-level sexual harassment is something I'm willing to overlook in return for photocopying.

Of course, being an English technician is not actually a real job. But then Stan is also Mr Hughes's twenty-two-year-old nephew. The whole English faculty ignore the blatant nepotism. Because Stan has a bottomless pit of laminating pouches, and you just don't look that sort of gift horse in the mouth. I just mumble a thanks, determinedly ignoring Stan winking at me. He can only half-manage it anyway. His other eye closes a bit too much. A timely reminder that there's always someone less competent at being alive than me.

Kaz is ready for work when I get back to the flat.

'How do you look like that for nights?' I ask, dumping my bag on the island in the kitchen.

Kaz has her red hair in a messy bun. Strands fall artfully around her face. She's leaning against the island, scrolling. Gran once described her as 'bright-eyed and bushy-tailed,' which seems apt. In contrast, 'drawn' is the adjective most used to appraise my own appearance.

'I eat vegetables occasionally. You should try it. There's aubergine pasta in the fridge.'

'Thanks.' I put the bowl straight in the microwave and retrieve the cheese. Kaz never adds enough.

I'm gazing intently at my phone, waiting for the microwave to ding. I took a picture of the mind map from first period today, with all the things that make someone's life interesting.

'Emily, *Emily*!' Kaz says.

'Huh?'

'We're nearly out of loo roll. I see you're still being slightly more weird than normal. How're you feeling?'

I take a dramatic breath.

'So, as you know I've been having something of a life crisis.'

She puts her phone down.

'On account of the fact that I am an exactly average, completely boring human.'

'Right. But *you* aren't boring.'

'I am. So, I've decided to do something about it. Have you seen my new stationery?' I'm rummaging through the kitchen drawers.

'What for?'

'For my list.'

'Your list?'

'Yes, the list I'm going to write to make my life interesting.'

I let out an involuntary squeal when I spot the notebook Kaz got me for Christmas. I sniff the first page.

'Yes, because nothing screams, "look at my extraordinary life" like a well-formed list in a new notebook that you just sniffed.'

'You know, you're onto something there.' I point the pen at her before starting to copy down the ideas.

'Fascist?' She peers over my shoulder.

'Ah, you're distracting me.' I quickly draw a line through *fascist*, annoyed that I've messed up the first page.

I add 'do nots' and underline it.

Do not meet future husband.

Kaz snorts.

'What? Look, the average person gets married for the first time at thirty-one, right. And you've got at least a year-long engagement because weddings are so bloody expensive these days, and a two-year relationship before that, so technically speaking, I should be just about ready to meet my soulmate any day now.'

'And that would be awful because—?'

'I refuse to do it. I will not be average anymore.' I slam the pen down. Point made.

The microwave dings and I add copious amounts of cheese. Cheese never lets me down.

'And this has all come from some programme that you watched and not the fact that it's twenty years this year since Claire died?'

Kaz rests her arms on the kitchen island and narrows her eyes at me. I flinch under her steely gaze.

'It's absolutely not that. Just the programme.'

There's no way that I'm admitting that this list is about Claire. To anyone. I'm already perilously close to pointing out how much better at being alive she would have been.

'If you say so.'

It doesn't sound like she buys it.

God. I wish this *was* as straightforward as a midlife crisis. If I were fifty, perhaps I could buy a red sports car and be done with it. No one would ask too many questions. But can you have a plausible midlife crisis at twenty-eight? A third of a life crisis, perhaps? Either way, I can't afford a sports car. I can barely manage the upkeep on my Ford.

Kaz walks over to where I'm stood frozen and waves her hand in front of my eyes.

'Are you having a seizure that I need to be aware of?'

'Don't think so.'

'Good. Shall we resume your breakdown on Friday at that new bar in town? I need to get ready.'

'Isn't it another Wetherspoons?' Kaz isn't a Wetherspoons person.

'Come on, we haven't been out for ages. I said I'd meet Brian there.'

'Brian?'

'Met him while I was getting rid of that dresser.'

'So, just to clarify, you met him at the tip.'

'It's not like he lives there. Don't look so horrified.'

She gathers up her phone and heads to the stairs.

'Only you could go to the tip and come away with a phone number.'

'Why, thank you.'

'Why do you need me though? Sounds like you're past the wingwoman stage if you already have his number.'

'He's just got a job there. Said I'd wait for him until his shift finishes. Apparently, his brother will be there too.'

'Now it makes sense. I'm babysitting the brother so that you and Brian can get it on.'

She pauses, a foot on the bottom stair.

'No one has said that since the eighties. Come on, what's the worst that could happen?'

'I fall head over heels in love with said brother and he tricks me into marrying him in three years.' I look down pointedly at my list.

'Well yes, that would be awful. And maybe illegal, if you're forced into marriage against your will. But seriously, what are the odds? Anyway, we can make a night of it. Before we meet them. I thought I was dealing with a new Emily here?'

I swallow.

'Okay.'

'Great. I'll see you after work and I'll do your hair in a way that screams "soulmates not welcome, everyone else please form an orderly queue".'

'Okay. Oh, I know, I can show you my finished list by then.'

'Deal. I'm a good friend. I can support you through this crisis.'

With that she bounces up the stairs.

I move to the couch to finish my pasta. Taking the notebook with me. The list is sparse, no doubt about it. With a sinking sensation I realise there isn't enough here to see me through another fifty-four years.

I decide to watch the programme again. Take notes this time.

Kaz leaves, shaking her head as I perch on the edge of the sofa, metallic notebook in one hand, remote grasped firmly in the other.

I fast forward to the right bit, with the presenter churning through all the stuff about an average adult. I scribble notes. Pausing it when I need to. I finish, ignoring the final third of the programme about old age. Hopefully I'll have already smashed life by then and I'll just have a rest.

My notes are more of a 'what not to do'. I do, however, pick up on a number of salient points.

Average human (AH) visits seven countries in their lifetime.

Okay, I'm not particularly average here. I actually hate the thought of going on holiday. I've only ever been to Ayia Napa, and that was with Kaz when we were eighteen. And I'm not sure spending seven nights pissed in the Temple of Doom nightclub even qualifies as having visited Greece. Technically then, I'm actually behind on this one.

AH has seven sexual partners and spends around 117 days of their life having sex.

So, I've had two and a half. The half being when, at the Year 11 prom, I'd accidentally brushed Jason Stanford's penis during an overly enthusiastic attempt at the macarena. We'd been dancing opposite each other, and he was freakishly tall. Unsolicited gropings aside, I can't imagine my experience thus far would amount to even seventeen minutes, let alone anything more. I've no idea what all the fuss is about.

I'm starting to think that even average is a lofty height that I have yet to attain.

AH spends 180 days exercising in their lifetime.

Moving swiftly on.

AH spends forty-one per cent of waking hours looking at technology.

Hmm, I'd long since disabled those judge-y little screen-time notifications from my phone so I'm not sure on this one. I've learned from experience that it's hard to scroll and teach. However, instinct tells me that I'm more than making up for this in my free time. Even now my thumb is liking of its own accord. I'm still not entirely sure how I ended up so engrossed in the life of a God-fearing Texan mum of seven.

I've filled two pages with random facts. Nothing which resembles a proper list has emerged yet, though. No wonder I've been boring for so long; interesting requires serious dedication and effort.

Claire was the remarkable one. The extrovert. I'm the other one.

It dawns on me. Without her there's been no one urging me on these last twenty years. Making me do stuff I don't want to do. Grief really has to be the sneakiest of the human emotions. It's the twist in a story you never see coming. I rub away tears and try to get back to my list.

At university I'd had an 'out there' university lecturer who'd made us walk around for all of our seminars. Apparently, Frederick Nietzsche had once said that all great thoughts are conceived while walking. I would challenge both Professor Stebbins and Nietzsche on this. I would argue that all great thoughts have already been conceived and uploaded onto Google to peruse at our convenience. No walking required. Bleary-eyed, it is to Google I turn next.

There is nothing that our supreme overlord Google does not know. That I haven't considered this solution before astounds me. But still, I'm here now. *What makes a person interesting?* I type. Pleasingly, there are many millions of hits. I will be interesting in no time.

With the sheer volume of information out there, I feel the need to expand beyond the confines of my notebook. Grabbing the Post-it Notes, I begin a visual mind map of different ideas, wading through hit after hit until I find what I'm looking for. *Be spontaneous*, one site tells me. *Explore*, says another. *Embrace the past*. I ignore that one. I add my own notes and start sticking ideas to the coffee table. I feel no guilt here because it's only plastic.

A number of sites harp on about the importance of opening ourselves up to love. One has the audacity to point out that love and loss go hand in hand. 'Despite the risk,' it declares, 'love is perhaps the most meaningful facet of the human experience.' I close that site with an angry click.

An hour later I sit back, exhausted. To the unsuspecting eye it might look like I'm an amateur detective, hunting a pattern in the murders of a serial killer. But it's all there. Everything I need to embark upon my new, interesting life.

I pause for a moment, turning to a fresh page. Every good list needs a title. After a moment's more indecision, I add, 'The Life List' to the top of the page. Goodbye, dreary existence. I have a list against you and I'm not afraid to use it.

The Life List, by Emily Turner

Be Spontaneous

- *Spontaneity might include things such as saying yes to questions which hitherto would have been met with reluctance.*

Be Successful

- *Leave teaching to fulfil a greater ambition/cause.*
- *Discover what aforementioned ambition/cause is.*

Be Brave

- *This could include a bungee jump. But only if other opportunities for bravery fail to present themselves.*

Be Compassionate

- *Become vegan unlike 93 per cent of the UK.*

Be Inspirational

- *Unlikely to master Fortnite to professional level. Consider some sort of sporting achievement as a last resort.*

Be Helpful

- *Ensure this is highly visible in order to receive proper recognition for efforts.*

Be An Explorer

- *Travel to other countries and once there commit to visiting places beyond local nightclubs and McDonald's.*

Be Authentic

- DO NOT FALL IN LOVE.
- *Be authentic and show everyone the 'new' Emily.*

Chapter Seven

Kaz is in a contouring frenzy. Her nose has shrunk. There's a glow around her hairline. She's wearing a tight green satin dress that would look horrific on me. It's always something of a relief leaving the house with her looking like this. Literally no one pays me any attention when I'm out with Kaz.

She's sat in front of the mirror propped against my bedroom wall (nails and screws both having been expressly forbidden under the terms of our tenancy agreement).

'What were you planning on wearing?' she asks.

'Jeans and a nice top?'

'Your purple top? The one you always wear?'

I nod mutely.

She lets out a frustrated growl. 'You know, I reckon you're right.'

'About what?'

'Maybe you do need to shake things up a bit.'

''Course I'm right.'

My phone dings.

Mum: Did you get my message yesterday love? Xxx

I scroll up. Also **Mum:** Hi love, hope work's okay.
Your gran had her toenail done. I was thinking
of setting a date for the family meeting for the
memorial. We mentioned it last Sunday. Did you
want to let me know when you're free? Xxx

I am normally a very fastidious replier on account of the fact
that I almost never have messages worthy of a reply. NatWest
text me more than anyone else, to tell me that I'm using my
overdraft. Yet I've virtually no recollection of Mum's first
message. If I leave it any longer, she'll call the police, so I
fire one back.

Sorry, Mum, must have missed your text. Glad
Gran's toenail is sorted. I'll check my diary and get
back to you with some dates. Off out with Kaz xxx
Mum, approximately one nanosecond later: Okay,
love! Have fun! Xxx

'Bad news?' Kaz asks. I'm staring at my now-blank phone.

I give my head a shake. It does nothing.

'No, just Mum. She wants to have a family meeting about
the memorial.'

There's only Kaz and her mum so she finds my family's
penchant for a family meeting highly amusing. However, on
this occasion she doesn't even begin to wind me up. Instead,
she pauses blending and turns to me.

'Ah. You know, Em—'

I cut her off. 'I don't want to talk about it. I just want to get this evening over with.'

'Okay. But try to rein in your excitement, will you? It's almost overwhelming.' She's blending again.

I huff like a moody teenager. 'If not this one,' I hold up the floaty halter neck top that's so well worn it's gone bobbly, 'then what shall I wear?'

Kaz pads through to her own room, returning a few minutes later with something akin to a tiny piece of chainmail.

'This, with these.' She holds up a seems-like-metal-but-isn't-proper-metal dress and black heels. I gulp. Visibly apparently. 'Go on, you'll look good.'

'No chance.'

'Do you trust me?'

'Will you be offended if I say no?'

Kaz is very much in the single digits when it comes to clothes sizes. In contrast, I am very much not.

'How about you try it with tights. You can always take it off?'

'All right, fine.' I take the offending dress. *Be spontaneous*, I chant on my way to the bathroom.

'Are you talking to yourself already?'

I stop chanting.

In the bathroom I pull the dress on. It's tight in places it probably shouldn't be, but not completely indecent.

I give myself the once-over, doing my best to ignore the bits that I wish were just a little bit bigger or smaller, depending on the bit in question. Body positivity is exhausting.

Life was so much easier when we were all slaves to diet culture. We were hungry, but at least we didn't have the energy to think.

Kaz whistles as I go back in the bedroom. 'You look hot.'

'I've never looked hot in my life.'

She's busy dousing the room in perfume and walking through it.

'Please. False modesty has had its day.'

I ignore her and instead look down at my dress.

This is the sort of thing the new Emily would wear. Bold, daring. The dress rattles and I can't quite decide if I'm shaking or a bit cold.

'Come here and I'll sort your hair out.'

I pad over obediently to sit in front of the mirror.

I'm normally a nondescript bobble type of girl. So it's really no surprise that Kaz is better at doing my hair than I am. She's plaited it and twisted it around the top of my head. If I were in lederhosen, I'd look like a gone to seed Heidi.

'Fit.' Kaz heads for the door. 'Let's make sure you meet anyone *but* your soulmate tonight.'

'One sec, let me get my notepad. Remember, you promised we could talk about my list.'

Her eyes roll so far back in her head I'm surprised the retinas don't detach.

'Can I order a cup of tea?'

'No, you cannot.'

'But that old lady's having one?'

59

'She's here for Fish Friday. It's part of the deal.'

I groan, shaking with the cold. My edgy resolve had all but withered and died around three metres from our front door, when I'd realised that it was January, and I was essentially naked on the streets of Huddersfield.

'Let's huddle together for warmth.'

The new Wetherspoons looks decidedly like all other Wetherspoons. If a bit cleaner on account of the newness.

Kaz and I are clinging to each other like a pair of weirdos when a scruffy-looking bartender approaches. His hair is slightly long and there's a faint scar under his eye. I can spot Kaz's type a mile off.

'You made it.' Bingo. Brian.

'What time do you finish?' Kaz asks, leaning across the bar.

'Ten. Josh is meeting us here.'

Oh yes. I'd almost forgotten about the brother.

'What can I get you both? It's on the house.'

I keep quiet about the fact that it's potentially unwise for Brian to be offering free drinks so early on in his bartending career. Mainly because I really want a free drink.

A stern shake of the head from Kaz ends my cup of tea fantasies once and for all.

'Um, a glass of red wine please.'

'Make that a bottle.'

'Any specific type?'

'Er, just a warming one.'

'No problem.'

He busies himself.

'He seems nice.' Over the years I've learnt not to grow too attached to any of Kaz's flings because she's determinedly anti-relationship. I would say it's because Ben Stevens broke her heart in sixth form. She would say that she just prefers one-night stands. Either way I admire her for it. Like I said, I don't see what all the fuss is about.

'Honestly, who cares. It's been too long.'

'It's been three weeks since Steve the lorry driver.'

'Exactly, too long.'

Brian reappears with our wine.

'See you later,' he says, looking incredibly pleased at this fact.

'Is it me or is it very bright in here?' We peer out from the bar, searching for a table.

'I think we're just a bit early, that's all. Maybe it'll get going later on.'

It's only 8pm. I hear that kids these days don't go out till midnight or something. I won't last till then with these shoes on. It's like walking on glass. I hop from foot to foot.

'Come on, let's sit in that booth over there.' Kaz nods towards the corner and we head with intent to the safety of the table.

'Drink quick,' Kaz commands as we sit. 'It'll warm us up.'

We neck our first glass of wine. She's right, almost immediately I start to feel warmer. But there's also a wooziness in my head. Red wine is not a drink designed to be downed.

Kaz pours another glass.

'Right, come on then, time for the grand unveiling.'

I notice my hands are already a bit wobbly on the clasp of my bag. Surely that's impossible after not even two glasses of wine. I don't tend to drink much at home, not unless Kaz is with me. Drinking alone when your life is as miserable as mine is a one-way ticket to alcohol dependency.

'So, what I've aimed for are some general guiding principles and then the subpoints are the ways and means that they could be applied.'

'Hmm, good plan. Though I'd like to go officially on the record as saying that I think you're already very interesting.' It's a blatant lie. But she tilts her glass in a mock cheer and I follow suit.

Okay, half a bottle of wine. Now it's fine to feel a bit drunk. Even if it is only 8.30pm. At least I don't feel cold, or more sad than usual. Perhaps I've been too hasty in dismissing the use of alcohol as an emotional crutch before now. It's actually highly effective.

Kaz looks down at my list.

'Did you come up with all this?'

'God no. It's a mixture of the programme, my Year 11s and Google.'

She looks from the list to me and back again. I've added a flower border around the outside which I think sets it off quite nicely.

'Well, it's, um, very . . . expansive.'

I nod. 'I know. It needs to be. I am not to be trusted with any aspect of my fate.'

'You're like Stalin, but with an eight-point plan.'

'And a penchant for mass murder.'

'Are you going in order?'

I shake my head. 'I thought I'd go for one or two a month.' I swallow hard. I'd been so focused on coming up with The List, I'd not really worried sufficiently about actually doing it. I muster my best fake smile. 'Hopefully by the time summer comes, I'll be living my new life, authentically.'

'I see. So you're going vegan?' She's still looking at The List.

'I can still eat chips.'

'This is very true.'

'And I'll have time to say an emotional farewell to cheese.'

'Good plan.' I'm not sure if Kaz does in fact think this is a good plan. But she's at that cheery stage of drunk where she agrees with everything I say.

'You do know you already *are* some of these things, don't you?'

'Name one.'

'You're compassionate. You donate to the hospice. Money for sick kids. You are the epitome of compassion. You could skip the vegan thing.'

'The hospice doesn't count,' I whisper. 'And anyway, I'm not *visibly* compassionate. No one looks at me and thinks, wow, Emily is so kind.'

'Jesus would be rolling in his grave.'

'He *literally* resurrected himself, Kaz. That's the whole point.'

'You know, this here is the problem.' Kaz stabs at my still-open list.

63

'What, why?'

'There's too much pressure on us all these days. We've got to be amazing all the frigging time.'

'Maybe. But what's wrong with wanting a little more for myself?' I'm pleased that in my almost-drunk state I appear to be maintaining my lie.

'Nothing. It's just,' she waves her arms around in a gesture which could mean Wetherspoons, but probably means the universe, 'a hundred years ago, no one would have cared about being remarkable. People were more contented.'

She takes a big drink.

'Were they? I thought they were all dying of measles and tonsillitis. Anyway, isn't it a good thing that we're dreaming big now? Especially women.'

I take a big drink.

'Abso-fuckinglutely. But it comes with pressure. That's the price of it all. It's the curse of our generation.'

'Great, so even my third of a life crisis isn't particularly unique.'

'Well, other people probably think for a minute, "Hmm, I wonder what I'm doing with my life?" And then order a Chinese and go back to watching *Britain's Got Talent*. I'm not sure many would canvass a list from a bunch of random fifteen-year-olds and Google, and then use it as the basis for their entire futures.'

'Why, thank you.'

'You're welcome.'

I go to drink. 'Oh dear. It's empty.'

'More wine?'

'Absolutely.'

While Kaz is at the bar, and she's there for an inordinately long time, I think about her critique. She's right. Most people would have at least come up with their own list. Except life without Claire has always seemed so beyond me. So really, I needed the support. And anyway, it's surely the execution that counts. The List will be the making of me. My metamorphosis from sad little caterpillar to happy colourful Claire-shaped butterfly.

'Did you just say metamorphosis? You're not drunk enough yet.'

I laugh nervously to mask the fact that I might now be insane.

'You took your time.'

'Chatting to Brian.'

Brian is still smiling in a dumbstruck fashion at Kaz. He's ignoring the other customers. Poor love-struck fool.

Another half a bottle of wine and I'm slamming my glass on the table.

'I'm gonna do it!'

'Do what?'

'The Life List. And it'll be brilliant.'

'I thought we'd reached that conclusion several days ago but okay. Cheers to the Life List!'

We fake cheers. There's a chance we're shouting because people are looking our way.

'Let's take a selfie!' Kaz declares, phone in hand.

Rebecca Ryan

'Absolutely not,' I reply.

'Why?'

'Because we're twenty-eight and it's tragic.' I do my best to dodge Kaz's phone as she snaps away.

'Look, Brian is waving at us. Come on.'

'I need a wee. Wait for me at the front.'

I've not been this drunk for some time. And I seem to be getting drunker the more I walk.

On the loo I get another message from Mum with a massive of list of potential memorial dates she's canvassed from the rest of the Turner clan. I turn my phone off in defiance.

I find the idea of a memorial unfathomably hard. I have my own little routine around the anniversary of Claire's death. It involves getting steadily more depressed in the run-up to the day itself, and then going to see a musical. Last year I'd bawled my eyes out watching the local drama club murder *Annie Get Your Gun*.

Leaving the toilets, I seem weirdly angry. This week really has been a veritable onslaught of unwelcome feeling.

There's a guy leaving the men's loo at the same time. He does a sort of half-smile at me, revealing some rather appealing dimples.

I scowl at him.

I pick up the pace to get away from him, stumbling through the pub like a drunk Bambi.

Kaz is waving at me. And scruffy Brian is waving too.

That's nice. I've only met Brian once. I wave back and then stop when I realise that Dimples is following me.

We both come to a stop in front of Kaz and Brian.

'Argh,' I yelp and attempt to jump. It's an impossible feat in my shoes and I'm seconds away from face-planting on the Wetherspoons carpet. Dimples catches me, helping me to right myself. I jolt, realising that I'm holding his forearms in a vice-like grip.

Brian clears his throat. 'Kaz, this is my brother Josh. Josh, this is Kaz and . . . sorry I didn't catch your name?'

'Emily,' I say in a small voice.

Josh holds his hand out for me to shake. I chance a look at his face as I do. Nice blue eyes. Very nice, actually. And dimples. I never realised until now, but I really love dimples. He has a cowlick at the front of his hair. I resist the ridiculous urge to lean over and smooth it down.

I'm stood gawping at Josh. He's wearing a faded T-shirt and dark jeans. I think I'm staring and we're blocking the door, so Kaz pulls me to the side of the exit. Brian and Josh follow.

Oh fate, you wily thing you, you almost caught me there.

I turn to Kaz. 'No, absolutely not. We cannot possibly spend time with Josh.'

Josh is stood half a foot away from us and I'm definitely shouting.

'Er,' he says.

Kaz ignores me. In fact, in the seconds it's taken Josh to make a confused sound, she's begun kissing Brian.

I implore to a rather confused looking Josh.

'It's the dimples you see.'

'I don't actually.'

There has to be a way to make him understand.

'Here, this is it, the Life List. As you can see, it explicitly states no soulmates allowed. That's right, Kaz, isn't it?'

She makes a 'mmm' noise. I can't tell if it's encouragement or a groan.

Josh's eyes go wide.

'Right-o,' he chances. 'And you reckon that's me, do you? Soulmate?'

There's a cheer and a clunking noise as someone wins big on the slot machine. We're still tucked in the dark corner by the doors. With each passing minute, the pub seems smaller and smaller.

'It's the dimples,' I reply faintly.

He chuckles again.

There's a sound like a plunger being released. 'Look, can we get out of here?' Brian asks.

'Let's go back to ours!' Kaz declares. Traitor.

'Kaz, I've told you, I can't spend any more time with Josh.' I glance at him. 'No offence.'

'None taken. But could I just point out that, one, I'm seeing someone and two, you're not really my type. No offence.'

Plenty taken.

'All right, let's go back to ours,' I relent.

Josh looks like he would rather do anything, absolutely anything, than spend the rest of the evening in my company. And it's clear that it will be my company, as Kaz and Brian are dry humping as they push through the door. It's quite a feat of multi-tasking actually. The walking hump.

'You don't need to come,' I tell him as we emerge into the cold, arctic night. In my head I'm being kind, absolving him of his responsibility to tag along. In reality, I sound like a petulant teenager.

'It's okay. I said I'd wait for Bri. We're sharing a taxi.'

I can't think of a reply that isn't asking why a grown man needs a babysitter, so I just make a hmph sound. Undoubtedly enhancing his conviction that I'm not his type.

I chance a look at Josh as we walk. He's a bit taller than me. Average height or so I'd say. He catches me, so I style it out as a cough. I can't remember the last time I spent an evening with someone who wasn't a blood relation or Kaz.

It's going to be a long night.

Chapter Eight

'Here we are!' Kaz declares, taking for ever with the lock. Whether it's because she's still drunk, or because frostbite has begun to set in, remains a mystery. Personally, the cold to be very sobering.

It's 10.10pm. Our wild night out lasted a grand total of two hours and ten minutes. Well, my wild night out did, at any rate. It doesn't look like Kaz is planning on ending the evening any time soon.

We push through into the front room and Kaz and Brian collapse on the couch. A tangle of arms and legs. The fleecy throw we use to hide a red wine stain is on the floor in seconds. Josh hovers awkwardly beside our IKEA lamp.

'I'm, um, just going to get changed.' I stumble towards the stairs.

'Be quick, will you?' Josh is trying not to look at Kaz and Brian. Kaz is straddling him. My heart sinks. I'd actually been planning on hiding up in my room for the rest of the evening.

I bang around my bedroom, soothed by the familiarity of it all. I'm looking for my sprout pyjamas. They've got cute little sprouts with Santa hats on. And though it's January, for some reason it is imperative that I wear them. They're like a hug in pyjama form.

I hear the door slam along the corridor and realise, with relief, that Kaz and Brian have made it to the bedroom.

Catching sight of myself in the the hall mirror, I let out a yelp. I look wrecked. My mascara appears to be making a bid for freedom and bits of plait have escaped from the top of my head making it look like I've been electrocuted. My teeth are basically black from the wine. No wonder Josh said I wasn't his type. I am no one's definition of their type.

Back downstairs, I round on him. He's perched on the edge of the Poäng.

'For the record, my teeth are black from the red wine. I do not have tooth decay.'

Josh looks disturbed.

'Are those sprouts on your pyjamas?'

'Yep. And not just any sprouts – Santa sprouts,' I nod sagely. 'I wear them when I get my period.' Shut up woman. 'Plenty of room for bloating.' And to demonstrate I pull the waistband out, probably flashing my knickers, hammering the final nail in the coffin of Josh's attraction.

He looks suitably horrified.

'Anyway, moving on from my period PJs.' Why do I keep saying the word period? 'Do you, um, want to get a pizza? I think they'll be up there for a while.' I tilt my head back, gesturing upstairs.

'Sure.' Josh relaxes a bit. I think he'd been preparing to run. 'I'll do the honours – what type?'

'Pepperoni please.'

'No problem.'

I give him our address and he taps away on his phone. Once he's done, he sits on the couch. It's a really good job that he thinks I'm ugly. Because I can't help but notice that he is not ugly. Not even a little bit. There's nothing specific about him making him not ugly, he's just the sum of some really slightly above average parts. Like his eyes. Blue is top-notch as eye colours go. And the dimples are a positive addition to his face, no doubt. Actually, even his neck is better than most. Not too thick but not one of those weedy necks either.

He puts his phone down. I think I'm gawping.

'You want a drink?' I recover, padding through to the kitchen and taking the opportunity to gulp in some sobering breaths en route.

It's been a long time since I've entertained. Long time as in never.

'Sure, what have you got?'

'Wine, water or . . . milk?' I call through.

He laughs. 'I'll take some wine then, I guess.'

I return with one glass of wine for Josh and a water for me. Because quite frankly, I've had enough.

'So, um, do you have a job?'

He tilts his head to the side but answers anyway. 'Yeah, in IT. I work for Microsoft in their outreach team. Mainly I help with the installation of new systems in organisations all around West Yorkshire.' I almost nod off in the middle of his answer. His job sounds awfully boring. We're practically made for each other.

'And you say you're seeing someone?'

'Yep. Amy, it's been three years.'

'Wow, long time.'

Awkward silence.

'How about you?'

'Nope, single.' This revelation, I imagine, is a surprise to no one. The thing is, I've never actually wanted a boyfriend. Not really. I dislike the concept of sharing my innermost thoughts and feelings with another human on a fundamental level. Mostly I just get ghosted, which suits me fine.

'But you're expecting to run into your soulmate any day now?'

'Rubbish, isn't it? I've just got to keep my wits about me, make sure one doesn't creep up on me unawares.'

He laughs at that, even though I was being serious. Maybe I'm still drunker than I think I am.

'Tell me about yourself then,' he says. I don't even think *he* likes the question because he just winced. Though it could be at the mascara running down my face. I tried ineffectively to rub it off in the kitchen.

'There's absolutely nothing to tell, I'm afraid. I'm just like everyone else. Moderately sad.'

He frowns in a way that suggests that perhaps not everyone *does* feel like this. But we've just met, so he has to be polite.

'Okay, then what about this Life List?'

'I watched this programme and basically, it showed all the

average stuff that humans normally do, and I realised that I'm totally average. And that's a bit rubbish, isn't it?'

'I don't know, there's worse things.'

'Yeah, but only really bad stuff. Like being one of those people who fancy dead bodies.'

'You don't seem boring to me. You're wearing sprout pyjamas.'

I laugh nervously. I'm once again having to tiptoe around the fact that my dead twin would have been much better at being alive than me. I might not have gotten out much this last decade, but even I recognise that this isn't an appropriate revelation for a first meeting.

There's another awkward silence. The pizza arrives, which is something of a relief for us both. I wish I'd kept quiet about the sad thing. At least we have pizza. It's actually challenging to be even moderately sad in the company of pizza.

Josh dives straight in like an amateur.

I grab his arm to stop him. 'This is Fat Joe's, right?'

He nods.

'Thought so, I recognise the writing.'

Fat Joe has written our address on the box with a little x under it. I'm a very loyal customer.

'You need to leave it three minutes to solidify.' I lift the lid. 'See, it's so cheesy the pepperoni will run straight off at this stage, and then you've just got soggy tomato bread.'

'Okay.'

'The sweet spot is between minutes three and eleven, while the cheese is solid. After that it coagulates and might kill you. See it as a sort of competitive eating challenge as opposed to an enjoyable meal.'

We sit diligently waiting for the three minutes to be up. 'Tuck in.'

Cheese makes everyone happy. I read once that it sets off the opioid receptors in brains. Basically, it's as addictive as crack.

Josh goes to speak. 'What'll you do first – from The List I mean?'

I hold my finger to my lips. Conversation will have to wait. Already the stuffed crust is turning solid. You can tell by the amount of torque required from your jaw to chew.

When the game is lost, I pick up the conversation where we left off. It's been a gallant effort.

'No idea. I'm going to aim for one a month though.'

'So, you'll be interesting by . . . ?'

I feel that he may be mocking me. 'July.'

'Right.'

Josh is still trying to chew. I can see his jaw straining. Fool.

Upstairs there's a slap, followed by a shriek of laughter from Brian.

'Why did you come?' I ask too loudly.

'Pardon?' he replies, equally loudly.

'Tonight. It was obvious that those two were going to keep each other busy.'

'Oh, I, er . . .' He looks uncomfortable and I feel bad.

'You don't have to tell me, obviously.'

'No, it's just I wanted to make sure Bri got home all right. That's all.'

I don't think that is all, but I don't push it. Chances are that after tonight, I'll never see or hear from Josh or Brian again.

I feel an odd mixture of relief tinged with sadness at the fact.

'Do you want to watch a musical?' I ask.

'Er, okay.'

He says it in a way that screams, I'm just being polite, please don't make me watch one. But I ignore his silent pleading and put on *La La Land*. And really, he should be grateful that I've gone for one of the trendy musicals. He could be about to watch *Brigadoon* if I were feeling that way inclined.

'They're my favourite genre.'

'An unusual choice for someone who claims to be sad.'

'Maybe. But I'm still putting it on. You might enjoy it.'

Josh's eyes, which I've been decidedly ignoring all night, tell me that he is very, very doubtful that this will be the case.

We're only up to the bit where Emma Stone gets ready for a night out before I feel sleepy. It's the Fat Joe's. The effort required to digest the volume of cheese means that non-essential functions are shut down. Like staying awake. And I've always slept better in the company of others. I just rarely get the chance. Now though, I must not go to sleep. I'm a drooler.

I'm awoken by Brian thumping down the stairs. The credits are rolling on *La La Land* and if I'm not mistaken, Josh has just wiped a tear from his eye. And even though toxic masculinity has done no one any good ever, I pretend not to notice.

'Ready?' Brian asks, beaming. He might as well just get a flashing sign that reads, 'I just had sex!'

Josh nods as I scramble off the couch.

'Nice to meet you both, Josh, Brian.' I hold my hand out for them to shake in an oddly formal move.

Josh smiles and takes my hand as Brian heads to the door.

'See you around. And good luck with The List.'

'Why, thank you. Bye, Josh.'

'Bye.'

Well, and I don't resort to swearing lightly, thank fuck that's over.

Chapter Nine

1997

'But Mum, I don't want to go to school without Claire!'

'Don't be silly, love. Your other friends will all be there. Katherine from next door is starting today.'

I don't care about stupid Katherine from stupid next door. I don't want to go without Claire.

'Claire, CLAIRE,' I shout at her in the bottom bunk. She just rolls over to look at me and she looks really sick and I'm a bit scared then.

'Claire,' I whisper. 'Are you feeling all right? Do you want a glass of milk and a KitKat?' It's what we always have when we're sick. 'Maybe I could put *Annie* on?'

She just groans and rolls onto her side. Mum is frowning and that makes me frown too.

'Right, off you go to school, Emily. Katherine's mum is going to give you a lift.'

I make my legs all straight as Mum steers me out of the bedroom. Matt is already waiting at the door with his bag in his hand. He starts Year 5 today.

'Come on, Emily, we're going to be late.' I let him hold my hand.

Mum kisses us both. She's staying home from working at the big Asda today to look after Claire, even though normally when we're sick, Granny comes and watches us. Mum is pushing us out of the door.

'Enjoy, both of you, have fun!'

My new school shoes are stiff and squeaky and my uniform is a bit big. But Mum says I'll grow into it, so that's all right.

We knock next door and wait.

Matt tells me that there might be cornflake cake and custard for lunch today because he knows that's my favourite.

Katherine opens the door. I already know who she is because me and Claire have played dressy ups once, and pirates three times, with her since she moved in when we got back from Butlin's. Claire said we had to be her friend because she doesn't have any friends like us and she isn't a twin.

Katherine doesn't have a dad, only a mum. But my mum says that's okay and that not everyone has to have a mum and a dad. She said some people might have two mummies or two daddies and that it doesn't matter either way. I'd like two mummies, but not two daddies. Because Dad doesn't cut the crusts off bread like he's supposed to.

'Hi,' Katherine says. 'We're ready now.'

Katherine's mum comes bustling out of the door. She's always in a rush. She wears blue pyjamas to work because she's a nurse. Katherine says her mum works with people who don't get better. But that seems like a really silly place for a nurse to work.

'Come on then, you three.'

She shoos us into the car.

'How's Claire?' Katherine's mum asks.

'She's got a headache again, that's all. Except this one seems worser. I told her to have a glass of milk.'

'Again? She's had other headaches?'

'Yup, she's had them all over summer. Even on our last night in Butlin's. I thought it might be because she keeps falling over but I'm not sure.'

'Falling over . . .' I'm not sure if Katherine's mum is still talking to me or to herself now.

Katherine's mum drives like she's in a rush and taps her finger on the wheel when we have to wait at a red light. 'Here we are then.' She pulls up in front of the gate in the bit that you're not meant to stop in. 'Be good today.'

We climb out. Matt goes towards the juniors building but me and Katherine go the other way because we're still in infants. Infants is better than juniors because we have hopscotch on the floor of our playground, but they don't have anything.

'Are you sad because Claire isn't here?' Katherine asks.

I do a big sniff and nod.

'You can call me Kaz,' she says as we walk up to where the other Year 1s are lining up.

'Okay, Kaz.' It sounds like a grown-up name. Not a name for when you're five, nearly six.

Mr Jones, our new teacher, rings the bell and we all line up like we've been taught to. Mr Jones walks down the line and I think he notices that Claire isn't here because he looks at me for a little bit longer than everyone else.

I sit next to Kaz through carpet time. And at playtime we share our crisps. She has prawn cocktail and I have Quavers.

We do sums and make butterflies and I make mine purple for Claire. It's not too bad doing things with Kaz, but it's not as good as playing with Claire.

At the end of the day, me, Kaz and Matt stand next to each other waiting for her mum to come and pick us up. We're the only people left, aside from Mr Jones. It's a bit odd because Kaz's mum is always in a rush so she shouldn't really be late.

The secretary comes running out of school and whispers something to Mr Jones. But even though she's talking to him, she's looking at me and Matt.

'Okay, I'll take them,' he nods.

Mr Jones seems quite nice but I'm not sure I want to go anywhere with him. I want to go home to see Claire and give her the butterfly I made for her.

'Right, folks. Bit of a change of plan. Your mum and dad have had to take Claire to the hospital. Katherine, your mum is there too. So, I'm going to give you a lift over.'

Matt just says, 'Yes, sir,' but I want to cry.

Mr Jones's car is long and gold. My legs kick the seat with a *thump, thump, thump* that makes Matt look at me.

We get to the hospital and Dad is waiting for us outside

some big glass doors and I almost jump out before Mr Jones's car has even stopped moving. Dad's eyes are all red.

Dad shakes Mr Jones's hand, and Mr Jones says, 'If there's anything I can do to help, please let me know.' Which I think is odd because we've only just met him today.

Dad holds my hand, I hold Kaz's.

I want to run away from the hospital. But instead, we go through the glass doors. I want to take Claire and go far, far away where it doesn't smell like cleaning bottles that we aren't allowed to touch. And where people wear proper clothes, not pyjamas.

I don't think I'm going to like this hospital one little bit.

JANUARY

Be Helpful

Chapter Ten

By the time I drag myself downstairs in the morning, Kaz is just getting back from another parkrun.

'Do you even sleep at night, or do they just plug you in to reboot?'

'The rebooting thing.'

She plonks some orange juice down in front of me. 'Stopped at the Co-op, thought you'd need this.' I nod, grateful.

'So, good night then?' I hazard.

'Mm-hmm. Brian was surprisingly . . . agile.'

I briefly wonder what agility has to do with it.

'I don't want to know.'

'Suit yourself. You and Josh, huh?' She wriggles her eyebrows at me.

'Me and Josh nothing. He's seeing someone, he said I wasn't his type and I made him watch *La La Land* while gorging myself on pizza in my period pyjamas. If he didn't fancy me at the beginning of the night, I'm sure he now finds me nothing short of repulsive.'

'I thought you made a nice pair.' It's testament to the fact that Kaz is my best friend that she doesn't give me any stick for the aforementioned weird shit I did last night.

'No way, he's totally out of my league.'

'Not true at all.'

She pulls the orange juice towards her.

'Anyway, he's way too normal. He works in IT, for goodness' sake. I don't do normal anymore, remember? Any future boyfriends will be something interesting, like a surfer, or at least have a noun for a name.'

'Okay, so we're looking for a surf bum called Chair, even though it's three hours to the seaside from here. Even then, *do* people surf in the North Sea?'

'You're being pedantic. He doesn't have to be called Chair.'

She laughs.

'Tag me in some pictures from last night, will you? Anything that screams, "I love my new, extraordinary life" will do.'

'I see. *Do* you love your life?'

''Course not. It's a shit show. So long as I *look* happy.'

'Well, fat chance of that, you dodged all of my selfie attempts.'

'Damn it. I was sure you caught me in one.'

'Mostly I got an ear and half an eyebrow.'

Kaz scrolls through the pictures on her phone.

'I look excellent in this one?' She holds the screen for me to inspect. She does look excellent. Her arm is round my shoulder and her head tilted to the side. My eyes are halfway between closed and open.

I mean, on the one hand it's probably irresponsible to peddle the myth that our lives are as good as they appear online. But then on the other, fake success might be as close as I ever get. In which eventuality—

'Yes, that'll do.'

'Okay, weirdo. What's your plan for today?'

'Get rid of this awful hangover for starters. Pass me the paracetamol, will you?' I don't tell Kaz, but I can't stop thinking about Claire. It's like my alcohol-weakened brain is under attack from Claire-based memories. I've been humming the theme tune to *Annie* all morning. It's imperative that I begin the Life List at once.

I take a huge gulp of orange juice and swallow the tablets before going to retrieve the calendar from the kitchen wall. The glassy eyes of January's cute kitten, playing with a ball of wool, stare back at me.

'Pass a pen, would you?'

Kaz obliges.

'What're you doing?'

'Making a plan.'

The calendar is divided into four columns, a sort of family planner if you will. Kaz has one for her work shifts and one for socialising. I just have one. It's wholly devoid of engagements.

I retrieve my notebook, wondering where to start.

I close my eyes and jab the pen at my notebook, as good a strategy as any for life-altering decisions. It lands close to Be Helpful. Be Helpful gets a little tick in my notebook and the January column is filled.

Be helpful. Nice and easy to get me started. There's only a week or so of January left; surely even I can manage some visible helpfulness in a week.

I'm not sure which to put next.

Kaz comes to stand behind me.

'You know, you'll only be able to explore when you're off work. Easter holidays?'

'Might be a bit soon.' The thought of exploring seems like a big step. 'Half-term?' May seems pretty far away.

Before I can talk myself out of it, I've turned to the May cute kitten and written Be An Explorer on my column. Another tick.

'I need another easy one for February. Just while I'm getting into it.'

'How about spontaneous. If you're really stuck, we'll just shave half of your hair off or get you a face tattoo.'

'Good idea.'

I add Be Spontaneous to February, silently vowing not to be in a situation whereby I involve Kaz on that one.

'I thought Be Brave might be a good one for June.'

Kaz nods, she understands.

'What've we got left then?'

I check the Life List. 'Be Successful, Be Inspirational, Be Compassionate, that's the vegan thing remember, and Be Authentic.'

'Well, you can't be authentic while you're in the middle of this thing. I say have authentic last.'

'Agreed.' I flick to July.

'Em, if you're going by one a month, the last month will be August.'

'Will it?'

'Eight points on The List, eight months. August.'

'I told Josh July.'

'I don't think he'll be back to check on your progress.'

After last night he won't be back at all.

Still, I liked the thought of being done for summer.

'Maybe I could do two one month. Like in May, I'll only be able to explore during half term anyway. Surely I can manage another that month.'

'Hey, it's your rodeo.'

I add Be Successful to May. Because I think I'm going to need quite some time to work on that one.

'Right that just leaves Be Inspirational and Be Compassionate.'

'And you've got March and April left to fill.'

'I think I'll put off the vegan thing for as long as I can.'

I turn to March, adding Be Inspirational. April gets Be Compassionate.

'Looks like you're all set. How're you going to go about being, what do you call it? Visibly helpful?'

'No idea.'

Now that I have a plan, and there really is nothing stopping me from getting on with it, I'm terrified. I flip backwards and forwards through the calendar like a maniac. I am not equipped to do any of these things.

I slam it shut.

'Oh no you don't. Come on. It has to be now or it you'll never do it.'

She sounds so much like Claire that a spontaneous sob almost escapes. Kaz is eyeing me warily.

'I suppose I *could* go into town, see if there's anyone that needs my help. So long as I remember to take a picture for Instagram, I'd be all set.'

'It would make a nice change from all the pictures of cats, I'll agree.'

I still don't move.

'That's it then, I'll go to town.'

'Right you are, best go get dressed, hadn't you?'

'Yep.'

I move slowly. Even for me. Upstairs I pull on my jeggings because I could do with an elasticated waistband today, and a nice jumper that belongs interchangeably to Kaz. Just the act of getting dressed makes this one of my most productive Saturdays to date.

Huddersfield Town's claim to fame is that it's one of the largest towns in England. Which is like winning the prize for having the biggest turnips at a village fair. Literally no one cares, but you become inflated with a sense of self-importance regardless. British towns are mundane at the best of times, with the same shops all selling the same stuff. But on a grey January day, with that rain that gets you especially wet, it seems extra dreary here.

Perhaps it's just that I've never left. Not even for university.

Kaz had begged me to apply to Sheffield with her. But I just couldn't bring myself to do it. So, I'd stayed put and felt guilty about the fact that I hated every minute. It was genuinely one of the best days of my life when Kaz moved back home. I only stopped crying when I overheard Kaz on the phone to Mum questioning whether I might be having a psychotic episode.

We only live a five-minute walk from the centre. In one of those soulless new build blocks filled with people for whom the housing market is about as tangible as Narnia. In no time at all I'm surrounded by shops.

I wander through the Kingsgate Shopping Centre first. Except most of the shops in here are chains, which will no doubt not require my services. Even I'm not about to barge into Topshop and offer to help in there. I've long since stopped shopping with them. They have someone with a malevolent sense of humour in charge of their sizing.

Instead, I head towards the increasingly dilapidated high street.

'Emily! Long time no see!'

Percy the pie shop man greets me. He's busy sticking a big 'sold out' notice over a Today's Special blackboard. Percy gave us free pies for Claire's *thing* and I, of course, like pies. Only psychopaths don't like pies.

These facts alone mean that Percy is potentially one of my closest acquaintances. I give him a sort of half-wave before abruptly changing direction.

'Ah, careful!' I crash into Josh. I mean obviously. Because

the universe clearly hates me. And though this is small fry compared to some of the shit it's pulled on me, it's still highly inconvenient. It takes me a moment longer than it should to let go. He's so solid and warm. For a split second I imagine never letting go at all. I could spend the rest of my life gazing into his blue eyes. I notice a few flecks of darker blue. Well, they're very good—

'Hi, Emily.' Josh has a crease between his eyebrows.

Huh. In my head, the way last night went down made me seem quirky. Mildly unhinged at best. But Josh scowling at me like he is makes me think I have a very generous recollection of events.

'Fancy seeing you again!' I nudge his elbow and do an exaggerated wink like I'm Dick Van Dyke, the nineteenth-century chimney sweep version.

'Yeah well, I, er, better go.' He pokes his thumb over his shoulder as if someone with my mental faculties might struggle to understand the concept of the word 'go'.

''Course, 'course. Places to go, people to see.' Why are my arms waving about so much?

'Josh, who're you talking to?'

A woman appears to stand next to him. Something that feels like a brick lands in my stomach. Josh and I freeze, as if we've just been caught in the middle of a diamond heist. In three steps she reaches us. Handing her shopping bags to Josh, who takes them without a word. I hadn't realised but he's quite laden down already. The woman is almost as tall as he is and she's absolutely gorgeous. With long blonde hair that looks like it might be naturally wavy in a way that would take a team of professionals to achieve on me. Josh wasn't kidding when he said I wasn't his type.

'Emily, this is Amy. My girlfriend.'

Amy frowns at me and wrinkles her nose as if I smell. Which I may well do.

Attractive people are so lucky, not having to bother being polite like the rest of us.

There's some definite tension in the air which I ease by saying, 'Pie's so good, don't you think?'

They both look at me blankly. And I suppose without being privy to my innermost thoughts a couple of moments ago, the question is a bit odd.

Josh huffs out a laugh but stops at the death stare Amy gives him. Well, this has been lovely. Lovely.

'Right,' I spring suddenly into action. 'I've actually got to go and meet some friends,' I gesture into the middle of the high street. 'Over there.'

'I think they're Jehovah's Witnesses.' Josh looks towards a group of men and women in suits handing out leaflets in the rain.

'Yeah, well I'm, um, thinking of converting actually.' I practically sprint towards the group leaving Josh and Amy behind. And unless mine ears do deceive me, they bicker as they walk off.

Jesus. Leaving the house is a very stressful experience.

Chapter Eleven

I pull up a metre short of the closest Jehovah's Witness and make an abrupt turn in the opposite direction.

There's the faint heckling of someone calling, 'The living are conscious they will die, but the dead are conscious of nothing at all,' after me, when my tolerance is at an all-time low.

I hurry toward the more decaying end of the high street, catching my reflection in the window of some abandoned shop. I look shell-shocked.

Claire would have been much more adept at this than me. Even *I* used to be more adept at this than me. Claire was the more outgoing one, but I wasn't totally at the opposite end of the spectrum. I guess it's just that over the years I've done less and less and without realising it, I've sort of meandered into a semi-reclusive lifestyle without giving due consideration as to whether the hermit life is the one for me.

I come to a halt outside the last shop on the street. A charity shop. Cat rescue, to be exact.

Now there's an idea.

Helpful people give to charity shops, don't they? Really helpful people might even volunteer in them.

I mean I *am* the sort of person who gives to charity. I was coerced by one of those street sellers five years ago into setting up a direct debit for the Snow Leopards Trust. Despite the fact that my finances are often stretched so thin they're translucent, I will not cancel. The snow leopards are depending on me and my £7.99 a month. It's a pity I can't post a picture of my bank statement online. However, even I know that is an open invitation for fraud. I'd spend the next decade convincing the bank that I hadn't in fact bought a diamond anklet in Bora Bora.

And then there's what I give to the hospiceeach month. Enough to ensure that I'm always mildly poor. Though I'm not about to start broadcasting that.

This cat sanctuary shop could very well be my best hope of visible helpfulness.

Before I can talk myself out of it, I open the door. Everything smells of cats, even though, from what I can discern, no cats are kept on the premises. A woman with an absolute mane of black hair is barking orders at a thin sullen young man who I would not expect to be volunteering here. If I was judgemental like that. Which I clearly am.

'All right, love?' she asks. There's so much dust it hangs in the air, undecided as to where to settle. It looks like the rails of clothes haven't been updated in decades.

'Yes, I, er, was just having a look.'

'Well, welcome. I'm Sandra.' She offers her hand.

'Um, nice to meet you. Emily.' I shake back, feeling self-conscious.

I walk between the rails, not touching anything. It takes approximately thirteen seconds before I'm stood gawping weirdly at Sandra again.

'Get over here, will you? See if our customer needs your help!' Sandra barks at the young man before whispering conspiratorially, 'They keep sending criminals but between you and me, they're absolutely flaming useless.'

This clearly isn't between me and Sandra, as said criminal is stood about two feet away from her. I wonder what he's done but presume it's a bit rude to ask.

'You buying owt then?' he demands.

'Er, no I don't think so.'

'Then what the fuck you doing?'

'Language, young man.' That comes from Sandra, not me. I'm busy trying to back out of the door. I crash into a rail.

'Sorry to waste your time, I was just, um, wondering if you needed some help, but you seem to have everything under control.' I'm tangled in something that looks like an old fur coat. Or else a spare bit of carpet.

Sandra comes to my rescue, clapping her hands together. 'How wonderful! We *could* always use an extra pair of hands. How do Saturday mornings sound?'

I'm finally free of the coat.

'Er.'

'Fuck's sake,' the criminal mutters.

'Do you like cats?' Sandra asks.

I let out the breath I didn't realise I was holding. I *do* like cats. 'Actually, I do. Have you, um, seen that YouTube of those kittens dancing to "Gangnam Style"?'

'Of course, who hasn't seen that?' she laughs and I feel myself relax a little.

The criminal rolls his eyes pointedly.

'How many do you have?'

'None, actually. My landlord won't let us have them. I would if I could, though,' I add hastily. Sandra strikes me as the sort of person who doesn't trust anyone who doesn't like cats.

Criminal now releases a breath very slowly. It looks like a technique from some sort of anger management class.

'It sounds like you're the perfect fit.'

There's an exceptionally good chance that I've just been manipulated in some way, shape or form. But Sandra's right, so I just nod.

Criminal, whose name I really must get so as not to dehumanise him further, is scanning the room. Presumably for materials with which to inflict bodily harm. On us. On himself. Who knows at this stage?

I clear my throat. 'Next Saturday, you say?'

'That's right. 9am. This muppet will be here too, mind.'

I feel a pang of pity for the young man, now busy making rude hand gestures behind Sandra's back.

'Great. Well, since we'll be work chums,' I'm starting to

think that my Van Dyke persona emerges when I'm nervous, 'you'd better tell me your name?' I do my brightest smile and realise that I haven't smiled particularly brightly for quite some time. I think my lip has split.

Criminal narrows his eyes at me. 'It's fucking Leon innit.'

'Nice to meet you, fucking Leon innit.'

He glowers at me.

'It's just Leon.'

'Gotcha, just Leon.'

The joke is wearing painfully thin but still, at least he isn't audibly grinding his back teeth anymore.

I say a self-conscious goodbye and turn to leave the shop. Outside, I take a quick selfie, flinching when I see it. And not just for the normal reason. My pupils are massive, and my cheeks are flushed. I look like I've just stumbled out of an opium den. I'll have to filter the hell out of it. Maybe add one of those snapchat things so that I have a crown of flowers to distract people from the state of me.

It strikes me that Claire probably wouldn't have expended quite so much energy trying to muster up a bit of visible helpfulness. In fact, she probably wouldn't have had to try so hard at the visible part at all. She *was* helpful. Like the time she watered all of Mr Tibbit's houseplants when he went on holiday. He was our neighbour across the street and lived to be 103.

I couldn't pick my current neighbours out of an identity parade.

I need to go lie down but at least I've done it. I've sweated more than I hoped I might and the run-in with Josh had been unpleasant, but I've found a way to be visibly helpful. Emily Turner, saviour to the cats of Huddersfield, has quite a nice ring to it after all.

Chapter Twelve

'So, let me get this straight,' Matt says for the fifteenth time. 'This list or whatever it is you're calling it.'

'The Life List,' I reply, also for the fifteenth time.

'Is designed to make you less boring, somehow.'

Matt is like me. Supreme accountancy skills aside, for the most part he got the dull genes. Actually, aside from Claire and Gran, the whole family seems to suffer with a chronic case of average-itis. He's dutifully engaged to Sarah. How he managed to convince the extremely timid woman into agreeing to marry him is beyond me. In my head, it's a sort of Princess Andromeda and the Kraken situation.

'We're ever so proud of you, you know that don't you?' Mum says for no discernible reason.

''Course I do. You're my parents. Genetically programmed to be proud of me. You'd say that if I'd dropped out of school to be a crack whore.'

'Who's a crack whore?' Gran chelps up, trying and failing to secretly screw the lid on the hip flask she always brings. In exchange, the rest of us pretend not to notice.

'NO, MUM,' Dad shouts, even though there's no medical

evidence that Gran is hard of hearing. 'Emily said SOME MORE!' He gives me a pointed look that says 'crack whore' is not appropriate Sunday lunch conversation. I'm feeling particularly irritable today. Probably Matt's incredulity at my list. And the fact that I didn't sleep well last night.

Ever since I came up with the Life List, I can't stop thinking about Claire. Imagining Claire doing the things on The List. It's unnerving. I'm usually much better at controlling the extent to which she can invade my brain. My skin feels all hot and prickly.

It's always been this way. At school, I'd been forced to visit that awful woman in the little office off the library who only ever wanted to talk about Claire. Of course, now I know that she was a child psychologist or something of a similar ilk. She was relentless. Talk about Claire. Read stories about people like Claire. Paint a picture of Claire. Claire. Claire. Claire. But she didn't break me. Not once did I do as she asked. Not that she ever got mad or anything; they aren't allowed to, I don't suppose. And after a year or so, she gave me up as a lost cause. It did give me lots of practice, though, at controlling my Claire thoughts.

In contrast, Matt had done exactly as he was told. Annoying do-gooder that he likes to pretend to be.

'More mash, anyone?' Mum carries on as if the last two minutes haven't happened.

'I just don't understand,' Matt continues. 'Why wouldn't you want to be normal? What's wrong with it?'

He seems genuinely concerned. As if the equilibrium of

the universe is about to be disturbed because I'm volunteering at a local charity shop. But then Matt is a man who has a spreadsheet for every aspect of his life. Even I'm not *that* dull. Excel strikes fear into my heart.

Obviously, I had uploaded the picture of myself outside the cat shop. Heavily filtered and resplendent in flower crown. It's truly a terrible thing, doing good for the sole purpose of telling other people about it. The important thing is that I recognise that.

'There's nothing wrong with it. Nothing at all,' I almost snap. 'I just want to try something a little different. Push out of my comfort zone.'

'It's what Claire would have wanted,' Gran adds. Gran has devoted most of her eighty-odd years on earth to saying whatever is most likely to make the maximum number of people uncomfortable in any given situation, so her comment about Claire isn't wholly unexpected. Still, everyone nodding around the table is really annoying me. And the nervy glances they're giving me are especially irritating. It's like they know. They know Claire wouldn't have needed a list.

I stuff a bit of Yorkshire pudding in my mouth and chew angrily, just for something to do.

'I think volunteering is a lovely idea. We organise lots of placements like that at work. For community payback,' Sarah squeaks and then looks down at her plate. We just ignore her. She seems to prefer it that way.

'What else will you try, love?' Dad asks.

'February is dedicated to doing something spontaneous, so

I can't really plan that one too much. And then in March I'll need to do something inspirational. I was thinking a sporting achievement of some sort.'

I stuff yet more food in my mouth. Anything to distract from the fact that Dad has just reached for Mum's hand and given it a squeeze.

'Work are doing a sponsored walk. For Alzheimer's UK. Tag along if you like?' Dad offers.

'How far is it?'

'Just a mile. But posties all around the country are doing it with some folks from the old biddies' home.'

I think back to Steven Whitward's Facebook photo. It looked like he'd done a lot more than walk a mile with a load of octogenarians. Walking a mile is surely only impressive for those with plastic hips.

'I'm not sure it's far enough, to be honest.'

'What about that thing in the Lakes? Rough Mudder or something. I always think they're very impressive, covered in mud like that.'

Mum is right. There's a Tough Mudder every year during our annual family trip to Keswick. I've scoffed at the finishers, hobbling through the streets, on a yearly basis.

But a picture finishing a race like that would surely be inspirational, if clearly very, very painful.

'Yeah maybe,' I add vaguely.

'Well, don't forget to tell me when you're free for the family meeting, love. You didn't reply to my text.' My mum. A woman who cannot read a room.

My pulse starts to pound. 'I think I'll be busy until after the Tough Mudder,' I blurt out.

'I ran a 5K last year to raise money for AstroTurf,' Sarah says, her eyes darting about like she can't believe she's just spoken. I've absolutely no idea why she'd be raising money for AstroTurf. However, I'm far too self-absorbed at the moment to ask questions.

'That's nice, love.' Mum pats her arm.

'So, that's it then, that's the one you're doing?' Matt asks. He tucks a strand of Sarah's hair behind her ear, and I narrow my eyes at the pair of them. Gentle Matt unnerves me. I much prefer the robot persona he reserves for me. I push his arm with my index finger. He swats at my hand.

'Mum,' I whine, 'the robot brother is malfunctioning again. He's showing love.'

'Stop bickering you two, honestly.'

I surreptitiously check the race using my phone under the table.

It's a Tough Mudder classic. Ten miles. That doesn't sound too bad.'

'You got my dates for the meeting?' Matt asks Mum, his voice dripping with condescension.

'Yes, love. It's just Emily we're waiting on.'

'Honestly, Mum, I think it'll have to be after the Lakes now. I'm going to have a lot on, training for this race.' I'm a terrible daughter. Mum, however, is an excellent mum. She ignores my blatant delay tactic and instead says, 'Do you think it's safe?'

'It's got to be. These sorts of things are on all the time.'

'It's all about the training,' Matt adds unhelpfully, the human definition of raining on a parade. 'You've got to prepare your circulatory system for the increased activity. Without proper training, people have died.'

I gulp. Surely ordinary people don't die doing this sort of thing. We're far more likely to be taken down by something mundane. No one with an average number of bodily moles – thirty, I checked – would give out crossing the finish line of a race.

'I don't think it's worth the risk, poppet,' Mum says.

'Me neither,' adds Matt.

'Uh,' offers Dad.

Gran takes a swig from her flask. 'Worse ways to go.'

'Thanks for the vote of confidence.'

'We're just looking out for you, love.' Dad locks eyes with me.

'Well, I'm an adult. Maybe I don't need so much looking out for.'

This is the closest we've ever come to outright confrontation. Sarah's knuckles are white around her knife and fork.

'Look.' My tone softens. It'll really take the shine off my Life List if the mere thought of it gives a close family member an aneurysm. 'If I can't run the race, I'll walk it. We walk loads in the Lakes anyway. This is just different because it's called a race. But I'll not be racing anyone. And you can all come and watch. Honestly, it's no big deal.'

If they realise that the 'walk loads' part of that sentence

only applies to Matt, Dad and Sarah, they don't let on. Mum and I mainly eat scones. It's just the way of the world. Proving her credentials as a top-notch mother, Mum relents. 'I'll have to remember to take my camera.' She nods to the wall of photo albums behind the dining table.

'That's the spirit. Now, can we get on with lunch? There is honestly no need to worry.'

Chapter Thirteen

'A Tough Mudder?! What the hell were you thinking?' Kaz asks as I gaze down miserably at my List.

'I've honestly no idea. Will you help me?'

'I'm not sure I can. Park run's only a 5K. This is way beyond my pay grade. You know there are obstacles and all sorts, don't you?' Kaz is the *only* person I know who runs anywhere on a voluntary basis. I personally gave up physical activity years ago. Bleep tests in PE were enough to put me off for life.

''Course I do,' I lie. I'd been hoping that the 'tough' part of the title implied that you'd feel tough at the end of it. Not that it was, in a literal sense, tough.

It's Sunday evening and I'm exhausted. When people say, 'push out of your comfort zone,' they don't let on that you'll be uncomfortable *and* knackered.

I collapse over the breakfast bar.

'What possessed you to commit to it? I thought by "sporting achievement" you meant like a sponsored walk.'

'I wanted to really challenge myself.' Another lie. I'd essentially pledged myself to crawling through mud for ten miles as a way of avoiding talking about Claire. I need professional help.

'It's not till the end of March though. I can forget about it for a bit till then. I haven't even planned in something spontaneous for February.'

'You can't wait till March to start training.' Kaz is holding a mug of tea between her hands. She blows on it and then takes a sip, leaning back against the countertop. She looks me dead in the eye. 'It'll kill you otherwise.'

Why does everyone keep saying that?

'So, you've got what?'

'Eight weeks.'

'Eight weeks! You'd better get running.'

I grimace. I'd already tentatively checked online. There are none of those *Couch To* things that cover this sort of eventuality, *Couch To* being able to run without feeling like you'd punctured a lung. It was useless. And I'd already started to wonder if helping the Huddersfield cat population was a good enough go at helpfulness. Cats are the sort of species that plot to enslave all humans in their quest for world domination, aren't they? When we were kids, our neighbour's cat had lived for half a decade with one eye and a thyroid problem.

And now it seemed that the general consensus was that the cost of being inspirational would be my untimely death.

'I know! You should do a boot camp.'

'Er—' There is very little I would rather do less.

'It'll be good for you. You might even make some more friends.'

'I have plenty of friends. I've got you and Sandra and Leon.' I trail off. Okay, I don't really have friends. Being so closely related to tragedy makes people wary. You're suddenly the black cat in the room. The dark cloud on the horizon. You make people nervous. I'm doing the world a kindness by staying away.

'Two of those you met yesterday.'

'And Brian. I'm friends with Brian.'

'That's a stretch at best.'

I reach for another Hobnob, still full after lunch but unwilling to pass up on a mealtime.

'Here, look.' Kaz holds her phone towards me. 'Birkby Brutal Boot Camp. Meets every Tuesday and Thursday at 6pm in the town centre. All abilities welcome.'

'And by all, do you reckon they mean none?'

'Everyone's got to start somewhere.'

'It's not for me. The name quite clearly states that it's brutal. And anyway, two nights a week is a big commitment.'

'You literally have nothing else on. And you need brutal. Brutal is what will prepare you for this thing.'

'I'll think about it,' I lie. There is absolutely no way I am signing up to boot camp.

By Tuesday night I am considering the drastic step of severing all ties with Kaz. If it weren't for the fact that she's the one who knows the Netflix password, she'd be dead to me.

Not only has she signed me up for this god-awful boot

camp group, she's gone to the trouble of emailing the leader pretending to be me.

'Just go once. If you hate it, don't go again. Simple.'

'But I don't want to. Not even once. Everyone will laugh at me.'

'No one will even notice you. Everyone will be sweating too much.'

She starts ushering me towards the door.

'I read once that too much exercise is bad for you.'

She hands me my keys.

'Uh huh.'

She shoves me outside. I grab at the door frame, clinging on.

'Think of my arthritic knees!' I implore.

Kaz steps back.

'Suit yourself. Just so you know though, Brian is coming round. We've discovered this great new move. All it takes is for me to find his—'

'Okay, okay, I'm going.' I hold my hands up. 'For the record, you are a terrible friend.'

'I can live with that. History, I believe, will judge me kindly.'

Half an hour later I find myself huddled with a small group at the entrance to the old church in town. Like moths, everyone vies for the brightness of the lights coming from the front of the church. Except me. I keep a good distance from the rest of the pack and send up a silent prayer that the darkness takes me.

At least it's more of a mixed bag here than I'd anticipated.

Sure, there are some keenos who look like they could kill you with their calf muscles. They're decked out in what I presume to be the latest hi-tech gear, all glowing in the dark with actual torches strapped to their heads. But there's also a range of ages. And different shapes and sizes too. Perhaps this will be survivable, if not enjoyable.

My optimism is dashed almost instantly.

'Evening everyone! And welcome to the newcomers.' I presume that is just me as everyone turns to gawp for a second. I fight the urge to run away.

The group leader inspires no confidence that I will make it out of the next hour in one piece. He's wearing army trousers and a tank top. In January. A luminous orange whistle hangs around his neck. Veins burst out of his arms, as if they're being squeezed out by all the muscle packed in there.

'For those who don't know me, I'm Bruce. It's just the usual this evening,' Bruce smiles, adding extra strain to his neck. 'We'll do a quick warm-up and then get straight into the HIIT training. High intensity interval training is essentially short bursts of intense activity followed by periods of rest.'

A chuckle ripples through the group at that, making me even more uneasy.

I could run home now. Surely, I'd outpace this Bruce guy, even if he gave chase. I'm amazed he's still standing he's so top heavy.

A whistle pierces the air.

'Marks, GO!' he barks. Before I have chance to even realise what's happening, the whole group takes off at a run.

I don't move. I'm rooted to the spot.

'I said go, Turner, GO!' He blows the whistle at me. Bruce is no longer smiling. Instead, his neck has expanded further, and his face is contorted in anger.

I don't understand what's happening. I don't want to run but there's a giant army man shouting in my face.

'Come on!'

Someone grabs me by the arm and pulls me off. My legs move of their own accord. I think I'm in shock. I no longer feel the cold.

'It's better if you just do what he says. Once he's in the zone he doesn't like people who dilly-dally.'

I glance over. My guardian angel is wearing workout clothes that I've seen in Primark. I think I love her. We run alongside each other in silence. Down the high street. Past Percy's and the cat rescue shop.

For a moment I think I'm doing it. Spurred on by the mortal fear that Bruce will catch us, I'm actually running. I chance a glance at my rescuer; she's pumping her arms, breathing hard. I try to copy her arm movements. Unfortunately, they don't have the desired effect of propelling me any further forwards.

Within five minutes my jogging bottoms and fleece are soaked with sweat. I wonder if I'm going to sweat profusely through every point of the Life List.

Argh. A stabbing pain hits me right below the ribs. And not like the allegorical one you get from guilt.

Every breath is painful. *Stab. Stab. Stab.*

I double over, limping as we come to a stop on the lawn outside the old church again.

Panic consumes me. I'll never be able to escape in this state. *Stab. Stab.*

'That's the warm-up done. Hit the floor. Sit-ups, sixty seconds. GO!' The whistle screeches. Everyone dutifully lies down and begins furiously sitting up again. Bruce circulates, abusing people. This is the state of the world. People are now willing to spend their hard-earned money being insulted on a Tuesday night.

I manage one sit-up.

'And REST!' That whistle again.

Almost everyone jumps straight up and starts jogging on the spot. The antithesis of rest.

I don't budge.

'I'm Sophie.' The woman who rescued me is also still lying down.

'Emily,' I pant at her. 'Have you been coming for long?'

'Second week. I need to lose an inch for my wedding.'

'Right.' Losing an inch sounds like a serious commitment. Sophie has big dark eyes and is fifty times more attractive than me. She doesn't appear to have an inch to spare.

The whistle. 'SQUAT!'

I try to copy the moves of some of the more seasoned squatters. If I were ever to return, which of course I won't, I'd be expecting a little more guidance on form.

Instead, what I get is Bruce shouting in my face. 'Deeper!' he yells.

I've genuinely no idea what he's talking about.

'Lower! Harder!'

He's not making any sense. How exactly do you squat harder?

The stress at being singled out starts to engulf me. I freeze again.

'What are you doing, Turner?' I'm seconds away from crying. Only shame is keeping the tears lodged in their ducts.

'I . . . I . . . I—'

'I can't be arsed either.'

Sophie has ceased to squat. The leader rounds on her before a little beep on his watch prompts him to blow his whistle again.

'REST!' he screeches.

'Come on, let's get further back.'

Sophie and I move backwards as everyone else jogs on the spot. Some of them are laughing. My lungs feel like they're on fire. If this is the cost of being inspirational, it isn't worth it.

The rest of the session passes in a blur. Voices echo around me, but I hardly hear them. If Sophie asks me a question, I don't reply. I'm constantly five seconds behind everyone else.

The only thing I feel is pain. My legs are shaking. Long-forgotten muscles scream for release. My fleece and joggers cling to me. No wonder they say exercise is good for your mental health. My brain is currently incapable of any thought, depressive or otherwise. It's shut down entirely.

'I'm dying,' Sophie pants.

At this stage I would consider death a sweet release.

Two blows on the whistle.

'Session's up, folks! Great work.' Bruce is no longer shouting at us. He's smiling. Only a throbbing vein on his forehead suggests that just moments before he was yelling at a sixty-odd-year-old woman, telling her nobody loves a lardarse. I deduce that he must have a personality disorder.

'Remember, we're running on Thursday so bring your backpacks please. And don't make me fill them for you,' he laughs, waggling his finger. The others laugh back. It's like I'm in the twilight zone. I check the sky for a full moon.

'He means it.' Sophie is speaking. I turn slowly towards her. Because slowly is all I can manage. 'Last week I just brought an empty bag and he put a kettle bell in it.' She gulps at the memory.

'I'm not coming.'

'What, on Thursday?'

'Ever.'

'Great work tonight, ladies.' Bruce appears as everyone else is walking off. 'Remember, when you're squatting, your knees need to stay behind your feet. You'll give yourself an injury otherwise.' This seems like advice that would have been better conferred about forty minutes ago. 'And you might want to invest in some breathable gear.' He nods towards my fleece, which is now so sweat-soaked it feels like someone has added a lead lining.

I just nod, not trusting that he isn't about to morph into crazy army man again.

Sophie hands him five pounds.

I've brought the same amount. I reach for my pocket, but Bruce holds out a hand to stop me.

'You've paid for the ten-week block in advance, remember?'

'I have?' I stutter.

He laughs like I'm joking.

'See you Thursday, girls. Nice to meet you in person, Emily.'

And with that, he sprints off.

Some people are very odd.

'How come you said you weren't coming back if you've already paid?' Sophie asks.

'I've er ... I was just joking about not coming back.' In actual fact, my plan is to get home, remove all traces of Kaz from my life and then emigrate to Australia. I'll feel much happier with a couple of continents between me and Bruce.

'Thank fuck for that. You're already the only person I even remotely like at this thing.'

I'm almost certain that Sophie's compliment is based purely on the fact that I'm as inept as she is. It's definitely not my sparkling personality.

We head off the lawn. In my head the silence is long, awkward.

'So ... when's ... the ... wedding?'

'June.'

As a rule, I don't like June. Claire died in June.

'You need a lift home?' Sophie asks.

'Thanks, but I'm, um, only five minutes that way.' I suddenly want to be on my own.

'Okay bye, see you Thursday.'

I limp home, mildly regretting declining the lift.

This evening could hardly be considered a roaring success.

I do a big sniff. The cold night air makes my watery eyes sting.

Chapter Fourteen

'Just give that shelf a dust, would you?' Sandra asks.

I'm in the cat shop and the shelf Sandra is referring to is covered in an assortment of knick-knacks, a sizeable proportion of which I recognise as Happy Meal toys from bygone eras. There's a hand-drawn sign just above them which reads, 'Everything 50p.'

Still, despite the minute stature of the obstacles faced by my dusting cloth, this task may genuinely be beyond me and my riotous arm muscles. Against the better judgement of every fibre of my being, I had attended the next boot camp running session on Thursday. Partly because Sophie had added me as a friend on Facebook. My first genuine friend request in at least half a decade. Partly because to quit the Life List after four whole days seemed beyond pathetic. Definitely *not* because I discovered that Kaz had forked out a hundred quid in signing me up to ten weeks' worth of sessions.

If Dante had been around in the twenty-first century, he'd have chosen hill reps as a circle of hell. There's a lovely, if slightly sinister come night-time, canal path in Huddersfield. It's flat. Why we couldn't run along that I'll never know.

Instead, Bruce had had us powering up hills as if we were preparing to tackle Everest. He'd followed Sophie and I up each one, hurling abuse at us, before ending the class and enquiring politely about whether we'd seen the latest episode of *Call the Midwife*.

One might assume I'd fall into an exhausted slumber after that carry-on, but I can't get a good night's sleep. I see Claire everywhere. My own reflection catches me unawares. The sweet shop down the road has her sweet of choice, strawberry laces, on offer. There are more ginger kids about – *Annie* was her favourite film.

I've been silently musing for an inordinate amount of time.

We've had not a single customer. I've been here over an hour and no one is talking. Sandra seems unperturbed by the silence. She's wearing a stripy linen dress, a couple of sizes too small, without a bra I might add. Thick white socks and Velcro sandals finish the look. She sits at the counter reading *The Communist Manifesto*. In contrast, Leon is definitely on the lanky side. He's kitted out in a suspiciously pristine track suit and enormous white trainers. He has those lines shaved in the side of his hair, the ones that are basically a prerequisite for a life of crime.

He occasionally walks from one end of the shop to the other. But that's about as exciting as it gets.

I check the clock on the wall. Nine minutes have passed since I last looked.

'I'll go and put the kettle on, shall I?' Sandra closes her book suddenly. 'Why don't you two spend some time getting better acquainted? I've been thinking, since we have some extra human power these days pardon me if I don't use the phrase "manpower", Leon – perhaps we could spruce the shop up a little. Try to drum up some business. Get your thinking caps on.'

'What, with her?' Leon barks.

Sandra ignores him, heading instead for the tiny kitchen out back. Leon and I look at each other. His is more of a glare but it'll pass for a look. He's young. Maybe only a year or two older than the kids I teach.

Something inside of me relaxes a bit at that. He's just a kid. And I get on well with kids like Leon. The ones no one else seems to like. If anyone understands how it is to be on the outside looking in, it's me.

'I bet you've never even nicked a sweet from the pick 'n' mix. You look like a right boring cow.' Leon continues to be mildly abusive.

'Uh,' is all I manage to say out loud before he's talking again.

'At least I've lived a little.'

Ah, he thinks I'm judging him.

'What in prison, where hopes and dreams come alive? It's not Disneyland, Leon.' I huff out a laugh.

I can't quite decide if Leon is about to punch me, but instead he starts to laugh too. And even if the exchange had been wholly offensive and cast aspersions on my entire life, before I know it there's tears rolling down my cheeks. I think I'm delirious.

'So, is it normally this quiet?' I ask, finally coming up for air.

'No, we're normally fucking overrun.'

'Watch your lip, young man.' Sandra re-emerges from the kitchen.

Leon sighs.

'We don't get a lot of customers, no,' Sandra says. 'Mid-morning, I take Fred his breakfast and a cuppa.'

Fred is Huddersfield Town's resident homeless man. Of course, there are many more, which is quite frankly a travesty. But none quite have the charisma of Fred. He holds a sign asking for gluten-free food donations only. Rumour has it that he was disowned by his millionaire family over an affair with another man. I could see he and Sandra being chums.

'I thought that while I was gone, the two of you could come up with something of an action plan. You must both know what young people want to see in a shop these days.'

The smirk that Leon pulls suggests wanton lack of security is top of his list.

I nod. I'm here to be helpful and helpful I will be.

'Leon, be a dear and run and get the flipchart from the back. Won't be long.' With that, Sandra leaves the shop.

I wait by the counter for Leon. Digging around in my bag, I manage to locate some spare board markers.

'Fucking tragic,' is all Leon says. I'm assuming it's in relation to the pen situation.

He drags the rusty old flipchart in front of the till. Clearly there is no chance of an actual paying customer arriving.

'So, what's your skill set?' I ask.

'Don't have one.'

''Course you do, everyone does. What are you good at?'

'Nicking stuff. But ain't nothing I want to nick from here.'

'Do they send people to prison for nicking stuff these days? Seems harsh. Though obviously, I disapprove of larceny.' I twist the pen round in my hands.

'Obviously.' He gives me a look. Leaning his elbows on the countertop. He's practically horizontal. 'Nah, you just get community payback for nicking stuff. Prison was for summit else.'

'Really?' I lean in a touch.

'I know you're begging to ask what happened.'

'I am not.' A pause. 'Okay, I am a little bit.'

He rolls his eyes.

'Nothing mega. You know that sandwich joint, Time for Lunch?'

'Leon, please tell me that you didn't go to prison for holding up a sandwich shop?'

'Wasn't me proper. I was just there for the till money. But there was a few of us and it turned a bit dodge when the guy wouldn't hand it over.'

'Sorry that you got caught up in it all.'

I clear my throat.

Leon does the same.

'How long did you get?'

'Twelve months. Served six.'

I cough.

'Okay, so the plan is to make this place somewhere people *want* to steal from.'

'You're mental.'

I ignore him. Unclicking the lid off the pen. 'How about we do a sort of brain dump of our different ideas?'

'Knock yourself out, posh girl.'

If only he could see the mould currently staging a hostile takeover of my bathroom.

'I know – how about we update the window displays, make them a bit more, um, fashionable?'

A single nod. I add it to the board.

'Right. Your turn.'

'I've got nothing.' He holds up his hands.

'Hmm, and maybe we could spruce the place up a bit?' The walls are a sort of baby blue colour. Except the paint has started to crack and a leaky pipe has resulted in a trickle of yellowy mould down one wall. 'A nice purple or something?'

Another nod.

'And the changing room should be a bit more private perhaps. In case all our new customers want to try something on.' At present the changing room is simply three stud walls semi-surrounding an office chair. A curtain covers half of the opening.

'Any ideas of your own, Leon?' I'm in full teacher mode.

'Nope.' Excellent.

Sandra returns, beaming at our three-pronged plan of attack. 'Perhaps that's enough to be getting on with for now?' Sandra asks.

'Okay,' I nod.

'Tell you what, why don't you both make a start on the window this morning?'

'Okay.'

'Leon, will you help Emily find some clothes for the mannequin?'

He grunts, which I take as a yes.

'I'll go and put the kettle on.' This appears to be 99 per cent of Sandra's job role.

Leon and I start moving through the rails.

'What am I looking for?'

'Something people might want to wear now, seeing as it's still winter. Jumpers, that sort of thing.' I lower my voice to a whisper. 'If Sandra would wear it, put it back.'

That gets a smirk out of him.

We're busy pulling a maroon jumper onto the mannequin when Sandra re-emerges. We've managed to find some jeans and brown boots to match. I hang a dusty tan coat over the shoulders and add some fake amber beads.

'That looks wonderful. A job well done.'

'We done then?' Leon asks.

'How about we tidy the shelves a little bit, clear some space ready to paint?'

He nods and we work in what is potentially a companionable silence. Well, he's silent. I'm doubtful it's companionable. And I'm doing what any educated verging on middle-class person would be doing. Coming up with ways to save him.

Could he come and live with me a la *The Brightside* with Sandra Bullock? No. I'm literally mid-breakdown.

Could I use my contacts to find him a deep and meaningful job that he loves?

Seems unlikely. I rent a run-down two-bed flat. And my contacts haven't even meant that *I* have a deep and meaningful job. I have no contacts.

'I can hear you thinking from over there. Just quit it.'

'Quit what?'

'Whatever you're planning.' I'm starting to think I have a very readable face.

'Ooof, Emily, look, it's past twelve o'clock. You get off now.' Sandra re-emerges.

I discover that I haven't checked the clock for the past hour and a half. I wonder if that means that I've enjoyed myself. It doesn't particularly feel like it.

'Leon, will you clear some space in the storeroom this afternoon? We're expecting a delivery.'

He grunts, which I already recognise as his yes.

'You're good with him,' Sandra says, following me into the back to collect my coat. 'It's true,' she adds. 'I've barely heard him say two words before today. He likes you.'

I shrug, wondering how Leon behaves if he doesn't like you.

'Am I okay to come half an hour late next week? We've a staff meal out on Friday night.' The English faculty staff meal is perhaps my only recurring social engagement. It's actually our Christmas meal, but the fact that the head of English insists on full attendance means we haven't been able to find a date until the start of February.

"Course. Just this once,' Sandra replies indulgently. I resist the urge to remind her no one is paying me to be here.

Walking home, I realise my stomach is in knots. The staff meal out heralds the start of February and yet another challenge on the Life List. I've no idea where to even begin with being spontaneous. I remember the time Claire tried to pierce our ears with Mum's sewing kit. Or when she coloured in her hair with a yellow highlighter she found. The most spontaneous thing I've done so far this year is to order a thin crust pizza from Fat Joe's. I was trying to be healthy. Even then I regretted it.

I sigh. My earlier good feeling is disappearing as quickly as a puddle in the desert. The Life List is revealing my life to be more rubbish than even I'd realised. That and it's given me mild insomnia and an almost permanent dull headache. I walk on, wondering how the hell I'll get through another six months of this thing.

Chapter Fifteen

1998

Claire sits up in her big hospital bed as we come in. Mum jumps. She's been snoozing in her chair, but she pretends like she hasn't been.

'Em, please tell me you brought the books, I can't live without them for another day.'

I hold up the Tesco carrier bag with all the library books I could carry in them. She squeals with happiness.

Claire has been spending lots of time in the hospital. Ever since our first day of school. She has her own room now and it's quite big, but it doesn't have bunk beds like our bedroom at home. She was in hospital when it was our birthday and we turned six. Claire was too sick to have any cake on that day, so I didn't want any either.

And Claire was in hospital for Christmas too. I was worried that Santa wouldn't know where to bring her presents, but Mum said not to worry because Santa knows everything. It wasn't very fun, waking up with just Dad and Matt on Christmas Day. But then we went to the hospital to have our

127

dinner with Claire. No one made her eat any sprouts because she was too poorly, so she just had jelly.

Now the medicine is starting to work. I don't mind Claire being in hospital if the medicine works. She's getting better because the cancer in her head is going away. The doctors tested me with a needle too. They thought me and Claire might be the same. But I don't have anything in my head, so we aren't.

'So, what's happening at school? Tell me everything – all I can do here is read.'

Me and Claire always liked story time before but now it's all we do. Cartoons are only on at teatime.

Dad makes me wash my hands again, even though I only did them a minute ago. Then I'm allowed to go and sit next to Claire.

'We did cooking. We made fruit salad. Christopher Simmins got some orange juice in his eye and cried. Sir made him hold a paper towel to it.'

She laughs and I feel happy.

'What else?'

Claire starts coughing and Mum has to tell her to lie down a moment.

'Do you want to watch cartoons?'

Mum says this means that Claire is too tired to talk anymore so I sit next to her, and we watch *The Animals of Farthing Wood* even though there's lots that I'd like to talk to her about.

Like how it's really lonely when it's just me, Matt and Dad

at home. And how I've had Happy Meals for tea four times this week, which doesn't sound too bad. But after number three, I had a tummy ache.

And how I can't go to sleep at night because I don't like how quiet our bedroom is without her.

And how I really miss her. And Mum. Because Mum is always at the hospital when Claire's here. She doesn't even go to work at the big Asda or anything.

Some doctors come in. You can tell that they're doctors because they have long white coats and stethoscopes around their necks.

They all go and wash their hands too. Everyone is always washing their hands in Claire's room.

'And how's our favourite patient doing?'

Claire beams. Her smile is extra big in her face now.

'I like your scarf today.' Claire has on a red and white spotty scarf that would make her look like a pirate if she had an eye patch too.

'Mum says everyone will be wearing them to copy off me.' Claire coughs again.

'I bet they will.' The doctors read some paper from a little bucket at the end of Claire's bed.

'Good. Very good, still.' They talk to Mum and Dad.

'When can I go home?' Claire asks. 'Only, I really don't want to stay here much longer because I have important things I need to be doing.' The doctors laugh at Claire, but I don't know why because she didn't tell a joke.

'Not quite yet. There's still another treatment cycle. And

we need to make sure your immune system is strong enough to fight off whatever germs might be lurking out there.'

I didn't like the thought of germs lurking like that. Maybe I could walk in front of Claire from now on, so that if the germs come, they get to me first.

Another doctor is busy checking the machines beeping around Claire, listening to her heart beating and putting light-up pegs on her fingers.

'All fine here.' One doctor nods to the other doctor.

'We'll get you home soon.' He pats Claire's foot.

Everyone in the room is smiling and I'm so happy I could shout really, really loud. Soon.

They said Claire was coming home soon.

FEBRUARY

Be Spontaneous

Chapter Sixteen

The week passes in a sleep-deprived blur. My weakened body is accosted by thoughts of Claire. I hardly even try to ward them off anymore. I find myself raking over memories when I should be teaching and, instead of my usual mirror avoidance tactics, I now spend an inordinately long time staring at my reflection. It is taking an excessive amount of effort to continue to behave like even a slightly normal person.

This week has also heralded the start of February, normally something to celebrate. January, the month which lasts at least four times as long as any of the good months, is over. The half-term holidays, and the promise of a week on the couch, are in touching distance. But this year February is looking like January's poor relation. In hindsight, I see that being helpful was in fact much easier than spontaneity. After all, we live in a woefully unequal society – there are always people in need of help. But as for being spontaneous, I really don't know where to start.

*

The staff night out on Friday creates something of a buzz in the English faculty pod. Honestly, it's no wonder our pupils think we're a load of saddos. The prospect of spag bol and a glass of red wine down Danchinos is enough to get everyone giddy with excitement.

I am, at best, ambivalent about attending. On the one hand, Danchinos' spag bol is a pleasure to behold. On the other, I could be wearing my slipper socks for an evening on the couch.

But time spent under the duvet on the couch is no longer the sanctuary it once was. Wherever I go, I can't escape my brain.

So, it would seem that I'm going.

Stan the English technician slinks into my room at the end of period five on Friday. I'm packing up as quick as I can, hoping to fit in a power nap before I have to get ready. The fact that my body is fighting sleep, fundamentally one of its most basic of functions, is highly annoying.

'Hi Emily, I've got your photocopying ready for next week.'

'Stan, you ... you ... shouldn't have.' Stan is being extra diligent with my photocopying at the moment.

He puts the neat pile of papers on the nearest desk.

'So, you still on for tonight?'

He slides his arm up the doorframe. I presume he's going for provocative. It would work for someone else, but not Stan. For one, he's called Stan. Secondly, he's several years younger than me, with black hair that reaches his shoulders. This in itself would not be an issue; what is, is that he uses several handfuls of gel to slick it back every day. It's either that, or it's incredibly greasy.

'Yup. You?' We know this. We had the same conversation at lunchtime already.

'Yeah. I'm really looking forward to it.'

'Me too.' I smile my fake smile. I walk this tightrope with Stan on an almost daily basis. He has a crush on me. Not in a bigheaded way. He sticks Post-it Notes to my printing that say STA hearts TUR, our staff codes. I can neither encourage his crush nor extinguish all hope. I don't want to go out with him, but I don't want to be responsible for my own laminating either.

'Um, I best dash then. See you later.'

'You know,' he whispers as I pass, 'we could always carry on the party. After.' His voice has dropped a few octaves.

I'm not sure that the English Christmas do really counts as a party. I give a non-committal hum.

Stan doesn't move as I squeeze through the door past him. He smells quite nice actually. It's not that he's physically repulsive or anything, hair aside. I'd just never consider seeing anyone with whom Mr Hughes shares genetic material. I've rarely considered anyone at all. Hence the 2.5 sexual partners.

Sex.

I smack my hand to my forehead in a *why didn't I think of this before* move. Stan could be my ticket to spontaneity. And a way to bump my numbers.

After all, I'd never consider a relationship with Stan, but if I closed my eyes, I think I could manage some other stuff. It's been a *very* long time since I did some other stuff. Surely my brain would have to shut up for a bit then. Perhaps this could be a win-win situation.

I mull the thought over on my way home. There are definite merits. If nothing else, I might get a good night's sleep with someone else in the room.

'Kaz,' I burst into the hallway, which also serves as our living room, 'guess what? I think I'm going to have my first spontaneous one-night stand tonight.'

Kaz, who has been watching *Friends* – 'The One with George Stephanopoulos', presses pause. 'I feel like this conversation deserves my full attention. So, who is the lucky man you're planning to spontaneously sleep with?'

'Stan, you know, the English technician?'

'Greasy Stan?'

'I think it's gel actually.'

'I see. And what has made you reach such an important decision? Life List might I hazard?'

'Yep. February's challenge. Be spontaneous.'

'Well, this plan sounds *very* spontaneous. It's only the third of the month. Are you sure you don't want to wait a bit? Consider something less drastic? I still reckon you'd look good with pink eyebrows.'

I move to sit on the Poäng, dropping my bag on the floor next to it.

'Just think about it, if I have sex with Stan, I not only get to be spontaneous, I also edge closer to being a better than average sexual person. There's still a way to go but now seems as good a time as any to make a start. I just need to take the bull by the horns.'

'I don't see Stan as particularly bullish, but you never know, sometimes the little ones surprise you.'

I ignore her.

'Anyway, you can't dye my eyebrows pink. I'd get the sack. It's in the staff handbook.'

Every year on the first day of term, Mr Hughes makes us study the staff handbook and do a pop quiz on it. On the welcome back schedule, it's marked as the 'fun activity' for the day.

Kaz gives me a look. 'I think you're missing something really important here. Do you actually *want* to sleep with him?'

'I don't not want to. I need to do something unexpected. And actually, I haven't had sex in a long time.'

'This is very true. But you do know that you can't tell anyone about this. You're not planning on adding it to your Facebook bio are you?'

'No. But *I'll* know. This one's for me.'

'You're sure?'

Absolutely not. 'Yup.'

'Then I'm all for it. What's your plan of attack?'

'It sounds borderline illegal when you say it like that. What do *you* normally do?'

'I just tell them I'd like to have sex with them.'

'You do not!'

''Course I do. What else am I going to say? I need to feel your intriguing length inside me?'

I stick my fingers in my ears and bounce backwards and forwards on the Poäng.

'I can't do that. I'll have to rely on my feminine charms.'

'Pray tell. What feminine charms shall you unleash on poor Stan?'

'I don't know. I'll just touch his arm and laugh extra hard at his jokes.'

'Well, it'll be clear as day that you're after a shag.'

'That's how it works in films.'

'You only watch musicals, Em. No one has sex in musicals.'

'Sometimes they kiss. You just wait.' I begin the process of hauling myself out of the chair. 'Me and Stan. Tonight. I'm calling it the Stan Plan. By tomorrow I'll have been spontaneous and I'll be on my way to the average number of sexual partners. After Stan, the sky's the limit.' I finally manage to extricate myself.

'Your parents would be so proud.'

I'm running late. Instead of napping, I'd spent a solid two hours wondering if Claire would approve of my Stan Plan. It's very strange and also highly inappropriate to spend any amount of time considering the sexual prowess of your twin who died as an actual child. All I do know is that Claire once punched Tyler Moore for trying to kiss her during an errant game of 'What's the Time, Mr Wolf?'. I'm not sure if the memory bolsters or weakens my resolve.

Unhappily, I'm a complete flustered mess by the time I start to get dressed. It takes an inordinately long time to scrub my cheeks free from tear-stained mascara and then it turns out that I own not one set of matching underwear. When I finally arrive at the restaurant, everyone else is seated at a long table. Someone has put tinsel down the middle as a nod to this being our Christmas party. There's only one seat left right at the end. No one has saved me one obviously. To my dismay (and slight relief), I'm several people away from Stan.

I put my coat on the back of the chair next to Ebony, the newest member of the department.

Ebony has only been teaching for seven months. She's full of teaching and learning initiatives at department meetings and has been known to squeal when one of her pupils makes beyond expected progress. She does, however, wear an 'I heart books' pin badge every day, and I admire that in a person.

'Emily,' she turns to me immediately. 'You've got to tell me what strategies you use for Tim O'Hara.'

Oh no. The only thing worse than a teacher night out is one where you talk about teaching all night. I pour an exceptionally large glass of red wine from the bottle on the table, looking forlornly at Stan several seats away.

'Tim from Year 11?' I stutter.

'Yeah. He's making more progress in your lessons than any others. I checked the data. And I saw you engaging with him in the corridor yesterday. He's in your form, right? Personally, I find his behaviour incredibly challenging.'

I don't mention that Tim has started an illicit trade in bonbons, after the school canteen banned anything even remotely sugary. I was forced to confiscate a bag in return for £2.50.

'He can be a bit cheeky.'

Ebony reels off a list of other pupils whose behaviour she deems 'challenging and disruptive to the learning of others', pausing only to place her order. Spag bol.

I order the same. The waiter leaves, giving Ebony free rein to launch into her concerns about how Tim's negative attitude might affect her whole class progress score. There is genuine fear in her eyes.

I take a big gulp of wine and resist the urge to point out that seeing Tim as a means to a progress score is probably not the way to win him round.

'So, is he challenging for you too? What strategies do you use?'

'Er, I quite like Tim.'

Ebony looks like I've just called her mum a whore. I glance at Stan again. He's tucking into the breadbasket, laughing at something. Everyone at the table is having more fun than me.

For Ebony's sake, I backtrack. She's actually a good teacher. 'I mean, don't get me wrong, Tim can be a pain.' She visibly relaxes. 'But, um, I suppose he has a lot going on at home. Sometimes acting out is a way to get attention.'

'Does he? I never realised.'

I nod, encouraged. 'Dad was never about. Mum's not about much. He has three brothers, and they all live together in those council flats over the road from school.' I take a bite of bread.

'You're absolutely right. I need to connect with Tim some more, get down to his level.' This isn't what I meant exactly, but I'm keen to end the conversation now.

An uncomfortable silence ensues.

Clearly we've run out of things to say. Ebony turns to Mr Nichols to ask him about his questioning techniques.

Hopefully I'll be left to eat my food in peace.

I manage a few blissful mouthfuls, keeping one eye on Stan. The man must have the bladder of an ox, he hasn't been to the loo once yet. But then Ms Carroll, the head of English, is leaning forward to talk to me. She's halfway down the table so she has to talk in her loud teacher voice.

'Emily, I was just talking to Jan. I have a favour to ask you.'

Ms Carroll's question makes me immediately suspicious. Favour requests from your boss are essentially orders masquerading as something nicer.

I just nod.

'Excellent! I told Jan you'd be just the person.'

I've never been 'just the person' for anything.

141

'For what?

I stuff more food into my mouth to buy me some *thinking up an excuse* time.

'To help with the school play. Mrs Thomas the food tech teacher has had to pull out and Jan needs support.'

I indicate that I'm chewing and so can't reply. When I finally swallow, I say, 'I ... I ... don't think I have time.'

'Nonsense. You were the only person who could make any of the dates for the Christmas do. It's only two nights a week.'

'What days?' Everyone along the table has stopped talking to watch us.

'Mondays and Wednesdays.'

'Er—'

'Excellent. We'll count you in. It'll look very good on your appraisal, you know.'

I resign myself to my fate.

'What's the show again?'

'*Little Shop of Horrors.*'

Apt.

At that moment, I notice Stan get up and head for the stairs leading to the toilets.

'Excuse me.' I scramble out of my chair after him. This is a terrible idea.

'Stan, STAN!' I catch him at the top of the steps.

'Emily, you look lovely tonight.' He doesn't even attempt to hide his eyes roaming up and down my body. I plough on before I can fully acknowledge my irritation.

'Thanks, um, so do you.'

I do my own more subtle scan and Stan does look all right actually. His jeans are a bit low, but he has a clean black shirt on and so long as I don't concentrate on his hair, the whole effect is not displeasing.

'Well, er . . .'

Stan goes to make for the door, and I realise that the Stan Plan stands no chance of success outside the toilets. There is only one thing for it.

'Standoyouwanttocomebacktominetonight?' My heart is thumping in my ears. All the blood has rushed to my face. I'm surely moments away from spontaneously combusting. Which would be ironic, given the month's aim. Stan's eyes go so wide, it looks like he's been drugged.

'God, I'm so, so sorry.' I turn to run.

'YES.'

It's emphatic. I'll say that.

I fiddle with my hands and tuck a few stray strands of hair behind my ear. Just for something to do. Stan recovers quickly. Zeroing in on my lips. I'm not there yet. I start to talk.

'Look, I only live a five-minute walk from town. When everyone's finished, just, um, follow me?' I breathe out the words so fast I'm amazed he can make them out.

He just nods. Slowly.

'Okay.'

'Okay.'

Our conversation is sparkling.

I push into the ladies, just so I don't have to watch Stan's reaction, not at all convinced by my grand plan.

If it's anything like the other sex I've had, at least it'll be over quickly.

I immediately feel guilty. The suffragettes would all be rolling in their graves.

Chapter Seventeen

It's at this point in the Stan Plan that I realise it's been quite some time since I last had sex. I hide in the toilets trying to get enough signal to load up a bit of explanatory porn for so long that my spag bol has been cleared away by the time I re-emerge.

It didn't even help me brush up. I only got as far as an invite for Kelly's webcam party. Kelly wasn't exactly leaving much to the imagination in said advert, so I did wonder what the party would entail. But still, though it would be nice to be a bit more clued up, watching some middle-aged woman from Blackpool masturbate probably isn't the way to go. Pleasure Beach indeed.

I'm on edge the second half of the evening. I fidget constantly while Ebony grills me some more on teaching and learning strategies for difficult pupils. What I want to say is, *try being nice to kids who have a horrible life*. What I actually say is a series of 'ah's', 'uh's' and 'um's.'

It's hard to concentrate with Stan staring at me in open-mouthed reverence. He attempts to seductively dribble a bit of tiramisu into his mouth. It lands with a splodge in his lap.

And then the meal is over. We all throw our respective £20 notes onto the silver platter and grab a minty chocolate. I once saw an article about how sweet treats that come with the bill should be avoided at the end of a meal because of the calories. However, passing on one would seem very much like shutting the stable door once the horse has bolted.

I see Stan take one too. Watching me as he puts it in his mouth. I've never seen a man attempt to eat an After Eight mint seductively. The increasingly disintegrated square that he keeps displaying is not doing it for me at all. But gold star for imagination and effort.

Maybe I should have had more wine.

Stan catches up to me as I round the corner away from the restaurant.

'I think I got away without anyone noticing.'

'Well done.' I give him a double thumbs up as if he's five.

We don't talk much on the way home. I manage a few sideways glances at Stan. He's wearing a trench coat with the collar turned up. Like a sort of polyester spy.

Confidence in the Stan Plan is fading fast. I need to get him inside.

In only a few minutes more, we're at the flat. Stan waits behind me as I fumble with the keys.

'So, there's just the two of you here?'

I nod. 'Mm-hmm, me and Kaz.'

'That's so cool. I'm hoping to move out of Mum and Dad's place soon.'

I'd forgotten how young Stan is. Not problematically young. But still, young.

We're in. Thankfully Kaz has made herself scarce.

'Can I get you anything to drink? A glass of wine?'

'That would be great, thanks.' He shrugs off his coat and lays it on the back of the sofa.

I down half a glass in the kitchen before topping it up and taking it through along with Stan's. They spill over as I put them on the coffee table by the couch. Stan comes to sit next to me. He looks a bit sweaty but his smile is kind.

I'm not sure of the etiquette. Do we make small talk for a while, or should we get it over with and just start going at it? I've obviously spent too much time thinking because Stan says, 'I'm going to kiss you now, Emily.'

He says it like we're in the original *Star Trek* series and he's requesting to 'Beam me up Scotty.'

Still, I stutter out, 'okay.' I can feel my pulse in my temple.

He leans in and I do the same. I close my eyes and his lips are on mine. They're quite soft, smoother than I would have imagined. He slides his tongue in. Coffee breath aside, it's not too bad. As kisses go. He weaves his hand into my hair, and I wonder if I should follow suit or if the gel would mean there isn't much give.

He pulls away and starts to kiss my neck. I've no idea how to respond. Should I still have my eyes open by now or not? Do I add in an encouraging moan? I think I'm sat up too straight. There is nothing even close to resembling a spark.

My neck just feels a bit cold, from where he's slavered on it and then moved on.

Stan murmurs into my shoulder. 'Yes, Emily, yes. I need this.'

I'm no longer so sure about the Stan Plan.

'I can't wait to feel your—'

Okay, that's enough.

'Stan, no, wait.'

He pauses with his hand on my boob. I bat at it like it's a pesky wasp.

'Emily, what's wrong? We're moving too fast, aren't we? I didn't want to push you. It's just, I need—'

'Please. Not that again. I'm sorry, Stan. I don't want to do *this*,' I wave between us, 'anymore.'

'I see.' Stan doesn't move. The Stan Plan is falling apart at the seams.

'Er, do you want to go home, then?'

'I suppose I'll have to, won't I?'

'Um, yeah, I guess so.'

Stan doesn't move. He just sits opening and closing his fist. There's a noise behind us.

'You heard the woman. Time to skedaddle.' Kaz appears in the doorway to the living room. She's wearing satin pyjamas and her hair is wrapped up in a plastic bag. Still, she narrows her eyes at Stan in a look that makes even me want to bolt.

'Fine. I'm going,' Stan huffs.

'I'm really sorry,' I say again.

'Don't you be apologising,' Kaz interrupts.

Stan and I both look down like we're errant pre-schoolers who've been caught crayoning the walls.

After a few beats of silence, he moves to gather his coat.

'Bye, Stan. See you Monday.'

He slams the door. Or at least he attempts to. It's swollen over time and now fails to slam. He does three firm pulls before abandoning it only half in its frame. Kaz goes over and shoves it shut with her shoulder.

'That sounds like it went well?' Kaz comes to join me on the couch.

'I got it so wrong, Kaz. I don't even know where to start on how wrong it was. I couldn't go through with it. But also, I was going to use him, wasn't I? That's bad, Kaz. Really bad.'

Kaz takes a gulp of Stan's wine. 'It's a little bit bad, I admit.'

'I'm going to throw The List in the bin. What good's it done so far? We've yet to have a customer in the shop; I'm basically failing to help even the cats of Huddersfield. And I've just been really, really shitty with Stan, haven't I? Plus, what is there to look forward to? A race through mud that I've virtually no chance of finishing. I can't even manage one push up. Not one. And Kaz, I started with the easy stuff!'

I think I'm having some sort of attack. It feels like I can't get enough air into my lungs. Who fails at life when they have an actual list telling them what to do?

Kaz moves my wine away. 'I'm getting you some water. Just concentrate on your breathing for now. In through your nose, out through your mouth. Shut everything else out of that brain of yours.'

My brain doesn't work like that.

Still, I try to concentrate. Nose, mouth, nose, mouth. My breaths start to get deeper as Kaz rubs my back. I lift up my hair. I've sweated so much it's stuck to the back of my neck.

I gulp down some water.

'Better?'

'A bit, thanks.'

'So, the Stan thing probably wasn't your finest hour, admittedly.'

I go to reply but she holds up her hand. 'You just keep going with the nose, mouth routine.'

I nod.

'But don't you go beating yourself up over it. You weren't going to use him; he was as into it as you. More so, by the looks of things. And obviously, you can change your mind. Obviously.'

I nod. Because she's right. She carries on.

'I don't think The List is quite the disaster you're making it out to be. You're volunteering at the cat shop. I know you don't hate that Leon dude.'

My internal monologue stops wailing just enough to appreciate what Leon's reaction would be to being called, 'that Leon dude'.

I smile a bit as Kaz carries on.

'Plus, you've made friends at boot camp.'

'A single friend.'

'It's still increased your friendship circle by fifty per cent. I don't think you're giving yourself enough credit. You can't quit yet.'

I really should tell Kaz that I don't feel right. That ever since I started the Life List, I feel worse, not better, about my life. I don't sleep. It's like my brain is agitated. I was used to the loss. The existing without Claire. But now I can't even make a cup of tea without questioning what tea Claire would have drunk. *Would* she have been a Tetley's person? Probably not. She'd have drunk Hibiscus flowers from one of those fancy see-through teapots. I just know it. Like how she'd declared that passionfruit was her favourite ice cream flavour after she tried it once. Every time we'd gotten an ice cream after she'd complained about the lack of passionfruit.

Obviously, I don't tell Kaz. Because it's one thing feeling like you're going insane. It's quite another admitting it out loud. So, I do my very best to put a lid on all the emotions threatening to explode. I attempt something that I hope looks like a smile and say, 'Okay, I won't quit yet. If you think it's helping.' Obviously, I could just quit and not tell Kaz. Maybe I'd just pretend to do the run. I could roll around in some mud and then get a taxi to the end. I'll look into that.

'I do.' She's looking at me through narrowed eyes. 'And you know, make sure you give over some time to thinking about *why* you're actually doing this.'

She's onto me.

'I told you. That programme I watched.'

'Hmm.'

151

There are a few moments of silence.

'Did you wait up because you knew my plan was doomed?'

'Not exactly doomed. Just a bit unlikely.' I detect the beginnings of stifled laughter.

'Okay, so I see this is something you're already happy to joke about. My being a useless sex person.'

Kaz rearranges her expression into something more akin to the deathbed of a relative.

'Perhaps I should just accept that I'm inept. I will channel energy hitherto earmarked for sex into other pursuits. Like the race.'

'You just need to find the right person. But speaking of the race, I meant to say, I've booked the weekend off. I'm coming. So, you'd better finish.'

I hug her then. Without warning. Even though her coming makes my plan to cheat all the more challenging. She's wilier than the Turner clan. I catch Kaz off guard with my sudden burst of affection. I'm not by nature a hugger. In fact, I'm highly suspicious of people who are. But she doesn't say anything. She just squeezes me back.

'Right, enough soppiness. I'm going to wash this hair mask off. Don't spend the night wallowing. Everyone fucks up occasionally.'

'Poetic.'

'Thank you for coming to my TED talk.'

And with that she heads upstairs.

Chapter Eighteen

Come morning, I wake up wondering if I've even been to sleep at all. Still, I resist the urge to mindlessly scroll and drag myself out of bed.

Catching my reflection, I let out a silent cry. There are black rings around my eyes and my hair looks like it's trying to consciously uncouple from my scalp. I'm basically *Beetlejuice*.

I embark upon attempting to remove last night's mascara from under my eyes. I'm only partially successful. Though it's hard to tell where the mascara ends and my eye bags begin. Chances are I'm attempting to scrub off my actual skin.

At least the only place I have to be is the cat rescue shop. No one expects charity workers to be glamorous. Resigned, I throw on jeans and a University of Huddersfield hoodie that I extract from a could be clean, could be dirty pile on the floor.

Hunting for my keys in the kitchen, I pause. There are murmurings coming from Kaz's room. Male murmurings. How on earth she managed to find someone so late in the day last night, I'll never know. The woman could manifest a willing willy out of thin air.

I chuckle to myself.

The murmurings halt. Replaced instead by the soft thud of Kaz's headboard. I pick up the pace of my key hunt.

There's a groan.

Keys sourced from down the side of the couch, I make a dash for the front door. Closing it behind me and breathing a sigh of relief.

There's a car idling on the kerb by our door. I begin to march past it because every woman knows that dawdling around idling cars is a one-way ticket to Murderville. I hear the window coming down slowly and get ready to stab whoever it is in the eye with my keys.

'Emily! Is Bri nearly ready?'

I spin round.

'Josh! How lovely to see you again. My voice drips with insincerity even as my stomach flips at the sight of him. 'Man sat in car' is quite an unusual kink to have, I reckon.

'Er, yeah, you too. Did you see if Bri is in there? I've been messaging him, but he hasn't replied.'

I wonder again why Josh is fussing like an old mother hen. But he keeps looking at his phone in his lap. Seemingly stressed.

'He's fine,' I reassure him. 'Better than fine really. He and Kaz were, um . . .' I sort of wave my hands about. I consider a pelvic thrust to get my point across but thankfully, my brain shuts down the notion.

Fortunately, Josh gets what I mean from the hand action and the fact that I've gone puce.

154

We just sort of stare at each other then. Between my encounters with Stan and Josh, I'm beginning to think that those feminists who want to wipe out men and grow babies in fish tanks are onto something.

I'm suddenly painfully aware of my eye bags and my horrific hair.

'I'm sure Brian will be out soon. I'd better go.' I jerk my thumb over my shoulder. 'I have a shift.'

Josh looks confused.

'I thought you were a teacher?'

'I do. I mean, I am. I volunteer at a charity shop on Saturdays.'

Josh tilts his head and I think he's impressed. It's no wonder men have done a number on us all these years; one head tilt and my stomach swoops. I think of Stan's wet kisses last night. There, spark extinguished.

'Okay, bye then.' I march off.

'Bye,' he calls after me.

I hurry down to the cat rescue shop, late after my run-in with Josh. I reassure myself that I probably don't look as bad as I think I look. You're always harsher to yourself, aren't you? But then I know it's bad because when Leon sees me, he doesn't even say anything. His eyes glass over with the strain of attempting to summon the perfect insult.

'Don't worry, I already know I look a state. I had an awful night and a stressful morning, in case you care.'

'I don't,' he replies. But then ten minutes later he does put a cup of tea in front of me, so I think he might care a little bit. Men are a headfuck. It'd be much easier if they came with a little inbuilt QR code to give us a sense of what we're dealing with. A quick scan and you know they're *nice*. Or else a *player*. Or else someone who *looks all right but likes to wear an adult nappy and be fed baby food*. That sort of thing.

'Fucking hell, it's only a cup of tea.'

I smile at Leon and raise a silent cheer with my giant Sports Direct mug.

'Let's get on with this painting then, shall we?'

The thought of seeing Stan on Monday morning makes my insides squirm. Surely he'll behave like a proper adult.

'Won't he?' I implore Kaz on Saturday night, a slice of Fat Joe's pizza hanging from my hand.

'Don't know. Men are aliens,' she replies, filling me with zero hope.

'Speaking of men, I ran into Josh on Saturday morning. Brian again?'

'What can I say, my hair looked excellent after the mask,' she shrugs.

Sleep is even more elusive than normal, my thoughts flitting unhelpfully between the fact that I failed to be spontaneous and the lengths I was prepared to go to in a bid for said spontaneity. In an effort to kill time during the early hours of Sunday morning, I bake approximately four hundred cookies. Kaz blinks hard twice when she comes downstairs to see every surface covered in baked goods.

'What are you doing?' she asks.

'I believe it's called having a mental breakdown,' I reply chipperly.

No one talks about the benefits of insomnia. I've never actually baked anything before, and they're god-awful. But still, they've kept me busy.

At Sunday lunch I'm so delirious I talk incessantly. I only stop when Mum clutches Dad's forearm and the table falls silent.

'Are you okay, Emily, love?' Mum says.

'Absolutely great, thanks.'

Problem solved.

Come Monday morning, I'm wondering whether I should have attempted to contact Stan to clear the air. I don't have his number, but I do have him as a friend on Facebook. I just don't know if the kids are still using Facebook Messenger these days. Obviously, the main thing is that we just behave like reasonable adults. Okay, the main, main thing is that he keeps doing my photocopying, but the reasonable adults thing is important too.

These hopes are somewhat dashed upon entering my classroom.

The neat pile of photocopying that I'd left on Friday night has been scattered around the floor. And someone has gone to the quite considerable effort of putting a line through each page with a black marker.

I throw down my bag and go in search of him.

The hunt takes all of thirty seconds. There really aren't

many places to hide in a school, when your job is to photo-copy. Stan and Ebony are by the English copier as it churns out page after page.

'Stan,' I venture.

He looks round. He and Ebony scowl at me. This, I feel, is a little unfair. I didn't try to use Ebony for her body.

'I've nothing to say to you.'

'I understand, but there's something I'd like to say to you.' I've practised this bit.

'Say it then.'

'Er, here?' I hadn't banked on Ebony's presence, but she doesn't move an inch. I know what she's thinking. She's doubting my Hufflepuff credentials.

Stan nods.

'I'd just hoped that we could put Friday night behind us. We've always been chums,' seriously brain, 'and I wouldn't want whatever happened or didn't happen to end that.'

Stan scoffs.

'Come on, Ebs, I can't listen to any more of this.'

I'm really wishing that I'd gone for Kaz's version of the speech now. It had the words, 'consent bitch' in it quite a few times.

Anyway, I haven't really prepared for Stan not to agree with me, so I don't say anything. I just stand there as he and Ebony stalk off together.

To make myself feel better, I confiscate another packet of Tim's bonbons for £2.50. On top of my run-in with Stan, I have my first rehearsals for *Little Shop of Horrors* tonight. I have a feeling I'll need the sugar.

'How're your brothers getting on, Tim?'

'They're all right, miss. Dan, the middle one, he's got that dyslexia now. Had the proper test last week.' I teach Dan, he's in Year 8. Quite frankly it's ridiculous that it's taken this long to accurately diagnose him.

'And Stevie's a right little gobshite, but he's the brainy one, I reckon. He's coming up next year. I'll tell him to go easy on you, miss.'

'You're going soft in your old age, Tim.'

'Nah, I'm not really, you're just not too much of a knob for a teacher.'

As soon as he leaves, I start to weep. It's possibly the nicest thing anyone has ever said to me.

After school I make my way down to the hall. All the chairs normally laid out in neat rows for assemblies are pushed to the side and a gaggle of screaming kids crowd around Jan, one of the other English teachers.

Jan is as short as she is wide and can only just be made out among the melee. She has an arm raised above her head, waving what might be scripts, or else the white flag of surrender.

I wait at the edge of the pack until Jan sees me.

'Miss Turner, oh thank god. They're feral!'

It's no surprise that the school struggles to get enough staff to help with the play. Still, I'm not sure what Jan wants me to do. If she's expecting me to be the authority figure here, she's about to be sorely disappointed. I exist in direct opposition to the words 'authority figure'.

Jan disappears under a herd of stampeding teenagers once more. Mr Barnes, the newly qualified music teacher, is sat at the piano, his head in his hands.

My head is pulsing; the dull ache I carry around now has progressed to a full-on throb.

I need to make the noise stop. Acting on autopilot, I haul myself up onto the stage and shout 'HEY!!!' while waving my arms around. No one pays me any attention.

'MR BARNES,' I shout. 'MAKE SOME REALLY LOUD NOISE ON THE PIANO!'

'WHAT?'

It's no use. I walk over to where the piano is perched close to the edge of the stage and run my fingers along all of the keys as aggressively as possible.

Finally, some of the kids start to look my way. More demented noises and hand-waving and I finally have their attention.

'LISTEN,' I shout, 'LISTEN!!!'

They're all looking up at me now. Jan, released from the mob, is panting.

'Right, everyone,' I shout, standing at the edge of the stage. 'I can tell you already, this show is going to be absolutely rubbish. A total and utter pile of ... rubbish.' I draw a big breath and plough on. 'If you carry on like this, no one will want to come and see a play here next year, or the year after. Is that what you want?' To the unsuspecting ear, I actually sound like I'm exerting control over the situation. 'How about you?' I start pointing randomly at pupils, 'or you?' They all shake their heads, eyeing me warily.

'Okay, well unless you want to be part of the worst show in the school's history, this has to stop. No talking unless you're asked to talk. Understood?'

A half-hearted nod.

'I said, understood?' I sound like every teacher I ever had.

Enthusiastic nodding. Better.

'Ensemble, come and stand over here.' I wave my right arm. I'm a lion tamer now, dizzy from the power I wield. 'You're going to go through the dance routines with miss. Quickly. That's right.'

'Main characters to me. Get a script, we'll run your lines. Does everyone know where they need to be?'

En masse, eyes turn towards the floor.

'Excellent. Let's make this happen, people.' I clap my hands frantically like a flamboyant director. All I need now is one of those pointlessly narrow scarfs and a monocle.

Somehow, I've gone from unwilling participant to supreme play overlord. There's no time to consider it as several pupils extricate themselves and make their way onto the stage. Jan is looking at me like I'm the second coming. I inhale several fortifying bonbons.

'So, tell me your name and who you are in the play. Obviously, I know some of you.' I nod towards the two pupils I teach. 'Amy, who are you?'

'Audrey, miss.' Good choice. Amy is hard-working and she'll learn her lines. I've heard her humming in class and she can carry a tune.

'And you, Steven?'

161

'Seymour.'

'Okay'. Steven is two years younger and several feet shorter than Amy. So, they'll be an odd pairing for the romantic leads, but that doesn't matter.

'And the rest of you?'

'Dev, I'm the dentist.'

'Love that part.'

'Uzefa, shopkeeper.'

'Good.'

One pupil remains, he must be in Year 7. He's a tiny little thing with massive glasses and teeth that one has to hope he'll grow into. I didn't think there were any more main parts though.

'Cade. I'm the plant, Audrey Two.' His voice is squeaky. Just speaking makes him turn a worrying shade of red.

'Course you are.

'Right, well from now on, in rehearsals I'll only be calling you by your character names. That way it'll help you stay in the zone while you're here.' They all nod.

'I tell you what,' I carry on. 'Shopkeeper and Audrey, you go and run lines together in the corner. Dentist, I think the dancers are doing your song so you might want to join them. Seymour and Audrey Two, let's go through the scene where the plant is asking Seymour to feed him blood, that's a really important one. We can make do without the piano.'

They all go off dutifully as I've asked. Ebony is right, getting the little buggers to behave does seem to be my thing.

I turn to Seymour and Audrey Two.

'So, this scene is when the relationship between the plant and Seymour really changes. Audrey Two has grown so big that he's now making demands on Seymour and asking him to do things that aren't, um, particularly nice.'

'It's a bloodbath, miss.' Eyes light up in a way that I may well be retelling in court in twenty years' time.

'Well, quite. But really it's about how Seymour changes from a good person to a person who is willing to do whatever it takes to keep his plant happy. Because Seymour wrongly believes that the only interesting thing in his life is the strange and unusual plant he found during that thunderstorm.' My encyclopaedic knowledge of musicals is really coming into its own here. Claire would be so proud. I sniff.

I look at Cade, aka Audrey Two. 'Think you can pull it off?'

'Absolutely,' he squeaks, somehow becoming redder.

Hope withers and dies inside of me.

'So, let's take it from the bit where Audrey Two, the plant, starts asking Seymour to feed him. Ready?'

They nod.

'You might like to face each other. And remember Seymour, he's asking you to do something you really don't want to do. Just picture being given eighteen pages of maths homework or something.'

He screws up his face.

'That's perfect. Go.'

I honestly don't know what happens then. I can only assume that some musical spirit akin to *The Phantom of the Opera* invades Cade's vocal cords. Because when he sings '*Feed me, Seymour*', I swear the stage rattles.

'*Feed me, Seymour, feed me all night long,*' he carries on. Seymour isn't managing much of a grimace. Like me, he's gawping at the noise coming out of the four foot of nothingness that is Cade.

'Is that okay, miss?' His voice ratchets up a few octaves.

'Okay? You're absolutely brilliant, Cade!'

'Fist bump, miss?'

'Of course.' We bump fists. 'You're going to make an excellent Audrey Two. Where did you learn to sing like that?'

'Me dad was in a band before he bust his back and went on universal credit.'

'Well, you've obviously inherited his talent. Now Seymour, remember you need to look like you're being asked to do something you'd rather not.'

We run the scene again, all the way through this time. Now he's over the shock of Cade's voice, Seymour is doing an excellent job at looking aggrieved.

'Fantastic you two, you've both found your characters. Seymour, you looked horrified!'

'I was imagining your lessons, miss, when you make us do Shakespeare!'

I suppress a groan.

'Do you still think it'll be the worst play ever, miss? Because I was in *The Crucible* last year and that was pretty bad.'

It had been bad. Jan clearly had a taste for the macabre. *Little Shop of Horrors* was a dark comedy, but at least we weren't burning Year 7s. The year before that had been *Bambi*. Complete with a projected abattoir-themed montage.

'It will definitely be better than last year.' I say this with some confidence. 'Come on, let's go join the others.'

The dancing, from what I can tell, is a bit of a hodge-podge. Some kids have obviously spent years training and are kicking and leaping with the flexibility of a slinky. Others, clearly here for the time out of lessons a commitment to the play entails, just sort of walk around waving their arms a bit. And speaking of pupils avoiding lessons . . .

'Tim, I didn't have you down for a thespian?' Tim is sitting on the floor with his back to the wall. I fear he's come to flog bonbons to the flagging dancers.

'I'm lighting, miss. Four years now.'

'Ah, I see. And you being here has nothing to do with missing half a week of lessons to rehearse, would it?'

He pretends to be offended.

'Me? 'Course not. You know I love learning, it's what I live for.'

'Hmm. Well, go and make yourself useful – start sorting through the costume cupboard. We need something that could resemble a giant blood-eating plant.'

He huffs, but goes anyway.

I head over to Jan, still waving her arms frantically at the dancers.

'Oh thank you, Emily. I don't know what I'd have done

without you.' She grabs the tops of my arms so hard her fingers turn white.

'No problem. I've quite enjoyed myself actually.'

'Have you really?' She looks like she might cry.

I nod, surprising myself.

Chapter Nineteen

1998

Claire is home.

I keep saying it over and over in my head because that makes it feel more real. When I get home from school today, Claire will be there. In the bottom bunk.

Granny picks me, Kaz and Matt up from school.

'Katherine, love,' Granny says from the front seat, 'your mum's next door helping Claire get settled. You'll want to come in and wait for her.'

Kaz nods. Kaz is my second-best friend now, after Claire. She says I'm her first-best friend, but she doesn't mind that I have a different first-best friend. And then we have Charlotte and Haffsah and Ruby, who are our next friends from school.

I'm sitting on my hands now because I'm so excited to get home.

I charge through the front door and don't even take my shoes off like I'm meant to before I stomp upstairs. Kaz is right behind me.

Granny shouts, 'I'll stick the kettle on,' and heads through to the kitchen.

I push the door to our bedroom so hard that it bangs the wall behind it.

Kaz's mum is fixing cushions behind Claire's back, and my mum is standing to the side looking like she might cry again, but Claire is there, she's really there!

'Hand wash, girls,' Mum instructs, and we do as we're told and wash our hands in the bathroom.

'Emily!' Claire wheezes. Now that she's back in our bedroom, I notice how much Claire doesn't look like Claire at all. And she definitely doesn't look like me. And a little bit of my happiness goes then because I think Claire doesn't look like she belongs in our room anymore. With its purple wallpaper and floor that looks like wood but isn't really.

But Mum says that Claire's hair will grow back properly. And her eyebrows will be where eyebrows are supposed to be again.

'That feel all right, Claire?' Kaz's mum asks.

'Yes, thank you.'

I'm not sure what to do.

'Em, Kaz, why don't you sit on the floor by Claire's bed, then you can all talk properly.'

We walk over.

'Now you see this button?' Kaz's mum points to a little remote with a big red button on it, on our desk under the window. Claire could reach it from her bed. 'This button will let us know if there's something wrong with Claire. So, if ever you're all together and she seems sick, you just push this button. Do you understand?'

We nod.

'And, Claire, remember sweetie, if you don't feel right, even in the middle of the night, don't worry about waking anybody up. Just push the button, okay?'

Claire nods too. Then the grown-ups go and it's just me, Claire and Kaz, just how I like it.

'What did you do at school today?' Claire asks. She always asks this first and I think she might be a little bit sad about not going to school. Even though we like it best when we're on our holidays, normally.

'We played tig at break and learnt a new song about Jonah and the Whale. Jonah got eaten by the whale, but he was all right in the end.'

'That sounds like a funny song.'

Claire shuffles on the bed a bit and scrunches up her eyes like something might hurt.

'Shall I press the red button?'

'No! I just needed to sit up a little bit. You and Kaz can play Barbie if you like, I think I might just close my eyes.'

And Claire closes her eyes even though it's not bedtime and we don't normally like to go to sleep for as long as we can help it and Dad has called us pests.

Me and Kaz play Barbies, but we talk in our quiet voices because Claire has gone to sleep. I wonder if she'll go to sleep tonight as well because that seems like a lot of sleep for one person.

Downstairs, Kaz's mum says that Claire will probably sleep a lot over the next few weeks because that's when the body heals itself and Claire's body has a lot of healing to do after the cancer. So, after that I think that it's a good thing that Claire's sleeping. I tell Mum that I'll be extra quiet whenever she's asleep so that her body can do all of its healing and her hair can grow back.

Mum starts to cry then. Except I don't know what I've said to make her sad.

MARCH

Be Inspirational

Chapter Twenty

I'm sobbing hysterically.

'Stop being a baby and let me pop it.'

'No, it'll hurt.'

'It's just a blister, Jesus. Who gets a blister the size of Scotland after a two-mile run?'

I perch nervously on the rim of the bath as Kaz edges towards me with the needle. Okay, it's a safety pin. But still. She runs the flame of a lighter along it in a very menacing fashion.

It's March. Which means I need to become suddenly inspirational. Essentially February was a disaster. I had spontaneously hugged Kaz but wrought untold damage to womankind by failing to stand up to Stan. On balance it was impossible to call the month a success. My sanity has continued to slip further away and I'm yet to have a good night's sleep.

But this month holds some promise. Despite my better judgement, I'm still attending boot camp. If I finish the race, I will be inspirational. During the early hours of the mornings, I spend my time looking through Instagram posts of sporting people. They look incredible when they finish. Like the knowledge that they are just better than other humans seeps from their every pore. These are the people who could flee an axe murderer without breaking a sweat. Spanx are just something Bridget Jones once wore to these people. I need to become one of these people.

During one particularly long night, I go to the effort of superimposing my face onto a couple of shots. I can't tell if it's myself or Claire that looks back.

Claire was sporty. She smashed the reception egg and spoon race on sports day and had three swim badges to my one. She *laughed* when she ran. Perhaps then this is the month that I will finally make peace with my own reflection. One can dare to dream.

But first, this demon blister.

'You know I'll faint if it bleeds.'

'What happens when they do the blood test?'

'They only test me every three years. And I take a drowsy hay fever tablet to take the edge off.'

Because we were twins, Claire having cancer means that I have a higher chance of getting it too. So that's nice. It's another thing I determinedly don't think about.

'Jesus.' In one swift movement she grabs my foot and spikes the blister on my heel.

'OWWW! Ahhh, that feels better.'

'Told you.' She holds some cotton wool to the wound, read, small hole – and pushes down.

'I know you're enjoying this.'

'It's satisfying, that's all. So, enormous blister aside, how's the training going?'

'Well, I'm better equipped now, that's for sure.'

My hours spent trawling Instagram mean that I now have an in-depth knowledge of the absolute best gear for athletic prowess. I've been influenced, and I'm not even ashamed to admit it. As such, over the last few weeks a steady stream of sporting wares have arrived. Stuff I didn't even know I needed. Like nipple tape. It was tagged in a number of posts. All men. But better to be safe than sorry, especially where nipples are concerned. And I wore some fancy new socks yesterday. They're responsible for my mega blister. Basically, I am now cash-poor, but sporting-equipment rich.

'Do you think you've gotten the bug then?' Kaz sticks the blister plaster to my wound.

'I want to have the bug, I really do. But if anything, all this working out is putting me off exercise. I just want to get this thing over with. Get my picture and have at least one person call me inspirational.'

'How long till the race again?' Kaz sticks a blister plaster to my heel.

'Two weeks.' The thought makes me feel queasy. I hadn't even jogged all of the two mile 'run' I'd just been on. And I'm still stuck at nought point five of a push-up. I'd avoided watching any of the promotional videos for the Tough Mudder, banking on the premise that it's right what they say about ignorance.

Kaz sits back on the bathroom floor.

175

'Good for you. I've never seen you apply yourself to anything as much as this. You're inspiring me even.'

'Oh shut up. It doesn't count when you say it.'

'I mean it, I've never seen you with so much on.'

She speaks the truth. Between running club, show rehearsals and the cat shop, I'm veritably busy.

So why on earth I haven't started to feel like I'm living a fulfilling, happy life is something of a mystery. In fact, at times I have the sense that I'm not even living my life at all. It's more like I'm watching myself live it. As in *The Truman Show*. Except it's me. I'm Truman.

Basic daily tasks take four times as long as they used to. Last Sunday, it took me two hours to make a breakfast that consisted of two pieces of toast and some Coco Pops. Literally no one would want to be me. I don't even want to be me.

I reassure myself that it's just because my List has proved to be harder than I expected. Once I've finished the race and become an inspirational person, I'll feel better about life. More like Claire would have felt.

'Right, you're all set,' Kaz says, slapping her thighs.

'Don't make me go.'

'I'm really not making you do anything.'

'The leader bullies me.'

'I think that's the whole point.'

'He finds the biggest hills for us to run up, just to punish me.'

'Punish you for what?'

'Being feeble.'

'Maybe he wants to help you improve?' she counters.

'No, he hates me. Come with me?'

'No can do, I'm afraid. Brian's coming round.'

'What, again? I didn't realise you were still seeing him.' I normally know everything about Kaz's love life. And it normally entails a steady stream of men who last a matter of hours, depending on their stamina.

'I'm not. Well, I haven't seen him in a couple of weeks. He just suggested we hook up and I've no objections.'

'Interesting. Very interesting.'

'Why are you doing your evil genius face?'

She uses the edge of the bath to haul herself off the floor.

'We are in unprecedented territory here.'

'We are?'

'Mm-hmm. You have never liked someone enough to see them so many times.'

I fight back the urge to cry as a future scenario in which Kaz is happily married to Brian flashes through my brain in a series of freeze-frames. Kaz and Brian frolicking in long grass. Kaz and Brian brunching. Not that Kaz and I have ever brunched, but we might do, one day. Kaz and Brian on a tandem bicycle. I squeeze my eyes shut to block out the, admittedly random, thoughts. I cannot add terrible friend into the shitshow that is my life at the moment. I need to support Kaz.

'That's great!' I beam. I sound like the Frosties tiger.

'Oh Jesus, stop panicking. I'm just horny.'

This seems like an inappropriate time to ask her how exactly that feels.

At least *I'd* been extra vigilant on the soulmate front. I acted upon the premise that they were like rats, never more than two metres away and had been on high alert. Ever since fate had tried to slip Josh, who didn't fancy me, under my nose and my ill-fated encounter with Stan, I hadn't even spoken to another man apart from Leon.

My wanton cynicism is the *only* thing about my new life that I embrace with open arms. I fast-forward the love songs in musicals. I research divorce rates to bolster my theory that love achieves nothing. I horrify my unsuspecting Year 7s by introducing the story of Romeo and Juliet as that of two randy teenagers who got in a bit too deep and engendered a murderous family war, culminating in an unnecessary suicide pact.

Kaz is staring at me as I continue to ruminate on the theory that love is death.

'All this exercise is addling your brain. Go on, you're going to be late.'

'That is in no way a bad thing.' But still, I slip on my new Asics jacket. I am the living embodiment of the phrase 'all the gear, no idea'.

'See you later,' I call up the stairs to Kaz, who is still in the bathroom; I presume to prepare for Brian's arrival. Even though we are both feminists, body hair is still the enemy.

Wincing at the pain in my heel, I walk along to the spot in front of the old church. Sophie is already there, doing some strange stretch with her legs apart, face screwed up in pain. Bruce is chatting and laughing away with some of the more dedicated members. I think he's telling them about his new puppy. If I'm ever murdered, I hope the police go straight to him.

'Hi, Em. How's things?' Sophie asks.

'Fine,' I lie for approximately the millionth time in my life. 'Are *you* all right?' I move to stand next to her. Normally a grimace of this magnitude is reserved for beyond the warm-up. We haven't even set off yet.

'Uh huh.' She tries to shake off her legs as Bruce takes his place on the steps in front of us.

'So, we're on hill reps today, guys. Last one to the top has to do fifty squats!' He laughs but zeros in on me, I'm certain of it.

'Marks, set, GO!' he blasts.

Sophie grabs my arm. 'Em, I can't do it.'

'We can make it together. We'll go slow.'

'No, I mean I actually can't do it. I've wrapped cling film around my thighs. I think it's cutting off the circulation to my feet.'

'Cling film?'

'I thought it'd shave a few centimetres!' Everyone is setting off. 'Help me.' I can see the whites of her eyes.

'You want to skip?'

'Please,' she begs.

I should feel guilty. The run is in two weeks and I'm woefully under-prepared. But I can hand on heart say that all I feel is absolute joy at having an excuse to avoid hill reps.

'Okay, here's what we'll do. The warm-up run goes

straight past that new Wetherspoons. If you can manage it that far, we can just dive in as we pass the doors and hopefully no one will notice.'

'I don't think we're actually forced to stay here but your idea sounds fun. Let's go.'

We begin a slow jog. Sophie's face contorts in pain as the cling film pinches tighter and tighter. It's a good job, really, that I watch so much *Grey's Anatomy*. If this turns into a medical emergency, I am more than prepared.

We round the corner, Wetherspoons up ahead. We need to speed up, Bruce is looking back at us. If we're too slow he'll join us and start hurling abuse.

'Just a bit faster if you can.'

'Fuck, it hurts,' she grits her teeth.

'Okay, nearly there. On three then, one – two – three!' We dive. Flying through the doors and earning a few glances from the clientele sat nursing pints on a Tuesday night.

'Toilets,' I say, casting a nervous look over my shoulder. Sophie waddles past the bar. I grab a knife from the cutlery station. Ready to saw her out.

In the loo we squish into a cubicle and Sophie yanks down her running leggings in a way that people who don't have cellulite are able to do.

'Ouch!' The cling film has wound into a tight strip digging into her thighs. The skin underneath is white and all around it is red and puffy. It looks pretty painful. Armed with my knife, I begin to cut.

'This looks sore.'

The cling film is no match for my blunt knife. It springs free from the first leg and Sophie's eyebrows unknot a touch.

I set to work on the other one.

'Ahhhh, that's better.' It comes off too. There are angry welts around both of her thighs. She rubs them with the palms of her hands. 'I saw in *Marie Claire* that exercising in bin bags could help you sweat more. But I couldn't turn up in one of those, so I thought cling film was the next best thing.' She pulls her trousers up, her eyes filling with tears. 'And now it hasn't worked, *and* I've missed training. Emily,' she grabs my shoulders, 'I'll be a fat bride!'

I begin to stutter, tragically under-prepared for this kind of female bonding conversation. But Sophie is depending on me. I try to imagine what I might say to Kaz. *Is* this the time to share my wholehearted belief that fatness is merely a societal construct perpetuated by a multimillion-pound diet industry designed to keep womankind poor, weak and miserable? Or is that a bit heavy for the Wetherspoons' loo?

'You're being ridiculous, Sophie. I'd kill to have legs like yours. But even if you had the shortest, stubbiest legs on the planet, which you don't, there's worse things you could be. Like those people who don't wait in a queue of traffic but speed along and try to cut in. Everyone hates them.'

She looks at me, surprised. 'Huh, I never knew you were funny. You're right though, they're scum.'

'Maybe the reason you can't lose any more weight is because there's no more to lose? Your body is clinging on to every last pound. It needs them. It wants them. Don't deny it.'

She laughs again. 'Do you want to get a drink in here tonight? And maybe some food. I skipped tea.'

I hadn't skipped tea; in fact, I'd had two portions. But I figure that this is not a moment for intuitive eating. Hunger cues are overrated anyway.

''Course, whatever you fancy.'

Chapter Twenty-One

Two hours, three portions of nachos and a bottle of rosé wine later and I'm heading for either a serious cardiac incident or a terrible hangover. Whichever comes first.

'Ohmygod! And then I did this keto diet where you make pizza out of eggs. But I started to smell funny, so I stopped.'

'Yeah, no point in being thin if you stink.' I shove another nacho in my mouth, having fully committed at this stage.

Sophie's phone beeps.

'It's my friend Amy. She's just broken up with her boyfriend – do you mind if she joins us for a drink?'

''Course not, I'll get more wine.'

'And more nachos!'

I hand my card over at the bar, with only a fifty-fifty chance of it being accepted, thanks to my sporting equipment splurge. There are a few minutes' quiet while the bartender goes in hunt of a bottle of rosé.

My head swims and I have to pick my way carefully back to the table.

By the time I make it, Amy has already arrived. Her eyes

are rimmed red, and her face is blotchy, but still, I recognise her straight away.

Amy.

Josh's Amy.

'Amy, this is Emily.'

'We've met actually,' Amy sniffs, squinting at me. 'Don't you know Josh?' The sniffing has stopped, and her voice has an accusatory air.

'We met once. My flatmate is seeing Brian. At this very moment, in fact.'

She looks me up and down before nodding once. It strikes me that Amy likes Josh to only make the acquaintance of a certain type of woman. And whatever level of unattractiveness she deems necessary, I've clearly just surpassed it. She gives me a nod before turning back to Sophie.

'Is it definitely over this time?' Sophie asks. I pour three glasses of wine, making Amy's the biggest by some margin.

'It's over, yes. He said for certain.' Sniff. I deduce that we aren't just dealing with a break-up, it's a *dumping*. I've never coached someone through a dumping.

Happily, I've watched a lot of American sitcoms. They should help me here.

'You know he's been staying at Brian's for months now. So I gave him an ultimatum. Either come back and fully commit to making me happy or it's over. I just never expected . . .' A lot more sniffing.

'He said he didn't care enough to want to try. And to think I had laser eye surgery for that man.'

'He doesn't deserve you.' It's my first contribution. Straight off the script of *New Girl*. On reflection it's perhaps a little odd, since I don't know Amy at all.

They both ignore me. Sophie rubs Amy's back.

'Yeah, but at least now you have this amazing vision. You got the last laugh, hun.'

'I just thought we had something. Three years. How can he say he doesn't want to move to the next stage of our lives together after three years? I thought he loved me.' Amy is crying now, well it's more of a wail really, and I feel a bit guilty at how nice I was to Josh that night. I let him watch *La La Land* and told him the optimum method for eating a Fat Joe's. It took me years to hone that technique. He did not deserve such magnanimity. Not if Amy had to have lasers beamed into her eyeballs to make him happy.

Amy starts necking her wine. Her face contorts from sad to frowny. I think we may be about to move from sadness to anger, *à la* Rachel and Ross break-up number one in *Friends* series three. She slams the glass down.

'You're right – what's your name again?'

'Emily.'

'You're right, Emily.'

I'm on a roll. 'You're better off without him,' I throw out there.

I line up, 'He doesn't know what he's missing,' and 'It's his loss.' I want to smile at how well this is going for me. But that would seem insensitive to Amy. So I park it, settling instead for an expression which I hope conveys anger at Josh and solidarity with Amy all rolled into one. A sort of frowning nod.

'And he used to leave the toilet seat up all the time. You know how I feel about germs.'

'I do, babes, totally inconsiderate,' Sophie soothes.

'And that toe hair? Would it have been too much to wax it, for *me*?'

'He doesn't know what he's missing.' Me again.

Amy hiccups and looks set to resume crying. Instead, she drinks some more. Which really is a fantastic idea.

It is some time later that we're evicted from the pub.

I stagger home. The cheese and wine swirl around in my tummy as I pause only to heave by the bins.

Somehow I make it into the flat. It's all very quiet, meaning that Brian has either left or Kaz has him gagged somewhere. Taking no chances, I launch straight into bed. I accept my fate. The morning will be bad, I know that. For now, all I can do is try to sleep.

Chapter Twenty-Two

I'm obviously dead. And I've gone to hell too. It seems that my particular punishment for all eternity is to have someone hit my head with a hammer while blasting a deafening noise in my ear.

The noise sounds again. It is suspiciously like my phone alarm. You have to admire the Prince of Darkness for his attention to detail.

'Em, are you up yet? You're going to be late!'

Kaz. Is she in hell too? How sad that we both died young.

'EMMMM!'

I lick my lips. Desperate for moisture. I try to swallow but my throat feels like glass. I'm so very thirsty. So very, very thirsty. I'm fading again.

'Em – oh my god, you're wrecked!'

'Am I dead?'

'No, but you'll probably wish you were.' I try fruitlessly to lift my head from the pillow.

Normally my wake-ups these days are punctuated by a crushing sense of failure. Today it's punctuated by the crushing sense of my own skull.

'Hang on, I'll get you water and tablets.'

With no fight left in me, I just lie waiting for Kaz to return.

'Here, drink this and swallow these.'

'What time is it?' Unfortunately, I'm forced to accept the fact that's it's possible to feel like this and still be alive.

'That was your third alarm. You've got fifteen minutes to get ready. Do you need help getting in the shower?'

Fifteen minutes. Work.

'No time. But could you help dress me?'

I don't move as Kaz pulls my workout gear off and shimmies my school trousers up my legs. She doesn't bother to change my underwear because well, that would be weird. Half-a-day-old underwear will be the least of my problems today.

Once she's had a go at brushing my hair, it becomes apparent that there is simply nothing more she can do while I'm face down on the bed. I have no choice. I have to get up.

We do a, 'three, two, one' as if I'm about to be moved off a gurney in an A&E department, and Kaz hauls me up by my arms. I swing my legs down and the room lurches.

Sitting on the end of the bed, I throw up. Kaz holds a Tupperware container as I puke, splashing bits of nacho sick on my black trousers.

'Do you want to change again?'

'No time. Can you get my toothbrush?'

I chew on the toothbrush for a minute.

'You can't drive. I'll run you in.'

'Thanks. Did you have a good night with Brian?' I slur.

'Not as good as you by the looks of it. Come on, you're already late.'

The car journey is painful. My stomach rolls with every turn. I have to make it to briefing. Mr Hughes made a very pointed remark that I hadn't been attending on my learning walk feedback sheet. It's Wellness Wednesday. Last week Mr Hughes had treated us to a slide show of him wild swimming in some Speedos. Just the memory is enough to make me retch again.

Kaz passes me some water and a packet of paracetamol.

'Good luck.' Next, she hands me some chewing gum. 'You'll need this.'

I nod, swallowing down some more sick, and hobble my way to the front doors, resting on car bonnets for support. The sun is annoyingly bright today, shiny little bastard. I put my sunglasses on, wondering if I might be able to keep them there through the whole day.

I stumble into the staffroom through the back entrance and collapse into the nearest chair. Still a seat nomad, today I'm relying on the fact that if I *am* in anyone's chair, they're unlikely to approach me and ask me to move. I sip at my water.

Mr Hughes assumes his position at the head of the room.

'Good morning, everyone,' he begins. 'Finally, the big day. As you know, today we officially become a Microsoft school.' I have no recollection of this being discussed, ever.

'In order to get the new system up and running as quickly as possible, we will be without technology for most of today. Please send paper registers to pupil services.'

No IT. I groan. Luckily, there's no one in earshot. Computers are to teachers what chocolate is to periods. We *can* manage without them. We'd just rather not.

'I for one am looking forward to the challenge.' Mr Hughes doesn't teach any lessons, so I'm not sure which element of the challenge he means. 'Just like the good old days when we taught using our minds and a piece of chalk.'

A sycophantic titter ripples around the room and I swallow yet more sick.

He carries on. 'Secondly, please may I also introduce Mr Smith. He has been loaned to us by Microsoft's outreach team for the next term or so while we make the transition.'

I'm so busy concentrating on blinking that I don't see Mr Smith stand up. He's doing an awkward wave by the time I look.

Josh.

No, this cannot be.

Josh is coming to work at my school. Josh with the really average surname who goes around forcing women to beam lasers into their eyeballs before he'll go out with them.

I try to shrink into my chair.

Today now has a new mission. It is no longer simply about survival. I now have to avoid Josh at all costs.

Mr Hughes is still talking.

'As you all know, today is our final Wellness Wednesday of the term and word on the street is that a great sporting achievement is set to take place.'

I look around, wondering who or what he could be talking about.

'I know better than most how physical activity benefits both mind and body and now our very own Miss Turner is taking part in a Tough Mudder race! Stand up, Miss Turner. Tell us what inspired you to do it.' He laughs as if the obvious answer is *him*. The only thing Mr Hughes might inspire me to do is to put my head in an oven.

I freeze. The staffroom is silent aside from someone who whispers a little too loudly, 'Who's Miss Turner?'

An age passes. Heads, including Josh's, turn to look at me. Still, I don't move. What do I say? *That I'm working my way through a Life List because my life is so ordinary that I'm convinced I've failed my dead twin? That I need to somehow prove to myself that it wouldn't have been better if she'd survived and I'd died instead?* Of course, trying to say anything without simultaneously vomiting is tantamount to my ability to do those weird press-ups where they clap in the middle.

A millennium passes. Everyone is still staring at me.

I take off my sunglasses, half-blinded by the strip lighting in here. From my seat I mutter, 'I just quite like running.'

Mr Hughes frowns. I've no idea how he even knows about the run. Maybe I mentioned something to Jan at rehearsals. I can't be sure. 'Well, best of luck, Emily.'

I nod. This morning couldn't have gone any worse if Lucifer *had* taken the time to rise from the depths of hell, crawled out of the gutter, and escorted me personally down to the underworld.

'And that's us! Have a good day everyone. Two more sleeps.' Mr Hughes always says this in the week approaching a holiday.

Everyone troops dutifully out towards their classrooms. I make a break for it, determined not to talk to Josh. Seriously, what are the odds that he'd wind up working here? In its weakened state, my brain has no chance of working out the chances of two people in a town of over one hundred thousand constantly meeting each other. Even on top form it would be beyond me. But surely, it's got to be somewhere on a par with Netflix commissioning *Chernobyl the Musical*.

I survive all the way to my classroom. Pulling down the blinds and turning the lights off. The darkness eases the pressure behind my eyes.

In a rare moment of good fortune, I have a free period. I move to the back of my room and put my head on a desk that has a deformed penis carved into it. I won't nap. Just re-group.

The bell for first lesson goes. Inside my actual skull, I'm sure.

'Hi, Emily. Um, is everything okay?'

Josh.

He's hunted me down.

'What are you doing here? Are you following me?'

'Did you hear Mr Hughes? I work here for now. And I, um, I'm not following you. You just didn't hand your laptop in to be updated.' He's already carrying two laptops. Why am I noticing how attractive he is in a shirt and tie – why?

'Sorry, I didn't hear that part of the announcement.'

'Rough night?'

'Not as rough as Amy's.'

He winces.

'I didn't know you knew her?'

'Friend of a friend. I train with Sophie.'

'Ah.'

I hold my hands up. 'It's really none of my business.' I say this when really, I'm fully embracing Amy's Josh-hating mania. Or else the rosé wine has killed off the bit of my brain responsible for appropriate behaviour. I plough on. 'You know, though. Some people have a genuine fear of toe hair.'

'Pardon?'

'It's one of the lesser-known phobias, I'm sure. The opposite of a foot fetish.' What the actual fuck am I talking about?

Josh looks confused but regroups quickly. 'I don't mean to be rude,' he says. Though this is literally the first thing people say before they are, in fact, rude. 'But I'm having a shit day. And you have toothpaste in your hair.'

Touché.

With that he walks over to my laptop, picks it up and leaves. Somehow, I feel even worse than I did five minutes ago.

Obviously, I have to apologise to Josh. It really *is* none of my business what happened between him and Amy. I'm not sure I even like Amy. It's just at the minute I don't know my arse from my elbow, as Gran would say.

The day is long.

By period five my head feels set to implode. Shakespearean soliloquies should not be tackled with a hangover. It's hard to disagree with one disgruntled pupil, fed up with Hamlet's indecision, who declares, 'Couldn't he just make up his fucking mind?'

Suffering from post-Hamlet stress disorder, I set off to find Josh. I'd taken lunch as an opportunity to lie down at the back of my classroom and so I haven't eaten all day. I have a craving for hot chocolate. My stomach growls. A desperate craving.

Josh is in the staffroom. I keep a respectable distance, regretting not changing out of last night's underwear.

'Hi, Josh.' He's busy fiddling with the printer. He looks at me but says nothing. I've considered my apology in fits and starts all day.

'If it's broken, you just need to kick that drawer there,' I offer up helpfully. 'That normally sorts it out.'

'Actually, I think that's probably why it's broken. What can I do for you, Emily?'

Awkward. 'I just, um, wanted to say sorry for this morning. It's really none of my business what happened between you and Amy. I hardly know either of you. I just, um, met Amy last night and got caught up in what she was saying. And I'd had a lot of nachos and jalapenos, which make me jittery, you know? I've never met anyone else who has that reaction, but anyway. And then there was the wine. So, I've not been feeling my best self, but I still shouldn't have taken it out on you. I'm really sorry.' I finally come up for air. Wondering how I'd veered so far from the apology I'd planned.

'Okay, that's fine then. Very thorough apology accepted.'

'Really?'

'Really. It was an interesting move, blaming the jalapenos.'

I wince and he laughs.

'Right, well, I'm, er, going to go get a hot chocolate.' I've little to no idea why I'm telling him this.

'Okay.' Josh blinks at me.

'Do you like hot chocolate?'

'I guess so.'

'You should have some too.' He flinches. 'Not with me!' I shout at him. 'I don't mean you should have hot chocolate with me. I just mean that we should go our separate ways, and each enjoy liquid chocolate on our own. In separate locations.'

'I mean, I'm up for a trip to Costa if you like? You seem really keen for some hot chocolate.'

I don't want to go. I look a state. I'm the *before* in one of those extreme makeover programmes. But I've completely lost my faculties.

'What like, together? Go together?'

'Just a friendly drink.' He shrugs. Poor beautiful Josh. I really must stop forcing him to remind me that he doesn't fancy me every time we meet. I compose myself.

'Um, I don't know, I should probably get home. I'm not sure anyone would want to be seen in public with me.'

I'd already cried off show rehearsals. Judging by Jan's

sympathetic entreaties, she'd had no trouble believing that I was at death's door.

'My social standing will survive it. Come on.'

We walk to the Costa down the road. I try to keep a distance.

'How was your first day?' I ask overly loudly to distract from my growling hunger pangs.

'Not too bad, recent break-up aside. Hughes is a bit full on. There were some funny noises coming from his office at one point.'

'Like a grizzly bear in the throes of death?'

He laughs. 'Yeah, sort of like that.'

'It's him and Higginbottom. I warn you, never disturb their eleven o'clock meeting.'

'I'm glad I didn't find that out the hard way.'

I nod.

'So, you're living with Brian now?' That's it. I'll just keep shouting questions at him.

'Yeah, just till I find somewhere else. The lease is up on mine and Amy's place in a month. I said I'd still pay the rent till then. Normally, workwise I'm based around Leeds, so I'll probably look there.'

My stomach rumbles angrily again. Josh is either hard of hearing or tactful, saying nothing.

As we walk into Costa, he says, 'What can I get you?'

'This is on me.'

'Don't worry about it.'

'Okay. But just so you know, I do not support

perpetuating the patriarchy. I'm only agreeing because I've been having some issues with my card ever since Leon tried to defraud me.'

'Who's Leon?' he asks with a frown.

'He's the criminal I volunteer with. He felt quite bad about it after.'

'And you say your life is dull,' he mutters.

'I'll have a hot chocolate please.' I fear that this is what a child would order. A woman with her shit together orders a latte or something, surely. But we are all here under the pretence of hot chocolate and anyway, I don't have my shit together.

I sit in the furthest corner, already very aware that half the school are in here. I've nodded to a number of 'hi, Miss Turners' by the time I eventually sit down. I fully expect to be faced with the rumour tomorrow that I'm pregnant with Josh's triplets.

'They seem to like you?'

'I like them.' I can't help it; I squeal when Josh sets the tray down. Clearly, he'd listened to my silent pleading. Or my stomach. There are four cakes.

'I wasn't sure what you'd like but your stomach was rumbling pretty loud, so I thought you'd better eat something.' They could bottle me up and sell me as man repellent. A female antidote to Lynx Africa.

'Thanks,' I spit through a mouthful of blueberry muffin.

'Better?' he asks as I'm halfway through cake three. I catch his eye, noticing all the different shades of blue. They really are very appealing. His cowlick is a little droopy today. Sad Josh.

I dab at my mouth with a napkin in an attempt to regain some sense of decorum.

'How come you want to leave teaching if you like the kids?' Josh asks.

'Spoken like a man who knows nothing about teaching. Sorry.' I realise that once again I've been mildly insulting. I carry on, hopeful that he won't notice. 'It's not the kids. It's all the other stuff. The data.' The word sends a chill through me. 'The acronyms, oh lord, the acronyms. It's failing a learning walk because you have the wrong colour on the background of your PowerPoint slide. Mr Hughes closing the school library to make way for an isolation unit and filling it with kids who've bought a blue instead of a black pen.'

I come up for air and the realisation that I'm not in fact Martin Luther King giving a speech to thousands jolts me into embarrassment. 'So, yeah, I um just don't like that stuff,' I finish with an uninspired squib.

Josh is looking at me funny. 'Makes sense when you put it like that.' My insides squirm.

'So, is it just you and Brian then?'

'Yep. There're a few years between us but we've always gotten on all right. Mum lives over at Mytholmroyd. Dad died a few years back. His heart.'

'I'm sorry.'

'Thanks. Things were really tough for a while. For Bri especially. He struggled to accept it. Got in some trouble.'

I nod. 'It's hard to care about being a good person when you're pissed at the universe.' I pause and do a small cough. 'I mean, I bet that's the case. That grief makes you angry.'

Josh looks at me and I can feel a red stress rash working its way up my neck.

'You're spot on.'

I do a nervous half-laugh.

'And how about you? An only child?'

This should be safer ground. Except, of course, it isn't.

'No, I've a sister and an older brother, Matt, who's getting married next year. I'm yet to fully ascertain whether his fiancé is under some sort of hypnosis.'

'That bad huh?'

'I mean, he's not a monster or anything.' I adopt the accent of a 1920s American gangster before quickly snapping out of it. 'Just a slightly more annoying version of an annoying big brother. All Matt wants is to be married, two point four kids, white picket fence. The whole shebang.'

'Do people have white picket fences anymore?'

'Maybe not, but Matt will.'

'What's so wrong with that?'

'Nothing at all. If that's what you want.'

'And what about your sister?'

'No, marriage is, um, not for her.'

Ouch. Stabby guilt pain. It's just easier for everyone this way.

'You, okay?' Josh asks.

'Yeah, brilliant thanks!'

He pauses for a moment and I do my widest smile. There's a good chance I look deranged.

'Is the race part of your Life List then?'

I try to shake off the veil of sadness that's just cloaked me.

'What, because I don't look like I've had a lifelong commitment to competitive sports?' I wave my hands up and down my body, immediately wishing I hadn't. I've only drawn attention to the sick.

'I didn't mean that.'

'I'm kidding. 'Course it's part of my List. I hate running. My legs are too short.'

He laughs and I feel a bit better. 'Still, a Tough Mudder's pretty impressive?'

'Thank you,' I beam.

'Do you think you'll finish?'

'I don't know. Sometimes I think I'll finish if it kills me and then at other times, I think what's the point? Why am I putting myself through this? I'm in agony. Being boring is dull but at least you have all your toenails.'

'I don't think you're boring.'

Wow, I should not be experiencing a little zap of happiness at that. Just because something is not an insult doesn't make it a compliment.

'That's because the only two times we've met I've either been drunk or hungover. You probably think my life is all rock and roll. When really it's more Ben and Jerry's and *Les Misérables*.'

'We've met three times. The second time you were

meeting your pals, the Jehovah's Witnesses.' I cringe. I'd forgotten about that.

'They're good people.' I nod solemnly.

'And that time I picked Bri up.'

The morning after Stan. 'Okay, that time I just straight up purged from my memories.'

He laughs. I laugh too, though mine sounds more forced because I really like the sound of his laugh. I like it a bit too much. The realisation jolts me into action.

'I think I'd better head home. Today has not been a roaring success.'

'Wow, thanks. *I* enjoyed my drink at least.'

I stand up, now distinctly more nervous than I had been on the way here.

'Thanks for the drink and cake, I mean cakes. See you around.'

'Yeah, see you soon, Emily.' He smiles.

Fuck.

Fuck.

Fuck.

What the hell was I thinking?

Going out for a drink with Josh. Chatting to Josh. Even if I did railroad him into coming. I do a quick search on my phone. Of course, Costa fucking Coffee is the most popular coffee shop in the UK. I bet most marriages start there. It's like the universe is determined to drag me back to mediocrity and I just walked right into the trap.

Without a car I decide to walk home. Try to clear my head

a little. Except in a spectacularly inept move, I take a wrong turn somewhere. Essentially, I'm lost in the town I've never left. I have to Google Map the way to my own home. I'm flustered and my head is pounding by the time I get there over an hour later.

My phone pings. It's not from Natwest either.

> **Unknown number:** Hi Emily, hope it's okay, Brian got your number from Kaz. Just checking that you got home okay. I think I drove past you looking a bit stressed by the canal. Was nowhere to stop and wasn't sure it was you.

The canal is in the complete opposite direction to home. I'd stopped there to implore to God about being lost.

> **Me:** Hi Josh, yes thank you. Just fancied a walk.
> **Josh:** Good stuff. Let me know if you fancy another drink one day.

I stare at the message while the butterflies in my stomach lose the plot entirely.

> **Me:** Will do! Hope you have a nice Easter.

There. Breezy. I am chill. Totally chill.

> **Josh:** Thank you, you too.

Argh.

Seeing Josh's name on my phone comes with a serious serving of guilt.

I delete the messages. I've made a commitment to staying single. *Not* finding my soulmate is the only part of my Life List I should have no problem sailing through.

Chapter Twenty-Three

Josh, Claire, Josh, Claire. My brain is at war with itself. Try as I might, I'm struggling to quash all Josh-based thoughts. I don't even know why I'm worried when he clearly doesn't see me like that. I blame the eyes. No wait, the dimples. Life would be much easier if he'd been maimed by a dog.

It is now the night before the race. All my research suggests that I should be eating pasta and feeling zen. At least I have excelled in the pasta-eating.

'You okay over there? You were a bit quiet at tea,' Kaz asks from her bed. We're in the bed and breakfast we have for the weekend. My race gear is all laid out on the floor between our twin beds. I've seen other runners do this online; as if in the morning I won't even want to expend the energy it takes to look for my socks. The lights are off. I know I need to try and sleep, it's just that the unadulterated terror currently coursing through me is not conducive to the fact.

'Yeah, I'm fine. Fine!'

Kaz flicks the bedside lamp on. My knuckles are white, clutching the flowery duvet.

'You do realise you sound hysterical, right?'

'Do I?' My voice is so high there's a chance only the bats will hear me. I attempt to bring it down a few octaves. 'Probably just running nerves. Ten miles is an awfully long way, don't you think?' Now I sound like a man. A pensive sea captain perhaps.

'*Is* it just running nerves?'

'Yes,' I lie. I mean they're definitely in there. I'm woefully under-prepared. 'What if I don't finish?'

'You will.'

'But what if I don't? What if I can't? What if I get stuck in the first patch of mud I see and then get trampled by all of the other runners in a stampede-like situation? Better men than me have been trampled.'

'Like who?'

'Mufasa.'

'So long as you're maintaining a sense of realism.'

I wonder how it'll feel if I fail. Of course, it's not myself I'm bothered about, I'm used to disappointing *me*. But Claire …

I remember the little plaque the primary school had put up in the hall after she died.

In memory of Claire Turner. Reception egg and spoon race record-holder.

Kaz still has her head turned to me.

'I went to Costa with Josh.'

'No wonder you're having a breakdown. You should have just said.'

'You don't understand.'

'That's quite evident. Was it really such an awful date?'

'It wasn't a date.'

'I see.'

'Just a drink. But Kaz, that's not all.' My voice drops to a whisper. 'He texted me after. To ask if I got home okay.'

'Wow, really. I'm surprised your knickers didn't just burn right off. All that dirty talk, oof, how do you stand it?'

I start to cry then. I do my best to make it a silent cry. But a few sobs escape.

Kaz comes and sits by my bed.

'Hey, I'm sorry. I didn't mean the knicker thing. What's brought all this on? You're about to do something really fantastic. You're helping people. You gave me that spontaneous hug. You're really doing it, Em. And if you like Josh then—'

'No.'

'No what?'

'Don't finish that sentence. Don't give me permission.'

'I just don't understand why?'

'Because I can't. I've no room for someone like Josh right now. The Life List has to be my sole focus.'

Claire deserves that at least.

Claire. Claire. Claire. Every time I think about Josh, I betray her. My hands aren't tight on the duvet now. They're covering my face while I cry. The pain is physical. Visceral. It claws at my lungs. It's astounding, really, that grief can still do this. Kaz opens her arms and I crawl in.

'Twenty years, Kaz.' I don't elaborate further. Just squeeze my eyes tight shut, sure they're a portal for the pain.

'Shhh, I know.'

My sobs become gulping breaths.

I do a massive sniff, sure that I've left a trail of snot across Kaz's shoulder.

'I shouldn't have said anything. It's not about that.'

I half-want Kaz to force the truth out of me. That it's not about some programme. It's about Claire. I want her to tell me that I'm wrong to doubt myself. That of course I can live life just like Claire would have done. That it isn't the wrong way round, that I'm the one who's been left behind.

But she doesn't. So I don't.

'I think you'll feel better tomorrow. Once you've finished the run.' She's trying to sound confident.

'Yeah. Probably. We should get some sleep.'

She goes to move back to her own bed but stops herself. 'You'll be okay, you know.'

'Mm-hmm. I'm pretty tired now though.' It sounds a bit forced.

'Okay, if you're sure.'

'I am. Night.'

'Night, Em.'

I lay still, listening as Kaz drifts to sleep. When I'm sure she's off, I retrieve the Life List from my bag as carefully as I can. I know it off by heart by now. But still, I read each word carefully. The List tethers me to Claire. It's all I have left.

I pad through to the bathroom, use my phone torch to look at my reflection in one of those tiny, round pull-out mirrors.

Claire looks back.

I nod.

The List. It has to be The List.

Fortunately, as I stand at the start line come morning it is quite clear that for the next several hours, survival must be my only endeavour. I can't be sure whether I slept at all. Kaz had pretended not to notice as I'd been forced to surreptitiously slide my notebook back in my bag. In my somewhere state between awake and asleep, I'd been clutching it to my chest.

We're all penned in just behind the start line. It's also the finish line because the route is circular. I was hoping to have some beautiful fells as the backdrop to my inspirational 'crossing the finishing line' photo. Instead, what I look out upon is best described as something akin to the trenches of the First World War.

There is mud everywhere. Wet mud. Muddy hills rise out of flatness and drop into mud lakes. I see netting, covered in mud. What appears to be a gallows looms in the distance. Straight bits of rope dangle down over yet more mud. And this is just what I can see. I've no idea what the rest of the race has in store. Suddenly, my strategy to avoid all promotional videos seems completely stupid.

Almost my whole family are here. Aside from Gran, who declined on account of the fact that she was 'in the middle of a Jill Mansell' and Sarah, who is coming later today. Apparently one of her clients tried to escape or something similarly strange. I'm way too preoccupied to be thinking about Sarah right now. Instead, Kaz's final words of wisdom haunt me. 'Whatever you do, don't poo yourself.'

Do people poo themselves during races like this?

None of the Instagram posts had mentioned that this might be a possibility.

I can't google my way out of this one. Kaz has my phone. And anyway, I'm distracted as a massive truck-type thing roars past as we approach the start. It revs hard, sending a spray of mud from underneath huge wheels. Everyone around me cheers, making me even more nervous. I've signed up to a race with people who get turned on by wet mud.

There's a communal warm-up. Dance music blares from giant speakers as everyone jumps and stretches with gay abandon. Some of them are laughing. A group of women are wearing tutus over their running shorts. I haven't moved a muscle yet. I'm as far from warmed up as it's possible to be.

But then, my legs start to bob in time with the beat. Awkward jolts morph into a more fluid bend as something bordering on excitement works its way into my limbs. I stretch along with everyone else, wondering if this is what it feels like to be psyched.

'RUNNERS, ARE YOU READY!!?' I want to shout 'PROBABLY NOT!' But everyone around me starts a sort of haka chant. 'Mud, mud, mud!' They bash their chests, gearing themselves up. Never mind seeing your dead sister in the mirror. This, this is what insanity looks like.

My teeth start chattering even though it's quite a nice spring day.

'TO THE START LINE!'

The crowd surge forward as one, dragging me with them.

'Good luck, Em!' I hear Kaz shout from the distance.

'On your marks, get set, GO!' Someone somewhere blows a horn and people shoot off, immediately slipping and sliding on the wet mud.

I place a tentative foot on the ground beyond the start line. Attempting to run on this seems like a completely futile endeavour. Instead, I move as far to the side of the path as I can and begin to wobble my way along. Run seems like a completely erroneous description of what I'm currently doing.

Other people barge past me. The first 'challenge', a massive mud hill, looms just ahead and they seem desperately keen to get there. They fall down and laugh as they slide along like penguins. There are already other competitors scrambling up the hill. I see now that ropes have been hidden in the mud to help our ascent. I develop a plan. I will go around it.

I'm at the back of the pack as it is. So a few minutes seeking out a more cunning route is really neither here nor there.

About halfway round the base, I come across some sort of giant. He has the words 'Marshall' emblazoned across a black outfit. I peer around him. Instead of speaking, however, he points up the hill and crosses his arms.

Marshall looks like a fairly immovable object. I decide to cut my losses and try the other side of the hill. But either Marshall is exceptionally speedy, or they've cloned him and plonked him either side of the hill to make sure people, paying customers I might add, are forced to go over the top.

I'm completely alone now. So, I've no trouble getting a rope. It's already caked with wet mud. My hands start to slip. I take three steps. As soon as I try to move my hands up the rope, I collapse in a heap. Damn it. Why the hell did I wear new gear to this thing?

I look behind me. The start line is depressingly close. I check the Fitbit I had to use my credit card to buy. Apparently I've already been going forty minutes. I'm not entirely sure what all the other information it's giving me relates to.

I'm left with no choice. If I want to finish this thing I will have to crawl. I remember the finishing photo that I superimposed my face onto. I keep it to mind as on my knees I drag myself up a muddy hill. My arm muscles scream in pain. I sweat so much that my vision blurs. I wipe my eyes and smear mud across my face.

Finally, I reach the top of the hill and peer down. The other side is just as steep, and I wonder how the hell you're meant to make it down in one piece. I grope about on the ground in search of a hidden aid, the prospect of getting any muddier now completely irrelevant. There's a grunting behind me and I turn to see two men and a woman powering up the hill.

It seems highly, highly unlikely that they've somehow been slower than me.

'Um, where've you come from?' I ask the first man to make it to the top.

He doesn't even look at me but grunts, 'second lap,' before skidding down the hill on his bum.

Second lap. As in, there are more laps than one.

The woman appears at the crest of the hill.

'How many laps are there?' I ask. Frantic.

'Four.' She throws me a funny look and I suppose I must seem a little odd, my hands sunk into the mud at the top of the hill having some sort of breakdown. She also skids down on her bum. I look once more towards the start. A steady stream of racers makes their way towards the hill again.

I should stop. There is clearly no way that I'm going to finish.

I try to imagine how everyone would react if I walked back along to the start. They'd all try to make me feel better. Which would probably be worse than if they just came right out and said what was true. That I'm a total failure.

There are more racers now, ascending and descending the hill, making it look easy. A couple of them glance at me but say nothing.

I sit on my bum and try to sort of shuffle down the muddy hill. It doesn't work and I go skidding down, landing with a thump at the bottom. Setting my shoulders and tapping into hitherto unknown reserves of determination, I set off again. Towards the next hurdle. It's quite literally, a hurdle. One that lands in a pool of watery mud to wade through. My legs and arms are already aching, but I force them on. Even if it kills me . . .

*

Six hours later and it is abundantly clear that finishing this thing will in fact kill me. It's late afternoon now. I'm about to embark on my final lap. Alone. Everyone else has finished.

In fact, there's a good chance that the race is over, and I've been disqualified. In an official capacity at least. Even Marshall has gone home. All that remains of the viewing stands are a few race stragglers and my family. They cheer as I set off again. It's the saddest thing I've ever heard.

I pick up my knees one at a time and plonk them forward towards the hill once more. It seems to take four times as long as the other rounds to make it. I'm lightheaded with weariness. I've eaten all my glucose gels. The effects on my energy levels have been negligible. All that's left are those tiny packets of Haribo that you get. Two days ago, out of sheer panic, I'd stuffed them into every pocket of my running leggings. At the foot of the hill, I take one out. My fingers are unwieldy and stubborn, but I manage to tear the little packet open. I pour them all in my mouth and only half-chew before I swallow.

The ascent is slow. I'm urged on by the comforting thought that I'll never have to climb another hill for as long as I live. By the top I'm wobbly again. I ran out of water at some point in round three. I take another shot of Haribo to stabilise myself before free-falling down the hill.

By the time I make it towards the final hurdle, a muddy mesh net that racers have to climb under, I'm fairly sure I'm having an out of body experience. My vision is blurry and despite my determination to keep going straight, I seem to be weaving about the path. I'd given up walking some time ago, in favour of a crawl, but even this I can't seem to manage with any sort of purpose. Time has ceased to have meaning. I've no idea how long I've been going at this last lap. I'd check my Fitbit, but it's so caked in mud that I won't be able to see the screen. Anyway, I can't expend the energy it would take to lift my arm.

Finally, my hand touches something that feels like a muddy mesh. With a grunt I throw it over my head and begin to slither. The urge to go to sleep is overwhelming. I wonder if the race organisers would let me rest here for the night and then pick up the race tomorrow. As I'd set off for round three, they'd been busy deflating the finishing line. So honestly, they've probably gone home.

The plan is a solid one. I'll rest a bit. And when my eyesight returns, I'll finish it off.

I slump down, my face in the cold mud. I don't mind anymore. They say it's good for the skin, mud. So really, I'm getting a facial and a rest. I close my eyes and fall into a strange dream.

I'm being pulled out from under the mesh. It's effortless. I glide across the mud like an ethereal being.

'Up you get.'

In my dream, two men hook an arm over each of their necks and begin to drag me towards the end. I don't move my feet. I don't have to. My head lolls to the side and I bump into a shoulder.

'Argh.'

'Don't worry, you're almost done.'

Part of me desperately wants to believe that this is still a dream. I'm not being carried towards the finish line by two men who look like extras from the cast of *Vikings*.

'Hang in there,' the other one says. And hang I do. Even awake I make no effort to move my legs. My Viking rescuers are doing a sort of squat run at a pace I've never been able to achieve, even before Tough Mudder broke me.

I hear a cheer and try to raise my head and my eyes roll backwards. Before they take up residence at the base of my skull, I make out Mum and Kaz clapping and Dad taking pictures on his phone. I open my mouth to protest: *this* is not the sort of finishing photo I hoped for, but no words come out.

Mouth open, we cross the line. The Vikings deposit me at the foot of my family and Dad thanks them. Kaz rushes to wrap me in a foil blanket. I hear them talking in worried tones as everything fades to black.

Chapter Twenty-Four

'Arrrgggghhhhhhhh.'

Kaz sits up. Blinking. 'What's wrong?'

'I think I have that locked-in syndrome.'

'What?'

'You know. Where your body is immobile, but your mind works fine. Don't turn off life support, I want to live!'

It's the next morning. I'm lying in bed completely frozen. I can't move a muscle. I've only the faintest recollection of how I got here. I seem to remember someone feeding me chips on the way back to the Bed and Breakfast. Someone else, hopefully Kaz, trying to get my clothes off and clear some of the mud. Most of the night, however, is something of a blur.

'Kaz, what happened?'

'Oh you know, nothing special. You did a ten-mile run is all! You were amazing, Em! They could make a film out of you doing that race.'

'Would they edit out the bit where I was carried over the finish line?'

'That was like the last few hundred metres max. You did

it! And I got your medal. The organisers gave it to me before they went home.'

This is pleasing. Clearly there are to be no inspirational pictures of me actually doing the run, but if I can post a picture of my medal, all the strangers on my Facebook will know how impressive I am.

I try to sit up, keen to inspect my medal. Hard evidence of my achievement. Unfortunately, I still can't move.

'Maybe you've seized up while you slept.'

We're in the attic bedroom and there isn't much room for manoeuvre.

'Just swing your legs round and sit on the edge of the bed.' Out of the corner of my eye, because I can't turn my head, I see Kaz get up and pull on her dressing gown.

I count myself in, one – two – three – and try to swing my legs but my whole body goes flying onto the floor, whacking my head on the bedside table on the way down. Once I hit carpet, I flop around like a dying fish.

'God, Em!' Kaz is right next to me. 'You're completely stiff. You need a bath.'

This is a good idea in more ways than one. I'm still fifty per cent mud.

Kaz has no option but to leave me on the floor as she goes to run a bath.

'Can you sit up?' she calls, coming back to get me. I blink twice. 'What's wrong with your face?'

'Once for yes, twice for no. You're a nurse and everyone knows that. How am I meant to get to the bath?'

'I'll have to drag you. Hold my hand.'

I don't particularly like the sound of this, but I'm willing to give it a go.

I'm just relieved that no one can see Kaz dragging me across the bedroom floor. I get some serious friction burns from the pink nylon carpet en route.

'Ow ow ow ow,' I yell.

By the time we make it to the bathroom, the bath is already almost full. Kaz pours salts into it while I lie on the floor.

'What if I bring that chair over and help you onto it? Then you can just sort of roll into the bath?'

She turns off the tap.

'Good idea.'

'I can just help you undress, you know. I'm a nurse. I've seen many a wonky boob.'

'Hey, they're not that wonky. And even if they *were*, it's actually common to have one bigger than the other. Average even.'

'Like I said, I know.'

'I can manage, I think, just help me onto that thing.'

Pulling under my arms, Kaz yanks me up and onto the chair. My legs won't bend.

'Will you put my medal over there?' I point towards the fold-out mirror. She hangs it so that I'll be able to see it from the bath.

'Call me if you start to drown.'

'Will do.'

I've got just enough movement to shimmy my nighty down my legs. Gripping the edge of the bath I dive headfirst, landing on my side and whacking my knee. But I'm in. And it is glorious.

'Still alive in there?'

'Only just.'

The bath water turns a bit murky, but I don't care. I can feel the heat seeping into my muscles as they start to relax. Gazing at the medal, I swell with a little pride. And with fluid retention, but mainly pride.

So, I needed a little help with the last 200 metres. That doesn't detract from my achievement. At least I don't think it does. Okay, so perhaps I wasn't that inspirational to all the other people who didn't need carrying over the finish line, but someone outside the world of competitive sports would be inspired surely.

And Claire . . . A memory of her running around the back garden slams into my brain. Laughing. Her head thrown back to the sun. It's followed by another. Of us crossing the finish line together. Mirror smiles. A lot less mud. Perhaps then, Claire would be inspired too.

'Are you coming down for breakfast?' Kaz calls through the door.

Relieved to no longer be alone with my own thoughts, I pad through the bedroom, pleased to have some movement back in my limbs.

I pull on joggers and a hoodie. They seem to offer the path

of least resistance clothing-wise. Kaz helps me with my socks. There's no way I'm putting a shoe on.

'Here she is, our little athlete!' Dad stands up proudly clapping my hobbling entrance to breakfast. The other diners look down into their meals, embarrassed. I pretend not to know him.

'Er, full English please,' I wince at the waitress, tentatively lowering myself into the chair, gritting my teeth as my bum makes contact. My bum muscles really hurt.

'Poached, fried or scrambled? White toast or brown? Tea or coffee?'

So many options. 'Er. Whatever's easiest.'

'She doesn't like poached eggs. And it's white toast and tea. She'll swap the black pudding for an extra hash brown too please. I'll have the same.'

The waitress nods, clearly assuming that Kaz is some sort of custodian.

'How're you feeling, love?' Mum asks from the table next to us.

'You were so impressive out there!' Dad chimes.

'Ten miles, I can't believe it. Can you believe it, Pete?' Mum again.

'Certainly can't.' Dad.

My parents are smiling so much it looks like their faces might split in two. Clearly, after such a drought of their children doing anything noteworthy, they're now ready to explode with parental pride. Maybe that's why Matt is shovelling sausage into his mouth like his life depends on it.

Sarah is wearing a dress with a pattern to match the flowery wallpaper of the breakfast room. Like a human chameleon. It's only the whites of her eyes that allow me to even spot her.

The niggle that my efforts are not really worthy of such adulation is still there. I put three sugar cubes in my tea and stir miserably.

Dad's phone pings.

'Twenty-seven likes already!' He holds the phone out for Mum to inspect.

Twenty-seven. None of Dad's inspirational quotes ever garner enough likes to make it out of single digits.

'And I only posted it less than an hour ago.'

Kaz seems very interested in her tea all of a sudden.

'Dad,' I ask, full of trepidation. 'What is it that you've posted, exactly?'

'Here. Have a look, love,' he beams.

'Are you sure you want to, Em?' Kaz reaches for my arm before I take the phone from Dad. She's being ridiculous. How can it possibly be that—

Oh sweet mother of Jesus.

For reasons that shall remain a mystery on a par with crop circles, Dad has posted a picture of my limp body being half-dragged across the deflated line. I've raised my head just enough for him to get a full-frontal snap of my face. I look like I've died. Several days ago, in fact. I'm almost bent double. One foot trails behind the other. My arms hang limp by my sides. And my face is contorted in agony. Like a photographic version of *The Scream*.

Kaz reaches over and squeezes my arm. 'Just remember, you ran a really, really long way.'

I'm speechless. I've *seen* running pictures. People sprinting across the line, tired but glowing.

I look like I'm being dragged from a war zone.

I'm covered in mud. My face is luminous red aside from strange white circles around my eyes and mouth. What the hell? That is not a thing.

He hasn't filtered it. Not even a glow.

Dad shifts uncomfortably in his chair.

I round on him.

'How could you do this to me?'

'We're just so proud of you! We wanted to show off.' Matt is smirking and Kaz looks stricken. She knows it's bad.

I force myself to look at the picture again. It's worse on second inspection.

WE ARE SO PROUD OF OUR DAUGHTER EMILY TURNER FOR COMPLETING KESWICK'S TOUGH MUDDER. WE'RE SURE IT'LL BE THE FIRST OF MANY. GO EMILY!!

And just to add insult to injury, he's tagged half the universe into the post. Including the school account.

The damage is done. Everyone knows that once something is online it takes on a life of its own.

The drive back is not a pleasant one. I go from checking Dad's post, which now has 117 likes and five re-shares, to complaining about how much my muscles hurt. For long stretches of time, I stare aimlessly out of the window. I've failed. Again. All that effort and for what? The photograph would surely put people *off* sports, instead inspiring them towards a lifestyle of starchy carbs and Netflix binges.

I smack my head against the car window.

'You all right?' Kaz asks.

'Yeah. Just trying to distract from the pain in my legs.'

'Look, Em. I know the picture isn't what you wanted.' I'm sure she's fighting down a laugh. Traitor. 'But you *did* finish a pretty mega race. I couldn't have done it. You should be proud of yourself.'

That's the thing. If I were just doing this for me, I probably *would* be proud. I've never done anything even remotely like that before. But this has nothing to do with me. And it just wouldn't have gone that way for Claire, I'm sure of it.

I do a sad nod in an effort to get Kaz to stop talking and turn up the radio.

It's impossible not to dwell on just how different things would have been if Claire were here. Maybe *we'd* have been the ones helping other people. I wouldn't have noticed the pain because it would have been a thing we'd done together.

I imagine Claire in the car now. Here but not. What she'd say.

'*I gave you one job, Emily.*'

'I know. I'm sorry. It's really hard without you.'

'*Don't you care enough about me?*'

Ghost Claire is still eight years old.

'Of course I do. You're all I care about.'

'*Prove it.*'

'I'm trying.'

Ghost Claire doesn't answer. She knows I'm not enough.

That's the thing about grief. You don't just grieve for the person who's died, you grieve for the person you might have been with them here. For the life you might have had.

I'm angry then. At what, who knows? At Claire, maybe. At the universe, probably. At myself, definitely. I slump my head on the window again and close my eyes tight. The last thing I want to see right now is my reflection.

APRIL

Be Compassionate

Chapter Twenty-Five

I wish I'd never done the run. That's what I think as I hobble into the staffroom on Monday morning to see that someone has blown up the picture of me finishing and projected it onto the whiteboard. I now feel immune to just how bad it is. And anyway, I spent so much of the night obsessing over yet another failed endeavour on my Life List that I think I'm going blind from tiredness. My eyes are scratchy. But I see other people grimace as they catch sight of it. So, I know it's still bad.

I don't know how this has happened. I was so sure that I'd feel amazing once I'd finished. Instead, it's like I'm on the world's shittiest version of *Wheel of Fortune*. But instead of cash, every spin reveals that there's a surfeit of gloom awaiting me.

I should quit. I *want* to quit. And actually, I have no problem with quitting at things under normal circumstances. I feel, if anything, that quitting gets a bad rap.

I'd even gotten as far as hovering over the bin with my Life List-containing notebook at some crazy early hour this morning. But I couldn't do it. My fingers had remained stubbornly grasped around the spine. Another body part refusing to do as it's told.

I take a seat at the back of the staffroom.

'Welcome back, everyone,' Mr Hughes chimes. 'As you can see,' he waves a hand at the picture. It's totally unnecessary. You can't not see it. 'Miss Turner completed her race on Saturday. How's that for a motivational Monday, ey? Can we have a round of applause please!' Everyone dutifully starts to clap.

'Stand up, stand up, Miss Turner,' he calls over the claps. I'm genuinely not sure that I can. I just sort of grip the side of the chair with one hand and manage a little wave with the other.

I can see Josh at the front. He's clapping but I'm sure he's laughing at the picture too.

'It turns out that we are quite the hive of sporting achievements.' I presume in this instance Mr Hughes is using a royal 'we'. Despite his escapades into the world of wild swimming, the man still looks like he'd keel over running to open the door for an Ofsted inspector.

'Our very own Mr Turnbull tells me that next weekend he will be running the Three Peaks, dressed as a bird and eating only bird food. If anyone would like to donate to the RSPB in his name, the sheet is on the wall.' Everyone claps again. Mr Turnbull, a PE teacher, goes a bit red. Fuck off. Why is there always someone waiting in the wings, ready to outdo you?

'Very good,' Mr Hughes carries on. 'Now the IT system

should be up and running as normal today. Any problems and Mr Smith here will bob up and help you. And don't forget Year 11 reports are due this week.' A stifled groan.

We trudge out. I try to move quickly, hoping to avoid Josh.

'Congratulations on the race.' He catches up to my elbow.

'Thanks. It wasn't too bad actually.' A bare-faced lie.

'Kaz came round last night.'

'In which case you'll already know that I was manhandled across the finish line. Mostly unconscious.'

He barks out a laugh. 'Saw the picture too.'

I groan.

'How're you feeling now?'

Like I want to saw off my own legs rather than keep walking on them.

'Been better. As you can probably tell from the state of me.' I wince from trying to pick up the pace.

'You look fine.'

Hardly the compliment of the decade but I feel a blush creep across my cheeks. Damn you, average complexion.

'Well, this is me.' We finally arrive at my classroom. There's already a long line of Year 11s waiting by the door. 'You're all here early.' I address no one in particular. No one arrives early for Life Lessons.

'Sex ed, miss,' Tim chirps up. 'You promised us some porn.'

My third and most vociferous groan of the morning.

In the haze of the run and my Claire versus Josh dilemma,

I'd completely forgotten that we were moving on to sex education in Life Lessons.

'Let me know if you need anything today,' Josh says. Still smirking at me like he knows I'm an antelope with a broken leg in a lion's den.

'Like what?' I'm all flustered.

'Er, like IT support.'

'Oh right, of course.'

Tim laughs at me. Stopping when I shoot him my best teacher look.

'Right, let's get this over with. In you go, everyone.' I wave them towards the classroom, hobbling over to turn on my laptop.

Except the screen remains black. I don't have time for this today. I jab the on button again. Still black. I do what any computer-literate person would do in this situation. I press control, alt, delete and then when nothing happens, I start punching the on/off button with my aching index finger.

'Miss, I'm sure that IT guy is just outside, shall I give him a shout?'

'No thank you, Tim!'

'But I'm desperate to get on with my learning today, miss.'

One more unsuccessful punch.

'Right, fine, go get him!'

Tim makes for the door.

'IT MAN!' he bellows down the corridor. I hear a door slam shut in protest. 'MISS TURNER NEEDS YOU BAD!'

Tim cocks an eyebrow as Josh walks back through the door.

'Problem?' The class are all silent. They're watching me again.

'It won't turn on,' I grit.

'Here, let me have a look.'

He bends down to fiddle with the wires under my desk. Brushing past me I realise he smells quite nice. Like wood and maybe a field or something. I do a quick sniff before I hear a snigger and realise that thirty sixteen-year-olds are looking right at me. I blush again, deeper this time.

If Josh notices the awkward silence, he doesn't let on. Just keeps fiddling with wires.

'Right-o, everyone,' I jump suddenly to life, most likely inflicting lasting muscle damage in the process. 'So, this morning we're moving on to sex education.' There's a snigger at that. My efforts during the Year 10 sessions to roll a condom onto a banana were the stuff of school legend. 'Like last time, we'll have an anonymous question and answer session at the end. So, grab a Post-it Note and write down anything you'd like to know, and I'll have a go at answering them later on.' I will my voice to remain calm, but beads of sweat are working their way down my spine. Kudos to my body for mustering a bit after the weekend's sweat fest.

'Miss, how do you spell gonorrhoea?'

There's a bang from under the desk. Josh's head.

'Just have a go, Tim.'

I start to fan myself with my teacher planner. If Josh doesn't get my laptop fixed soon, I'll have to freestyle it rather than use the pre-prepared PowerPoint. I am not, in any way, qualified for this. My only experience of porn is watching Kelly of Blackpool finger herself.

The last Post-it Note is folded and my form are all staring at me expectantly. Waiting for the good bit to start.

'So,' I flounder, 'let's start by thinking of some of the positives and negatives of watching pornography. Chat about it to your partner and then we'll share with the class.'

There's a burst of excited chatter.

'All done.' Josh emerges from under the desk.

'Oh, thank God!' I say with such conviction that a couple of heads turn to look at me.

Josh pushes himself up.

'Let me know if you need anything else, won't you?' He smiles as he leaves.

'Miss, weren't you and sir down Costa together the other week? Millie in Year 10 saw you.'

'Urgh, I don't think so.'

'She said you ate, like, fifty cakes.'

'Come on, let's talk about porn.'

'You survived, then?' Josh hovers in my classroom doorway at lunch.

'Only just. There was much discussion of genital herpes. Much. I'd been hoping for a bit more focus on female empowerment, that sort of thing.'

He laughs. And then moves to sit at one of the desks. I'm taken aback. I always eat lunch on my own, catching up on other people's lives via social media. Except in the wake of photogate, I've sworn off Facebook. And all the sporting accounts I follow on Instagram are a taunting reminder of my own ineptitude.

'So, what's next on The List?'

I take a massive bite of my cheese and crisp baguette.

'I'm going vegan in a bid to be more compassionate.'

I'd thought about it in lessons all morning. Yes, the urge to stop is strong. But it's hard not to worry about the shadow such a monumental amount of failure would cast over the rest of my days. And the next point is food-related. If anyone can smash a food-based challenge, it's me.

The more I consider it, the more confident I am that Claire would have been a vegan. She loved animals. Even the ones no one else likes. Like those flying daddy longlegs that are all kinds of nightmarish. When we were little and next door's one-eyed cat had taken to sitting under our bird table, waiting for the baby birds to try and fail at their first flight, Claire had sat there all day next to it. In a staring contest with a cat. She'd only moved when it'd gotten dark, and Dad promised to take over in her stead.

I often think of Claire when I do my bit to save the Tibetan snow leopards.

'Vegan, huh?'

He looks pointedly at my cheese baguette.

'I'm not one yet.' And I plan on eating a lifetime's worth of cheese over the next few days.

'When do you start?'

'April the first, this weekend. I might go on a cooking course or something. Really do it properly.'

I'd spoken to Casey with the dreadlocks after period one and she'd said that she and her mum had done one in town. As I had already let my Year 11s direct vast quantities of my life thus far, it seemed only sensible to continue in this catastrophic vein.

'Sounds good.' Josh takes out his lunch. Apparently he's staying. 'What's on the agenda for this afternoon?'

'Er, more lessons.'

'I figured. What're you teaching? Nothing as exciting as porn surely.'

I check my teacher planner.

'Poetry with Year 9. We're doing Dylan Thomas. Do you know him?'

He nods. 'A-level English. *Do not go gentle.*'

'That's the one.'

Josh tilts his head. His cowlick is almost flat today. 'You look sad.'

'Do I?' My voice sounds far away. 'It's a great poem. I get that it's about his dad dying; it's just that it makes it seem like dying is a battle, like we have a choice in the matter when really, we don't. I mean, people wouldn't leave if they had a choice, would they?'

Josh just looks at me and I get that feeling. The one which tells me I'm like a dark cloud on the day of a picnic. Today was all light and full of porn-based jokes until I started talking about death. This is why I don't bother with people. Because who wants to be around some-one who starts harping on about dying on a Monday lunchtime.

'Anyway, you'll probably want to get off,' I tell him after too long in my own head.

'I get it, Emily. My dad, it was pretty recent,' is all he says.

We are, quite literally, saved by the bell.

The ten-minute warning bell sounds, signalling that the end of lunch and freedom is nigh.

'I meant to say,' Josh carries on, getting up, 'you're really good with those kids, you know? I see them in other lessons, and they aren't like they are with you.'

'Thanks,' I say, going to stand up and then remembering that I'm already in my classroom and so don't actually need to go anywhere. I try to style it out as an extreme yawn and stretch.

'But yet you want to leave?'

'Mr Hughes' forty-two-point plan for progress makes me come out in hives.'

He laughs and some of the tension in the room lifts.

'Well, see you around, Em.' Josh leaves, looking a bit con-fused at the fact that my arms are still in the air.

'Bye!' I double-handed wave.

My phone buzzes and I'm relieved that I get to stop being weird for a moment and check it out.

Mum: Now that the run's over, I wondered if
we could have that little get together to discuss

the memorial? How does this Sunday sound?
Black Bull? Xxx

Urgh.

There's no getting out of it this time.

Chapter Twenty-Six

1999

This Christmas is going to be our best one ever. Not like last Christmas when Claire was at the hospital. She still has to take some medicines, but she doesn't sleep so much in the day. And Mum says she's going to be coming to school some days when we go back after the Christmas holidays. I think that's the best-est news I've ever heard. I can't wait to show her our classroom.

Mum says you can see our house from space. Dad spent all day up a ladder hammering lights to the front. And inside the tree is full too. We've got gold streamers criss-crossing the ceiling, and Mum has blu-tacked tinsel around all our pictures. Gran said we'd go up like Guy Fawkes.

'Is everything ready for Santa?' Dad asks.

'Yes, Dad,' me and Claire laugh. I don't know how I'll ever be able to get to sleep tonight. We do one last check of the mince pie and carrot and lager we've left on a plate for Santa by the front door before Dad shoos us up the stairs. 'Remember, Santa won't come until he knows you're defi-nitely asleep.'

'Night, girls!' Mum shouts. She's in the front room eating all the purple ones out of a box of Quality Streets. She's been peeling and chopping all day today because she doesn't like to be a slave to the kitchen on Christmas Day.

Abbie Browning in our year said that Santa wasn't real. But she got it wrong and after she talked to our teacher, she said she'd changed her mind.

Me and Claire brush our teeth because even on Christmas Eve you have to brush your teeth. When we get into our bedroom, we climb up on the desk to look out of the window in case we can see Santa. Claire's hair is growing back, and it covers her ears now.

'He's not here yet, I don't think,' I say.

'Maybe he's over France.' Claire knows more about countries than I do because she's been learning about them while I've been at school. She still loves books even though she can do other stuff too now.

'We should go to sleep so that we wake up faster.'

Claire nods and climbs into her bed. The big red button is still there but we never have to press it.

'Do you think Santa definitely got our list?' I ask. I really, really want a Furby.

'Yes, he must have done. Because even if he didn't then he'd wonder where our list was, wouldn't he? He wouldn't just bring us no presents. Everyone says how good I've been with all the brain cancer. So I'll probably get more than normal. I bet Santa's worried I'll relapse, like Mum is.'

I scrunch up my face because I don't like to think about

that word. We heard Mum and Dad talking about relapse. So, we asked Kaz to ask her mum what it meant. Claire just said it was no big thing.

Claire won't get a relapse though. Not now she's better.

We shut our eyes tight. It's like I've gone to sleep already. Now that Claire's home I go to sleep really easy every night, just like I used to. Even with nasty words like cancer and relapse in my brain where I don't want them.

'Em, EMILY!' Claire is on the steps up to my bunk. 'Wake up, it's Christmas DAY!!' She starts dancing around the bedroom then and I go from asleep to awake really quickly, which never happens when I have to get up for school.

We put on our matching dressing gowns because it's still dark and a bit cold and then we go to wake Mum and Dad up.

Dad says, 'For God's sake, it's 5am!'

Mum says, 'Don't be a grouch, get up.' And they're both smiling even though Dad's a grouch. And when they look at me and Claire stood together at the bottom of the bed, they smile even bigger.

We all try to pile into Matt's room, except he has the box room and it's a bit too small for everyone. So, Claire makes me go in because she says that Matt never gets mad at me. I don't think he's gotten mad at her since she got sick either, but I don't argue with her because it's Christmas.

Claire goes first down the stairs. 'Look! He's eaten the mince pie, and the lager. Rudolph must have gotten full up of carrots, though.' Claire's right. Rudolph only took a little bite out of the end of the carrot. I hope he wasn't hungry because he had to fly a long way.

'HE'S BEEN, HE'S BEEN!' Claire opens the door to the front room and there are presents everywhere. I don't think Santa has ever brought us this many presents. Claire was right. There are two big piles for me and Claire in purple wrapping paper because Santa and his elves know everything. And then there's another pile of blue wrapping paper for Matt. And our stockings are full too.

'Well, I think that Santa obviously knows what good girls and boy you've been this year.'

Claire is jumping up and down. 'Can we open them now? I can't wait.'

'Just give me two ticks to put the kettle on and get my camera.'

It takes Mum a lot longer than two ticks to get her and Dad a cup of tea.

The room fills up really quickly with wrapping paper and every now and then we have to stop while Dad packs it up in a black bin bag so that we can see our other presents. Mum takes lots and lots of pictures.

My favourite present is my Furby, he's yellow with purple eyes. Claire got one too, which is purple with yellow eyes. We're going to decide on names later because we're too busy now. I also got a Blast Box, a nail set, three new beanies, a wedding Cherished Teddy; a silver locket that Claire got half of; some new trainers that flash lights when I walk and a My Little Pony house.

On top of her Furby, Claire gets a tattoo studio, a Mr

Frosty, a globe that lights up the dark, a dancing Cherished Teddy, some dress-up clothes, and a Barbie Porsche.

Claire seems a bit worn out by all of the present opening, so Dad clears us a space on the couch, and we watch Noddy in Toyland, even though we're a bit old for it, because there's nothing else on.

And then Claire says she's feeling a lot better and shouldn't we go and get ready for the day.

We take some toys to our bedroom so that we can get another look at them. Claire does matching tattoos on our faces, and we both put clips in our hair and wear the same dresses that Mum bought us from the big Asda where she's working again. Except Claire's is red and mine is green because Mum says that purple isn't really a Christmas colour. And Claire's is smaller because she's smaller than me now. But aside from that we're starting to look like mirror twins again.

Then Gran comes over and we have even more presents and we eat our Christmas dinner. Mum and Dad have wine. Gran has a little glass. We're allowed some Coke even though Mum says it'll send us barmy.

Mum takes another picture of us all in our paper crowns. All the grown-ups keep saying they couldn't eat another bite, but they manage to. Mum says Claire only has to eat one sprout so she holds her nose and shovels one in. And then she eats more and more because she says they aren't so bad once you're holding your nose. I don't think they're too bad anyway, but I laugh with everyone else.

*

That night me and Claire sit in the dark with her light-up globe and she points out some of the countries she's learnt about. 'This big one is Australia, that's where kangaroos come from.'

I know that they do but I don't say anything because I don't want to come across as a smarty pants.

'And this is the North Pole. When I grow up, I'm going to go and see every country on the world.'

It seems to me that there are too many countries for one person to visit. Especially when we're already six and we've never even been on an aeroplane.

'Do you really think you will?'

'Oh definitely. You'll have to come with me though. We'll go exploring together.'

Actually, that sounds like really good fun.

Chapter Twenty-Seven

'Emily, love!' Sandra effuses. 'We saw the photo on Facebook! Didn't you do well?'

'Course they saw the photo. Not a single person in the Northern Hemisphere missed that bad boy.

Obviously, I've quit boot camp. Sophie has been sending me increasingly threatening messages about the fact. I surmise that there must be something permanently wrong with my brain because a tiny part of it *has* missed having Bruce scream at me that I'm the scum of the earth as I star jump.

Leon looks like all of his Christmases have come at once; I presume at the prospect of being able to ridicule me to my face for the photos.

'Oh, shut it,' I say before he can start insulting me. 'You're literally a criminal. You don't get to mock anyone.'

He just laughs at that. It's a sign of how far we've come.

'Here, help me with these boxes. I need to leave on time today.' As usual, there's a pile of boxes full of old clothes waiting for us. Really, when people say they're giving to charity, what they really mean is that they're going to chuck out any old trash.

'Hot date?'

'No, I've got a vegan cooking course.' Leon rolls his eyes but then I've seen him eat one of those knock-off KFC buckets full of deep-fried animal parts for breakfast.

Sandra has, as usual, gone to put the kettle on.

'How long do you have left, anyway?' I ask Leon, scrunching my nose at a pair of paint-splattered dungarees that someone has kindly 'donated'.

'Just another sixty hours and I'm done.'

'But what will you do then?'

'Dunno. I'm a criminal. Crime stuff probably.' He narrows his eyes at me. 'Are you going to try to save me?'

'How else am I going to get my damehood? Is there really nothing else you want to do?'

'You know,' he looks abashed, 'I used to write poems.'

'Wow, Leon, you should have said! I won a poetry competition once. Well, runner-up but it's the same thing really, isn't it?'

''Course I don't want to be a fucking poet.'

Oh. We continue to sort.

'In all seriousness though, you should go back to school, finish your qualifications. The tech offers catch-up courses.'

'I never even started my qualifications.'

'Don't they have lessons in prison?' I whisper the word prison.

'Yeah. But we had a different teacher every week. One guy couldn't even spell February, never mind teach us what a fucking adverb was or any of that shit.'

'Language, Leon. And I can teach you what an adverb is, I actually have a very catchy song. It's to the tune of 'The Skeleton Dance', you ready? *The adverb's connected to the verb, the main verb's basically a doing word—*'

I stop. Mainly because there's a vein in Leon's forehead that looks set to explode.

'I know what an adverb is. But that bit where you tried to squeeze an extra syllable into "verb" in that first line was really special.'

'Right. I just thought you said—'

'Just an example.' He narrows his eyes at me before stretching his neck side to side. 'You're a teacher, aren't you?'

'For now. I'm still looking for my own purpose in life.'

In reality, I've made absolutely no progress on the big career move. It had seemed quite far away in January, 'Be Successful by May'. Now, with only a month to go, I've done a few preliminary searches. Trouble is, I hardly even recognise some of the jobs out there. Obviously, I'd filtered them by income, but even after an evening's research I was no closer to working out what a hedge fund manager did. I figure, in that instance, it probably isn't for me. And I don't have the spatial awareness required to be a pilot. I can't even parallel park.

'Fair enough, couldn't pay me all the money in the world to spend every day with a load of little shits.'

'It's not that. It's more just that I can't summon the energy to care about all the ridiculous stuff that goes with it. The jumping through hoops. The target setting.'

'Yeah, sounds shit.'

'You know, if you swore a bit less you might be a more appealing job applicant.'

He gives me the finger.

We continue to rummage through boxes for a while. The discarded pile is a mountain. The 'to keep' pile consists of a single black T-shirt from Primark.

'I've always liked music. DJing, like.'

'You any good?'

'I reckon so.'

'Well, there you go. Can't DJ from prison, can you? So keep your bum out of there.'

I manage to leave only ten minutes late from my shift and so run to the Half Moon Café for our vegan cooking course. At £70 a person, it wasn't exactly cheap. But they'd promised cheesy pasta and chocolate cake.

Kaz is waiting outside.

'Ready?' she asks.

'Mm-hm, I'm starving.'

I've never been to the café before, but honestly, it really does tick every vegan cliché. There's an abundance of tie-dye for one. What sounds like whale song drifts softly from speakers in the corners. Nap-inducingly peaceful. Maybe I could ask for the CD.

'Take a seat anywhere, ladies.' A waif of a woman with long blonde hair waves her hand around the café. A man sits typing on his MacBook, teenage girls drink moss-coloured smoothies, women in workout clothes have avocado on toast. This is promising. I need to make these people my people.

'Actually, we're here for the vegan cooking thing,' Kaz offers.

'Pardon?'

'The vegan cookery course. Pasta and cake?'

'Oh right, of course.' Realisation crosses her face at the most ethereal pace. 'Come through, come through.'

We duck through a curtain of beads separating the kitchen from the café.

'Tony, these ladies are here for the course.'

'Right you are. Welcome!' Tony is also waif-like. In the credits to a movie, he would appear under 'vegan chef'. Neither of them look like they partake in much pasta or cake. He has short brown hair and an impressive beard.

Tony leads us to a workstation with two sets of ingredients laid out. How we're going to create cheesy pasta from something called nutritional yeast is anyone's guess. It sounds like something you'd treat with Canesten.

Kaz throws me a dubious glance.

'So, as you might already know,' Tony begins, throwing a tea towel over his shoulder in a way that is no doubt mandatory training at chef school, 'veganism is the fastest-growing food trend there is. There has been a 350 per cent increase in the number of vegans in the last five years.'

Brilliant. Even in my attempts to be unique, I've managed to jump on a bandwagon.

'A vegan diet protects the environment. It takes almost

two hundred times more water to produce a pound of meat than it does a pound of vegetables.' Tony sounds distinctly bored. Like he can't believe that he's still having to regurgitate this crap. 'On top of that,' he soldiers on, 'vegans live on average ten years longer than non-vegans.'

Deep down I probably already know that eating ten tonnes of meat has had its day. I mean, I've seen *Cowspiracy*. Perhaps being vegan was maybe something that would make me interesting *and* do some good. It really speaks to how much of a terrible person I've become that this is my first time considering this.

Kaz nudges me. I've zoned out for a good chunk of Tony's speech.

'So, you ladies get on with that, I'll just whip up this salad.'

'What are we doing again?'

'Making cheese. Out of cashew nuts.' Kaz dutifully pours a bowl of wet cashew nuts into a blender, adding the nutritional yeast and a few other bits and bobs.

I copy and as we blitz, I wonder on what planet nuts are meant to taste like cheese. Like everyone else, I know that nuts are good for me. I know I should be snacking on them through the day. But let's be honest here. A nut is no crisp.

We put the cheese, in the loosest possible sense of the word, to one side and get started on the cake. Tony does a grand unveiling of our second box of ingredients. Well, he pulls a tea towel off them at least.

We were promised chocolate cake. But I cannot see anything here that resembles chocolate. One thousand batch of cookies aside, I'm no baker. But surely a chocolate cake needs chocolate. Instead, there's agave nectar, cacao nibs and – my heart sinks – an avocado.

We start by mushing up the avocado. I've no idea why people on Instagram go bat shit crazy for these things. It's so slimy it turns my stomach.

'You always want to wait until they're a bit overripe, like that,' Tony adds.

We combine the unique set of ingredients and then pour them into a cake tin. I'd assumed we'd get a cake each for £70. Clearly not.

Then it's back to the cashew cheese. We chop and fry vegetables, some of which I've genuinely never heard of. Romanesco. Case in point. Looks like the spawn of a broccoli and a cauliflower. I interrupt Tony's instructions with questions designed to ascertain which foods count as vegan. He gets a bit terse after I enquire about ketchup.

Kaz does announce that she heard Oreos are vegan, which makes me feel better.

Finally, the pasta has boiled and we're stirring everything together. I've had enough now. The chances of me being able to replicate these recipes at home are slim to none. Not because I'm stupid. Just because I already know I won't want to.

Everything is plated up, including the cake.

'Here you are, cheesy pasta and chocolate cake. Easy as you like,' Tony states.

We've used four thousand ingredients and the kitchen looks like a bomb has exploded. Kaz narrows her eyes at him.

Tony is still watching us, so we've no real choice but to tuck in. The cheese is very nutty. And there are far too many vegetables in the pasta. Pasta is an ingredient that can hold up on its own in my opinion.

'What do you think?' Tony asks as I try discreetly to scrape away the nutty cheese.

'Yeah, it's um . . .' We start on the cake.

I remember Claire and the sprouts. Or the time she worked her way through half a pint of passionfruit ice cream. I take a bite.

In the end, it's not the avocado that ruins it. It's the lack of sugar. Sugar is vegan. If there is one thing I will take away from this course, it's that there must always be sugar in cake.

'I think we're done here, Tony.' Kaz nods at him, pushing the cake back across the counter. Tony looks genuinely gobsmacked that someone might find sugarless avocado cake unappealing.

He has no time to dwell. There's an urgent order for zoodles. Kaz and I make our way back through the restaurant and emerge onto the street.

'That was a bloody disaster – seventy pounds and I'm starving.'

'Me too. Do you think we're cut out to be vegans?'

'I'm *not* going vegan. But I reckon it's like anything, there's real hardcore ones and then there's some who eat chips and normal stuff.'

'You're probably right. I thought he was going to burst a

blood vessel when I asked if gin was vegan.' We're heading towards the high street now.

'You never know. Honey isn't.'

'I know. I was there when Tony told you.'

We arrive to stand in front of Greggs. A choir of angels might well start up any moment now. Because there, in the window, is a sign for the vegan sausage roll.

'Kaz, do you see it?' I'm like a wise man pointing to the North Star.

'I do see. Piers Morgan hated them.'

I clap my hands together excitedly. Piers Morgan is my very own moral compass. I just take whatever stance is in opposition to him on everything we're meant to have an opinion on.

'God, this is amazing.' I'm halfway through my first vegan sausage roll and finally come up for air. We're sat on a bench that's approximately three metres from the entrance to Greggs. I didn't want to wait. 'And vegan donuts too. Why are people milking cashew nuts when they could be eating this?' I implore.

I go in for another bite.

'So, you're planning on sticking with it then?'

'Can I eat these for every meal?'

'Might get scurvy.'

'Worth it. But yeah, I think I will. It seems like this is maybe a good thing; you know, a bit less self-involved than being inspirational, at least.'

'I agree. But you're going back to boot camp?'

'Undecided.' I inhale some delicious flaky pastry and cough. Death by Greggs vegan sausage roll. A glorious ending by any standard.

'So, you're volunteering at the shop, you've run a mega race and now you're vegan. Your life has gone from distinctly meh to pretty full on in a few short months.'

'Meh?'

'Not you. Just your life always just seemed quite small. In relation to you, I mean.'

Funny, I'd always thought my life was bigger than me.

'Anyway, you're massively overplaying my Life List successes so far. I'm sort of volunteering, Leon spends all morning abusing me.'

Kaz goes to interrupt but I keep talking.

'The less said about February's endeavours to be spontaneous, the better. And I was at best, moderately inspirational. I haven't even gotten started on the harder stuff yet.'

I think of Claire and am enveloped in sadness. It's always the same when my shortcomings are laid out so starkly. God, grief is draining. It would be much easier to pick a team – happy, sad, confused, lonely – and just stick with it.

'You'll nail this challenge at least. And what's next month, be an explorer?'

'Mm-hm. And the Be Successful one. Which quite frankly I regret adding to The List. Remember, May is the double whammy.'

'Where will you go? Travelling, I mean.'

I start on the doughnuts and groan.

'I think I'll just go to the airport and get on the first plane, you know?'

'Wow, that *is* explore-y.'

'Want to tag along?'

'I'm not a teacher. I don't spend half my life on holiday. And anyway, I think it'll be good for you to go alone, you know.'

I couldn't disagree more.

Chapter Twenty-Eight

'Emily, EMILY!' Josh catches up with me at the door to my classroom on Monday morning. He's like a celebrity death, you never see him coming.

'Hi, Josh.'

'Good weekend?' He follows me inside.

'Yeah fine.' It had been the family memorial meeting in the Black Bull. We'd agreed on purple balloons and photos in the first five minutes, but I'd avoided a breakdown so I'm taking it as a win.

'How was the cooking thing?'

'Expensive. But I did have my first vegan sausage roll. Hang on, I bought one for you to try.'

I rummage in my bag and produce the grease-stained paper bag bearing the sausage roll, holding it out on my hands like I'm Mary and it's the baby Jesus. I hadn't in fact bought it specifically for Josh. But I'd reached my sausage roll wall after eating eight or so over the weekend and had a few going spare.

Josh smiles and I swear his cheeks go a bit red. Surely buying him a sausage roll is not admitting to fancying him.

Which I don't. Because I'm EXTREMELY focused on my List. Anyway, no one sensible declares their love with out-of-date fake meat.

'Thanks very much. I'll eat it at lunch. See you then?' After that first day, Josh has taken to spending all of his lunchtimes in my classroom, making me think he wasn't as put off when I'd randomly started talking about dying, as the rest of the population might have been. So, I have a lunch buddy. Buddy being the key word, because, as I remind myself for the millionth time, Josh doesn't fancy me.

'Yep, see you.' He turns to leave.

Stan chooses this moment to stalk through my open door. He throws Josh a pitying look and scowls at me, shoving a pile of photocopying into my hands. Stan taking my refusal to have sex with him as a personal affront is so wrong it's not even funny.

'What's his problem?' Josh asks as Stan leaves.

I pinch the bridge of my nose. In the emotional roller-coaster that is my day-to-day existence, I don't have much capacity for Stan.

'It's a long story.' And one which I plan on telling Josh round about never.

'Right – okay, well, have a good one.'

'This is really good.' Josh dutifully eats my Greggs offering at lunch.

'I know, right.'

'There's this new vegan place opened in Leeds. We could check it out if you like?'

I nearly choke on my crisp.

'Are you okay?'

'Yeah.' My eyes water. 'Bit of crisp went down the wrong way.' God I'm sexy. I take a big drink. 'You were saying about the vegan place?'

'It's in the Arcades. Maybe one night after work?' I swear Josh's cheeks are tinged pink again. I home in on them, hopeful that they'll give me a clue as to what is actually happening here. Because it sounds like Josh is asking me out. But he had declared loud and clear that he didn't fancy me. And I looked significantly more attractive that night in Wetherspoons than I do the rest of the time.

I've been quiet way too long. We're friends. I think. Friends can go out for tea with other friends.

Stop thinking and say something.

People don't marry someone they're only friends with. You need to be having sexy times to get married.

Speak!

I hear myself say, 'Why yes, Josh. That would be lovely, thank you.'

If he's disturbed by my overly formal reply, he doesn't say so.

'Great, how about tomorrow night?'

'Sorry, boot camp on Tuesday.' I've committed to return. I don't know why. Though it might have something to do with Sophie's ever-increasing stream of aggressive memes. In the last one, a cartoon dog was being strangled.

'Wednesday?'

'Okay. Yeah. Cool.' I aim for breezy.

'We could get the train after work if you like?'

'Sounds good. I have rehearsals for the school show on Wednesdays. You could hang around if you like, wait until we're done. Or not. If you wanted to leave it until, um, a different time.'

'No problem, I'll hang around.' The bell rings. 'See you later.'

At least four pupils ask me why I'm being weird for the rest of the day.

'Hi, Soph.'

I jog up to her in front of the church. It's a mark of how far I've come that this alone hasn't finished me off. In fact, Sophie and I have both improved significantly. We're still a long way from being 'good' but we're no longer shit either.

'Fucking finally.'

I let out a nervous laugh. The closer we get to Sophie's wedding, the more unhinged she seems to be. 'It's hill reps tonight. Though he did suggest we do something called fartlek training. I ignored him.'

'Good.' I begin my stretches.

Something akin to a good mood lingered all day yesterday *and* today. It's been punctuated by the odd bout of mild desolation. But definitely less than usual. Plus, I've not touched a single animal product. Even my shampoo is now vegan.

'How's the wedding planning coming along?'

'Nightmare. My half-sister and her husband are refusing to come because we've decided on a no kids policy. Hers are three and five, and they're absolutely fucking awful. They've ruined her life. And I don't even want to tell you what happened to her front bum after she had the last one. Episiotomy *and* forceps. He was ten pounds.'

I'm struggling to keep up with the story. I don't know how we've gotten to her half-sister's vagina so quickly. Still, this is the nice thing about talking to Sophie. She does most of the talking.

'You'd think she'd want a break from them. Anyway, so I thought she was bluffing at first but she's not. And now it's too late to get a refund so I've basically paid £200 for a pair of empty seats. I could have put that money towards my Invisalign.'

'That's awful, Soph.'

'I know, right. It's *my* wedding. If I don't want a load of gross sproglodytes ruining the meal, then it's up to me. We said they could come to the fucking disco if they had to.' Sophie is a nursery nurse.

The whistle blows and we start to jog. These days we keep to the middle of the pack. Like those penguins who stand for four months in the Antarctic, it's always the ones on the edge that die off first.

'Hey Soph, Amy's ex, you know, Josh. I was just, um, wondering what happened between them?'

I've replayed Josh asking if I wanted to go eat with him

over and over. I'm no closer to working out whether he meant it as a date or not. Either way, I decide to gather intel.

Sophie looks puzzled. But if she's surprised by the sudden change of topic, she doesn't say so.

'He's the worst. Treated Amy so bad, you wouldn't believe.'

'Really? I can't picture it.'

That earns me a look.

'Months ago, he said he thought he didn't see a future and wanted to move out. Poor Amy didn't see it coming at all. She had a Pinterest board of wedding stuff, and he was plotting his escape.' She's breathing heavily, though whether from the jog or her hatred of Josh and his evil deeds, it's hard to tell.

'Then, after Amy begged him to try a break instead of breaking up proper, he strung her along for months before finishing things once and for all. And he was invited to the wedding. Luckily, they broke up early enough so that I got my deposit back on his place, not that he knew that, mind.'

This insight doesn't seem like Josh at all. I can't help wondering whether Amy really is as much of a victim as Sophie is making out. Amy looks like she could kill a man with her acrylic nails alone.

Our conversation means that we have drifted to the back of the pack. And like the cold arctic night, Bruce swoops in to terrorise us.

There's a moment, just before the apex of the hill, as Bruce is shouting that we will die fat and Soph is replying that she wishes she were dead, when I genuinely wonder whether I make good choices.

And then it's over. I force my shaking legs into a series of stretches that have thus far proved to have zero impact.

'Nice session, girls!' Bruce beams. I eye him warily. 'I just wondered if you ladies would be interested in a fun run we're putting on. No obstacles, smallish hill, should be no problem for you both these days.' He smiles.

'Um, I think I'm busy that weekend,' I say.

'And I just don't want to,' Soph adds.

He laughs as if we're joking. He obviously doesn't know us at all. My quest to be inspirational is over.

'If you change your mind, here's the details. We're going to make a day of it. There'll be all sorts on. I think some people are going to collect money for charity.' He hands us a flyer and we both look shamefaced, as if by declining to participate we are single-handedly responsible for the financial shortfalls in the charity sector.

He jogs off and I tuck the leaflet in my jacket pocket. No doubt the next time I see it will be as mush in the bottom of the washing machine.

Soph puts her hand out to stop me. 'Em, you know I've just had a thought.'

'About the run?'

'Shit, no, I'm not doing that. About the wedding. You should come! And you can bring a date!'

I decidedly ignore the fact that I'm only getting an invite because someone else is refusing to come. I've never actually been to the whole day of a wedding. The closest I've come was to the evening do of a random member of the English department. There'd been a hog roast and even in my pre-vegan days, I'd wondered as to the symbolism of having a rotating burnt pig to celebrate your day of love.

'Wow, really? I'd love to come, thank you so much!'

She claps her hands really fast and dances on the spot.

'And you already know Amy, she's a bridesmaid. Like I said, you can bring a plus one. My sister-in-law is going to flip her lid when she finds out I've given her place away. So, you'll definitely come?'

'Wild horses couldn't keep me away.'

'Haha, you're funny. Like an old person even though you're young.'

I sort of half-laugh because her observation seems halfway to an insult.

'Let's go get a drink to celebrate.'

Three drinks later and I stumble through the front door to the flat. Fortunately, I'd started having flashbacks from our last night out and put my foot down after one bottle of wine. I'm feeling woozy but with all the drinking I'm doing these days, my blood alcohol tolerance has improved significantly. No wonder Gran could knock back half a bottle of Baileys with lunch. You just had to have commitment to the cause.

Kaz is on the sofa watching *Line of Duty*. She is the only person I know who looks good in loungewear.

'Kaz, I need your help with something.' I sound a bit slurry, but not too bad.

She cocks an eyebrow. 'What – now? It's the series finale.'

'Can you pause it for a minute? I need to do a Facebook stalk.'

Her eyes light up. A real testament to the generational gulf that exists these days. My gran had kids by twenty-five. Kaz and I consider a Facebook stalk a legitimate way to pass an evening. No wonder there are genuine fears for the future of the planet.

She whips out her phone. This is something of a forte for her.

'Who are we hunting?'

'Er, Josh. Do you have to make it sound so predatory?'

Another cock of the eyebrow. 'As in, Brian's Josh?'

'He asked me out. We're going for tea tomorrow night.'

'Sounds like a date.'

'It didn't sound date-like when he asked.'

I'm so muddled I'm actually confusing myself. Obviously I don't want Josh to ask me on a date. Because I'm avoiding anyone with the potential to be my soulmate. Yet I feel a bit disappointed with that line of thought.

'For argument's sake, say it is a date, what about the whole soulmate avoidance strategy?'

'Don't worry, I'm still committed. I have until July for the authentic thing. Still, it'd be easier if we found something really dark on his Facebook. Fingers crossed he's a big game hunter.'

'You're weird. Brian said he's had a rough time of it lately. His ex was a bit of a psycho by all accounts.'

'She's friends with Sophie,' I nod.

'Apparently she squirted fake tan foam onto all of his white shirts. And she cooked his phone. Like, actually boiled it in a pan.'

Okay, that does sound mildly unhinged.

'So, what's his surname?'

'You don't know Brian's surname?'

'Why would I?'

'Smith. It's Josh Smith.'

'You're kidding me, right?'

'Nope. I'm going out with a man whose surname is the *only* one more common than my own.'

'Brilliant, there are four hundred Josh Smiths. We'll have to go through Brian. Now let me just triangulate . . .'

She scrolls a bit and then holds her phone high up as if getting inches closer to an orbiting satellite might help.

'Got him. He's got pretty tight security settings. I'm not sure I can hack too much.'

'He's in IT, I suppose. He probably reads those new Terms of Agreement that Facebook send out every now and then. Let's have a look at his profile picture.'

Even that's a bit blurry. But from what I can tell, it's a picture of Josh in a field. It doesn't give much away.

'Maybe Brian will have some stuff on Josh.'

Kaz begins to scroll.

'Here they are.' There's a picture of Josh and Brian inside

a club. They're both holding bottles of Bud. Josh has dark denim jeans and boots with one of those faded T-shirts he likes. My tummy does a little flip at the sight of him.

We look some more.

'This must have been their dad,' I say. It's a testament to just how far back we go that we find a picture of a much younger Josh and Brian with their dad. They're at the top of some hill in walking boots. Brian looks more like Josh in the picture. His hair is shorter, and I can't see any tattoos. Kaz scrolls back to the top.

'He is handsome, isn't he?' she says.

'Who, Josh?'

'No, Brian. Though Josh is all right too.'

I'm forced to agree. And what's worse, there's nothing to suggest they're members of a cult, unfortunately.

'Are you going to bed, Em?' Kaz asks completely out of the blue.

'Er, yeah, I was planning on at some point.'

'Off you pop then, I think I'll see if Brian wants to come round.'

'What, now? It's nearly ten o'clock.'

'Exactly, the night is still young. But you, you've got a big date tomorrow. You need your beauty sleep. You'll thank me in the morning. Wear the purple dress.'

'You don't think that's a bit OTT?'

'What else are you going to wear, your work suit?' She's jabbing away on her phone.

It pings.

'He's on his way. Off you go. Actually, let me use the bathroom first.' She pulls me up the stairs by my arm.

'Okay, okay, I'm going. Have fun with Brian.'

'Don't worry, I intend to.'

I really wish I hadn't heard that last part.

Chapter Twenty-Nine

1999

It starts with a headache.

Kaz's mum let her come to Butlin's with us that summer and we'd all done the talent show together. And then we'd gotten matching friendship bracelets because we'd won again. Claire's hair was long like mine, and everyone was saying over and over how good it was to put this cancer malarkey behind us.

Then we'd had our eighth birthday party at McDonald's. We both got a Tamagotchi and some matching roller skates. Mum was so scared when we went out on them that I wondered why she'd bought them for us in the first place.

But now Claire says she has a headache.

At first, I don't know if it's true. We're meant to go visit Aunty Nelly in the old people's home that smells of gravy later. Claire doesn't like it there. Except I think it must be true because Claire doesn't want to play in the garden with me and Kaz either. Instead, she goes for a lie-down while we play handstands.

But then I think of the cancer that was in Claire's brain and a good twin would go and double-check that Claire is all right, and I really want to be a good twin.

Me and Kaz go upstairs. Mum is in the kitchen and we can hear her singing along to 'Mambo No. 5' on the radio.

'Are you okay, Claire?' I ask and push the door open. Except Claire doesn't answer because she's on the floor with her eyes shut, moving her arms and legs and twitching. I run to her and try to wake her up, but I can't, so Kaz pushes the red button that we've never pushed before, and grown-ups start pouring into the room.

Mum's holding Claire and saying, 'Oh no, oh no, oh no.' Over and over again. I feel like the room is shaking. I go really cold, and I open my mouth to scream but no sound comes out. My arms and legs don't work properly anymore. I can't move. The ambulance comes and takes Claire away and still my scream is stuck in my throat.

Chapter Thirty

I have a fitful night's sleep. A faceless doctor follows me down endless corridors. I wake up unsettled.

Getting dressed, I think about my might-be-a-date-but probably-isn't-a-date with Josh later. There's no way I can keep convincing myself that I don't fancy him. I think about him way too much. Hopefully tonight will reveal that Amy was right, and his personality is awful. I have a feeling it won't.

I run through all of my previous half-baked relationships, dwelling on Sam. We'd been casual acquaintances at uni and he'd eventually asked me out. The date had lasted eighteen minutes. I mentioned Claire, Sam went to the toilet and never returned. We had to spend the next two years avoiding each other in the library.

Thoughts of Sam fortify me.

Even if the date that probably isn't a date *does* turn out to be a date, there's no way anything with Josh will last until July. It can't. And anyway, if I have to choose, dead twin trumps dimples any day of the week.

As Kaz suggests, I pack my lucky purple dress and borrow

some of her wedges. Then for good measure I add a hair-
brush, perfume and half my make-up to the bag for life I'm
planning to take into school. I'll have to hang the dress up
when I get there, it's satin with a chiffon overlay and a tie
at the waist, so it would be a crime against fabric to let it
languish in a bag for life all day.

At three o'clock, Josh is waiting for me outside my classroom.

'Sorry, rehearsals are on three o'clock till four, I thought
I said,' I mutter.

'You did. I thought I'd come and watch.' He's taken his
suit jacket off and rolled his sleeves up. His cowlick is stood
almost on end, freed at the end of the day.

'Nice dress.' He nods towards my arm, the dress draped
over it, as we walk towards the hall.

'It's purple.' I sound like a moron. There's no way I'm
going to be able to concentrate on rehearsals with Josh here.

'Tim, come here,' I beckon as soon as we make it to the
hall. 'This is Mr Smith, he knows about IT things.'

'I remember. All right, IT man.'

'He *also* has A-level English.'

Josh looks mildly alarmed.

'Tim is our lighting guy. Except the lights are just "on"
the whole time. He's here to bunk off lessons.'

'Miss, you wound me.' Tim makes as if I've shot him.

'I've plastered the walls of the lighting booth with anthol-
ogy quotes that Tim needs to learn for his GCSE,' I tell Josh.
'Maybe you could test him a bit?'

Josh now looks very alarmed. Tim is smirking.

'Don't worry, Tim won't cause you any trouble.' I tap the side of my nose. 'I know where he keeps the bonbons.'

Tim laughs. 'Come on then, IT man, let's get this over with.'

Without Josh and his arm veins following my every move, rehearsal goes well. We manage a roaring rendition of *Skid Row*, which lifts my mood significantly, and then we practise feeding various cast members to the plant. We've rigged a short play tunnel to the base that Cade, aka Audrey Two, is going to stand on. Cade still looks terrified whenever he has to speak instead of sing. In fact, he couldn't be less like a manipulative blood-eating plant if he tried. I order some green face paint with the aim of at least hiding how red he goes. It arrives alongside my order of twenty litres of fake blood. Jan and I have decided to save that until the actual performances, when cleaning it up will no longer be our responsibility.

I still have some concerns that the whole thing is somewhat dark for a school production; essentially every main character meets a gory end. But it's too late to change the salient points of the musical now. We're in twenty litres of fake blood too deep.

Bag for life in hand, at four o'clock I make a dash for the loo. I brush out my hair and add another layer of make-up on top of the one I've already got. I shimmy into the dress and spray some perfume.

I have a moment of crippling self-doubt as I look in the

mirror. Partly because no matter how hard I try, I can't see Claire looking back at me today, I'm on my own. There's also an incredibly good chance that Josh and I are going to a café as pals, and I've wholly overdone it on every front. However, as my work clothes are now in a scrunched heap, I have no choice but to stick to Kaz's guns.

I leave the bathroom.

Josh is standing on the other side of the corridor. He's opened his top button and taken off his tie. I am weak at the knees. Well, I would be if that was a genuine bodily reaction.

He just stands there staring.

But then he says, 'Wow, Emily, you look amazing.' And he coughs as if he can't really believe that I could look like this, which could be taken as an insult if I were feeling that way inclined.

'I'll just dump this bag in my classroom, one sec.'

I meet Josh again at the entrance.

'Are you okay walking to the station?'

''Course.'

We walk in silence. Josh has his suit jacket over his arm. I want to talk to him just so I can look at him, but it's as if the part of my brain used to form words has shut down completely.

'So, did you, er, always want to be a computer, um, person?' I go for the record of the dullest question ever asked on a date.

'I went through a stint of wanting to be an astronaut. But then I threw up on the Oblivion, you know that rollercoaster with the vertical drop at Alton Towers? After that I thought computers seemed like a safer bet.'

'Interesting. I feel like computers don't like me on a personal level. Those little caterpillar rollercoasters used to make me nauseous though, so I know what you mean.'

'You think computers don't like you?'

'Yup. Ever since I started, the school printers have had a vendetta against me.'

He laughs like I'm joking.

'Aren't you a bit young to be a technophobe?'

'Don't get me wrong, I can social media stalk with the best of them.'

'Is that so?' He gives me a look that says he knows I've tried to hack him.

'Yup. So long as the stalkee doesn't have levels of security akin to the head of MI5.'

He laughs and we're at the station.

There's only a five-minute wait for the train but the platform is rammed. It's commuter time, after all.

We squeeze on and Josh gallantly offers up the only seat we come across. I take it and then immediately regret my decision because I inevitably spend the whole of the journey making conversation with his crotch.

I fear I'm looking a bit frazzled. My only hope is that at least one of the layers of make-up is still attached to my face.

'Shall we go and get a drink first? I made the reservation for 6.30.'

That sounds like something you'd do for a date.

'Great,' I smile, clandestinely trying to see if I've got sweat patches. When Josh catches me, I slam my arms down by my side and vow never to raise them again.

I order a gin and tonic at a trendy bar because my commitment to authenticity does not extend to abandoning gin, the drink of my generation. Josh has a bottle of beer, and we sit outside. It's nice. Too nice. Before I know it, I'm three gins in and talking him through my Cherished Teddy collection.

I'm fairly sure he's feigning interest. But he looks sympathetic, if mildly disturbed, when I recall how I got a duplicate teddy for my ninth birthday and cried. I leave out the part about lying about the incident to my child psychologist. I still haven't told Josh about Claire. He'd been down with my death chat but it's impossible for people not to look at you differently once they know you've been through something like that.

'Shall we head to the restaurant?'

I nod. Josh offers me his jacket for the walk as there's a chill in the air now. I take it with the chant of *date, date, date* in my head and hope he doesn't notice me sniffing the sleeve.

'Do you like the smell?' Busted.

'Are you kidding? I want to snort you.' I silently vow to lay off the booze because even if this is a date, that was a very weird thing to say.

The restaurant is in the Arcades, which have always been

my favourite part of Leeds. The glass ceiling is teaming with fairy lights and someone is tinkling at the piano in front of the fountain.

We take our seats. There's a string of lights in a jar on the table and the waiter passes me a menu from which I want to order everything. So engrossed in the menu am I that I don't pay much attention when Josh asks what wine I like and then orders a bottle of white.

We place our order. And then, because I'm still me, I manage to ruin things by saying cheerfully, 'I knew you weren't horrible.'

His eyes go wide, and I rush to undo the damage.

'God sorry. It's just we've been spending all our lunches together and if you are a bit awful, you're really good at hiding it. No, actually that's not it either. Ignore me.' I really must stop talking. I take a gulp of wine.

'Amy, right?' he asks.

'Yeah, but you don't have to explain yourself. It's none of my business, like I said before. We're just mates, aren't we?' Why I feel that this is a good opportunity to test out my using the word 'mate', I'll never know.

He pauses for a second while I gulp yet more wine. We never have this sort of chat at lunchtimes.

'I don't know how to say it without sounding like a dick, but Amy, er, struggled to accept that we were over, even after I moved out.' He runs his hand through his hair. 'I was worried about Bri and distracted, but I should have realised earlier than I did that we weren't on the same page.'

I nod but then shake my head and attempt to shrug at the same time.

'Seems fair enough. No more explaining required.'

'Now it's my turn.'

'Oh, there's nothing to tell about my love life, all distinctly mediocre.'

'Is that so?' His eyes fix on mine and my stomach starts flipping involuntarily. He goes red. 'So, what's the deal with you and Stan?'

I groan and bash my head against the table. The waiter reappears and I have to reassure him that everything is all right. I really need to rein in my dramatic gestures.

'What makes you say there's anything going on between me and Stan?'

'Your reaction for one,' he smiles. Those dimples. I start wafting my cheeks with my hands. 'And he sort of scowls at you a lot. Did you two . . . ?' He just raises his eyebrows. Eyebrow sign language for jiggy jiggy.

'No. Absolutely not. I, um, just considered it. But then I changed my mind. Stan has taken it as a personal affront.'

Josh's jaw twitches. 'What a dick.'

I can't make eye contact. I feel like the ground is shifting under Josh and me, and there's nothing I can do to stop it. I'm saved from considering further by the arrival of our food. I let out a cry of happiness as the waiter puts a massive chicken burger in front of me. It has cheese and BBQ sauce and onion rings and is so big that it has one of those sticks holding it all together.

I have never in my life used the phrase food porn. But here I am, rolling it out.

Josh, I notice, has gone for some sort of pasta dish that looks much more straightforward to eat. I tuck in. It's amazing. I'm so enthralled with my burger that I forget about Josh entirely. If the burger asked me out, I'd accept.

'So, tell me about your brother and sister?'

I'm dragged back to the moment.

'Who, Matt? There's not much to tell. He's four years older.'

'He's the one getting married next year, right?'

'That's it. To Sarah. Matt's like those people from *Star Trek* who don't feel emotions; Sarah's Ariel after she gave up her voice for a man. I can't imagine either of them ever having an orgasm.'

'And you think about your brother orgasming often, do you?' I can tell he's about to laugh at me. And who can blame him. My chat is unbelievably poor. This is what a lifetime of avoiding going out gets you. Talking about your brother's sex life of a Wednesday evening.

'Ha, no, not often. I'm not weird or anything.' Why oh why do I even try to interact with normal people?

He takes a bite. 'Sometimes I wish Bri were a bit more boring, to be honest.' I swallow hard but Josh carries on, 'He went through a bit of a wild patch, after Dad died.'

I nod. 'I understand. Grief makes us crazy.'

Josh looks at me and I know it's time.

I take a deep breath. I can do this. 'I was a twin. My sister, Claire, died when we were eight. Cancer.'

'God, Emily, I'm so sorry.' I try to read his face for signs of discomfort but can't spot any. I forget about the chip I've speared ready to eat.

'Thanks. It was a long time ago. Twenty years this June.'

'Still. You don't get over something like that.'

'No, you don't. Or if you do, I never have.' I want to keep talking. To tell Josh that losing Claire has been the central fact of my life. The sun from which all other life events orbit around. I want to say that the Life List is basically Claire. That she was all the things that I'm not. The things on my List. They're her. I want to tell him that my darkest fear is that it would have been better if Claire had lived, and I'd died.

'Purple was our favourite colour.' My voice sounds small. I look down at my dress, blinking hard.

'It looks beautiful on you, Em.' Josh reaches across the table. We both watch his hand advance like it's not attached to the rest of his body. When it closes around mine, a sigh escapes me. I wonder if Josh would have held my hand if I hadn't told him about Claire. I shrug the thought off.

We talk easily for the rest of the meal. Josh wins brownie points for suggesting that we share desserts after it takes me an inordinate amount of time to decide between lemon drizzle and chocolate fudge cake.

The restaurant has emptied around us. We argue for so long over who gets to pay the bill that the waiter proposes that we arrange another date and take turns. I say, 'It's not a date,' even though I think it might be a date and Josh frowns.

In the end I relent and let Josh pay. I catch sight of how much the meal cost and think myself lucky. Josh suggests that I see it as recouping a bit of the gender pay gap.

And then we're outside the station. My train is in five minutes. We do that awkward thing where we stand looking at each other and my brain screams RUN, RUN, you idiot, you're going to fall head over heels in love with this man. RUN, I tell you.

But my legs have clearly had enough of my brain ordering them to run and they don't budge.

And when he says, 'Emily.' I just nod.

He puts a hand on my back, and I let him tug me close. 'You said it wasn't a date.' He sounds a bit sad.

'I didn't think it was.' I'm not sure why we're whispering. 'I didn't think you liked me like that.'

He scrunches up his face in thought. Without thinking, I reach up and smooth down his cowlick. He captures my hand and presses a chaste kiss to my palm.

The sky is clear and starry. We are the perfect Valentine's Day card, framed by the light from the station. And when Josh leans into me, I close my eyes. Even the homeless guy yelling, 'Go on lad,' doesn't ruin the moment. I feel like I'm melting. My skin is so hot. When we finally break apart, my heart is racing, and Josh's pupils have gone all big.

'Sexy eyes.'

'What?' he murmurs.

'Your eyeballs are just so . . . sexy right now.'

He laughs and rests his forehead against mine.

We stay like that. My heart beating hard until I finally pull away.

'I should go . . . my train.'

'You better had. Keep the jacket.'

MAY

Be Successful, Be an Explorer

Chapter Thirty-One

After what has to be my first proper night's sleep in months, I wake up to a message the next day.

> **Josh:** How's your head? I had a really nice evening x
> **Me:** Better than I expected. Good job I ate so much.
> Me too 😊 It's so easy to be vegan these days. I
> have vegan soap now and everything x
> **Josh:** Glad to hear it. We should go again, try some
> of their other food.

My fingers almost type YES! of their own volition. But I pause. There can be no denying last night was a date. I can feel Josh's kiss like he branded my lips. And I'm already questioning whether things will peter out like I expect them to. I'd told Josh about Claire and he still kissed me. He didn't run away or attempt to talk about something else. I've never been kissed like that before. I can see how it could become challenging to give up kisses of that calibre come July.

Josh (again): Though other vegan options are available x

Me: Ha good one. Jesus, who types that in a message. I'd love to go out for another fake meat-based meal at some point in the future. It's just that I've a lot on with the school show at the minute. Plus, I'm auditing my clothes to check for animal products in them.

So far, I'd discovered that almost everything I owned was synthetic. I keep typing.

But maybe once I'm done with the play and the audit? X

I'm aggrieved at my reluctance to break things off entirely. Fucking dimples.

I sit nervously watching my phone.

Josh: Sounds good to me. Let me know if you need any help with the play? If you need me, I'll be hauling my leather sofa down four flights of stairs.

I decidedly do not swoon at the image of a shirtless Josh being all manly and lifting a sofa.

Me: HA. No seriously, please don't get rid of it on my account. I mean, the cow already died so . . .

Me: And I may have a job for you re: the play. Leave
it with me x
Josh: Sorry. Can't talk. Sofa hauling.

Several weeks pass after the date. It's now May, which means I have the double challenge of suddenly becoming Phineas Fogg and a successful careers person all at once.

Josh hasn't asked me out again, which is totally fine. I only think about it every half-hour tops.

However, today all thoughts of Josh and the Life List are on temporary hiatus. The school show is two days away. And I am one sequin away from my last nerve.

'My fingers are bleeding,' Josh complains.

We're in my room at lunchtime as usual. I'm eating a pasta salad that's 99 per cent pasta.

'I told you to use the thimble. Don't get blood on the costume.'

He holds the lime green jumpsuit he's been painstakingly sewing sequins to for the past three weeks at arm's length.

'Remind me never to volunteer to help you again.'

'Head of haberdashery is a very important role in a school production.'

He goes back to sewing, appeased. Though I'm sure he mumbles something that sounds like, 'I've lost the bloody thread.'

Neither of us talk for the next few minutes. Josh sewing while I Amazon Prime another few litres of fake blood. Just in case.

Josh breaks the silence.

'Er, it's my last week this week, you know?'

I swallow a big mouthful of pasta.

'I didn't.'

'The new systems are all up and running.'

'Oh.'

For some reason, the thought of going back to Facebook browsing of a lunchtime makes me feel somewhat bereft.

'I think a few of us are going to go out for some drinks on Friday after the final show if you fancy it?'

'How have you managed to make more friends in half a term than I have in several years here? I'm fairly sure no one would turn up if I had a leaving do.'

'I don't know. Stan might, but only to pluck at your hair for his Emily-shaped voodoo doll.' He jests but I've seen Josh narrow his eyes in Stan's direction more than once. And he's taken to collecting my photocopying and bringing it to me himself, minimising my interactions with Stan. The cave woman part of me enjoys that.

'Funny. You're a funny guy.'

'So, you'll come?'

'Um.'

'I mean you do owe me a drink.'

'All right, fine. Now back to the sequins. And Audrey's lace trim was sagging at the dress rehearsal last night too. Just so you know.'

By the time we're all huddled behind the stage on opening night, I'm actually quite nervous.

'Right, everyone, listen up. I want you to go out there and give it your all, you hear me? Who cares if expectations are really low. They're wrong, you're all amazing. So, go give it some welly.'

We do a group cheer and everyone goes to take their places for the opening number. I stand in the wings, Josh beside me. 'Doesn't Tim need you?'

'I think he's got it.' We can just see Tim in the box at the back of the hall. He gives us a double thumbs up.

The music starts up and the hall falls silent. The dancers begin to creep across the stage dressed in sparkling rags.

'*When you live—*'

'*Downtown,*' Cade sings from the wings, his deep voice making the audience chuckle already.

'Those sequins are quite something,' Josh whispers.

'They really are,' I agree.

The glittering dancers can-can along the stage, high kicking fake rubbish out of the way.

We get to the part where Cade, dressed in lime green as Audrey Two, starts to eat people. Josh and I throw buckets of fake blood across the stage. The effect is extremely dramatic. And also, incredibly slippery. Seymour goes down but styles it out, crawling on his hands and knees begging Cade not to eat him. Cade just laughs in a menacing sort of way. It's darker than it was meant to be, with Seymour's face dripping with fake blood, but I'm proud of his improvisation. I see a mother cover the eyes of her young child in the audience. I wonder if we'll get some parental complaints. I must be turning into an anarchist because I hope we do.

All in all, bloodbath aside, the first night goes off without a hitch.

On the second night Dentist almost rides the bike that we've decked out to look like a motorbike off the stage. I hear a family member scream. Dentist pulls off a very ill-timed, but nonetheless effective, wheelie to save himself a trip to A&E. Then Audrey One gets stuck halfway to being eaten and everyone sings the final song with her legs sticking out of the tunnel beneath Audrey Two.

On the final night they are perfect. No one puts a foot wrong. Cade, his confidence now sky high due to rapturous applause, wiggles his bum in his lime green suit and demands, 'Feed me Seymour,' with such conviction that you could hear a pin drop. Rather than social suicide, playing Audrey Two has propelled Cade to a god-like reverence among the other pupils. I've seen him fist-pumping his way along the corridors all week.

By the time they take their final bows, the audience are on their feet. There's blood dripping off the end of the stage but no one seems to mind. I sniff from the wings, a fleck of glitter in my eyes.

Then Mr Hughes is onstage thanking everyone and saying how wonderful the pictures will look on the school website and to any Ofsted visitors we might be expecting soon, which somewhat kills the mood.

Everyone troops off stage and I congratulate them all again.

'What will we do next year, miss?' Cade asks.

I can't answer properly. Because obviously I'm hoping not to be working here by then. Not that I've been able to give leaving much thought. I've been too busy. I make a mental note to dedicate some of my exploring time to considering how to become successful.

Josh sidles up to me. 'Almost ready?'

'I think so, that's the last of them.'

Cade has gone to meet his dad. Only Tim's left.

'Is there anyone here to get you home?' It's gone nine and I don't much like the thought of him walking home in the dark.

'Don't worry, miss, I only live in the flats over there.'

'Okay, go on then, we'll wait until you're in the building.'

He heads for the block of low-rise council flats over the road, their porch illuminated with a bright orange light.

Chapter Thirty-Two

'Pub?' Josh asks.

It's not lost on me that he's spent much of his leaving do watching the school play for the third time.

'Yep.' I've been so busy that it hasn't fully occurred to me that I won't get to see Josh every day from now on. The thought makes me feel strangely mournful.

By the time we arrive at the pub there's already a group of almost-inebriated teachers sitting around a sticky table. The combined effects of a Friday and the prospect of half-term.

'JOSH!' they shout in unison as we walk in, and I again wonder that he's been able to make so many friends so quickly. But still, he's IT isn't he; teachers gravitate towards IT people. They are the solution to the many technological problems that plague our existence.

'Drink?' he asks.

'Yes, but it's my turn to buy. You go mingle with your people, what do you want?'

'Pint of Kronenbourg, please.'

I order a gin and the lager for Josh. Wondering if this is what triumph tastes like. The show was great. I'm going travelling on Sunday. I'm not a successful career person yet, but I'll have time to consider it properly while I'm travelling.

The only fly in my triumphant ointment is the prospect of Josh leaving. I can't help but wonder if he's going to miss my lunch chat. I'm always at my wittiest after a carb rush.

I take Josh his lager and am forced to admit that I only recognise a handful of the people here. Josh is talking so I put his lager on the table next to him.

'You got any half-term plans?' Someone who I think might be an art teacher comes over, obviously taking pity on me. She has a short bob haircut and a piercing through the middle of her nose that I cannot believe Hughes has overlooked. I wonder if she's another relative.

'Er, I'm, um, going travelling actually. How about you?'

'Travelling, wow. Where are you headed? I did Asia on my gap year, and it was amazing. India especially. The people were just *so* warm, you know?'

'I bet. I'll, um, probably be staying closer to home. The continentals are pretty balmy too, I believe. Well, maybe aside from the Russians.'

'Good plan. Wasn't it you who did that Tough Mudder? It's hard to tell from the picture. Emily, is it?'

'Yep, that's me.' I aim for what I hope is a bashful smile. So, this is what it can be like then.

'Has she told you that she volunteers at a charity shop every week too?' Josh joins us.

'What are you, like a saint or something?'

'I'm not sure I was even christened.' Everyone laughs.

'JOSH!' someone shouts from across the bar.

'Excuse me a sec.'

'He's such a nice guy. Is there a thing between you two? Only you never normally come to Friday drinks.' So, this is obviously a regular gathering. If I dig deep in the part of my brain labelled work, maybe someone did mention it once. Years ago.

And honestly, I have no idea what's going on between me and Josh. There's still been a dearth of kissing so chances are I needn't have worried about being single come July. Chances are, I'd never really been anything but single.

'Me and Josh, oh, we're, um, honestly, I don't know,' I say.

She laughs. 'Men eh? I reckon he's into you though. He keeps looking over.'

'He does?'

'Yep.'

I twist around to look for Josh and catch him in the act. Something goes clunk in my chest. People are talking around him but he's looking at me instead. I just stare back. He gestures his head towards the door, and I nod. Putting down my glass and moving without saying anything.

My skin has started to burn again.

We don't talk as we make our way down the side of the pub by the bins.

It's warm out. In the streetlight, Josh looks extra handsome. His cheeks are a bit flushed from all the drinks people have been buying him.

I just stare wide-eyed at him.

'Emily,' he breathes, rubbing his thumb along my cheek. I lean into it. Only slightly, but Josh notices.

'I can't stop thinking about you.' He does a laugh that I know is his nervous laugh.

This is it. I need to shut this down now and get on with my Life List. The art teacher was actually impressed in there, maybe it's working after all. I order my brain to tell Josh that we're just friends.

My brain, unfortunately, is not the body part running the show.

I launch myself at him. Josh gets only a second of warning before I make contact. And if our kiss by the station was a first date kiss, this is definitely a second date kiss by the bins. His hands are in my hair, on my bum.

I have a desperate l urge to feel his skin. I shove my hands up his top and run them over his back. He shivers and I think I'm going to explode. Some hitherto undiscovered primal forces have taken over me. I'm not myself. I'm a woman possessed.

We finally surface for air.

Josh laughs a breathless laugh and I'm at him again. All thoughts of technique have gone out of the window. All I know is that I must not stop kissing Josh. If my life depends on it, I must not stop.

'Em,' he whispers. There's a groan. I don't know where the sound comes from. It could well be me.

We pull away, mainly because I fear one of us may become hypoxic if we don't take in some real air.

I wonder at the logistics of having sex in the alley. My tetanus is up to date.

We're kissing again. I'm not sure I know my own name anymore.

'What day are you going travelling?' He pulls away slightly, kissing my forehead.

'Sunday.' Undeterred, I'm in the crook of his neck, breathing him in.

'Spend tomorrow with me? I'll take you to the airport on Sunday.' I know I shouldn't. That now more than ever I should be putting some distance between Josh and me. But it looks like my brain has taken the whole night off. Here's to hoping it's on a weekend break.

'Okay.'

'We can just hang out.' I'm surprised my knickers don't disintegrate right off me at self-conscious Josh.

'I have a shift tomorrow morning. I could meet you in Leeds after.'

'Okay. I'll cook.'

'I like food.'

He presses his forehead against mine.

'So, I'll see you tomorrow then?'

'Yes.' I don't want to wait for tomorrow. But then I think if I stay much longer, we won't make it that long. And I have a long overdue appointment with some Veet.

'I'll text you when I'm on my way.' In what is no doubt a portent of things to come, it takes an enormous amount of effort to walk away from Josh.

Chapter Thirty-Three

'Someone's in a good mood,' Kaz greets me as I slink into the kitchen on Saturday morning. And slink I do. I've spent the past two hours buffing, shaving, moisturising. Not that I'm banking on anything happening with Josh, just that I don't want it to *not* happen because the last time I shaved my legs properly, Destiny's Child were still together.

'Thank you, Kaz. I am in a good mood. Actually, can I have some of that?' I nod towards the green smoothie she's decanting into a glass. It looks like pond water.

She pours me a glass and slides it across the island, eyeing me warily.

'Bottoms up.' I fake cheers. Wow, it's disgusting.

'What's brought this on?' Kaz asks, zipping up my running jacket. 'Can I borrow this?'

''Course. And what do you mean, brought what on?'

'Your unusually sunny disposition.'

'I can be sunny.'

'You are not sunny.'

'Oh I don't know,' I reply wistfully, as if I'm a lovesick

dame from the deep south. If my hair were in ringlets, I'd twirl them. 'It might have something to do with kissing Josh last night.'

'Wey hey. Good for you, Em. Much better to have a fling with someone you actually fancy.'

I do a nervous laugh. And then bark out, 'HA yes, a fling.'

Kaz finishes the last drop of her smoothie. 'Or is it more serious than a fling?'

'I'm not thinking about it.'

'You think about everything.' Kaz heads for the door.

'I'm a changed woman. My brain is on secondment.'

'Okay, weirdo. See you later.'

'Bye, Kaz!' I call after her.

The door shuts and I immediately pour the gross smoothie down the sink.

Kaz is wrong. I don't need to overthink this. I've committed to spending a day with Josh, not marrying the man. And if he asks me to marry him, I'll say no. There, totally rational thought processes.

I'm just going to go, have some fun and importantly, not think.

'So, Emily,' Leon asks, 'what would you say is the meaning of life?'

'Are you kidding me?'

'No, it's a genuine question on my application.'

The door tinkles shut. We've had a customer. The place still isn't exactly teaming; as Gran would say, you can't polish a turd. But we average two customers an hour, which is a significant increase in footfall.

'Your application for what – Mensa?'

'Nope, cardboard box factory.'

'They don't want much, do they?'

'Apparently, it's to get a "sense of us as a person". Should I write down sex, drugs and rock and roll?'

'Perhaps best to avoid the word "drugs" with a criminal record.'

'I don't do drugs. Never have.'

'No, you *feed* your addiction with baps, don't you? Get it? Because you held up a sandwich shop.'

I nudge him with my elbow and wink.

He throws me a scathing look.

'I got it, thanks.'

'You're welcome.' I hand him my phone. 'Here, google some quotes about life.'

He begins scrolling.

'So, that's what you're going for then? The cardboard box factory down in Fartown?'

'Probation set it up after I got rejected from the House of Lords. I'm done here after today. Officially a free man.'

I feel an odd sense of loss at the thought of not spending my Saturday mornings being berated and sworn at by Leon.

'Will you come back, do you think? You know, voluntarily?'

'Fuck no.'

Well, that settles that then.

How long Leon will last at a box factory, I don't know. He's way too bright.

'I've got one, how about this? *The dignity of a man lies in his ability to realise that it's all just meaningless.*'

'What a cheery prospect.'

'Or this, *Life is like an onion. You peel it one layer at a time and sometimes you weep.*'

'Wow, that's a really positive outlook you've gotten there, Leon. Here, pass it to me.'

I scroll through enough inspirational life quotes to feel slightly nauseous. Finally, I stumble upon one I think will fit.

'Here . . . *To be what we are, and to become what we are capable of becoming. George Stephenson.*'

'Is that like saying that what I'm capable of becoming is a production line operator at a cardboard factory?'

'Absolutely not. I think you've a lot to offer, you know that.' He puts his hand on his heart in mock thanks. 'But it's for you to remember, not them. You've got time.'

'*The trouble is you think you have time.*'

'Did you come up with that?'

'Nope. Buddha.' He nods to my phone.

'Well, Buddha dropped the ball on that one. You *do* have time, Leon. But not a limitless supply. You've just got to figure out what you want and go from there.'

Leon does an exaggerated wipe of a fake tear as Sandra appears with a tray of tea and cupcakes. She's taken to reading erotic novels in the kitchen for most of Saturday mornings.

This isn't something we've been forced to deduce. She came right out and told us.

'I propose a toast,' she says, taking a cup of tea. Leon and I follow suit. 'To our little Leon.' Leon is six foot four. 'Off out into the big wide world. Stay out of trouble.'

We chink mugs and I wince at the taste of my black tea. It's not particularly palatable.

'Here.' I write down my phone number on a scrap of paper and hand it to Leon. 'If you need anything, give me a call.'

'Are you hitting on me, Em?'

'No. But if you're thinking of doing something illegal, just call me instead and I'll try to talk you down.'

Sandra wipes a genuine tear from her eye.

'Like an AA sponsor?'

'Exactly.'

'I knew it, you've been trying to save me since the first day we met.' I notice that he pockets the phone number.

He's right but I can't help thinking that the chances are, he might just need saving.

Sandra is openly crying now. 'You two,' she says, pulling us in for a hug. I really wish she would start wearing bras.

Chapter Thirty-Four

2000

Claire has been moved to somewhere that's like the hospital but isn't. It's called a hospice.

I didn't like the hospital and I don't like it here.

Claire was still in the real hospital when the millennium happened and everyone thought all the computers would explode. Except us. We didn't have time to worry about that. I just went to bed as normal on the last night of 1999. The fireworks woke me up at midnight, and then I knew it was 2000. The computers didn't explode and nothing changed.

Anyway, everyone in this hospital that isn't a hospital keeps talking about making Claire comfortable and it's really getting on my nerves. She doesn't need to be comfortable; she needs to get better. Doctors and nurses make people better. Everyone knows that.

Mum and Dad cry all the time. And sometimes I hear Matt crying in his room too. Except he always shuts the door.

And once, when I knocked, he didn't answer so I don't think he wants to see me when he's sad.

When everyone's with Claire, they pretend like nothing's wrong and talk about daft stuff like how the cherry blossom will be on the trees soon, or how handsome Craig David is.

Kaz's mum takes me to school every morning now. I don't like school so much anymore. Except from Kaz, nobody wants to be my friend. I think it's because I feel sad all the time and people don't like sad friends.

Or maybe because sometimes my clothes are dirty. Like this morning when I went to get a shirt out of my drawer there were none there. I think Mum might have forgotten to do the washing again. Either that or we can't afford washing powder now that Mum has stopped working at the big Asda for good. I just pulled one out of the dirty basket and wore that. Scott Killen told me I stink so Kaz punched him in the nose. I told the teacher I did it because I never get in trouble at school, it doesn't matter what I do.

Every day after school I get to come and sit with Claire. Her room here is nicer than the one at the proper hospital at least. It has big windows and doors that open onto a little garden. They even said that one day we can have a sleepover. I still don't like going to sleep without Claire.

'How was school?' she asks when I come in today. She's sat up in her bed wearing her pyjamas. Mum had to get some new ones from Asda because Claire's gotten so small that her normal ones don't fit.

'Fine. A bit boring.' I want to tell her about Scott Killen, but I don't want Mum to hear.

'I think one day I might like to be a teacher,' she says.

I wrinkle my nose because I wouldn't want to have to wipe snot away like Miss does all the time.

'You'd get to read books and play games.' Claire keeps talking even though she gets out of breath now. 'It wouldn't be so bad. Or maybe I'll be a teacher for a bit and then I'll go and be a scuba diving instructor. I know! I might join the circus as an acrobat and travel to places like Malaysia, or Uruguay.'

Mum makes a choked sound and runs from Claire's bedroom mumbling something about needing to get a cup of tea. I don't know where she's gone for one though because there's a kettle and a little fridge with milk right next to where she was pairing socks.

'I knew that would get rid of her,' Claire says with her evil genius face. 'We need to talk properly.'

'But I don't want to talk properly.' I don't know why but I know I definitely don't want to.

Claire sighs.

'I punched Scott Killen in the nose today at school.'

Her forehead crinkles.

'You did? Why?'

'Because he said I stink. And it wasn't me really, Kaz did it, but I took the blame.'

She laughs at that.

'I knew you couldn't do it. You're too nice.'

'I am not.'

'You are, but it's a good thing, being nice.' She looks like she's thinking for a bit. 'Listen, Em, Mum will be back soon.'

I stick my fingers in my ears and say, 'LA LA LA,' which isn't very nice of me.

'Em!' She tries to pull my arm away, but she isn't strong enough anymore, so she lies back down. I still don't like to disappoint Claire, so I take my arms away by myself.

'Can you bring my stationery set tomorrow?' I wonder if that's the important thing she wants to talk to me about.

''Course I can.'

'But don't tell Mum or Dad. I want it to be a surprise.'

Claire loves surprises. She always has.

'Okay. I'll smuggle it in in my rucksack.'

'And I'll get rid of Mum again, so you can give it to me.'

Mum comes back in then. Except she doesn't have a cup of tea and her face is all blotchy.

'What are you girls up to?'

'We're just going to watch *Blue Peter*.' Claire flicks on the TV. It's on the wall still, but it's bigger than the one in the real hospital.

Claire falls asleep halfway through the programme. Mum is sitting in the little garden having her cup of tea finally.

Me and Claire don't look like mirror twins anymore. She still has the freckle on the other side of her face to mine. But her face is rounder now, and her arms and legs are so small, she's like a tiny little bird. I wonder if anyone would stare

303

at us like the lady in Butlin's did when we did the talent contest.

I used to hate people staring. But now I think I wouldn't mind it one bit.

Chapter Thirty-Five

Josh is waiting for me in Leeds Station. I've brought my suitcase because he did say he'd take me to the airport tomorrow.
However, now that I'm here it may very well look like my
intention is to move in with him.

'Here, I'll carry your case.'

'It's on wheels.'

'Then I'll wheel it.' He laughs his soft laugh. This is what
happens when you don't use your brain. You get Josh in a
faded T-shirt wheeling your case for you and laughing his
soft laugh.

I'm so close I can feel the heat of his body on my arm. I
don't even hide the fact that I sniff him. His pheromones are
like Pringles.

'What do you want to do?'

It's lunchtime and normally I am loath to miss a meal.
But my stomach has apparently accompanied my brain
on holiday.

'Can we go to yours?'

He nods, his jaw tight.

Josh holds my hand as we walk to his. I *think* I'm about

to be ravished. I've never been ravished before, but I am here for it.

His flat is one of those ones in the city centre that's all shiny and white. Some of his furniture is the same as ours, except his Poäng chair is brown leather as opposed to the standard cream.

'This is nice.' I run a finger along the white kitchen, which is at the end of the living area.

'Do you want something to eat? I don't have much in, but I could nip downstairs to Tesco. Or we can go out?'

'In, thank you. Definitely in.'

Josh gulps, visibly.

'No problem, back in a min.'

Josh leaves and I've got free rein to check out his belongings.

There's some elaborate shelving around the TV, which is mounted to the wall. It's all dark brown, very manly. I can see books, some IT and a couple of Robert Harris novels. He also has one by Barack Obama. Good, I can trust his politics.

I accidentally on purpose look in the other three rooms. Starting with the bathroom, Josh has red towels and a matching shower curtain. There's a spare bedroom. It has a lot of boxes, as if Josh hasn't yet properly unpacked. There are some hand weights too. They look a lot like the ones I own. As in, still in the plastic. No spare bed.

Then there's Josh's bedroom. It's a bit bare. There are no pictures on the wall, and a nice dream catcher wouldn't go amiss. But not too bad.

He is perhaps the most normal human I've ever encountered.

'Emily!' Josh calls from the door.

I freeze. He must have expected me to snoop a little bit, mustn't he? Bar hiding under the bed and pretending to have initiated an off the cuff game of hide and seek, I've no real option but to face Josh in the corridor.

I shut the bedroom door behind me, facing Josh and going very red in the process.

Josh must be really hoping to get laid because he doesn't say anything relating to the fact that he just caught me in his bedroom. Instead, he just smiles and says, 'Is a sandwich okay?'

'Yeah, great, thanks.'

I follow him back into the kitchen and watch as he assembles it.

At the sight of a fake cheese and crisp sandwich, my hands start making strange grabbing motions. Like a T-Rex with those pathetic little arms. Turns out my appetite hasn't quite left the building completely.

We move onto the couch, except Josh is as far away as he can be from me. It's significantly more distance than I was hoping for, but it does give me chance to check him out. His cowlick is a bit floppy today. Chilling for the weekend.

'What do you want to do after lunch?'

'Pardon?'

'After lunch. We could go to the cinema or for a walk?'

I'd really hoped that after lunch was when the ravishing would begin.

'Er, a walk sounds nice,' I hear myself say. Though really, I wonder if I'm capable of physical exertion without Bruce following me, hurling abuse.

We finish our sandwiches and I'm putting my shoes back on. Adding clothes, the exact opposite of what I want to be doing.

Josh's block of flats opens onto the canal, so we set off along it. We're holding hands so the proximity means that at least I get to sniff him some more.

'You know, I think Bri is seeing Kaz again this weekend,' Josh says.

'Is he? She's a sly devil.' That sounded less odd in my head. I rush to undo the damage. 'I just mean that Kaz never normally sticks with the same man for long. Not that she's easy or anything. And even if she was, that would be fine. Totally fine. It's a new millennium, you know. Women can be whatever they want.'

I'm breathing hard, but Josh just laughs.

'You done?'

I nod, no longer trusting myself to say even the inanest of sentences.

'I was going to say that I'm pleased Bri seems happy.'

A part of me seriously hopes that Bri's happiness is not dependent on Kaz's monogamy. But it's only appropriate to spend a certain amount of time talking about your best friend's sex life.

'You know, the protective big brother thing is hot.'

'Alas it may no longer be needed. The job at Wetherspoons is the first one he's managed to keep.'

Josh seems determined to keep our conversation polite.

'Hey, is that why you came back to ours that night? To keep an eye on him?' Josh goes red and I know I'm right. 'And here I was thinking it was my charming repartee.'

'That too, obviously. Can't remember the last time I was offered a glass of milk as a serious drink.'

'Just thinking of your bone health. You'll be regretting turning me down when osteoporosis hits and your femurs crumble.'

A little more of that night returns to me. Specifically, the part where Josh said I wasn't his type.

Josh reaches over and smooths the frown from between my eyebrows. 'What's wrong?'

'I was just remembering the bit of the night where you were quite emphatic in the fact that you didn't fancy me.'

Realisation seems to dawn as Josh says, 'Listen, Em, I was confused. Me and Amy hadn't sorted things out properly and then you came barrelling out of that loo.'

I cringe.

'The thing is I *had* been checking you out. A bit at least.' His cheeks flush. 'I thought I was busted so I covered as best I could. Didn't mean it though.'

'Good, glad we cleared that up.' I can't help the smile that I make. I've a feeling it lands somewhere close to 'Cheshire cat' on the smile spectrum.

'Shall we head back?' Josh asks. I nod vigorously and we turn around.

'Is pasta okay for tea?'

'Sounds great, but honestly you don't need to go to any effort.' Why is Josh still talking about food when it's the last thing on my mind. And food is never the last thing on my mind.

He lets us back in the flat and I decide that it's time to bring out the big guns.

'Do you think I could have a quick shower?' I ask.

''Course, bottom of the corridor.'

We both know that I know this already. But it's good that we've already moved on from my invasion of Josh's privacy.

I wish I could invade more of Josh's privates.

Okay, maybe I'll take a cold shower.

I figure out the tap and strip off. I wash with Josh's body-wash, pleased that I will now only need to sniff myself to get a whiff of him. Josh is being unusually restrained for a man who went in for a good old snog by the bins last night. I've brought my sexiest pyjamas into the bathroom, brand new with tags after a last-minute dash to New Look before I'd gotten the train to Leeds. I'm thinking now that I should have given over five minutes to actually trying them on. They looked like they might provide more coverage than they do on the hanger.

I think of Josh chastely holding my hand.

What if he isn't even expecting me to stay the night?

Obviously, I'd brought my suitcase. But maybe he thinks I'm booked into the Travelodge by the airport.

My suitcase is in the hall still, so I can't re-dress.

There's a hoodie on the hook in the bathroom. I put it over my pyjamas. They're so short that it now looks like I'm not wearing any trousers. There's no time to think though because the whole flat starts to BEEP. I emerge from the bathroom to a smoke-filled corridor and a frantic Josh waving a tea towel at the fire alarm in the kitchen.

'Sorry!' he calls. 'The labels on the bottom of the pans caught fire! They're new.'

He pushes a button on the fire alarm and the beeping stops.

I start to cough. It is quite smoky.

'Oh god, sorry. Here, have some water.'

'Honestly, I'm fine.' I swallow another cough, making my eyes water in the process. I don't want to make him feel bad. 'Why do you have new pans?'

'Well, uh, Amy took the ones we shared.'

'So, you bought a whole new set to cook for me?'

'I guess so.'

'That's very sweet.'

At this exact moment, Josh seems to realise what I'm wearing. His stares at my legs for a moment before turning suddenly back to the hob.

'I think it's ready. It's just pasta. Nothing special.'

'Pasta is always special.'

Josh wrestles new cutlery out of tiny plastic straitjackets.

He has basically stocked his whole kitchen. The thought makes me feel all warm and fuzzy. Like a Care Bear.

'We can put the TV on if you like.' He nods towards the sofa. I absentmindedly flick it on, settling on reruns of *Masterchef*, because who doesn't enjoy watching grown men and women sweat blood over truffle-infused foam with seaweed air?

We sit on the couch to eat our spaghetti. It's delicious enough to temporarily halt my dirty thoughts.

Once I'm two-thirds of the way through, I slow down. I'm very aware of Josh sitting on the couch next to me. He's closer this time. Inches away from my naked thigh.

Just in case this is where the ravishing starts, I begin a gallant effort to suck my teeth clean. Terrance from Berkshire has a full-blown breakdown because his pigeon compote has turned out too salty, but I hardly even notice.

'You can put your feet on me if you like,' Josh says. Our plates are on the floor.

I don't think. I just swing my legs around and plonk them unceremoniously on Josh's lap. My shorts ride up a couple of inches but I daren't tug them down and draw attention to the fact.

I've no idea what programme comes on the TV next. I'm now very aware of the contact between my feet and Josh. At first, he doesn't move. But then he puts his hand over my ankle and moves it up and down a little. This is what happens when you don't think too much.

Josh stares straight ahead at the TV as if this is an everyday occurrence, while I'm over here having some seriously non-PG thoughts. I remain frozen. Fearful that if I move, he'll realise what he's doing and stop. So, we stay there, in a state of suspended animation. My thoughts well and truly in the gutter. Josh watching TV and stroking my ankle. Except he's taking shallow little breaths. And his jaw is tight again.

Eventually, I can't take it anymore.

'So, about the sleeping arrangements . . .'

'I'll sleep on the couch. You can have my bed.'

What. That's a terrible idea.

Josh laughs and I've no clue whether that was in my head or not.

'No, honestly.' I sit up. 'It's just that this couch is tiny.' I nervous laugh. 'We can just sleep in your room. Together.' I wonder if this counts as coercion. 'I mean, nothing has to happen. It's just, like, a sleepover.'

'Sure.' Josh clears his throat. 'I mean, if that's what you want.'

I nod way too emphatically. 'It is. Actually, I think I'll go and brush my teeth now.'

It's 8pm.

Fortunately, Josh has never seen me act like a normal human being, so he doesn't seem fazed by my current state of madness at all.

My skin is tingling in the bathroom. I genuinely fear I may jump Josh in his sleep.

When I emerge, Josh takes his turn in the bathroom.

He finds me standing at the foot of his bed.

'Do you have a side preference or ...' I ask, looking up. It is very disappointing to see that Josh is wearing a serious amount of bedtime attire. He has thick jogging bottoms on and a long-sleeved top. No socks though. I peer over the end of the bed. An average amount of toe hair. Though at this stage he could have cloven hooves and I wouldn't care. It's the glasses.

'I didn't know you needed glasses?'

He sits down on the right side of the bed, so I move around to the left. His voice sounds like he's being strangled.

'I wear contacts through the day.'

'They're very sexy.' That is my attempt at talking dirty.

Josh doesn't appear to hear me. His eyes have gone wide as I've taken his hoodie off and am just in my skimpy vest top.

In a flash he's under the covers. He starts to breathe deeply.

'Josh, are you okay?'

His jaw goes tight again.

'I can go, if this is too weird.'

'God no,' he spits out. 'Sorry, I mean that's definitely not what I want. I'm just,' he pauses, 'trying to take things slow. You sort of freaked out after our date ... and your List. I'm worried if we, you know ... I'll never see you again. I'm trying not to be a dick. It's just really hard. Not being a dick when you look like that and you're in my bedroom.'

Poor Josh. I'm basically emotionally abusing him.

'But I really don't want you to go, Emily,' he finishes off.

'Hey, is that why you're wearing eighteen layers of clothes for bed?'

He laughs, busted.

However, even I draw the line at begging someone to have sex with me. So instead, I say, 'Maybe we could have a cuddle?'

Josh opens his arm and I slide into the crook of his shoulder. I fit perfectly. He snakes his arm around my shoulders. It feels like the safest place on earth. I will never leave.

I'm Dorothy and Josh's apartment is the Land of Oz. Here everything is bright and colourful. Outside these walls there are no munchkins, and my house has been levelled by a freak hurricane.

I don't know at which point Josh's touch starts to give me goosebumps. My skin is fizzing. I twist my head to the side and catch his eye.

'How do you feel about being just a little bit of a dick?'

Josh's resolve disappears with an almost audible snap.

'Emily.' He breathes my name and pushes my hair behind my ear. His thumb traces my freckle as he does it. It's such a sweet gesture that tears threaten to prick at my eyes.

I lean up and kiss the spot just to the side of his mouth.

It's meant to be gentle and for a nanosecond it is. But then Josh is kissing me back. Properly. He tastes of toothpaste. I melt into him.

He moves onto my neck, kisses from my jaw to my collarbone.

'Josh.'

He kisses down to my collarbone. I fumble to get my hands onto him. Working my way through the layers of clothes he's wearing. 'Ahh,' I sigh as I eventually make contact.

At the touch of skin on skin, it's like we've been charged with electricity. All of a sudden, I'm yanking his T-shirt off, and his hands are roaming around my back. I put my hands in the air and my top falls to the floor. None of my usual thoughts are there. I don't care how I look. All I can think of is how to get as close to Josh's skin as possible.

'Wow, Emily, god.'

He's on top of me. Everywhere he touches feels like it's giving off static. His hands, his mouth. It's too much.

I grope around for whatever inch of skin I can get. His sexy eyes are back. He's breathing hard.

'We can stop, it's only if you want to.'

'Josh, if you stop, I swear I will never, ever forgive you.' I grab onto his arms to drive my point home.

It's all the encouragement he needs. There's nothing between us now. And it feels exactly right, just as it should be.

Well, one thing is abundantly clear. Josh is some sort of Huddersfield sex god.

He clears his throat. 'Well, was that, um . . . ?'

'The best.' I feel him smile into my neck. 'Does it normally work like that for you?'

'Er, what mechanically or—'

'Don't answer, it was a weird question.'

'No, it's not normally like that. Especially not, um, first go.'

my (extra)ordinary life

I can't see Josh's face, but I imagine his cheeks are on their way to red.

'Do you want some water?' He looks down at me. We're lying like we were earlier. Only without clothes. And there's more sweat. I feel like I've done a triathlon.

He brings two glasses of water in.

'Hey, look, it's my very own naked butler.'

I gulp mine down as Josh sits on the edge of the bed next to me. It's late now and dark outside. Only Josh's bedside lamp lights the room.

'You're so beautiful, Emily.' It's a very flattering light. He's tracing little patterns on my skin with his hands, swirling them around my hips, my waist, my ribs. My skin is buzzing again already. His hands move higher still, and I stop talking completely. I actually think I've lost the ability to form words. Henceforth, I will communicate through the medium of groans. 'Ohh, ahhh, and oooo, that's so nice.'

He kisses my temple and I push my hands through his hair, amazed at how long it's been since I touched someone like this.

So, this is what all the fuss was about.

Chapter Thirty-Six

'And you're sure, absolutely sure, that there is nowhere else I could go?'

'I'm afraid not, Ms Turner, the only seats available are on flights to Alicante.'

In months gone by, a setback such as this would have had the power to unsettle me. However, today, I am still sex-drunk. I don't know if that's a real thing, but my limbs feel heavy, relaxed, and my lips are swollen.

'You've nothing to Eastern Europe?'

'No.'

'And the cultural capitals? Paris? Berlin? They're off the cards too?'

'Like I said, Ms, it's Alicante or nowhere. Now, would you like to step aside and consider your decision while I deal with the next customer?'

No, I would not. I've wasted time in this queue that could have been better spent in Josh's bed. Or in the shower. Or the sofa. Wow, I have the mind of a randy teenager. Josh dropped me off at the airport an hour ago. A tiny part of me hadn't wanted to go. To leave him. But the bigger part had bullied the tiny part into submission. I'm still determinedly *not* thinking about what the future might hold for Josh and I, but I can't sack the whole list off entirely. I couldn't live with myself.

'And when does it leave?'

'At 3pm.'

It very much looks as if my first day of travelling will be spent in Leeds Bradford Airport. But come hell or high water, I'm getting on a plane today. I imagine Claire's Facebook feed. Full of pictures of her scuba diving. Or else as an acrobat in Uruguay.

'Okay, I'll take it. How much?'

'Returning Wednesday or Friday?'

'Friday.'

'£420.'

'Wednesday.'

'£250. It's the bank holiday,' she explains.

I relent. Five minutes and £250 lighter, I have a return ticket to Alicante.

'Don't forget to download the app to get your boarding pass, and you can self-check your luggage over there.'

My luggage safely checked in, I head through security. Authority figures always make me feel immediately guilty and I'm unsure whether it's best to make eye contact with the security personnel or not. It's been a while since I've done this.

Obviously I'm not even remotely considering any terrorist-like activity, but it's still something of a relief to make it through security without having anyone who isn't Josh probe my orifices. Must stop thinking about Josh.

I take advantage of the airport's half-hour free Wi-Fi to google 'things to do in Alicante' and am pleasantly surprised. There's a Museum of Contemporary Art, an archaeological museum, a castle. This is looking promising. Maybe Alicante *would* have been somewhere Claire would have visited. Plus, it has a beach. Surely I'll be much more inspired to be successful on a beach.

The Wi-Fi runs out and there's still two hours left till my flight. I order large fries from McDonald's and take the opportunity to tell the server that I'm vegan. He is suitably unimpressed. I squeeze an inappropriate amount of ketchup from the little self-serve pump and sit by the window watching the planes take off and land while I eat.

The more I sit, the more confident I am that Claire would have done this. She'd have gone off on holiday by herself. There's contentment from being somewhere adult Claire might have been. It's a peaceful emotion, contentment. My phone pings.

Josh: Hope you have fun. Let me know if you want picking up when you get back x

Taxis round here are expensive, so for purely mercenary reasons I text Josh the day and time of my return. If he's shocked that my grand exploration of the globe amounts to a mini break in Alicante, he doesn't say so. Instead, he replies. Sounds great, have a nice trip x

I file Josh away under the *things to think about later* section of my brain which admittedly at this stage does still include my entire future. But everyone knows it's easier to think in the sun, by the beach.

I buy a couple of cheap paperbacks, the sort that would have made my university professors weep, and then head towards the gate. I'm about to embark on a cultural journey through Spain, a country I've never been to before. This is good.

There is a distinct possibility that I'm dying from heatstroke. The past four hours have been spent lugging my case around cobbled streets in thirty-degree heat. Sweat pools between my breasts and there's some very distinct chafing under my sundress. Every hotel I've tried is full. Bloody bank holiday.

I'm reconciled to significantly lowering my expectations as I stand outside Jaggers Bar. No apostrophe. It has a faux wood front, and one of the g's hangs perilously. But the last place I tried said there might be room at the Jaggers Bar-shaped inn.

A quaint little hideaway where I can find myself it is not. But Jaggers Bar is thirty euros a night and most importantly, it has a room. Granted said room has a shared bathroom and charges a supplement for a colour TV. But still, after traversing the streets of Alicante, my wish list has dwindled to only one word. Vacant.

'That's 90 euros, duck.' The owner is the antithesis of all things Spanish. 'And we serve the classics in the bar. Pie and peas, bangers and mash, fish and chips. No need to get homesick while you're with us.' He hands me the key and I wonder if it's actually possible to get homesick on the very same day that you left the UK. He pauses to shout at someone called Babs to make him a spam sandwich.

'Um, thanks very much. I think I'll try one of the restaurants by the beach tonight though. Perhaps tomorrow.'

'I ate down there once. Had right bad indigestion. Anyhow duck, breakfast deal is a fry-up and a pint for six euros if it takes your fancy.'

'I'll, um, give it some thought.'

I back away slowly, checking the number on my key. Room eleven is on the first floor, so I lug my case up a flight of stairs. The walls have black and white pictures of famous people. Well, old famous people. I imagine the aim is to give the misleading impression that they're somehow acquainted with the hotel.

The room is grim. There's a single bulb which casts a very unforgiving light and no air-con. The walls are lime green, and the carpet is blue, as if it's dedicated to Marge Simpson. I tell myself it doesn't matter. I'm not going to be spending any time in the room. I'll just sleep and wash here. It'll force me to really get to know Alicante in a deep and meaningful way.

I quickly change into another sundress and add some tactical shorts underneath before heading out again. I haven't eaten since my chip and ketchup marathon earlier and I'm half-starved. I head in the direction of the beach, trying to absorb the ambience as I walk. Mostly I notice that there are a lot of tourist shops here. I wonder that there's such an expansive market for Spain fridge magnets.

But still, this is nice. It's warm out. The sun makes everything more appealing.

I look up, the universal symbol for addressing dead loved ones, and think that right at this second, Claire would be proud of me. Then I realise that I've thought about Claire on two separate occasions today and felt happy. There hasn't even been one bout of weeping. Finally, the Life List is doing what it's meant to.

The bars by the beach are teeming. Families jostle for space on the pavement. Kids rush past me, a blur of brightly-coloured hair braids. The whole place smells of the sea and suntan cream. I see a group of smurfs, or whatever the plural for smurf is, sat nursing pints and looking worse for wear. Further along, someone has already started on the karaoke. They're busy murdering 'My Heart Will Go On'. It's like Butlin's on acid.

There's a long stretch of restaurants, which all look remarkably similar. Lots of outdoor tables that spill onto the already packed pavement, a striped awning-type thing coming from the front of the restaurant. There's a universal commitment to only selling burgers or pizza. Aside from yet more chips, which one low-budget maître d' is unable to reassure me have not been cooked in cow, it appears that my vegan options will be somewhat limited. I remember my List. I'm committed to eating something authentic, for tonight at least. Tomorrow I'll reassess the chip situation. Surely, there has to be one Spanish restaurant round here.

Right at the end of the strip, next door to an arcade,

I notice a small wooden building. It looks much simpler than the rest. A Spanish flag flutters above the door. I hurry onward.

I'm right. It's a Spanish restaurant. Next to the door is a printed picture of two paella dishes. One has a cartoon rabbit on it, the other a pepper. I think I might be in luck.

The Spanish restaurant is nowhere near as busy as the other places. It's actually empty, aside from the bar where a man sits slumped among a pile of shot glasses. There's lots of dark wood panelling.

'Hola,' I venture. 'Er, is it possible to sit outside?'

A woman appears from the kitchen. 'Si, si,' she gestures me with her hands outside and I'm not entirely sure whether I'm being thrown out. I step back onto the street. With the strength of a small ox, the woman follows, carrying one of the solid wood tables out of the door with her. She plonks it unceremoniously on the pavement and returns for a chair. Once I'm sat down, she asks, 'You drink?'

She moves her hand to her mouth.

'Yes please. Er, red wine please.' She nods. Though I'm not sure she has a clue what I've just said. She's as wide as she is tall in a black dress and a should be white but isn't any more apron. There's an even dirtier dishcloth over her shoulder.

'You eat?'

'Yes please. Er, paella?'

'Good, good. You want . . .' she makes a little *fi fi fi* noise with her hands in front of her like paws and I deduce she means rabbit, '. . . or no?'

'No, definitely no. Thank you.' Is rabbit paella a thing? I normally object to cultural appropriation on principle. But substituting chorizo for rabbit in paella is clearly one of the British's better moves. Obviously, it doesn't outweigh enslaving half the world for all those centuries but still, one point to us.

Spanish lady retreats indoors, emerging moments later with a carafe of red wine and a basket of bread. I scoff at the tourists eating their burgers three hundred metres away. This is where it's at.

I allow myself five minutes of phone time, because well, I'm here for enlightenment. There's a couple of messages.

> **Mum:** Remember the water isn't safe there. Use bottled to brush your teeth. Love you x
> **I reply:** I'm in Spain, Mum. No cholera. Love you too x

And another.

> **Kaz:** I'm wearing your dressing gown and there's nothing you can do about it x

One day. I've been gone one day. And finally,

> **Josh:** Hope it's nice and sunny there. Have fun and see you Wednesday x

I reply: Thanks, have fun too x. Which makes no sense.

I've no one else to message so I put the phone back in my bag and genuinely wonder what I'm meant to do now. How did people in bygone eras entertain themselves? Am I expected to think? There's nothing else to do so I'll have to give it a go.

It's Josh that I picture first. Josh and his sexy, kind eyes, and dimples and cowlick. Josh being lovely. Josh naked. Okay, this is not helpful. Goodbye naked Josh. I'll think about you later. I'm feeling less and less confident that this thing between Josh and me will fizzle out by July like I expect it to. Last night felt like the opposite of a fizzle.

And I still have no idea what my passion in life might be. It was a real oversight, adding 'Be Successful' to The List. No doubt, there are things I *like* about teaching. Really like, in fact. The kids. I *do* enjoy working with the kids. And everyone says I'm good at it. Well, everyone except Hughes and Higginbottom, but I value their opinion about as much as I'd trust Leon with the name of my first pet.

Leon. Though he's technically not a kid anymore, I enjoy something about talking to the likes of him.

I mull the thought over, munching my way through the entirety of the breadbasket.

What I don't enjoy is all the other stuff. The arbitrary target setting, the dreaded learning walks. The feeling that I'm actually rubbish at my job.

Mouth full of bread, it hits me. Maybe I need something that focuses more on the sort of kids that I enjoy working with, the troublemakers, the ruffians, if you will. Leon *did* mention that he'd had some subpar lessons in the Young Offenders place. I could be better than subpar. I'm almost certain of it.

I feel inordinately pleased with, what is most likely, my first own thought independent of Google since 2008. And the more I think about the idea, the better it sounds. I don't mind teaching lessons. Some of them I definitely enjoy. And coming up with that adverb song is undoubtedly a life highlight. Plus, surely helping young offenders would be a worthwhile thing to do with my life?

I teach in a young offenders institute. I say it in my head.

I've a big smile on my face as Spanish lady emerges with my paella. I'm seconds away from gnawing at the leg of the table so it's a welcome sight. It's in a big black pan, teeming with vegetables I hardly even recognise. There's some fake meat too. I'm happy to realise they have Quorn in Spain, too. I take my first bite and it's absolutely delicious.

After consuming what I presume to be a sharing paella and winning a small round of applause from Spanish lady, I ask for the bill. I offer up a sincere 'gracias' as I pay, riding a carb high. But not just that, I'm buoyed by the fact that I've managed to come up with a genuine semblance of a plan for the rest of my life.

Chapter Thirty-Seven

I'm about to leave when I remember the cube of veg chorizo I've tucked in a napkin.

'Excuse me?' The Spanish lady turns from the bar where she's been cleaning, in the loosest sense of the word, glasses with her dishcloth. 'What's this please? It's delicious.'

She peers down at my cube and starts to make *oink* sounds.

'Yes, I know it taste likes pig but what is it really?'

'No taste like pig. *Is* pig. *Oink oink.*'

My stomach rolls.

'But I thought you said no *fi fi fi.*' I emulate a rabbit.

'No *fi fi fi*, but *oink oink* and *cluck cluck* and *moo moo.*' It's like a demented version of 'Old Macdonald'.

I feel suddenly nauseous.

I ate meat until recently, so it really shouldn't be a big deal. But still, I feel a pang of solidarity for vegans everywhere. No one should have a smorgasbord of animal protein forced upon them against their will.

I jab at the picture – there's another, stapled to the bar. 'But look, vegetable.'

'Yes. This only *fi fi fi.*' She points to the other picture.

'This one,' she makes her arms wide and round as if to suggest that I've just eaten every edible substance on the planet *aside* from rabbit.

My stomach rolls again.

All of a sudden, the restaurant appears more grungy than quaint. There's a thick layer of dust on the bar and they've still not had another customer. I glance around, searching in nervous anticipation for a food hygiene rating. There isn't one, or at least not one on display.

It is becoming increasingly evident, however, that my most pressing concern is to get back to the hotel.

I hobble out onto the road, gasping in the fresh air. The pictures of burgers and pizzas outside the beachfront restaurants set my stomach off again. This is serious.

Suddenly I'm sweating, even though the air has cooled somewhat.

I just need to get back to the hotel, throw up and then I'm sure I'll be fine. It has to be my body rejecting the meat medley I've just eaten after weeks of vegan food.

I'm bent double by the time Jaggers is in sight. The bar is full. People gather round a TV mounted to the wall, watching the football. Someone scores and there's an almighty roar.

I obviously do not look good. As I half-crawl through the lobby, the owner shouts, 'Babs, block off the toilet on floor one. It's occupied for the night.' Which fills me with dread. Okay, maybe I'll be sick a few times. Tomorrow I'll be fine though.

I can feel the sick coming in my back teeth and I clench my jaw shut. Just a few more feet.

I dive for the bathroom, slamming the door behind me.

The avocado green toilet is all it takes to send me over the edge. I try to ignore the grit and hair on the floor and close my eyes. Because sicked up multi-meat paella cannot be a pretty sight.

Probably, it wasn't even the meat. Rice is temperamental, as foods go isn't it? Maybe it was the rice. Or the meat. Or just the lack of cleanliness in general.

It's likely a moot point at this stage.

I crawl back to my room. Tomorrow will be better, I promise myself, tomorrow will be better.

Tomorrow is not better. In fact, I've no real sense of when today actually became tomorrow. I'm sick almost constantly. So clogged up becomes the toilet on floor one, that I'm asked to be sick into bowls for a while, just so that they can clear the drains.

By midday I'm so dehydrated, everything starts to get a bit fuzzy at the edges. The walls are swimming, and the lack of air-con does not help. I'm covered in a layer of cold sweat. A woman with leather skin, blonde hair and fuchsia nails of equal length to her fingers, dabs a wet towel on my head. She tries to give me sips of water. Everything that goes in comes straight back out again and by the afternoon I'm seeing stars.

It's obvious I'm dying.

'Tell my mum and dad I'm sorry,' I tell Babs. 'And Kaz, she can have my dressing gown if she likes. Josh should know the sex was excellent. Really excellent,' I whimper. 'I've nothing to leave any of them, but if someone could pay off my credit card that would be nice. I don't want NatWest to think bad of me.'

'Don't worry yourself about that, duck. We'll get you sorted.'

'And can you tell them that I died doing something impressive, like saving a small child or a dog at least. Don't tell them it was the meaty paella.'

Everything goes black.

'Ms Turner, it would appear that you're dead. Technically, that is.'

'Claire?' I hazard weakly. She's more manly than I remembered.

'Guess again.'

'St Peter?' I didn't expect him to have such a thick Spanish accent. Or be wearing a paramedic's outfit. Did they have them in the BC years?

'Wrong again, Ms Turner. Your blood pressure is too low. It's stopping us from getting a good reading. We're going to have to take you in.'

'Take me where?'

'To the hospital.'

'Hospital? No, I don't need to go to hospital. I've only been sick. Though I think I've gone a bit blind if someone could look into that.' No one is in focus.

'You're severely dehydrated. You need a drip. Is this okay to you?'

Hospital. Drip.

No.

'No.' I go to sit up, the room spins.

'My insurance won't cover a drip,' I slur. 'Just patch me up here. Please don't take me away.'

Things go black again. In the distance I hear the paramedic say, 'We're going to carry you downstairs. We have an ambulance waiting. You understand?'

I can't even summon the energy to fight. Instead, I'm forced to let myself be hauled off the bed. The nice paramedic has to sidestep the bowls filled with sick to get to the door. I catch sight of myself in the mirror as we leave and scream internally. Because I don't have the energy for an actual one. My eyes roll back in my head.

I come around a bit more in the ambulance. There's a drip in my hand already and a monitor on my finger. I take it all in with barely-concealed terror.

'Things will be okay soon, Ms Turner.'

I attempt to take some deep breaths. It feels like there's an elastic band around my chest.

'Where are you taking me?'

'To the hospital.'

'No, please. You can't.'

The paramedic peers down at me.

'I need to fly home on Wednesday.'

'You speak to the doctor. I think food poisoning takes

only a day to pass.' The paramedic smiles, noting something down on a clipboard.

He checks my blood pressure again.

'This is a little high, but at least you're not dead.'

I start to pant, which earns me a raised eyebrow.

We arrive at the hospital, and I'm taken into a side room. My knuckles are white from gripping the side of the gurney. The urge to flee is overwhelming but my body is wrecked. I can't summon the strength to flee.

'Your heart rate is a little high, Ms Turner,' a doctor in a white coat says. I'm not sure when she got here.

'I don't like hospital rooms. Can I be moved to a ward at least?' I sound out of breath.

She looks at me curiously.

'Any medical history we need to be aware of?'

I shake my head. 'Never stayed in hospital.'

'How about immediate family?'

'My sister, she died when we were eight. Cancer.'

I swallow hard. I'd cry if I had any bodily fluids to spare.

'I see.' The doctor nods in understanding.

'I'm afraid we have no space on the wards, Ms Turner, but I can assure you, you will start to feel better very soon. You will need to stay tonight but tomorrow you will be able to return to the hotel, I think. You must take sips of water when you can. I will have one of the nurses help you to change; someone at the hotel sent some things for you.'

'Thank you, so much. I actually do feel a bit better already. Maybe I'll just head back there now.' I go to sit up, but the movement makes my head feels like it's about to explode.

'Lie back and rest. You will have quite the headache tonight. I will arrange some painkillers.'

'Thank you again.' My eyes muster a lone tear.

The doctor nods and then leaves. Moments later the door is open again and a nurse comes in clutching a plastic bag.

'Good afternoon, Ms Turner,' she smiles brightly. 'I've come to help you get a little more comfortable.' She holds out the bag. 'Some pyjamas, from your hotel. We'll just disconnect the drip while you change.'

Lying down still, I peel off my sundress. Sitting up slowly, I rummage in the bag for something to change into.

It's immediately clear that Babs has sent me some of her own clothes. There are bright pink nylon pyjamas, fluffy slippers and a matching satin dressing gown. I relax the smallest amount at the sight of them.

The nurse's eyes go wide once I'm dressed. I must look like some sort of Halloween Barbie.

'Now you should get some rest. Shall I just put your clothes back in the bag?'

'Yes, um, thank you.'

She smiles.

'You should stick to water for now, but tonight we will try you with some broth. See if you can keep it down.'

I nod. 'Your English is amazing.' I don't want her to leave yet. Not sure I can bear to be on my own.

'Thanks. I'm Selena, by the way. My boyfriend comes

from Rochdale. I met him when he was admitted for alcohol poisoning a few years back.' She pauses as if she's just recounted the greatest love story ever told. 'He lives here with me now, but he never learnt Spanish.'

I have the good grace to look a bit shamefaced on behalf of all British people who never applied themselves to languages back in school.

'How lovely.'

'You rest. I'll be back later.' I can't think of anything else to say to keep her here.

Once she's gone, gnawing panic about where I am returns. I close my eyes tight, determined to avoid having to look at the hospital room. Instinct tells me that my chances of sleep are slim to none; however, I must doze off because when I open them again it's almost dark outside.

A monitor starts to beep, and I jump. Determined to leave, I swing my legs off the edge of the bed.

Selena comes back in.

'Your heart rate is high again.' She looks a little confused. I will my breathing to return to normal. If I keep setting off machines, they'll never let me out.

The beeping stops.

'I've brought you some soup. Dr Cruz came to check on you earlier. She says if you can keep some food down, you can go back to your hotel tomorrow. Though you might feel a little unwell still. You will have to rest in bed some more.'

Great. Basically, my whole holiday.

I'm too weak to argue. Or to question what the soup is.

It tastes decidedly chicken-y. By the time I've finished the bowl, I feel energised enough to pad to the toilet and use the toothbrush Babs has bought me.

I try to take in as little of the room as possible. Still, I notice that I'm decidedly less terror-struck. In fact, I feel oddly numb. Not my head, that hurts like hell still, but the rest of me. My legs don't feel like my legs. I turn away from the mirror in the bathroom as I brush, holding my hand in front of my face. It doesn't look like my hand.

There's a gentle buzzing in my ears. Like white noise. Perhaps they drugged the soup.

I float back to the bed.

'Get some more sleep,' Selena says. 'We can see how you are in the morning.'

An odd sense of calm envelops me as I get back into bed. I don't panic about my cheapo insurance covering the stay, or about the fact that I'm taking up a bed with my dodgy paella. Instead, I just float into a tranquil sleep.

To my astonishment, the next thing I know, Dr Cruz is disconnecting my drip and telling me that I'll be able to go back to the hotel. It's morning. Someone has put toast and a tea on the little tray next to my bed. I chew without tasting anything.

'Er, excuse me,' I ask Dr Cruz. My voice sounds far away.

'Si?'

'How do I pay? Only I've left my credit card at the hotel.' It has a £1500 limit. And I spent £250 on flights.

'Pay?'

'Yeah, I'll have to pay, won't I?' I'd paid £4.22 for my travel insurance. Somehow the thought of it not even covering my breakfast doesn't stress me out. Kaz will Crowdfund me away from here if it comes to it.

'You have insurance?'

I nod, causing a shooting pain in the back of my head. 'Yes. I bet it was easier when we all had those little cards. Less paperwork for you all. Bloody Brexit. I mean I know we voted for it, though I didn't by the way, in case that affects how much you're thinking of charging me. Not that I hate people who did, my mum did actually and we've a very good relationship.' Dr Cruz looks up from the notes she's writing.

'It is fine. You will be able to claim on your insurance. Now, would you like more toast before you return to the hotel?'

I'm already off the bed.

'No thank you, I'll be right on my way.'

I hover in the entrance to the hospital waiting for my taxi, still wearing Bab's bright pink pyjamas. Nylon, I discover, is a very unforgiving fabric in the heat.

The taxi pulls up and acting on autopilot I dive in. If the driver thinks my outfit is odd, he doesn't say anything. But then I imagine he's seen all sorts.

At Jaggers Bar I ask him to wait while I go and grab my purse. Even after Babs informs me that I've been moved rooms, on account of the fact that my old room has required

Rebecca Ryan

a deep clean, it takes me ages to get the money I need. It's quite clear that I've lost some brain matter in the last two days. No doubt puked out and blocking Jaggers Bar's drains at this very moment.

My new room is like my old, except the walls are canary yellow, I presume in continuation of the *Simpsons* theme. I grab my purse and pay before promising Babs that I'll go change so she can have her clothes back.

'Don't you worry about that, duck. You have a nice hot soak in the bath. Leave the stuff on the floor, I'll get it when you check out tomorrow.'

Under all that leathery skin, Babs has a heart of gold.

'Thank you, Babs, and for calling the ambulance. And sorry about the, er, drains, and the room. I've caused you so much trouble.'

'Don't you be worrying about that. You gave us quite the fright. Here,' she passes me a bottle of water. 'It's on the house. Now go and rest up.'

It's a wonder that Jaggers Bar turns a profit if Babs is this charitable to all her guests.

Back in my room, my brain still feels like it's made of candyfloss. It takes me much longer than it should to assemble some clean clothes and put my phone on charge.

In the bathroom there's a bath, but no shower. Though there's some contraption attached to the taps that I think acts as a shower head, and most likely dates from circa 1810.

I stand in the bath in my flip-flops and run the water cold.

Freezing water rushes over me yet I hardly even flinch.

338

I feel broken. Wrung out and exhausted. Once I'm done, I stand in my towel and brush my teeth until my tongue is numb from the toothpaste.

I catch sight of myself in the dirty mirror above the sink and my eyes fill with tears. It could be that I'm finally rehydrated enough to rally some proper ones. Or that it's dawned on me that my grand plan to go travelling has been an absolute disaster from start to finish. There is not one good thing I can say about this trip.

I go back to my room and lean against the door. My chest feels tight again. I wish Kaz was here. I text her.

> **Me:** So long story short. Got food poisoning on my first night. Just got back from hospital x

I add a sighing face emoji to give the impression that I'm more despondent than hysterical.

> **Kaz:** What the hell Em! Are you ok? You need salt, and fluids and rest. I can't believe you've been in hospital on your own. Love you xxx

Well, that only makes me cry harder.

> **Me:** Yeah I'm fine, honestly. A total lie. But one that I'm sure I'm not alone in constantly telling. Was VERY sick for twenty-four hours. Needed a drip. The paramedic did tell me I was technically

dead though, so maybe I can trade off being a
medical miracle. Wish I was at home xxx

Kaz: Do you want me to pick you up tomorrow? I
can swap shifts xxx

Me: Yes. Please. Josh was meant to come for me
but I can't face him. xxx

Kaz: Don't worry. Rest up and I'll see you
tomorrow. xxx

I change into my leggings and a T-shirt and lie down on top of the covers because that seems like the most hygienic place to be.

Josh.

Something cracks deep in my chest.

I look around at the yellow walls.

How wrong I was to think that I could have something good like Josh in my life. People like me don't get good stuff.

I won't do this to him. I can't.

Me: Hi Josh, I'm sorry but I don't think things are
going to work out between us. I know it's really
crappy to say this over text but I'm a total coward.
So there you go. Please don't get in touch with me. I
can't bear it. Emily x

I sip the water Babs gave me and close my eyes tight against the tears.

*

A watery light streaming through the window wakes me up. I feel completely empty. Like a hollowed-out pumpkin. The sort you're meant to leave out for the wildlife but really just turn to mush on the pavement.

Babs sees me from behind the bar.

'Here she is! You look a lot better. What'll it be? A whiskey to restore you? On the house.' It's 8am. And even then, I imagine that whiskey is not on the prescribed list of things to drink following severe food poisoning and dehydration.

'Actually, could I just get an orange juice and another bottle of water please?'

'Right you are. How're you feeling, duck?'

God-awful.

'Fine thanks.' I offer up a half-smile.

Babs hands me my drinks.

I leave a twenty-euro tip and say my goodbyes.

'Thanks again, maybe I'll come back one day.' This is highly unlikely. But at the very least I intend to leave a good review on Tripadvisor.

'That's right, duck, you'll have to. You didn't even see the art museum or nothing!'

It's raining when I land. I mean, of course it is. I spent the whole flight with my head against the window crying my silent cry. The man next to me read the paper in a very determined fashion.

Kaz is waiting for me in the pick-up section of the car

341

park. I feel a pang that it isn't Josh. But as she envelops me in a hug, I realise there's no one I'd rather be here.

'How're you feeling?' Kaz asks.

'Not good.' I slump down into the seat.

'Not good, how?'

'I really don't want to talk about it. Can we just go home please?'

Kaz nods and sets off.

My phone is stubbornly blank in my hand. No message from Josh. He didn't even reply to the one I sent.

Tears prick at my eyes again. I'm not even sure what I'm crying about anymore. I mean it probably has something to do with the fact that I've failed at my big travelling adventure. Just like I fail at everything.

I was kidding myself, to think that I could live like Claire would have lived.

Suddenly, my hands are in tight fists. I'm inexplicably angry. At myself, at Mum, Dad. At everyone who ever thought that Claire would have been better at this.

And I'm angry at Claire. More than angry. I'm furious. Furious that. Furious that I'm the one who got left behind to carry on.

Dying is easy. It's living that's impossibly hard.

Chapter Thirty-Eight

2000

'Pst,' Claire whispers in the dark. 'Em, wake up.'

I open my eyes slowly at first because it's still dark outside. But then I realise that Claire might be sick, so I sit up really quickly, and my head goes all woozy.

'What's wrong? Should I get a doctor?'

Mum stirs in the cot on the other side of Claire's big hospital bed.

'Shh, no. Don't wake Mum.'

I hear Claire shuffle on her bed and gasp. It hurts even when she moves now. Though she'd never admit to it. The doctors come and give her medicines all the time through a special tube in her chest, so I think she'll start to feel a bit better soon.

We're having our sleepover. The one the hospice promised. Mum is here too, but she sleeps here every night anyway. We watched *South Pacific* and danced along to '*wash that man right out of my hair*'. Well Claire just smiled while me and Mum danced. And we had some popcorn. But when I noticed that Claire wasn't eating hers, I didn't have mine either.

My eyes start to get used to the light in Claire's room now. The machines make everything a bit green. The nurses were worried I'd get disturbed but Mum said I could sleep through anything and that I'd always been the same since I was a baby. I didn't tell Mum that I don't sleep so well anymore.

Claire has turned on her side towards my camp-bed. Her face is round and tight and shiny.

'Do you reckon they think I don't know?' Claire asks, slightly breathless even though all she did was roll over. I see her wince and think that maybe I should wake Mum up after all. I go to get up, but Claire waves her hand at me to sit down again.

'Know what?' I reply in a whisper.

'I'm dying, Em.' Her eyes are bright now and she has a bit of a smirk on her face, the one she does when she knows she's said a naughty word. Like that time she said shit in Tesco and Mum went beetroot red and dragged us out by the tops of our arms.

'You are not! Who said that?' I gasp. But it is as if all the air has gone out of the room. I'm suddenly shivering even though I was warm a minute ago. 'You've just got to keep taking this medicine and then it'll all go back to normal.'

'Nobody tells me anything. Mum and Dad go out to talk to the doctors and when they come back, I know they've been crying.' Her whisper has turned angry now. 'And Kaz's mum works here.'

'She's a nurse. They make people better!'

'Nope. Not her. Remember when we first met Kaz? She

said her mum worked with people who don't get better. And she works here, doesn't she.'

I'm out of breath. Because I do remember Kaz saying that. Except there can't be a world without Claire in it. It's not right to be alive as only half a person.

'You can't give up, Claire. I don't know what I'd do without you.' I can't stop myself from crying then. It's quite ridiculous really. When I'm the one who's perfectly alive and well. Not hovering somewhere between alive and not quite.

'I don't want to be sick, Em. I can't do any of the things I like to do. It's no fun being sick all the time.'

'I know.' My voice is so small, it's like it comes from somewhere far, far away.

'Do you think there's a heaven?' Claire asks.

'Yes, absolutely.' She knows I'm lying. We sing some hymns in assembly but that's as close as we've ever gotten to thinking about God. Well, except for that time when Kaz went on the aeroplane to Majorca. I asked her if she'd seen him sat on a cloud in the sky. She hadn't.

'Hey, you don't think they'll send me to hell for squirting Matt with that water gun last summer, do you?'

'No way. He totally deserved it.'

'Maybe for the Fairy Liquid that made his eyes sting so bad.'

'Okay, maybe for that.' We giggle then. And it feels like some of the air is allowed back into the room. I've been holding my breath. Mum rolls over again and we go still.

'Matt's sad,' I say.

'I know,' Claire replies. 'But Em, you'll have to do that sort of stuff when I'm gone.'

'What stuff? And anyway, I told you – you're not going anywhere.'

'Shut up. The exciting stuff. I don't mean to be bigheaded, but everyone's going to be pretty gutted when I die. They'll need a distraction. Promise me you'll make a massive deal of things.'

'Of what things?'

'You're thick sometimes. Your life, dumbo. I'm not going to be around coming up with all the best ideas anymore. I'm passing you the baston.'

'I think it's baton.'

'Whatever. How rude to correct a dying person, Emily!'

She points a finger at me. Her hand is tiny. It's not like a hand of someone who's eight, nearly nine.

'Sorry.'

'I'm kidding. Jeez. So, do we have a deal then?'

'I'm not sure,' I stutter.

'You've got to, Emily. Don't you see it's so important?' She winces again. 'You have to live enough for the both of us. That's the only thing that keeps me going. Knowing someone who looks exactly like me will still be alive. You'd better not end up boring.'

'I don't know how to not be boring.' My voice is even smaller somehow.

''Course you do. It's easy. Help people, be spontaneous. Inspire people! Go see the world, be mega successful!' I wonder then if Claire's been thinking about this for a long time. Her eyes are sparkling in the dark.

'I can't.' I breathe out.

'You can. Be brave, Em.'

'But it sounds like a lot.'

'Just be yourself, that way you can't go wrong.'

I want to shout *'No!'*

But instead, I nod. Because I'm a liar, liar, pants on fire. Claire slumps back on her pillow.

'There's just one more thing.'

'What?'

'There's an envelope, I put it in your bag when you brushed your teeth. Take it home and give it to Mum or Dad when I die. Promise me?'

'I promise.'

'Then my work here is done.'

Just then the door creaks open. Kaz's mum comes in to check on Claire and give her some more medicine.

I pretend to be asleep because I don't really feel like talking to Kaz's mum, so I roll on my side and cry all the way till it's morning again.

Chapter Thirty-Nine

It was never my list. I know it was never mine.

'Em, I think you'd feel a bit better if you got dressed.'

I beg to disagree.

'Brian spoke to Josh.'

There's only a mild prickle of curiosity.

'What did he say?'

'Not much, just that Josh was miserable.'

Followed by guilt. It's been a week since I spent the night at Josh's. A lot can change in a week.

'Mm hm,' is all I can manage. I cried so much the first few days that I've run out of tears. My activity of choice is now staring glassy-eyed at the TV. The couch has welcomed me back into its worn cushions like an old friend.

It's ironically impressive, the expansiveness of my failure. Except no one wants to be spectacularly crap. It feels like everything has turned dark, as if the world is perpetually on the brink of a thunderstorm. Even blinking seems to take more strength than I possess.

'Pizza or Chinese?' Kaz asks. She'd arrived back home from who knows where, taken one look at me in the same position I'd been in for the last ninety-six hours and declared, 'I'm staging an intervention.'

I ignore her.

'Chinese. I had pizza last night.'

The pizza box is actually still on the floor next to the couch, but Kaz pretends not to notice. Everyone needs a friend like that.

'I'll call it in. Veg chow mein?'

'I normally have chicken.'

'I know. I just thought with the vegan thing . . .'

'I told you already. I failed at that.'

'Did you fail? Or did you *accidentally* eat meat one time?'

'It wasn't just one bit of meat, Kaz, I ate the Noah's ark of paella.'

'Still an accident.'

'Anyway, doesn't matter.'

'But why did you want to be vegan in the first place?'

I humour her because she's sat in close proximity to the dressing gown I've worn for two days and nights straight.

'TV programme that revealed me to be the exactly average human. Life List. You know all this.'

'Any other reasons?'

'The stuff about the environment too, I guess. And maybe the animals a little bit.'

And because the memory of a four-year-old Claire in a face-off with the one-eyed cat had become branded on my brain. I clench my teeth to block out the memory.

'Why don't you be a part-time vegan?' Kaz ploughs on.

'I read an article. Apparently, they're called flexitarians. Be vegan when you can, but when you can't, don't worry about it. Beyoncé's one.'

'But it's not as impressive, is it? "Hello, I'm a flexitarian. I'm committed to trying only some of the time."'

'Emily, everyone only tries some of the time. And when it all goes tits up, they try again the next day. It's not all or nothing. It's what you can manage, when you can manage it.'

Okay, it's not a terrible idea. Flexitarian. I'll think about it.

'All right, order me the veg. Don't forget my sides.' This depth of crisis calls for at least one portion of salt and pepper chips.

'Right you are. There's wine in the fridge, go open it.'

I sigh. I've been limiting my fluid intake all day. No mean feat considering my food consists wholly of salty takeaways. It's been very inconvenient leaving my pit of misery to go to the loo.

'All ordered,' Kaz says as I put the wine on the coffee table and begin to pour.

'Did you sort the insurance claim out?' she asks.

'Yes. They're paying up.'

'Good.'

We lapse into silence, watching *Come Dine with Me* from the couch. I've already seen this episode, so I know the chocolate soufflés deflate. The credits roll and Kaz puts down her wine and turns to me.

'What happened, Em? Why did you end things with Josh

like that?' She's not angry at me. Kaz has always been on my side. But I don't deserve anyone on my side this time.

'I don't want to talk about it.'

'Very mature.'

'I never claimed to be mature.'

Kaz mutters something which sounds suspiciously like, 'give me strength.'

'Fine,' I huff. 'It was too good, all right?' I choke out. 'Now can we talk about literally anything else?'

Kaz gives me a pointed look while I try to take the conversation in a new direction. 'I think the bathroom mould is growing again, don't you? Can't be safe for our lungs.'

She ignores me.

'But if it's good, that's a good thing, isn't it?'

I release a frustrated growl.

'Kaz, please.'

'Tell me what you're thinking.'

'Kaz,' I whimper.

'Emily.'

'Fine,' I snap. 'It wouldn't stay good, I know it.' I take a breath. 'And even if it did, I'd be failing. I can't do it, Kaz.'

Knowing that on some level I've inflicted this upset on myself only makes it sting all the more.

'But that's what I don't understand. *Why* would you be failing? You like him, he likes you, what's so hard about it all?'

I sit and think about this for a few minutes. As if I've thought of nothing else for the past two days. Picking Claire and her list is the right thing to do. That's all I have. Claire. I can't turn my back on her now.

I offer up a feeble, 'I don't know,' saved from expanding further by the arrival of the Chinese. We spread it all out on the coffee table and I take an age piling different things onto my plate.

'Can you tell me *exactly* how you feel?'

'What's the point?'

'Humour me.'

Fine. I put my plate down.

'Well, mainly I feel like shit.'

Kaz shakes her head.

'Not what you think you feel. Go from the food poisoning.'

'I can't.'

Kaz puts her plate down.

'I just can't remember.'

'What do you mean?'

'It's all a blur really. I remember the paramedics coming, and absolutely shitting myself on the way to the hospital. Like proper terror. You know I hate them.'

'Yeah, I do.'

'But then it was like, I don't know, I was a bit numb when I was there. It was weird. I was all over the place, to be honest.'

I decide not to tell Kaz about the bit of time I spent railing against my dead twin.

Kaz picks up her plate again.

'So, I have a theory.' She spoons noodles into her mouth.

'How nice for you.'

'You, my friend, have been in shock.'

'In shock?'

'Not physical shock. Emotional shock. It can happen after a traumatic event.'

'Not sure food poisoning counts as particularly traumatic.'

'I'm not talking about the food poisoning. It'll have been the hospital. It doesn't take a genius to work out that you have a fear of them after what happened to Claire. You associate them with places people go to die.'

'Duh, they *are* places people go to die.'

'That's not true, Em. Most people get better and go home. It'll never stop being crappy that Claire wasn't one of them.'

I'm cross-legged and crying on the couch.

'But Em, you can't help shock. You weren't responsible for how you reacted. When you texted Josh, you probably weren't even thinking straight. Your body just did what it thought was best to survive. This wasn't you being a terrible person.'

'Argh, I don't know ...'

'Google it. Go on. If you don't believe me.'

I google *emotional shock*. I have to read every word three times before they go in. Still, maybe Kaz is onto something here. Not that it matters.

'What if you're right?' I sink further down the couch. 'It doesn't change anything.' I sniff. 'If Josh forgives me, I've still failed Claire. It would have been better if I'd died. Not her.'

353

I throw both hands to my face but it's too late. My darkest fear has entered the universe.

'Is that what you really think?' Kaz asks.

I nod through my hands.

'I knew it hadn't been about that bloody TV programme all this time.'

My head is still in my hands. The Life List has been the same as everything else. And everything has fallen short since Claire died. Every endeavour doomed to be only half-enjoyed because she wasn't here to experience it. I guess once you accept that your life will be colourless, it's hard to move from that default setting. The List was meant to add the colour back. To prove that my life could be technicolour, just like Claire wanted it to be.

Kaz wraps me up in a hug.

'So let me get this right, the Life List is full of qualities you associate with Claire, and you'd hoped that by finishing it, everyone would stop thinking that you're like a poor imitation of her?'

I can only manage a sad nod. There's no getting away from it now.

'It was Claire. Before she died, she told me I had to do all these things. But. I don't know. I just didn't. And then I saw that programme and freaked.'

Kaz looks like she's thinking. Neither of us are eating now.

'For the record, you got *her* spot on. If Claire were here, she'd be off riding an elephant around some country none of us had heard of. With pink hair and at least one life partner called Miguel.' I manage a weak laugh.

'But Em, the rest is spectacularly wrong.' Even in the midst of my breakdown, Kaz doesn't hold back. 'Claire wouldn't have been perfect. No one is. She just didn't get the chance to show how not perfect she was because when your death is so fucking tragic, no one cares whether you leave wet towels on the bathroom floor or never sweep up your toast crumbs.'

'Claire never did—'

'They're examples. Claire was great. You know I loved her. But she was more selfish than you. She was always making you do stuff you didn't want to do. You cried for a day before she made you get on stage at Butlin's.'

I'd forgotten about that.

'I was worried I'd let her down.'

The tears come harder now.

'Em, you're more selfless than Claire ever was. And you're caring and loyal.'

I can't speak for the tears.

'You don't need a Life List. You don't need Claire telling you how to live. And it doesn't mean squat that Claire's life might have been different to yours. No one, I repeat, no one thinks Claire should have lived instead of you. You're here. You need to get on with it.'

The enormousness of this seems insurmountable.

'I don't know. Claire was always happy. I seem genetically programmed to reject happiness.'

'One, I don't think that's a thing. And two, happiness is like an orgasm: if you think about it too much, it goes away.'

'Did you come up with that?'

'No, Tim Minchin did. Stands to reason though.'

'So, should I finish the Life List or not?'

'That is for you to decide, my friend. It's your life.'

I think back to all the things that The List has helped me with. I wouldn't know Sandra, Leon or Sophie without it. I wouldn't be able to do half a press-up. I'd never have learnt so much about the environmental benefits of veganism.

Kaz is still talking. 'One thing I am certain of is that you can't continue to wallow. Plus, you're starting to smell.'

'Your empathy astounds me.'

'I actually think I'm rather wise.'

I'm so confused. Could Kaz be speaking the truth? She's right about one thing: I'm here and Claire isn't. Surely I owe it to myself to at least *try* this happiness thing. It speaks to the depths of my emotional turmoil that I've only eaten two salt and pepper chips.

It's now or never.

'What do I do?'

'What do you want to do?'

'I think I want to get some help. Like proper help. Like go back to therapy.'

Even in my state of *emotional shock*, it's abundantly clear that I might have some stuff I need to work through. And

I can't live the rest of my life afraid. Still, I'm self-conscious now that I've said it out loud.

'I think that is an excellent idea.'

'You do?'

'Absolutely.'

I'm buoyed by her encouragement.

'And I want to text Josh.' This comes out without a thought. Josh is the person I want to see most. Preferably without his clothes on.

'Then do it.'

'Do you think he'll forgive me?'

'I don't know. But you've nothing to lose.'

She's right. Tears splash down onto my phone as I type.

> **Me:** Hi Josh. I know you probably don't want to hear from me. But I'm so sorry about the other night. Would it help if I told you I was lobotomised in Spain? I'd really love to meet up again so I can explain in person. Em xxx

Three kisses. Who wouldn't forgive three kisses?

I hit send. And then immediately stare at my phone waiting for a reply. The WhatsApp only gets one tick, so I know it hasn't been delivered yet.

'What else?' I'm on a roll here.

'This is your rodeo, you tell me.'

'My job! In Spain, before I got sick, I thought I might like to be someone who teaches young offenders. What do you think?'

'Honestly, that would be a perfect fit for you. Go on, get googling.'

'What, now?'

'As the adage goes, no time like the present.'

'Okay.' I get to googling.

'Oh, there's a Young Offenders Institute at Wetherby. That's not too far from here!'

The more I read, the more I'm convinced this sounds like the perfect place for me. The chance to make a real difference to kids like Leon.

'It doesn't say there are any vacancies. What do you think that means?'

'Er, it's a stab in the dark but I'm guessing there's no vacancies right now. Maybe you could email them anyway. Nothing ventured, right?'

'Exactly. I'll do it tomorrow. I'm back at work next week and we've got Sophie's wedding at the weekend, remember?'

'That's settled then. Now eat your takeaway. I don't want to be held responsible for you missing a meal.' She holds up her glass. 'To Claire.'

I chink back.

I'm a jumble of emotions. Sadness, obviously. But then, there's a bit of relief in the mix too. Relief that what happened has a name. Emotional shock. It feels less frightening, with a name.

It's overwhelming. But then maybe life is a bit overwhelming sometimes. Something tells me emotions rarely come neatly packaged, even the ones we manage to label.

They come like a tornado and rattle us about. All we can do is try not to be torn apart by them.

I check my phone before I tuck into the now-cold food. Josh still hasn't replied. But he will. Surely no great love story ended as a damp squib with an unread WhatsApp.

JUNE

Be Brave

Chapter Forty

On Sunday morning the sadness is still there. But it's duller now. More bearable.

To make up for cancelling yesterday's shift, I volunteer at the cat shop and nod along in all the right places as Sandra chats to me about the benefits of martial law.

In the afternoon, I pour my heart and soul into an email to the young offender's institute. There's an incredibly good chance I've come on a bit heavy, describing it as 'my life's dream' to work with young criminals. Obviously, I leave out how recently I realised said dream. I hit send and there's nothing more to be done.

Josh hasn't replied, but for some reason the message hasn't been delivered. I resend it as an actual text and spend the evening coming up with fanciful reasons as to what might have happened. Kaz comes home from her shift, and I pester her to text Brian and ask what's going on. Brian reveals that Josh isn't replying to his messages either. After further digging, we ascertain that Brian's WhatsApp ticks are turning blue, suggesting that his messages are being read and ignored.

I go to bed early and lie in the dark thinking about

Claire. I remember the Christmas where she gave us matching face tattoos, I remember the darkness after she was gone. I think that if Josh doesn't reply, eventually I'll probably be okay.

Come Monday morning, I wonder at the truth of this. Josh still isn't replying.

I'm forced to confront the fact that he may just not want to talk to me. At this point I decide to send message after message, hoping to carpet bomb him, in a messaging sense at least, into submission. I use the excuse that it is June this week. And though I no longer feel wedded to the Life List, it does help me to abandon all pretence of self-respect while messaging Josh. The messages are all different, but the core tenet is *I'm sorry. Please give me another chance.*

By Thursday I'm pretty miserable about the Josh situation. Sophie is highly stressed about her two-days-away wedding and snaps my head off when I ask if Amy has heard from him lately.

'She better bloody not have done, I don't got time for that crap,' she replies while adopting an almost Terminator-like stance and pelting up to the top of the hill we're doing reps up.

When Friday night rolls around, I'm looking for excuses to avoid the wedding. A day dedicated entirely to romance seems just a bridge too far given the current climate of my love life.

'Can't I just say I've got food poisoning again?'

'If you like. I don't mind either way. Though it is a day of free food and drink.'

'You're right. I overlooked that. And I actually think Sophie would spontaneously combust if I told her we were cancelling. She told me on Thursday that it had caused a major family rift, her giving her sister-in-law's place to us. She looked quite happy about the fact. Still, I can't help but wonder if, when they're still estranged in twenty years, she'll regret her choice.'

'That settles it. We're going.'

Come morning and we're all stuffed into a tiny little church on the top of a hill. It's very quaint. Sophie had confided in me that she doesn't actually believe in God but that she didn't feel that this should prevent her from having a traditional wedding. She and the groom have been attending services diligently for six months, such is her commitment. As it happens, she has no intention of continuing with this folly post-wedding.

'It's bloody freezing in here.'

'I know, quite the feat when it's so hot outside.'

Kaz is wearing a cobalt blue strapless dress, with tan shoes and several silver bangles. People turn to look at her as we walk in. I'm in a floaty yellow sundress. It's one of the ones that Kaz has bought under the pretence that she liked it, but in reality, it's so that I will have something to wear on occasions such as these. Still, Kaz has done my hair in a low bun and stuck a sunflower in it. So, however I feel, I *look* like a very sunny person.

The organ starts to play the wedding march and the brides-maids begin their entrance. There is evidently a dark green and pink theme. Amy looks gorgeous in a pale pink halter neck. And then Sophie enters on her dad's arm. She's so beau-tiful I well up. Her dress is all fitted lace and she's wearing a long veil that pools behind her. Her groom, a slightly stacked guy with kind eyes, is already openly sobbing up by the altar.

We sing hymns and there's a reading from *Captain Corelli's Mandolin*. Kaz hands me a tissue.

As they say their vows, gazing at each other like there's no one else here, it's clear that they are totally and utterly in love. I wonder what on earth I was worried about all this time. Claire loved us all so much. And who can blame her. Being in love looks like a pretty good thing to be.

Once at the reception, a massive marquee in a field next to the church with the poshest portaloos I've ever seen, I decide that eating my feelings is my only viable option. Kaz and I align ourselves by the back entrance, ready to intercept waiting staff bearing canapes.

The marquee itself looks nothing like I expected. There are actual chandeliers, and a black and white dance floor. A lit-up LOVE, each letter the height of a medium-sized child, reminds us of the theme of the day. There's a photobooth and a pick 'n' mix table. A cellist plays softly in the corner. No wonder Sophie has been stressed. She's essentially organised a small festival.

The canapes start to flow. I've asked for a vegan meal, so I don't feel too bad scoffing miniature fish and chips like they're going out of fashion. I'm an excellent flexitarian.

Kaz returns from the bar with two gin and tonics.

'It's a free bar for the first hour, then wine on the table and fizz for the toast.'

'Excellent.' We chink glasses. There is, of course, an unspoken rule that we must drink as much as humanly possible for the free hour.

I splutter.

'They're doubles,' Kaz laughs.

'Emily.' I turn round and come face to face with Amy.

'Hi Amy, you look gorgeous. I love your dress.'

'Thanks, yours is nice too.' I recognise an obligatory reciprocal compliment when I see one. 'And I didn't know you were a lesbian. You should have said.' She looks pointedly at Kaz.

'Um, I'm not. But even if I were, I don't think they're forced to wear badges or anything. This is my flatmate. Kaz, Amy. Amy, Kaz.'

'Ooh, are you the one shagging Brian?'

Kaz gives me a very pointed look.

'On occasion, yep, that's me.'

'Excellent. I actually came to say that we're on the same table, but this is brilliant. I don't know if you know but Brian's brother Josh, we were a thing for ever. We've hit a few bumps in the road but I think things are working themselves out. I'd love to hear your opinion.'

'Right.' Kaz looks like she'd rather sit through a meal on *I'm a Celebrity*. I'm not sure how I remain standing, such is my urge to fold into a tiny ball. I cling to Kaz.

I mean, Josh thinks I told him I wanted nothing to do with him, which technically I did, though not for the reasons he probably imagines. So maybe I've pushed him and Amy back together. As in, he's seen what's on offer in a post-Amy world and decided better the devil you know. My heart is pounding. Good job it isn't a fragile organ. I'm really putting it through the wringer. No wonder heart disease is the number one killer.

I eat another miniature fish and chips for the emotional support.

Amy wanders off. 'Just remember,' Kaz says, turning to me, 'what Amy thinks might be happening and what is actually happening here are not necessarily the same thing.'

I sort of half-agree, half-groan in reply.

Surely Josh hasn't gotten back together with Amy. I feel queasy. And it isn't the four gin and tonics I've managed to down during the hour of free drinks.

A man in a red suit comes and barks at us all to take our seats. We're at table *Number 44 to Birkby*. I see other tables labelled *Paris* and *Salendine Nook School* and I do my best not to wonder which key part of the happy couple's relationship took place on the number 44 bus.

The pink and green theme is carried on at the table. There's a big vase of flowers in the centre and battery-operated tea lights scattered about. Everyone has a pink or green macaroon in a brown paper bag with their name on.

Amy nearly takes out Sophie's great-uncle in her quest to sit next to Kaz. She quickly swaps macaroon bags and gives the great-uncle, who has a military medal pinned to his suit, a *do not challenge this* look.

Said uncle, resigned to his fate, takes the seat next to me as I pour myself an, admittedly very large, glass of wine.

'So, like I was saying,' I hear Amy start up with Kaz, 'I just really feel like me and Josh have this deep connection. Here, read these messages. What do you think?'

I silently pour Kaz an equally large glass of wine.

'Pass me a drop would you, love?' Sophie's uncle asks and I oblige, pouring him half the amount me and Kaz are currently necking, on account of the fact that he looks to be about a hundred and two and is pretty much bent in half. As if the keeling over process is being dragged out over many, many years.

'William,' he offers out his hand, 'but I go by Billy.'

'Emily.' I return the shake to William who goes by Billy. 'I like your medal.'

'This old thing. Sophie said I ought to be proud to wear it. I think she thought it would look good on the photos.' He does a soft chuckle.

'What did you get it for?'

'El Alamein.'

'You're so lucky,' is my entirely inappropriate response.

He laughs and our starters are delivered.

'The vegan option?' the server asks the table and I make a right song and dance waving my arms about. That the self-same server saw me mainline fish and chip canapes an hour ago doesn't seem to register. I've some Vietnamese spring rolls and honestly, they look better than everyone else's melon and posh ham.

'Now, I think you were about to tell me why I'm so lucky to have been in a war?' Billy asks. But his watery eyes are smiling.

'I just mean that you've had chance to do something exceptional, haven't you? Like you know your life has been worth something. Obviously, war is bad, very bad. But it's not like you started it. And if there has to be one, then you're better to come out of it a hero, aren't you?' I glug back more wine.

'Very interesting. Can I show you something?'

I nod. Because obviously you don't say no to a hundred-year-old war veteran and Amy is still talking animatedly to Kaz. I notice Kaz is rolling her bread knife between her fingers. I hope she's not going to stab Amy. Sophie would never forgive us if we stole her thunder on her big day.

Billy seems to take an age retrieving his wallet from his trouser pockets. His hands have lumps at the knuckles and don't seem to work particularly well. With great care though, he manages to extract a black and white photo. It is a much younger Billy in a suit on his wedding day. He's wearing the same medal he has on now and his bride stands beaming next to him in a pale two-piece with a little pillar box hat. They're so happy it radiates off them.

'Well, I'd do you. Both of you in fact.' Those doubles have a lot to answer for.

That gets a roaring laugh from Billy.

The servers clear our starters. Billy uses the time to regroup.

'Thank you. You're about half a century too late. And three-ways weren't really our thing.' He's still laughing.

'What was her name?' I presume we're talking in the past tense here. Because I very much doubt that Billy would be here without his bride.

'Our Edna. Prettiest lass I ever saw.'

I nod because Edna is no doubt a hottie. 'How old are you both here?'

'We're twenty-two. We'd just started courting when war broke out. First thing I did when I got home was ask her to marry me. That very day in fact. 'Course people got married younger in those days.'

'You look so happy.'

My butternut squash risotto arrives. Billy, I notice, has the same.

'I'm not so good at cutting beef these days,' he offers as an explanation.

'How long were you married for?' I ask.

'Sixty-three years. And every day I'm grateful that she was my wife. Even now, when life has gotten lonely and slow, I'm happy that we had each other. This,' he flips his medal, 'is nothing. This,' he pokes the picture on the table, 'is everything.'

I want to correct him. *Time* is everything. Time is the thing that not everyone gets. But you don't go around arguing with war veterans.

Fortunately, Billy is too polite to mention the fact that I'm weeping into my risotto. The only person still talking is Amy.

'The thing is, someone like Josh doesn't know what he wants. I mean, have you seen those old T-shirts he still insists on wearing? I don't even know where he buys them. Without me, it's like he's totally clueless.'

It could be Billy's *all you need is love* speech, or it could be my blood alcohol levels, but something snaps. I lean around Kaz.

'For the record, I don't think Josh is totally clueless. In fact, he's not even a little bit clueless.' I slam my hand on the table.

Kaz is in the middle of draining her wine glass, but her eyes go wide.

'No one asked for your opinion, Emily, thank you very much. You don't even know Josh.'

Kaz mutters something that sounds distinctly like, 'Oh dear.'

I pull myself up to full sitting height, which is admittedly still quite a bit smaller than the gazelle-like Amy.

'Actually, I know Josh plenty. Josh is funny and kind and thoughtful and yes, faded band T-shirts may have had their day, but if anyone can pull one off then it's him.'

'And how, exactly, would *you* know any of this?' Amy seethes. I'm actually a little bit afraid she's going to start pulling my hair.

I take a deep breath. 'Because he is the best man I've ever met, with perhaps the exception of Billy here.' Billy does a grateful nod.

'What?! That's it. Outside,' she shouts. People from other tables are starting to stare.

'God no.' I am in no way shaped for combat.

'I think we'd better go to the loo, Em, don't you?' Kaz asks, standing between Amy and I.

I stand up. Though inside I'm actually genuinely terrified that Amy might deck me. But I've seen Bear Grylls – you must not show fear.

'Emily.' Billy nods his head to me as we vacate the table.

It is perhaps the greatest exit I have ever or will ever make.

Kaz and I spend the remainder of the wedding sat in a field behind the marquee. She snuck in and retrieved our desserts. Apparently Amy was talking animatedly to Billy. Kaz reported that Billy had fallen asleep.

'So, do you love him?'

'I think so. Not that it matters – he's never going to forgive me.'

'You don't know that.'

'I do. He's blocked my number. If he hasn't changed his mind yet, he's not going to. And I don't want other people to have to convince him, either.' I cut across as Kaz goes to talk. 'It needs to come from him.' I'm not sure where my sudden conviction has come from. Maybe a bit of Billy's heroism has rubbed off on me. At least on the outside. On the inside, I think my heart might be breaking. Be brave, I remind myself.

Kaz just nods.

'But you don't think he'll get back with Amy, do you? I want him to be happy, but I couldn't cope with that. She said he'd messaged her.'

'I saw the texts. One-word answers, all of them.'

'Thank fuck for that.'

'What you need is a distraction, my friend.'

'Don't you think I've had enough of those lately?'

'Nope. Look, I'd hoped it wouldn't come to this.'

She unzips her clutch bag and hands me a flyer. It's the one from boot camp weeks ago.

'I found this in your jacket that day I borrowed it for the park run. I've been saving it for a day like today.'

'Do you remember what happened last time I attempted an organised sporting event?'

'Will you look at the bloody flyer, Emily.'

I unfurl it. *Birkby Boot Camp Family Fun Day! 10K race, stalls serving food and drinks, lawn games, tombola.* And then I spot it. *Bungee jump.*

'You're joking, right?' I hand the flyer back to Kaz.

'Be Brave. You said it yourself.'

'Personally, I believe I already have been very brave this June.'

'You could do it for charity. Mum says the hospice—'

'Guilt. I can't believe you're using guilt.'

'Trust me, this is what you need.'

I do a big sniff. 'I read once that there's a chance your eyeballs can pop out.'

'As a nurse I swear that it is anatomically impossible.'

My arms and legs feel a bit tingly. And not because I've been sat on the grass for several hours, hiding from Amy. The disco booms from inside the marquee.

'You really think I could do it?'

'I know you could. Prove to yourself that you're braver than you think.'

'Okay, I'll do it.' My alcohol consumption has a lot to answer for this evening.

'Promise?' Kaz holds up her little finger and we link. 'Excellent. You can't back out now.'

'When is it?'

'Next weekend.'

I gulp.

'Cheers.' We chink glasses. 'To best friends and being brave.'

'I'll cheers to that. Cheers!'

Chapter Forty-One

'You're doing a bungee jump?' Dad asks.

Mum has paused with her fork halfway to her mouth. Gravy drips back onto her plate.

Matt and Sarah gasp and Gran says 'fecking brilliant'. So, all in all it's a mixed reaction to my news. But mostly it veers on the side of horror-struck.

Kaz had wasted no time in setting up a JustGiving page which, apparently, she'd managed to digitally disseminate to the far corners of the universe in a little over twelve hours. She'd included a picture of Claire and some of her story, along with a link to Huddersfield's Children's Hospice where her mum still works. That, and not the fact that I was wildly popular in any way, meant that I was already at seventy-five per cent of my £500 goal.

'That's right. Don't worry, I've checked. They're very safe these days. Minimal chance of death.'

It strikes me that as bereaved parents, any chance of death might be a bridge too far for them. But it's too late to take it back now.

No one has spoken. I make a gallant effort to fill the silence.

'There's a fun run beforehand. I might as well give it a go too. Can't be as bad as the Tough Mudder, it's only 10K. And a tombola. You love them, Gran, don't you? And there's food stalls and stuff. Matt, Sarah, you like to eat, I think.'

Sarah goes to speak but Mum cuts over her.

'I suppose it'll be over quickly,' Mum offers. I'm not sure if she means the jump or the prospect of my death.

'That's the spirit.'

'And it's really lovely that you're doing it for the hospice.'

I swallow hard.

The table goes unusually peaceful as I continue to eat my vegan pie. It's pretty easy to be a part-time vegan. Thank heavens for vegan junk food.

'Oh, and I've emailed a young offenders institute over in Wetherby. I've decided I'd like to teach in a prison. It just seems that it'll be a chance to make a real difference, you know.' It seems that, if no one is going to talk, then perhaps I should just get all this stuff out in the open. Seems cruel to drip-feed them change when they're all so naturally averse to it.

'I have some contacts there.' The sentence hangs in the air as if the wind itself has whispered it. Then I remember that's not a thing.

My head snaps to Sarah, who looks down at her hands and says quietly, 'I could speak to Angie for you if you like?'

'You could?'

She nods.

I put down my cutlery to give her my full attention.

'Sorry, Sarah. Just to go over that again. Did you say you had contacts?'

'That's right.'

'In a young offenders institute?'

'Yes.'

'But what is it you do exactly?' It's admittedly very poor that I don't already know this.

'I'm a probation officer.'

'Fuck off.' I cannot imagine anyone less suitable to working with hardened criminals.

Dad clears his throat and Gran claps her hands together as if lunch just got interesting.

'Like you say, it's about trying to make a difference.' Matt puffs up his chest. Matt the accountant, I might add.

'So, could you put in a good word for me, do you think?'

'Yes. They get most of their teachers through a supply agency. I'll make some calls.'

'Thank you. I mean, thank you so much.'

'No problem.' She returns to neatly cutting up roast potatoes.

'Well then. I suppose that's . . .' Mum flounders around for something to say.

'Don't worry. That's all the excitement I have to share.' There's a communal exhalation. 'Well, aside from the fact that I'm planning to drink a lot more than normal this week, that is. I'm not too keen on the bungee jump idea myself.'

As it turns out, it isn't possible to remain permanently drunk, especially when you work with children. I'm therefore forced to endure the week more sober than I'd hoped. Every day that I don't hear back from Josh my heart aches a little more.

On Monday my class ask me why I'm being weird, and I blurt out about the bungee jump. It's their last lesson before study leave and I've abandoned all pretence of teaching them the prescribed Life Lessons on calculating interest rates. I've warned them off wonga.com, that'll do. Instead, I'm signing shirts and posing for pictures.

On Tuesday I go to boot camp alone, as Sophie is on honeymoon. She texted and admitted that she felt incredibly relieved that the ordeal, her word, was over. I manage three-quarters of a push-up and Bruce says I'm making excellent progress. He reveals that most of the proceeds from the family fun day will be going to support abandoned puppies.

On Wednesday I receive an email from the young offenders institute inviting me for an interview on Friday. I feel a rush of affection towards Sarah. Swiftly followed by guilt at what a poor soon-to-be sister-in-law I've been. Especially when she really has come through for me here.

I am now a person with connections. Who'd have thought it?

I divide my waking hours between panicking about the jump and the interview alternately. If I have a spare moment,

I take time to dwell on the fact that Josh doesn't love me and that my twin sister is still dead.

Come the morning of the interview, I'm a jittery mess. I call in sick at work and drive the forty-five minutes to Wetherby in a state of nervous exhaustion, running over the hundred and fifty flash cards I've written out, all with potential interview questions on them.

The recruitment process at my current school was a veritable gauntlet of tasks. I'd been so exhausted by the onslaught of challenges that I'd taken to bed for a week after it. Marking task, planning task, a task where they gave you a 'to do' list and told you to prioritise the most important, but then had parents pretend to call and yell at you. And that was before teaching a fake lesson and the actual interviews. Both student and staff. I'd hardly dazzled in any part of the process. And I'd stumbled through the interview with a series of 'ums' and 'ahs'. Thank heavens for a national teacher shortage or I'd still be unemployed.

I wait at the visitor entrance and try to look like a person who isn't deranged. I'm not sure I'm wholly successful in this endeavour as the receptionist gives me some nervous glances.

'Ms Turner?' A woman with short grey hair appears. She isn't wearing a suit. Instead, she has on a long blue dress and sandals.

'Yes, that's me. Pleased to meet you.' I hold out my hand.

'Angie,' she offers back, smiling. 'Sarah mentioned how

keen you were.' Good old Sarah. I've always liked her. 'So, what we thought for the day, if it's all right with you, is that Mo will show you around a bit. He's one of our supply teachers, and he's ever so good. And then we'll have a chat in my office after?'

This, I presume, is before the hardcore stuff begins.

'Yes, that sounds brilliant, thank you. And Sarah is right – I am very keen.'

I'm not sure how normal that sounds. But she smiles. 'Come on through then.'

There's a lot of buzzing and clunking as Angie opens door after door.

I feel a moment's trepidation at the thought that I'm heading into an actual prison. With real-life criminals. As if Angie can read my mind she says, 'You get used to all this. Ah, here's Mo. I'll see you back at my office.'

Mo is standing waiting for me outside one of the class-rooms. It has a painted blue door with a window in the middle, just like you'd see in a regular school.

'Ready?' he asks. I nod.

'So, this is the English classroom.' He opens the door. Honestly, I'd expected it to be a bit more prison-y but it looks almost identical to my current classroom, with rows of desks and mismatched plastic chairs. I assume that this tour is part of the recruitment process and endeavour to ask intelligent questions.

'Um, what sort of curriculum do the pupils follow?'

'Key skills mainly. Most of them have reading ages far

below their chronological ones, so there's not as much focus on exams as you'd get in a mainstream setting. There's a high staff turnover. Only Angie and Michelle, the art teacher, are permanent.'

'Why's that, do you think?'

'My son has additional needs. So I can't commit to a full-time contract. But as for the others, I guess most people would rather work in a normal school. Angie was considering advertising again, for a full-time member of staff. But it's expensive to put an advert out and most candidates aren't suitable or are only applying as a last resort. This isn't that sort of a place.' I stand up a little taller. I mean it sounds very much like I might be having some actual luck here. As in, they want a teacher and haven't advertised yet. This sort of alignment of fortune has never happened to me. But then my horoscope did say that I was going to have a good week. About time too.

'This is very much my first resort. I love criminals.' Mo gives me a funny look.

'There's a buzzer next to the desk that you can press at the first sign of trouble, but there are always officers stationed at the doors. If you come this way, some of the boys are in art.'

We close the door to the English room and walk along the corridor to another classroom; this one has officers outside it.

'And the boys are fifteen to eighteen?' I ask, even though I already know. I just want to show off my research.

'That's right.'

He pushes the door leading to art. Everyone looks up

for a moment and then goes back to what they were doing. They're all wearing grey jumpers and joggers. There's an art teacher, Michelle, I presume, sitting next to one of the younger boys, showing him how to sketch.

It strikes me how young they all are. I try to imagine myself at fifteen, away from my family and everyone I know, but it's impossible.

I walk over to a boy perched on a high stool.

'Hi there, what're you up to?'

He looks nervous, but Michelle gives him a nod.

'I'm just drawing the apple.' He nods towards an apple balanced on a book in the middle of the desk.

'It's excellent. I really love your use of shading.' I've no idea if this is an appropriate artistic compliment but he nods.

'You ready to move on?' Mo asks.

'Yep.'

Next, we take a look at the sports hall and the football pitches before finishing the tour back inside. There's two more classrooms, for Life Skills and Maths. Mo tells me that all the teachers pitch in and deliver Life Skills. It would be interview suicide to admit that I am definitely not qualified to deliver these lessons. I just keep quiet.

'I'll take you back to Angie now, if that's okay?' Mo asks. 'I have a lesson starting in a moment.'

'Yes, excellent. Thanks so much.'

'No problem, hope to see you around.'

We arrive at Angie's office. I hope I've done enough to make a good impression with Mo. I don't think I asked enough intelligent questions; I mainly just walked around with my mouth open because whatever I expected, this wasn't it.

It's actually really nice here. Not like a prison at all.

I knock.

'Come in!' Angie calls. 'The kettle just boiled.'

I sit across from her desk while she makes a cup of tea, wondering if this is all some elaborate ruse before the really torturous part of the process begins. Maybe someone will jump me while I'm here and I'll be expected to react. I glance around, nervous all of a sudden. Angie starts to talk.

'Of course, you'll be inducted with a course that covers personal protection and all sorts before you start. You might have to miss a few weeks of your summer holiday if you wanted to start in September? How does that sound?'

Confusing, mostly. Do I already have the job?

'Yes! Excellent. I never have anything to do in summer anyway.'

Angie chuckles like I might be joking.

'And things will be quite different to what you're used to. Our boys might be fifteen or over, but mentally, and from an educational standpoint, they're much younger.'

I think I may already have the job.

'That's understandable. They must have been through an awful lot.'

'You're not wrong. For many, this is their safe place. The boys most likely to cause trouble are those just arriving and those about to leave. But we have a weekly meeting to discuss all the clients, so we'll always know who might need that extra bit of attention.'

'That sounds sensible. Er, excuse me, but do I already have the job? I just feel like I might have missed something.'

Angie chortles.

'Teaching in prisons isn't the most sought-after role. And it's tough, I'll be honest. Most of our boys have had incredibly difficult childhoods and are confused and frightened. They have an acute sense that the world does not want them.'

I think of Leon. They're not wrong. It doesn't.

'Reoffending rates are high. This is the only chance we have to change that. So, if I get an email practically begging me to come and help, alongside a ringing endorsement from one of our most trusted probation officers,' I will kiss Sarah next time I see her, 'well, there's no way in heaven I'm turning it down.'

'But you haven't seen me teach, don't you want to observe me or something?'

'What you need to know, Ms Turner – actually, can I call you Emily?'

'Yes. Totally. Call me Emily.'

'All right, Emily, what you need to know is that this isn't a normal teaching environment. We're looking at the bigger picture here. *Are* you a good teacher?'

'Yes, I think so.'

'Good. But most importantly, could you come to care about the boys here?'

Already I can tell that I will. It doesn't seem fair to write these boys off when they still have time.

'Absolutely.'

'Then we'd love to have you. If you'll have us?'

I head out of the prison into a sunny day. Somehow, here feels like I'm exactly where I'm meant to be. And for the first time in a very long time, I feel happy.

Chapter Forty-Two

2000

'If you are reading this, I'm already dead. Don't worry though, lots of the best people die young. I've looked it up. That singer from Queen, Freddie, I think his name was, or Judy Garland who sang 'Somewhere Over the Rainbow'. I know none of them died as young as me, but that's not the point.'

Dad pauses to blow his nose into a hanky. He's cried so much that his face is all wet. Kaz squeezes my hand tight. Dad takes a deep breath and carries on.

'I know you're all going to be pretty upset. I think that's only fair. I'd be really annoyed if no one cared! Especially with me being such a good singer and dancer. Plus, I'd be upset if any of you died. I wouldn't like to live without Matt or Emily at all. Matt, I'm sorry about squirting you with Fairy Liquid that time and Emily, I'm sorry I made you do all those shows at Butlin's. I know you only did them because I wanted you to. I think it's important to say sorry when you're dying. Actually, it's important to say sorry even when you're not.'

People laugh at that, and the church is full of laugh-cries. I can only cry though. I want to pull the lid off the box that Claire's trapped in. Mum says she's wearing a special purple dress and her half of our matching locket, but it doesn't matter. Claire still wouldn't like to be trapped like that.

'But you know, I'd be really annoyed if you're all miserable for ever. Because being alive is so much fun. You get to eat fish and chips and tomato sauce on the beach. You get to drink red Slush Puppies, and even though Emily thinks that blue are best, she's totally wrong. You get to do things that you love all day every day. If I were going to be alive, I would be very good at it. And I expect the same from you all.'

Another laugh. I don't understand why people are laughing. Nothing about this is funny.

'So please don't make my funeral miserable. Everyone should wear their favourite colours. And none of those boring hymns either. Sorry Mr Priest Man. Musicals only please. Mum, I know you fancy Craig David, so I don't mind if you play one of his if it'll make you feel better.'

Mum's laugh sounds like she's choking.

'I can't really think of anything else that I want to say now, and my arm is getting very tired, so I think I'll leave it there. I'm glad it doesn't hurt anymore.

All my love, Claire Rose Turner, age eight and nine months.

P.S. Tell Emily she can have all my Cherished Teddies.'

Everyone starts to clap then, as Dad walks back to sit next

to Mum. Even the priest looks sad, and he must have been to hundreds of funerals.

Claire died on a bright sunny day. In the end, there wasn't much difference between her being alive and not. We were all sitting by her bed in the hospice and Kaz's mum said that she'd gone. Gone where, I don't really know.

All I could think of was that Claire wouldn't get a hug again. She'd never have another Chicken McNuggets Happy Meal. Never get to listen to a musical again. Purple wasn't her favourite colour anymore. But somehow, it's still mine.

After the church bit of the funeral, we go to the golf club. Mum says that we're having a party for her. Claire did like parties.

Percy from the pie shop in town brings some pies on a tray for everyone. I'm really hungry because there's no food at home. Because who cares about food shopping now anyway? So, I sneak a pie when no one's looking. When I finish it, I feel bad because Claire won't get any pies ever now. I wish I hadn't eaten it.

Then I stand next to Mum as people come over to shake her hand. Sometimes they give her a brown drink that she doesn't seem to like very much. But she always drinks it straight away anyway.

'Such an inspiration,' one person says.

'An inspiration to us all,' another person says.

But I can tell that people don't want to be around us for

very long. Because once they've said those things, they go away again really quickly. And when Granny took me to Tesco and I saw Haffsah, my fourth friend from school, Haffsah didn't come and say hello even though she was looking right at me.

I wonder if this is what it always feels like when someone dies. Grandad died too. But I was too little to remember it. And Dad's mum and dad died before I was born. But they all seem okay, so maybe they didn't care as much about it when those people died. Or maybe it's extra bad for me because me and Claire were mirror twins. And now there's no one with a freckle on the opposite side to mine.

In his little speech, the priest I've never seen before talked about Claire's soul. But I don't understand how her soul didn't die when the rest of her did.

'Do you think she's watching all this from somewhere?' I ask Matt.

'No,' he says. Matt doesn't really talk to me anymore. Not since Claire died. He doesn't really talk to anyone.

Dad comes over to stand with us then. Me, Mum, Dad and Matt. If anyone saw us, they'd think were just a normal family. Claire made us special. And now we'll never be special again.

Chapter Forty-Three

It turns out that getting a job by default because no one else wanted it does not detract from the feelings of glee that come from getting said job.

I'm happy enough to forget, for a moment at least, about the fact that I'm about to potentially jump to my death in front of a crowd tomorrow. I'm almost happy enough to forget about the fact that Josh still hasn't messaged. Almost. Of course, I'm a bit nervous. But overwhelmingly, I felt like that prison is where I should be. From a teaching perspective at least.

'I got the job, I got the job!' I happy dance around the kitchen when I get home.

'I knew you would! Congratulations!'

'I can't wait to tell Hughes to stuff his job where the sun doesn't shine.'

'So long as you're planning a dignified exit.'

'Shall we have a drink?'

I go to open the fridge, but Kaz slams it shut with her hip.

'No can do, my friend. One of us is doing a bungee jump

tomorrow and I for one do not want to see you spew vomit all the way down. Do you think it'd be okay if Brian tagged along? I'm thinking of introducing him to Mum.'

'Brian? Agile Brian? Brian who, now I think about it, you've seen on numerous occasions over the past few months?' I start singing Brian and Kaz sitting in a tree.

'Pack it in, will you?'

'But Kaz, this is a massive deal.' Kaz *has* seen a lot of Brian. Way more than normal. 'Just tell me honestly. Have you used my prolonged breakdown to sneak into a relationship?'

'Er no, I've told you every single time I've seen Brian.'

'Then does it mean I'm a bad friend for not realising?'

'It's okay. Watching your bungee jump tomorrow will definitely cancel out any hard feelings.'

'So here you are on a life journey of your own.'

'Er, I just like him a bit more than the others, that's all.'

'Oh. Why?'

'He's funny. And he can be quite thoughtful when he wants to be.'

'Kaz, are you in love?'

'God, I hope not.' She looks away though and I think she might be a little bit in love.

I'm happy for her. Obviously, I want to fling myself at her ankles and beg her not to leave me and run off with Brian. But I'm committed to minimising my dramatic gestures. So instead, I just say, 'I'd love him to come and watch me jump to my death.'

*

Come Saturday morning and it's quite clear that my morbid prediction will come true. Someone has driven a massive crane into the car park of the field where the family fun day is taking place. What possessed the crane operators to park on concrete when there are fields in every other direction I will never know. I suppose it doesn't matter what you hit when you're falling that far.

It's impossibly high.

'There you are.' Kaz has arrived with Brian. They're closely followed by Kaz's mum and my entire family. Dad is pushing Gran in her wheelchair. She has a tartan blanket over her legs even though it's boiling. She's not fooling me; I know she has her hip flask under there. Sarah and Matt cling to each other wide-eyed.

'Sarah!'

She flinches.

'Thank you so much for putting in a good word with Angie. She offered me the job there and then.'

'I really like Angie,' Sarah whispers.

'You need to let me buy you a drink. To say thank you.'

Sarah does a small smile and I wonder if perhaps we've not been the easiest family to join. I vow to make more of an effort.

Anyway, I'd already told almost everyone present my job news approximately three seconds after leaving the prison. Still, I bask in their exultations for a moment. When people turn to thank Sarah, she turns puce but manages to maintain eye contact; significant progress.

Rebecca Ryan

'The fun run's about to start,' Kaz says.

'Yeah, god forbid I miss that. I mean, this day is already exciting enough.' I wave frantically at the crane behind me, and everyone looks up. My voice has taken on an air of hysteria.

'You're awfully brave, love,' Mum says.

'Do you think it's safe?' asks Matt.

'I wouldn't know. I've been stood watching it for ten minutes and no one has been stupid enough to give it a whirl.'

There's a shout from somewhere that the race is about to start. At least the running will delay my jump.

'We'll wait by the finish, love. A few hours, do you think?'

'At least.'

'Do you want me to take a picture of you finishing?' That's Kaz.

'Don't worry about it. I don't think I care anymore.' This feels like some sort of seminal breakthrough. But I'm too full of dread to give said breakthrough the recognition it deserves.

At the start line, we're greeted by Bruce.

'Morning everyone,' he beams. 'Thanks so much for supporting the family fun day. I just know the puppies of Huddersfield will really appreciate it.'

There's an 'ahh' from the assembled crowd. Not one person gathered would believe me if I revealed that at a session this week, Bruce had dropped the C bomb at a diabetic who had stopped to check his blood sugar.

There's only about thirty of us, mostly people from boot

394

camp. I wish Sophie were here with me. I imagine it's something of a bonding experience, coming in last together.

'Ready, set—'

The whistle blasts and we head off. Bruce and his massive
muscles bounce ahead of us all.

It's flat to begin with and I'm relieved to find that there
are no obstacles. It's actually much easier to find something
akin to a rhythm when you aren't being forced to stop and
crawl through a muddy swamp.

By the first kilometre marker, I'm nowhere near the back
of the pack and I vow to slow down. If I burn out now it'll
be an embarrassing last, not just last.

We start to climb the hill. I'm panting hard but somehow
my legs are still going. It's like they aren't really my legs at
all. They propel me forward with a stamina that has thus
far eluded me. The top of the hill and the halfway mark is
already in sight. A little orange flag flaps in the slight breeze.
The flag is a bright light and I'm a moth, pulled by some
nonsensical force towards it. Just a few moments more and
I'm there.

I turn round and begin to jog back down, amazed at
how unwobbly my legs feel. I sip at my water. It's boiling
out. I actually pass people going up on the way down and
they look at me with something that might be jealousy. I
can't be sure as there's sweat in my eyes, but it does look
like jealousy.

It seems like no time has passed and I'm on the flat again.
There's only a kilometre to go now before the finish and

I feel good. I do something I have never in my entire life contemplated before this moment: I start to sprint.

I hear the cheers start up as I get near the finish. It spurs me on, and I speed up just as I cross the line.

I'm standing with my hands on my knees panting as everyone makes their way over to me.

'Em! You were brilliant!' Kaz says.

'We didn't expect you for another hour yet, love.' Thanks, Dad.

'That was actually quite good, Emily.'

'Woah, don't be too over the top, Matt. You'll give yourself an injury.'

'I think you were one of the fastest girls, you know, Em.' That's Mum.

I feel amazing. I mean, I must look terrible. I seem to sweat a disproportionate amount when I exercise. So I know I'll be red and puffy. But for the first time in my life, I think I'm close to psyched. And I never imagined that I would be associated with that word. I know exactly what I need to do.

'Come on then, let's get this bungee over with.'

'That's my girl.' Kaz smacks me on the back. I notice she and Brian are holding hands.

As we near the crane again, I realise that a small crowd has gathered around the base. I hope beyond hope that this means someone else is about to test it out.

'Hi, miss!' Tim waves.

'Tim!' And then I notice, it isn't a crowd of strangers here. It's the kids from school.

'What are you all doing here? And Leon?!'

'Me and Tim actually, er, know each other.' I ignore the criminal implications of his statement. 'Anyway, I wasn't going to miss the chance to see you shit yourself up there, was I?'

He makes a very valid point.

'It's so high, miss!' Little Cade squeaks.

It is. But there is absolutely no way I can back out now. Wordlessly, Kaz holds out my swimming goggles. I have decided that to be on the safe side, in the event that my eyes do pop out, they will be much easier to reinsert if they haven't rolled around on the tarmac.

I head over to the two men sitting by the foot of the crane. They have approximately three chin hairs between them and they're reading the *Sun*. They look as shocked to have a customer as I am to be that customer.

'You're sure?' man number one asks.

'Is it safe?'

'Think so,' man number two replies.

'Then yes, I'm sure.'

'We're meant to make a little promo video for the first person to use it. Do you mind?' Man one's voice breaks a bit mid-sentence.

'Wait, am I the first person today? Or the first person ever?'

'Yeah.'

On balance, I don't really want to know.

'Okay, what would I have to do?'

'Just let us film while we strap you in and take you up

and stuff. And then you give us a big wave before you bungee. You can say a few words if you like. It's meant to be two minutes.'

'And this video. It's going –?'

'Just on the website.'

I swallow hard.

'Okay, I'll do it.'

'We have our first customer, folks!'

I wish they'd stop saying that. Still, a cheer goes up from my assembled family and friends.

Cometh the hour, cometh the woman. I sit in the little cage and wait as man number one attaches some heavy-duty ropes to my feet. My breathing is ragged but for the sake of keeping up appearances, I try to smile and wave.

They switch over and man number two inflates a sort of flat bouncy castle under what I presume to be the drop zone. He calls it a bouncy pillow. It reassures me that if I do die, at least my parents will be spared the indignity of seeing my remains scraped off the asphalt. Being removed from something as innocuous-sounding as a bouncy pillow seems much more palatable.

'So, we're all set here,' man number one says, turning the camera on. 'When we get up there, best thing you can do is keep your eyes on the horizon and don't dawdle. We'll help you shuffle to the edge and count down from three. Don't think. Just jump.'

Just jump, just jump, just jump, I chant to myself.

'I wouldn't mind if one of you gave me a little shove, you know?'

He laughs. 'Sorry, it's got to be all you. You'll be fine. Just remember, three, two, one. Go.'

I nod. My heart is rattling around in my chest like it's making a bid for freedom. My hands are shaking as I stand up, so I secure my goggles and then clasp them at my front.

'And let's hear from her, ladies and gents, our very first customer!' He hands me a mic, which I wasn't expecting.

A camera is turned towards me. The crowd, a mere two metres away, falls silent. The wind whistles. But I've no idea what to say. I think my jaw is frozen in fear.

Every one of my pupils have their phones out taking pictures. At least they all look excited. My family all look a bit pasty. Except Gran, that is, who's sipping from her hip flask as if gearing up for a great show. 'Miss, any last words?' Tim shouts.

'Yes, I do actually.' The mic screeches and I realise that there is, in fact, a lot that I want to say.

'C.S. Lewis once said that no one ever told him that grief looked so much like fear. He's right. I've been grieving and scared for as long as I can remember.' My voice is trembling. I ignore the fact that the watching crowd is growing.

'My sister Claire was the bravest person I knew; she would have already jumped. No doubt about it. And not just that, her life would have been full of amazing things, and it is the most unfair, awful thing ever that she didn't get the chance to live it.' Dad has his arm around Mum. I attempt to stand up.

'Claire wouldn't have been too scared to fall in love. She'd have loved everyone and everything around her. She wouldn't have run away from Josh after they'd had sex. Twice.' Kaz puts her hands over Cade's ears.

'So, this is for you, Claire! And the money I've raised will be going to the hospice that took such good care of you all those years ago. I promise you that I won't be scared anymore.'

Everyone's mouths are hanging open as I plonk back down on the little seat.

Without a word, man number two moves a little lever and the crane starts to rise very slowly.

I think there's a cheer from the ground that sounds worryingly far away. The crane has come to a stop, and we are seriously high up. I look out towards the horizon. The sun is shining down on the hills. And though I don't believe in heaven, or in anything really, I feel like Claire's right here beside me. Holding my hand as I shuffle to the edge.

'Three, two, one, BUNGEEEEE!'

I don't think. Not even for a second. Without looking down once, I leap off the edge. My heart and all my other vital organs are in my mouth and I'm hurtling towards the bouncy pillow so fast that I'm sure it'll be the last thing I'll see. But then there's a pulling on my legs and I'm hurtling upwards again. And down, and up and down.

As I come to a stall, hanging upside down, I realise that it isn't just blood pumping in my ears. The now rather large crowd are jumping up and down cheering so hard, it's deafening. I'm gently lowered onto the bouncy pillow.

I lie there staring up at the sky and I know that more than anything, Claire would be proud of me. Heck, I'm proud of me. And from now on, that has to be all that really matters.

Finally, my legs are free, and I crawl off the bouncy pillow. Everyone watching is still cheering. You've got to credit their longevity.

'All right, that's enough.'

Mum is weeping openly, which has set Dad off. Kaz is asking Brian to check whether she has something in her eye and her mum looks on in wonder at the exchange. Gran raises one eyebrow, which could be a *well done* or could be an *is that all?*

Leon says, 'Not bad for a posh girl,' and Tim calls me an 'all right teacher', which is a high accolade indeed. I'm glad this is his final year; I actually think I'd feel a bit bad leaving him otherwise.

Man number one approaches and asks for fifty quid. Apparently, that's the going rate for near-death experiences these days.

I hand it over. Knowing that for now, I am done. I want nothing more than to eat and drink and to not do anything even remotely adventurous for the foreseeable future. It's nice that I've found my inner Claire. But I think, now, I might just need to be me. Brave Emily is exhausting.

'All those things you said about Claire, love,' Dad sobs. 'It's been such a long time.' I was riding something of an adrenaline high and can't quite remember the entirety of my speech. I sincerely hope I am imagining the part where I announced to my immediate family that I'd had sex with Josh.

'You know, Emily's inspired me.' Mum attempts to dry her eyes. 'I think we should have salmon for lunch tomorrow. What do you think, Pete?' That's it then. The culmination of attempting to alter my entire life is that I've encouraged Mum and Dad to branch out from their Sunday lunch meat rota.

'Definitely. We've a few things to sort for the memorial too. It'll be cracking. I can tell,' Dad says.

This prompts a fresh bout of weeping from Mum. 'It will. But Pete, remember we still need to find someone to do the music.'

'You need a DJ?' I ask.

'That's right, love.'

'Leave it to me. I know just the person.'

That night I'm sitting with Kaz and Brian. They're on the sofa, I'm on the Poäng. At the sight of them, I feel a pang of regret about what happened with Josh. But I know I'll be all right. Eventually.

We're watching *Grand Designs* and talking as if we're Kevin McCloud.

'I just think there's a real symmetry to the smoke alarm in here, don't you, Emily? It really speaks to me on an anatomic level.'

'I couldn't agree more. I'm ever so glad we managed to

find that extra million when we thought we'd run out of money. Of course, we've had to forgo the taps forged in the fires of Mordor.'

'Er, Emily.' Brian is flicking through his phone. 'I think you'll want to see this.'

Kaz's eyes go wide at whatever is on Brian's phone. I pad over.

'Ohmygod. Where did you get that?'

It's the video. The bungee video. Me being tied up in the crane, declaring to the world about Claire and Josh. I look more ridiculous than I could ever have imagined. My swimming goggles are way too small and make my eyes bulge out. And I'm a hot mess from the run.

We get to the part where I announce that me and Josh had sex twice and I scream.

'Get rid of it.'

'Em, I can't, it's on YouTube. I didn't even search or anything. It just popped up.'

I look at the screen. It's been viewed seventeen thousand times already. There's nothing left to do except fake my own death and start afresh in Yemen.

'How is that even possible?'

'It's gone viral.'

Whoever edited it has added music.

I'm furious. Now they're over the shock, Kaz and Brian, however, appear to find my humiliation amusing.

'It's not that bad, Em.' Kaz is openly laughing. 'Whoop, there she goes.'

I watch myself tumble like a ragdoll to the ground. They're both laughing now. Tears of glee roll down Kaz's cheeks. 'Bungee Mania', the most unoriginal name for a bungee company ever, is stamped on at the end in lime green.

'They said it would just be on the website.'

'Did you check which website?'

'No.' I feel like I've seen a ghost. Actually, some sort of extraterrestrial experience would be preferable to this.

'Come on, Em. It's funny.' The loop starts to play again and once more the crane begins its ascent. Thank goodness I quoted C.S. Lewis. I've always been drawn to that quote. At least it made me sound clever.

'Yeah, look at all these comments.' Brian proceeds to read out some of said comments.

'So brave, good on you! I hope Josh knows what he's missing. I lost my sister too, sending hugs. You got this hamstergirl.'

'What did she call me?'

'Well, you do look a bit hamster-ish with your goggles on.' Kaz is now on her hands and knees gasping for breath. This is what betrayal looks like, then.

I snatch at Brian's phone and mute myself mid speech. I read more of the comments. They are overwhelmingly nice. And okay, one or two mention a camel toe, inaccurately in my opinion, but there's no getting away from the fact that having hundreds of perfect strangers virtually pat you on the back feels pretty nice.

Scrolling back to the top of the comments, I notice there's a link. Someone has added my JustGiving page when they uploaded the video. I click on it, and then drop the phone.

Kaz is still laughing. 'What's wrong now?' She wipes a tear from her eye.

'I'm at five thousand pounds.'

'Huh?'

'The JustGiving page is on there. People have been donating. We're at five thousand pounds.'

'Ahhh!' Kaz screams and starts jumping around the living room. I join her.

Maybe even Josh will see it. I consider whether he might be the sort of man to look at YouTube videos of an evening. I'm not sure. If he did, then he'd know that running away from him like that was all because of what happened to Claire. Surely, he'd forgive me if he realised it was all about my dead twin.

My brain plays out a little scenario in which Josh turns up at the front door unexpectedly. He's holding a stack of cardboard scrawled with messages that reveal over several drawn-out seconds that he forgives me. And look at that, he's declaring his love. See, this is what I get for watching *Love Actually* year-round.

Still, my happy imaginings make me all warm. Basking in their good feeling, I go to bed.

Chapter Forty-Four

My incredulity at becoming an overnight YouTube sensation, albeit a comedy one, lasts for approximately four minutes into Monday.

'*Miss Turner to the Head's office please. I repeat, Miss Turner to the Head's office,*' the tannoy bellows. I'm never sure why the receptionist repeats things like that. Surely, if you're hard of hearing enough to warrant missing the first time it blasts out, you're unlikely to catch it the second time either.

I wait nervously outside Mr Hughes's office. I can hear him through the door barking orders at someone down the phone. I think he might have said, 'Good god, woman, just defrost the cod. We'll have it with the dill sauce.' But as it sounds like he was ordering the slaughter of all firstborn sons across the land, it's hard to be sure.

'Enter,' he beckons. I go in and sit, irritated that I'm having to give up my free lesson for this impromptu meeting. The Year 11s are now on study leave. Or 'holiday' as it's more widely known.

Mr Hughes glares across his enormous desk at me and I

begin an involuntary shake. I set my jaw. I will not be bullied by this man.

After an uncomfortable silence and yet more glaring, he barks, 'It has come to my attention that a certain video is circulating the internet.'

I swallow.

'Would you happen to know to which video I am referring?'

He swivels his laptop round on the desk. I'm forced to watch myself, once again, give my speech. He slams the laptop shut before we get to the bit about the sex.

'Now it is all very admirable, about this,' he waves his hand as if he's trying to find the words, 'deceased sibling. 'But it is clearly stipulated in the staff handbook, section two, sub section four point six that members of staff shall not partake in any lewd behaviour online.'

I'm not sure my bungee jump qualifies as lewd, but I'm so furious I can hardly speak.

'You are discussing your private bedroom affairs.' I actually snort at that. 'And this is simply not acceptable. Are you finding this funny, Miss Turner?'

'I find you funny.' It's a childish response and I'm not proud of it. I am, however, proud of how red he is becoming. I just need to make sure he doesn't keel over. The last thing I want is the vengeful ghost of this great oaf haunting me for the rest of my life.

'Well, I can assure you, the governors and I take such matters very seriously. I'm afraid this means competency.'

There is no way that I'm enduring that for my final few weeks here. Of course, Hughes doesn't yet know that these are my final weeks. He's probably imagining a decade-long competency. I'm absolutely livid.

'Actually, I won't be going on competency. Because I quit.'

'You can't quit.'

'Yes, I can. Section five of the staff handbook, subsection three point one. Any member of staff placed on competency forgoes the right to a period of notice if it is deemed necessary to terminate their employment. This also applies should a member of staff placed on competency decide to seek employment elsewhere. Thank your start of the year quiz.'

Capillaries appear like tiny little branches across his already flushed cheeks. A purple roadmap of stress.

'This! This is why you'll never be an outstanding teacher, Miss Turner.'

'I don't care about being an outstanding teacher! I care about the kids. You might want to give it a go sometime since you're in charge of an actual school, not a factory.' He goes to stop me but I'm on a roll. My first-ever argument. It's brilliant. 'And another thing. People like you are the exact reason why so many teachers leave. I thought I hated teaching. Turns out I only hate teaching under *you*. So, I will save you the hassle of firing me because I quit. Goodbye, Mr Hughes.'

With that, I push the chair back and storm out of his office breathing hard.

I can't believe I just did that. Okay, I obviously didn't

think the financial implications of this decision through, but it's two months max until I start my new job. Maybe I'll just sell some of my workout stuff. Or, failing that, a kidney.

I'm free. I'm actually free. I am also a woman on a mission and there's one more person I need to see before I leave. I find Stan by the photocopier.

'Hi, Stan.' I go to stand next to him.

'Emily.'

'Look, this is my last day now. Your uncle's probably about to set security on me any minute.' I laugh and glance around, sure Hughes is busy canvassing the local kennels for dogs to chase me from the grounds.

Stan stops photocopying; I have his attention.

'I just wanted to say, while I have the chance, that you have absolutely no right to be pissed at me about that night. And while I'm sorry if I hurt your feelings, women can *always* change their mind and we absolutely don't owe you anything. Especially an orgasm.'

Two impassioned speeches in one week. Who even am I?

'That's okay, Emily. There's no need for you to apologise, it's actually rather poor of you. As a feminist. The error was all mine. Ebony has been helping me to manifest higher expectations of myself. I apologise unreservedly for my behaviour.'

Okay, what?

'That's great,' I smile, despite the half-insult. 'Apology accepted. I just thought because you still weren't doing my photocopying that you must have really hated me or something.'

'No, I just didn't want to do it.' It seems inappropriate to point out that photocopying is the entirety of Stan's job description.

'Ebony's encouraging me to pursue a higher ambition. We're in a relationship now,' he announces. His ears go a bit pink, and I decide to forgive him the hours I've spent stressed out at the photocopier because he seems quite smitten with Ebony. And that's all anyone can ever ask for, isn't it?

It's hard not to wonder what could have been with Josh. Disappointment for an imagined future steals up on me, dulling my post-speech glow. Either Josh has seen the video and decided that I am not, in fact, the love of his life, or he hasn't seen it. Whichever way I spin it, he hasn't rocked up in the middle of the night with a cardboard placard declaring his undying love.

Sad Josh-based thoughts aside, I leave school, knowing that I'll never have to suffer another learning walk at the hands of Mr Hughes again. And even if I do spend the rest of my years alone, that is cause in itself to be happy.

Chapter Forty-Five

The Saturday following my grand exit from Mr Hughes' office, Kaz and I are getting ready for Claire's memorial. Twenty years have passed since she died. More than twice her lifetime. It's almost unfathomable.

'I think you should go half-up, half-down.' Kaz fiddles with my hair.

'Do whatever you think is best.' I can't decide whether to feel excited about the party or sad that we need to have one at all. If I've learnt anything about grief these last few months, it's that it's confusing as fuck.

We can hear Brian on the phone through the walls to Kaz's room. He's practically living with us, and I've heard more through those walls than I care to admit. I didn't even realise what half of it meant. Even after I'd googled it, I can't see how a *flat doggy* could work logistically.

'What's he doing in there?'

'Who knows?' Kaz won't quite meet my eye.

I'm wearing a new dress. It's white with little purple flowers embroidered onto it. Granted I absolutely couldn't afford it; even before I became unemployed it would have been a stretch. I think when the hunger sets in, in a few weeks, I'll just gnaw on the straps for something to do with my mouth.

'You guys ready?' Brian shouts.

'Almost.' I add my half of the silver necklace Claire and I got for Christmas when we were kids. It's too precious to wear these days, even if it did come from Claire's Accessories. But for today, it feels just right.

Incidentally, no one seems particularly surprised about my sudden, if temporary, joblessness; though, breaking the news to my parents the week they're contemplating twenty years without one of their three children probably took some of the heat off me.

Kaz has done my hair in loose waves and tied half of it back. She's fussing an extra amount today. 'Ready?' she asks. 'You look lovely.'

'Ready,' I nod. 'Thanks, so do you.'

We drive in silence to my parents' house. Brian is texting constantly. There's a purple balloon medley tied to the front door.

Inside people are already starting to gather and I realise we're actually a bit late. 'Emily, love, you look gorgeous!' I can tell that Mum has already done a good deal of crying. She's doing that fussing thing that mums pull off so well.

'Can you plate up those sausage rolls? Don't forget to put the little flag in so that people know they're the vegan ones.' I do as I'm instructed.

'And crisps! We need more crisps!'

I head out into the garden laden with food. Dad comes to my rescue as a bowl of crisps begin a precarious wobble.

'It's gorgeous, Dad.' I kiss his cheek. And I mean it. Mum and Dad have hung purple butterfly bunting across the hedges. Leon is in the corner, playing 'Magical Mr Mistoffelees' from *Cats*. He looks up at the sky, probably wishing that he too were dead.

Everyone we know is here. Our old teacher, Mr Jones, Kaz's mum and some of the doctors who looked after Claire. Sophie and her husband, just back from honeymoon, wave at us. Sandra and Gran are deep in conversation. There's also a couple of people from the hospice. The upside to my digital humiliation is that we raised £10,000.

A table groaning with food contains pictures of Claire from Mum's many albums. Me and Claire as babies, wrinkly and red. On the beach at Butlin's. Our first day of school. Playing shows in the garden. And then Claire ill. In the hospital. In the hospice. In every snap she has the biggest smile. It dawns on me then that all these years spent avoiding talking about the bad times means that I've missed out on reminiscing about the good.

A stray tear escapes and I sniff.

I've only been here ten minutes. Is there an etiquette for when it's okay to start sobbing?

'Emily.' Matt arrives to stand by my side.

'Hi, Matt.' I look up at the sun. 'Should you be out in direct sunlight? I thought your kind melted?' I'm proud of my ability to needle him even as I'm on the brink of crying.

He hands me a tissue to dab at my eyes.

'I'm wearing my biggest crucifix,' he replies.

'Matt, was that a . . . was that a joke?'

He clears his throat. 'That, er, jump, last week.'

I nod, still reeling from the joke. 'Well, it was better than quite good. It was very impressive. Brave.' Matt coughs.

'Thank you,' I smile.

'Do you miss her?' He tilts his head towards the pictures of Claire.

'Like crazy.' It's true. My grief for Claire is wild and untameable. It always has been, despite the lies I've told myself.

'Me too.'

'You know, I always had this daft thought,' I venture.

'Go on.'

'No, it's nothing.'

'Okay.' He doesn't leave though.

'I always had this silly thought that you'd wished it was Claire who was here now.'

I laugh nervously.

'What, just me?'

'No, all of you. Like maybe you talked about it when I wasn't there. Kaz says I'm being daft.' More nervous laughter. Except now it sounds like I might be choking too.

Matt looks surprised. I am too. It's possibly the most honest thing I've ever said to him.

'Never.'

'Pardon?'

'Never.' He does a little cough. 'It was just hard. There were two of you, and then there was one. I didn't know what to say. I was worried about doing the wrong thing. Somehow, we ended up here.'

I take 'here' to mean bickering like five-year-olds.

'I always thought you seemed so much better at coping than me.'

Matt shakes his head. He has a drink of the can of coke he's holding.

'I think it was just that I didn't want to make you even sadder. I learnt to hide it. Seemed like as good a way as any to cope.'

Things click into place in my brain. 'Tis the season for sharing apparently.

'You're preaching to the choir here, Matt.'

'Sorry if I made you feel bad.'

'I'm sorry too. Ceasefire?'

'What, no more taking the mick out of me? Whatever will we talk about?' He has a faint smile.

I reach up and feel his forehead with the back of my hand.

'Are you coming down with something? Two jokes in five minutes. Someone call 999!'

He barks out a laugh. It's such a Matt laugh. Contained. But it's real and that makes it nice.

'I'd better get back to Sarah. She gets a bit shy at this sort of thing.' We both look her way. She's trying to disappear into a hedge.

I nod. 'Thank you.' He just raises his can as he walks away.

I spend a few minutes pretending to decide what to eat. Though really, I'm just looking at the pictures of Claire. I must be overwrought; my appetite has abandoned me.

'She looks so happy.'

The shock steals my breath away. But I don't turn around. Just in case I've heard wrong.

'She was.'

I can feel the heat of his body behind me. His hand is on my elbow.

And now I'm crying.

'Shh, Emily.' He's closer still now. Close enough to wipe a tear from my cheek.

It's enough to convince me that he's not some apparition. Or else a figment of my imagination, I turn around.

'Josh! What're you doing here?'

He's stood right there, by the broccoli quiche. Blue eyes and dimples and cowlick galore.

I start laughing like I might have lost one or two of my faculties. 'Emily, I'm so sorry. I just ...'

He pauses to run his knuckles over my wet cheeks. Catching yet more tears.

Out of the corner of my eye, I catch Dad trying to watch us. 'Wait, come over here.' I pull Josh down the side of the house. We pass Kaz and Brian who high-five each other.

'What are you – ? I don't understand?' I can hardly form sentences. My heart squeezes at the thought that he's not here for the reason I hope.

'I had to come. Emily, I'm so sorry, I've been an absolute idiot. Can you forgive me?'

'Wait. What? *You're* sorry? I'm the one who ended things, remember?'

'But I shouldn't have let you go so easy . . .'

'Did you get my messages?'

'I blocked your number. When you asked me not to message you. I didn't trust myself.'

'I'm so sorry, Josh. Like a crazy amount. It's all been so messed up. Wait, how did you know I'd be here?'

'I saw the video.'

'Oh, you saw that, did you?'

'Only this morning. I wasn't answering my phone, even to Brian. He rang non-stop until I gave in. I can't believe you did that jump.'

'I can't believe you saw me with those goggles on. Does this mean you forgive me? Because I'm so sorry. Shutting you out like that was the most cowardly thing.' He goes to shush me with a finger to my lips. 'No, wait, let me finish. It was the best sex I'd ever had, but then I ate this weird paella and got food poisoning. There was sick *everywhere*. Babs had to hold my hair. They took me to hospital and I freaked. I'm going back to therapy,' I announce.

'Okay, that was a lot of information.' He pulls me in for a hug and I do the biggest most obvious sniff. 'You had all this stuff going on and I just ignored it. I should have known better than anyone. What it's like.'

I'm smiling now. My tears all dried up. Or else absorbed into Josh's T-shirt.

'You're forgiven. Now can you kiss me please? I'm going to die here.'

'Just one more thing. Can we just revisit something you said a moment ago? The best sex you've ever had?' I dive for him then. The kiss quickly descends from loving into something that is entirely inappropriate to be doing at your dead twin's memorial. Josh has me pinned to the wall of the house when Brian taps him on the shoulder.

'All right, you two lovebirds, your dad's about to make a speech. Em, he's asking after you.'

Josh and I have no choice but to follow Brian down the side of the house and out into the garden where everyone is already assembled. Kaz gives a little whoop and Mum claps her hands together. Leon taps on the mic to quieten everyone before speaking. 'Thanks for joining us, Josh and Emily of YouTube fame. Josh, you have lipstick across your face, and I think there's a bit on your neck too.' This is, I presume, punishment for his DJ set, which comprises entirely of musical theatre. Josh goes red as Dad takes the mic and sets about loudly clearing his throat.

Everyone stands, still clutching their drinks. Josh gives my hand a squeeze as Dad begins.

'They say losing your child is the worst thing that can happen to any parent. Twenty years ago, our daughter

Claire was taken far too young by a truly dreadful disease. I hate all those clichés people roll out about cancer. All the "she fought so hard" bollocks. Cancer is never a fair fight. If it were, Claire would be here with us now. Because that kid had more spirit and more fight than anyone I've ever known.

'The hardest thing about Claire's death wasn't her actual death. That was peaceful and calm, thanks to the support of some wonderful nurses,' he tilts his head to Kaz's mum, 'and the fact that I'm as sure as anything that Claire knew how loved and special she was.' He nods towards Mum.

'No, the hardest part of all of this is living through every day without her. Telling a joke and not hearing her laugh at it. Cooking dinner every night and her not being there to eat it. Claire was a force of nature, and I will miss her to the day I die.'

No one isn't crying.

'What I am eternally grateful for,' Dad carries on, 'is that Claire left us a little piece of herself in her sister Emily. Watching you and Matt grow up, Emily, has been the great privilege of our lives.' Mum is nodding along in agreement.

'We love you both. Now, I know if Claire were here, she'd be telling us all to get on with the party. So please, to Claire.' He raises his glass.

'To Claire,' we chant back.

Leon starts up the music and 'I'm gonna live for ever' begins to blast out. People are half-laughing, half-crying. That humans can be so unbearably sad and yet so ridiculously happy at the same time really is quite the feat of evolution.

'That was a beautiful speech, Dad,' I tell him. Josh is beside me, still holding my hand.

'Thank you, love. And for all that money you raised. They're going to install a new sensory room at the hospice, in Claire's memory.' I give him the biggest hug. I'd do that bungee ten times over for this to all happen again.

'And you must be Josh?' He holds his hand out for Josh to shake. Claire would have found the whole thing hilarious.

'Nice to meet you.'

'Great speech, Pete.' Kaz and Brian come over.

'Thanks, Kaz. And for looking after this one.' He nods towards me. 'You've been a good friend.'

'What can I say? She's the love of my life.'

'I'll leave you youngsters to it then. Looks like your mum might need a hand with the cheese sticks.'

Kaz rounds on Josh. 'You took your time.'

He holds up his hands. 'Sorry! I'd have been here a week earlier if I'd seen the YouTube thing sooner.'

'What, because I looked so irresistible?'

Sophie and her husband come to join us, looking tanned and happy.

'So, you two are a thing now?' She looks between me and Josh.

'Yep, we are,' he replies, with a slightly combative air.

'Hmm,' Sophie replies. I'm sure I can look forward to some trolling from Amy in the near future.

We stand there for the afternoon, drinking and awkward

dancing in the sun. I tell Sandra about my new job and she says she knew all along that I should be doing something like that. Apparently, that's why she always left me on my own with Leon at the shop. Not so that she could read erotic fiction in the kitchen, but so I would find my true calling in life.

She extracts a promise that I'll keep volunteering. I wonder briefly if I'm now a modern-day slave. But we are to have another convict soon. So, that's something to look forward to. Sandra heads over to Gran, a glass of sherry in each hand.

JULY

Be Authentic

*(Because being anything else is
absolutely bloody exhausting)*

Chapter Forty-Six

Josh and I are in his flat. We've been staying here more and more since Brian became an almost permanent fixture in mine. Those walls really are thin.

'I can't believe everything you've done these last few months.' He's kissing my collarbone on the couch. I'm only vaguely aware that he's saying English words. I saw a National Geographic programme about beavers; I have a lot of spare time now that I'm unemployed, and apparently, they mate for life. So, maybe us humans think we're all intelligent, with our opposable thumbs and computers. But really, we're not too far removed from the largest rodent in Britain. Dodging love, once you've found it, goes against every instinct we possess. That I managed to run away from Josh all those times is actually pretty impressive. Desperately sad, but impressive, nonetheless.

'Ah um, it's nothing special.' I'm keen to end the conversation and carry on with more kissing. 'Yes, do that a bit more.'

He smiles into my neck.

'Wasn't there a challenge for July?'

'Mm-hmm — be authentic. I thought it would be the

hardest but actually it's pretty easy. So long as you're only trying to be yourself, I mean.'

'I can't believe you've solved it.'

'Solved what?'

'The meaning of life.'

I laugh. Honestly, I still feel like I don't have a clue. But then maybe everyone's like that. Maybe living isn't something we should all be thinking about so much, but something we should just do.

By way of putting my money where my mouth is, or something to do with my mouth at any rate, I kiss him hard. Honestly, I feel like any life where I get to kiss Josh would be one worth living.

'What's for lunch tomorrow?'

'Apparently, Mum is trying her hand at a chickpea curry. She just texted her surprise that chickpeas come in a can. I really do apologise for this bit of her personal growth.'

Josh laughs.

'Actually, do you mind if we go somewhere I need to visit.'

''Course not.'

'Glad that's settled. Is there anything else you'd like to discuss?'

'No.'

'Good.'

I sit up so that he can undo my dress. Sexy eyes.

I lean back in for another kiss. I will never get bored of kissing this man.

He looks up at me and I feel like my heart is about

to explode, it's so full of love and grief and everything in between.

'Will you ever forgive me, do you think? For not talking about you all those years?'

I'm aware that conversing with a headstone is not the sanest thing a person can do. There's absolutely no way that Claire would spend eternity floating around a tiny patch of grass in Huddersfield. So it is, very much, simply a headstone.

Obviously, there's no reply. An old lady shuffles past, a bunch of white flowers in her hand. She looks at me sympathetically, the way people do when they see you sat next to a butterfly-shaped grave. In the hierarchy of grief, children rightly come at the top of the pecking order.

'What's been going on?' I pretend like Claire's just asked me a question.

'Well, I got a new job. In a young offenders institute. I think I'll really like it there. And I got a therapist. The adult ones are better, I think. They haven't asked me to draw you yet.

'Obviously, everyone misses you. Though maybe you already know that. Wherever you are. And I'm officially as vegan as possible. Fat Joe's are introducing a vegan pizza. Their profits took a real nosedive that month I gave up cheese.'

I'm blabbering. I need to get the next bit out.

'So anyway, I met someone. The right someone. Bang on schedule. And even though I'm not trying to live like you might have done anymore, I still can't help wondering if you'd be a bit disappointed in me. I hope not. Not since your list, which by the way was exhausting, but it really did help me so much.'

It's still silent. Except for the wind in the trees.

I'm not lying. There's no shame in admitting I was completely lost. Before Claire's Life List, that is. It saved me. Or else I saved myself. Probably it was somewhere in between. But now that I'm actually living, it's all pretty obvious. There's no magic bullet for this amazing life we're all meant to have. I get that now. You've just got to fill it. With as much good stuff as you can. For as long as you can.

And while today I feel happy, I won't always feel like this. But then that's okay too. Maybe humans aren't meant to be these eternally happy, grateful beings. Maybe we need to just get on with it a bit and take the rough with the smooth.

'Yeah, so Josh—'

'Are my ears burning?'

'There's just all this toe hair everywhere, like Frodo. I'm not sure I can live like that.'

'That's it. I'm getting it lasered off!'

I laugh and give him a kiss.

'You just about done? I can wait?'

'No, I'm done. I was just telling Claire – we're living the dream.'

'You mean the Netflix and takeaway dream?'

'It's the best, isn't it?'

He nods and kisses the top of my head. 'Fat Joe's tonight?'

'I thought you'd never ask.'

He pulls me up off the grass. I'll forever regret that Claire and Josh never met. That she'll only ever come to things in spirit. That dying means she really is gone for good. But grieving for Claire reminds me that she was here. She was a real person, and she was loved.

I look back at her butterfly as we leave the cemetery. I guess it's true what all those clever people said then. Love really is all that counts in the end.

Acknowledgements

I love reading other people's acknowledgements (maybe I'm just nosy), and being able to write my own was something that I dreamed of doing for a long time. Thank you, so much, to anyone who has read this book. Emily's story has lived in my head since I was a teenager. I hope you've enjoyed reading it.

My first proper thanks has to go to my lovely editor Molly. You always say that I can disagree with you and yet I never want to. Thank you for championing Emily's story from the start and for never tiring of bolstering my ever-shakeable confidence. Thank you for the pasta, the cake and for that weird foamy dessert. And for introducing me to Oliver Bonas. But more than anything, thank you for your feedback and guidance. This book is infinitely better because of your involvement in it.

To my agent Hannah, I always think that if this (my writing career) were a duck you would be the serene head guiding us in the right direction and I'd be the webbed feet just flapping about. Thank you for helping me to figure out what I was meant to write, and for patiently answering all of my many, many questions. I will never forget your Friday phone call (even if I did cry through most of it). Thank you so much.

I really lucked out in the friend stakes. But special thanks go to Laura, Amy, and Anwen, Evelyn and Penny. All of whom read very tentative early drafts and encouraged me to keep going. Laura, there's no one I'd rather have existential crises over text with. No one talks wedding chair like you do.

To my lovely colleagues at TSS. I'd like to go on record as saying this isn't about you!

To Mark, Gill and all the Keighly writing gang. You were the first people I read any of Emily to and the book is definitely better for your careful guidance and feedback. Thank you for not mentioning the fact that I became strangely breathless every time it was my turn to read.

Hayley, if I'm even close to capturing the essence of grief in this book it's because of your generosity and openness in sharing your grief for Ike. That you read an early draft of this means so much to me. You're a great friend. I hope you know that Ike won't ever be forgotten.

For the writing wife to end all writing wives, Vicky, I am eternally grateful that we had babies at the same time. I don't know what I did with my time before I spent it WhatsApping you, but what I do know is that you are the most selfless of friends. Thank you for being the first person to read whatever I write. If there's such a thing as friend soulmates, I'm pretty sure you're mine.

To Mum and Dad, thank you for the childcare! It really

shows commitment to being top tier grandparents that you moved halfway across the country to be closer to us all. There is no way I'd have been able to write this book without your support and even though I claim to hate it, I don't really mind the shameless bragging.

Speaking of top tier, thank you to Matt. As you know, I am rarely lost for words but it's hard to find the right ones for you. Thank you for going along with all my schemes, for encouraging me always, for giving me time to write even though we had no idea if it would pay off. You are the best of us, and we're very lucky to have you.

And finally, to Elodie, Hugo and Kit. This book is dedicated to you because without you there's no point to any of it. I love you. Always.